John Dos Passos was born in Chicago in 1896, thus becoming a member of the extraordinary literary generation that also produced F. Scott Fitzgerald and Ernest Hemingway. His father was a noted lawyer of Portugese descent, his mother was of distinguished Southern lineage. After graduating from Harvard in 1916, Dos Passos served as an ambulance driver and medical corpsman in Europe in World War I, traveled the world widely, and first won fame with *Three Soldiers* in 1921. *Manhattan Transfer* (1925) marked a further advance, and in 1930 *The 42nd Parallel*, the first volume of his *U.S.A.* trilogy, placed him among the century's major novelists. *Nineteen Nineteen* (1932) and *The Big Money* (1936) completed what was immediately recognized as an American classic. His subsequent novels included the *District of Columbia* trilogy—*Chosen Country, The Great Days*, and *Midcentury*—as well as several notable works on American history and the recent autobiographical *The Best Times*.

John Dos Passos

THE
42nd PARALLEL

FIRST IN THE TRILOGY U.S.A.

Illustrated by REGINALD MARSH
With an Introduction by ALFRED KAZIN

(Revised and Updated Bibliography)

A SIGNET MODERN CLASSIC
NEW AMERICAN LIBRARY

TIMES MIRROR
NEW YORK AND SCARBOROUGH, ONTARIO

SIGNET CLASSIC TRADEMARK REG. U.S. PAT. OFF. AND FOREIGN COUNTRIES
REGISTERED TRADEMARK—MARCA REGISTRADA
HECHO EN CHICAGO, U.S.A.

SIGNET, SIGNET CLASSICS, MENTOR, PLUME, MERIDIAN AND NAL
BOOKS are published in the United States by
The New American Library, Inc.,
1633 Broadway, New York, New York 10019,
in Canada by The New American Library of Canada Limited,
81 Mack Avenue, Scarborough, Ontario M1L 1M8

FIRST SIGNET PRINTING, MARCH, 1969

8   9   10   11   12   13   14   15   16

PRINTED IN THE UNITED STATES OF AMERICA

Introduction

John O'Hara once said that the development of the United States in the first half of the twentieth century is the greatest possible subject for a novelist. He left the implication that anyone lucky enough to have been part of this change, to have made the subject his own, had an advantage over the younger novelists who since 1945 have taken American power for granted and have missed the drama of its emergence.

Whatever else may be said of this proposition, or of the gifted but now "old-fashioned" and resentful novelist who made it, it is a fact that this faith in subject matter as the novelist's secret strength, especially in the "big change" as the greatest of social facts, does characterize the novelists born around the turn of the century—writers otherwise so unlike each other as John O'Hara and John Dos Passos. This faith also distinguishes them from those younger writers like Saul Bellow, Ralph Ellison, Norman Mailer, Flannery O'Connor, who grew up in depression or war, and have never thought the United States to be as unique in world history as Americans used to think it was in 1917. The younger writers have been impressed by America's resemblance to old-world powers, not by the legends of America's special destiny. History, as they see it, sooner or later becomes everywhere the same. And all history is essentially obscure and problematical, in some ways too unreal ever to be fully understood by the individual novelist, who will not feel that *he* can depend on "history" to hold him up, to supply him with material, to infuse him with the vitality that only confidence in one's subject can.

Henry James said that the "novelist succeeds to the sacred office of the historian." The old faith that "history" exists objectively, that it has an ascertainable order, that it is what the novelist most depends on and appeals to, that "history" even supplies the *structure* of the novel—this is what distinguishes the extraordinary invention that is Dos Passos' *U.S.A.* from most novels published since 1940. And it is surely because "history" as order—to say nothing of "history" as something to believe in!—comes so hard to younger writers, and readers, that Dos Passos has been a relatively neglected writer in recent years.

It is often assumed that Dos Passos was a "left-wing" novelist in the thirties who, like other novelists of the period, turned conservative and thus changed and lost his creative identity. *U.S.A.* is certainly the peak of his career and the three novels that make it up were all published in the thirties —*The 42nd Parallel* in 1930, *1919* in 1932, *The Big Money* in 1936. But the trilogy is not simply a "left-wing" novel, and its technical inventiveness and the freshness of its style are typical of the twenties rather than the thirties. In any event, Dos Passos has always been so detached from all group thinking that it is impossible to understand his development as a novelist by identifying him with the radical novelists of the thirties. He began earlier, he has never been a Marxist, and in all periods he has followed his own perky, obstinately independent course. Whatever may be said of Dos Passos' political associations and ideas in recent years, it can be maintained that while some (by no means all) of his values have changed, it is not his values but the loss by many educated people of a belief in "history" that has caused Dos Passos' relative isolation in recent years.

Dos Passos was born in Chicago in 1896, graduated from Harvard in 1916, and served as an ambulance driver in France and Italy before joining the American army. None of the other writers associated with the "lost generation"—not Hemingway or Fitzgerald or Cummings, though they were all close friends—had the passion for history, for retracing history's creative moments, that Dos Passos has shown in his many nonfiction studies of American history as well as in *U.S.A.* Alone among his literary cronies, Dos Passos managed to add this idea of history as the great operative force to their enthusiasm for radical technique, the language of Joyce, and "the religion of the word." Dos Passos shared this cult of art, and *U.S.A.* grew out of it as much as it did out of his sense of American history as the greatest drama of modern times. But neither Fitzgerald, Cummings nor Hemingway ever had Dos Passos' interest in the average man as a subject for fiction.

Most oddly for someone with his "esthetic" concerns, Dos Passos was sympathetic to the long tradition of American radical dissent, and he has always been hostile to political dogma and orthodoxy. *The 42nd Parallel* opens with the story of Mac, a typically rootless Wobbly and "working-class stiff" of the golden age of American socialism before 1917; *The Big Money* ends on the struggles of Mary French (and John Dos Passos) to save Sacco and Vanzetti in 1927. To round out his trilogy when it was finally published in a single volume, Dos Passos added, as preface and epilogue, his sketches of a young man, hungry and alone, walking the highways. "Vag," the American vagrant, is Dos Passos' expression of his life-long fascination with the alienated, the outsider, the beaten, the dissenter: the lost and forgotten in American history. Mac, the American Wobbly and drifter at the beginning of *U.S.A.*, is as much an expression of what has been sacrificed to American progress as Mary French, the middle-class Communist, is at the end of the book. These solitaries, along with the young man endlessly walking America, frame this enormous chronicle of disillusionment with the American promise much as the saints in a medieval painting frame the agony on the cross. The loner in America interested Dos Passos long before he became interested in the American as protester. And despite Dos Passos' disenchantment since the thirties with the radical-as-ideologist, the Communist-as-policeman (at the end of *The Big Money* lonely Mary French identifies herself with a Stalinist orthodoxy to which she will inevitably fall victim), Dos Passos is still fascinated, as witness his books on the Jeffersonian tradition, with the true dissenter, whether he is alone in the White House or on the highway.

It is in his long attraction to figures who somehow illustrate some power for historic perspective (no matter what solitude this may bring) that we can see Dos Passos' particular artistic imperatives. The detachment behind this is very characteristic of those American writers from the upper class, born on the eve of our century—Hemingway, Cummings, Edmund Wilson—whose childhoods were distinctly sheltered and protected, who grew up in stable families where the fathers were ministers (Cummings), lawyers (Wilson), doctors (Hemingway), the mothers the conscious transmitters of the American Puritan tradition in all the old certainty that Americans were more virtuous than other peoples.

To these writers of the "lost generation," brought up in what is now thought of as the last stable period in American history—before America became a world empire—"Mr. Wilson's War," as Dos Passos calls it in his recent book on this central episode in the life of his generation, came as an explosion of the old isolationism and the old provincial self-righteousness. "Mr. Wilson's War" tied America to Europe in a way that was to be stimulating at the time to Dos Passos,

Hemingway and Cummings, but it destroyed their image of America. "Mr. Wilson," the very embodiment of Puritan American high-mindedness and didacticism, managed by "his war" to rob America of its good conscience. From now on the old familiar identification of America with righteousness was a subject for the history books. It was the writers—and some political dissenters—who were the new elect and keepers of the American conscience. "Mr. Wilson's War," from *their* point of view, was a moral cheat and a political catastrophe; as they saw it, it would soon give free rein to the speculators, financiers, and other "rugged individualists" whose unbridled greed was a dangerous American tradition that only men of intellectual principle had ever kept in check. But the writers who went to war (symbolically as ambulance drivers) found in Europe the same detachment from American money-making that they had found in their sheltered childhoods in professional families—plus a passion for the new language of twentieth-century painting and literature. Dos Passos and his friends would yet create something human out of so much destruction.

To these gifts and postures of detachment, natural to creative individualists, Dos Passos brought family circumstances that were certainly distinctive among those members of his social class who also graduated from Choate, Harvard, and the very select Norton-Harjes Volunteer Ambulance Service. The novelist's full name is John Roderigo Dos Passos; his paternal grandfather emigrated to the United States from the Portuguese island of Madeira. The novelist's father, John Randolph Dos Passos, was born in 1844, fought in the Civil War (he was at the Battle of Antietam), and became one of the most famous corporation lawyers of his time, an authority on the law of the stock market (he wrote a famous legal text on the subject). He was a deep-dyed Republican stalwart when this really meant something, in the age of McKinley. He was fifty-two years old when his son was born in Chicago to Lucy Addison Sprigg, who was of an old Maryland and Virginia family. The novelist's complex attitude toward American society may have one source in this complicated heritage. Another source was probably the distant yet flamboyant presence of Dos Passos *père*, who by all accounts was a man of very great abilities and a pillar of Wall Street, but was not a Sunday-school type when it came to women. Both the exotic name and the sexual scandal in the background of Dos Passos' family history possibly explain why the autobiographical "Camera Eye" sections of *U.S.A.* dealing with childhood and early youth are deliberately evasive as well as blurred in the style of Joyce's *A Portrait of the Artist as a Young Man*. The impressionistic style which is Dos Passos' general inspiration enables him to field certain family embarrassments. The perhaps deliberate murkiness of these early "Camera Eye" sections is in striking contrast with the later autobiographical chronicle and the bristlingly clear prose of the "biographies" of famous Americans and the narrative sections proper.

Dos Passos was clearly brought up with the immense reserve of the upper classes in America, and readers encountering him are usually amazed by the contrast between the fluent fast prose he writes and the extraordinarily shy, tight, embarrassed self he shows to strangers. It may be that the concentrated sensitivity of his public personality helps to explain the "streamlined" and even gimmicky side of his famous book; the sensibility that conceived *U.S.A.* is obviously complicated enough to have produced this complicated division into "Camera Eye," "newsreel," "biography," and narrative sections. This structure is surely, among other things, a way of objectifying one vulnerable individual's experience to the uttermost, of turning even the individual life into a facet of history. The hardness behind *U.S.A.* is an idea, not a feeling; it is an esthetic proposition about style in relation to the contemporary world; Dos Passos carries it off brilliantly, but it always remains distinctly *willed*. Malcolm Cowley once pointed out that Dos Passos' college years were those of the "Harvard esthetes." He learned to think of experience as separable into softish dreams and hard realities, of a world coming down on subjectivities of the poet, thus leading him doggedly to train his "camera" on an external world conceived of as a distant *object*—necessarily separable from man's hopes for unity with his surroundings.

The creed behind Dos Passos' first novels—*One Man's Initiation* (1919),* *Three Soldiers* (1921), *Manhattan Transfer* (1925)—was learned at college and at war, supported by his "esthetic" training and his experiences as an ambulance driver and medical corpsman. The modern world is ugly, hopelessly corrupt, and is to be met not by love or social protest, but by "art." For the writers of the "lost generation," "art" was the highest possible resistance to the "swindle" of the social world and the ultimate proof of one's aristocratic individualism in the modern mass world. Art was the *nuova scienza*, the true science of the new period, the only possible new language—it would capture the discontinuities of the modern world and use for itself the violent motions and radical new energies of the post-war period. The new language

* Republished in 1946 as *First Encounter*.

was to be modeled on painting, sculpture, architecture—the arts that alone could do justice to the transformation of space. Dos Passos first went to Europe to study architecture in Spain, and drawing has been his "second" art; he has illustrated some of his early travel books. He saw Europe even in wartime as the unique treasure house of architecture and painting. His obvious imitation of the impressionistic word-ties of Joyce (and perhaps Cummings as well, another painter among writers) was surely motivated by the plastic sense of composition among those writers, like the Futurists, who admired the new technology, the twentieth-century feeling for speed. Dos Passos is actually one of the few American writers of his generation who has been inspired by the industrial landscape and he sought to duplicate some of its forms in *U.S.A.* He has taken from technology the rhythms, images, and above all the headlong energy that would express the complexity of the human environment in the twentieth century.

Dos Passos' first novels no longer have much interest for us today, for they are too moody, self-dramatizingly "sensitive," and marked by the romantic despair that is the individual's conscious sacrifice of his hopes to the world of war, modern plutocracy, the inhuman big city. But with *The 42nd Parallel* (which, coming out in 1930, is of course not a book of the thirties but of the individualistic twenties), one is struck above all by the sharp, confident, radical new *tone* with which Dos Passos gets his singularly new kind of narrative under way. The novel opens with the "newsreel" flashing before us the popular songs, headlines, and the national excitement as the twentieth century opens. Behind his "Camera Eye," Dos Passos first remembers himself as a boy with his mother in Europe, escaping a hostile pro-Boer crowd that thinks them English. The first character in the book is "Mac," Fenian O'Hara McCreary from Middletown, Connecticut, who will devote his restless, baffled life to the "movement." The first biography of an important maker and shaper of the new century is of Eugene V. Debs.

The material from the first is that of labor struggles, imperialism, socialism, war—and the personal sense of futility that expresses itself in whoring, violent drinking, and the aimless moving on of Americans that conveys the prodigality of our continent. With Mac, we start at the bottom of the social pyramid, among the Wobblies, "Reds," militant "working-class stiffs" who will be central to the whole long trilogy because "socialism" has been the great twentieth-century issue, even in America; the radicals in the book seal its meanings like a Greek chorus. These radicals, though they fail like everybody else, are a judgment on the profit system whose business is business, whose most dramatic form of intelligence is money making, and whose violent competitiveness always leads to war. But though Dos Passos' sympathies, at least in *The 42nd Parallel,* are clearly with radicals who are off the main track, he does not particularly respect them. It is inventors, scientists, intellectuals of the highest creative ability, statesmen of rare moral courage who are his heroes. There are no such figures among the characters of the novel; even among the biographies we see the type only in Steinmetz, General Electric's "Socialist" wizard. For the same reason, the tonic edge of the book, its stylistic dash and irony, its gay inventiveness, are the greatest possible homage to art as a new kind of "practicality" in getting down the facts of human existence in our century.

What Dos Passos created with *The 42nd Parallel* was in fact another American invention—an American *thing* peculiar to the opportunity and stress of American life, like the Wright Brothers' airplane, Edison's phonograph, Luther Burbank's hybrids, Thorstein Veblen's social analysis, Frank Lloyd Wright's first office buildings. (All these fellow inventors are celebrated in *U.S.A.*) *The 42nd Parallel* is an artwork. But we soon recognize that Dos Passos' contraption, his new kind of novel, is in fact (reminding us of Frank Lloyd Wright's self-dramatizing Guggenheim Museum) *the greatest character in the book itself.* Our primary pleasure in reading *The 42nd Parallel* is in being surprised, delighted, and provoked by the "scheme," by Dos Passos' shifting "strategy." We recognize that the exciting presence in *The 42nd Parallel* is the book itself, which is always getting us to anticipate some happy new audacity. A mobile by Alexander Calder or a furious mural design by Jackson Pollock makes us dwell on the specific originality of the artist, the most dramatic thing about the work itself. So *The 42nd Parallel* becomes a book about writing *The 42nd Parallel.* That is the tradition of the romantic poet, and reading him we are on every side surrounded by Dos Passos himself: his "idea."

The technical interest of *The 42nd Parallel* was indeed so great for its time that Jean-Paul Sartre, whose restless search for what is "authentic" to our time makes him a prophetic critic, said in 1938: "Dos Passos has invented only one thing, an art of story-telling. But that is enough. . . . I regard Dos Passos as the greatest writer of our time." Thirty years later, that tribute will surprise even the most loyal admirers of *U.S.A.,* for Dos Passos has been more involved in recent years with social and intellectual history than with the art of the novel. Yet he has so absorbed what he invented for

U.S.A. that even his nonfiction books display the flat, clipped, peculiarly rushing style that at his worst is tabloid journalism but at his best a documentary prose with the freshness of free verse. When we look away from his recent books and come back to *The 42nd Parallel,* however, we can see the real ingenuity that went into it. Though the trilogy gets better and stronger as it goes along, this first volume shows what a remarkable tool Dos Passos has invented for evoking the simultaneous actualities of existence.

The 42nd Parallel opens in 1900. It follows Mac the "working-class stiff" as he constantly moves about, recites the biographies of Debs, Luther Burbank, Big Bill Haywood, William Jennings Bryan, Minor Keith of the United Fruit Company, and ends with Charley Anderson the garage mechanic from North Dakota going overseas. (Charley will come back in *The Big Money* an airplane ace and inventor.) The other main characters are Janey Williams, who will become private secretary to J. Ward Moorehouse, the rising man in the rising public relations industry; Eleanor Stoddard, the interior decorator who will become Moorehouse's prime confidante; Eleanor's friend Eveline Hutchins, who is not as frigid and superior as Eleanor (and tired of too many love affairs and too many parties, will commit suicide at the end of *The Big Money*).

The important point about J. Ward Moorehouse's racket, public relations, and Eleanor Stoddard's racket, interior decorating, is that both are new, responsive to big corporations and new money, and are synthetic. J. Ward Moorehouse and Eleanor Stoddard are in fact artificial people, always on stage, who correspondingly suffer from a lack of reality and of human affection. But on the other side of the broad American picture, Mac the professional agitator has no more direction in his life; marriage to a thoroughly conventional girl in San Diego becomes intolerable to him, but as he roams his way across the country, finally ending up in Mexico just as the revolution begins, he is at the mercy of every new "comrade" and every new pickup. The only direction in his life seems to be his symbolic presence wherever the "action" is —he is in Goldfield, Nevada, when the miners go on strike under the leadership of Big Bill Haywood, and he is in Mexico because the Mexican Revolution is taking place.

With the same "representative" quality, J. Ward Moorehouse rises in the public relations "game" in order to show its relation to big business and big government, while Eleanor Stoddard's dabbling in the "little theater" movement represents the artiness of the newly "modern" period just before World War I. History in the most tangible sense—what happened—is obviously more important in Dos Passos' scheme than with whom things happened to. The matter of the book is always the representative happening and person, the historical moment illustrated in its catchwords, its songs, its influences; above all, in its speech. What Dos Passos wants to capture more than anything else is the echo of what people were actually saying, exactly in the style in which anyone might have said it. The artistic aim of his book, one may say, is to represent the litany, the tone, the issue of the time in the voice of the time, the banality, the cliche that finally brings home to us the voice in the crowd: the voice of mass opinion. The voice that might be anyone's voice brings home to us, as only so powerful a reduction of the many to the one ever can, the vibrating resemblances that make history. In the flush of Wilson's New Freedom, 1913, Jerry Burnham the professional cynic says to Janey Williams—"I think there's a chance we may get back to being a democracy." Mac and his comrades are always talking about "forming the structure of a new society within the shell of the old." Janey Williams' "Popper" notes—"I don't trust girls nowadays with these here ankle-length skirts and all that." Eveline Hutchins, who will find life too dreary, thinks early in the book, "Maybe she'd been wrong from the start to want everything so justright and beautiful." Charley Anderson, leaving the sticks, thinks—"To hell with all that, I want to see some country."

Yet more important than the sayings, which make *U.S.A.* a compendium of American quotations, is the way in which Dos Passos the objective narrator gets popular rhythms, repetitions, and stock phrases into his running description of people. Terse and external as his narrative style is, it is cunningly made up of all the different speech styles of the people he is writing about. This is the "poetry" behind the book that makes the "history" in it live. The section on J. Ward Moorehouse begins—

He was born in Wilmington, Delaware, on the Fourth of July. Poor Mrs. Moorehouse could hear the firecrackers popping and crackling outside the hospital all through her labor pains. And when she came to a little and they brought the baby to her she asked the nurse in a trembling husky whisper if she thought it could have a bad effect on the baby all that noise, prenatal influence you know.

Moorehouse will always be a parody of the American big shot—all "front"; so this representative figure is born on the

Fourth of July. Later in the book, when Eleanor Stoddard's "beautiful friendship" with Moorehouse helps to send Mrs. Moorehouse into a decline, we see all that is chic, proud and angry in Eleanor concentrated into this description.

She got into a taxi and went up to the Pennsylvania Station. It was a premature Spring day. People were walking along the street with their overcoats unbuttoned. The sky was a soft mauve with frail clouds like milkweed floss. In the smell of furs and overcoats and exhausts and bundledup bodies came an unexpected scent of birchbark. Eleanor sat bolt upright in the back of the taxi driving her sharp nails into the palms of her graygloved hands. She hated these treacherous days when winter felt like Spring. They made the lines come out on her face, made everything seem to crumble about her, there seemed to be no firm footing any more.

1919, the second volume of the trilogy, is sharper than *The 42nd Parallel*. The obscenity of *the* war, "Mr. Wilson's War," is Dos Passos' theme, and since this war is the most important political event of the century, he rises to his theme with a brilliance that does not conceal the fury behind it. But it is also clear from the greater assurance of the text that Dos Passos has mastered the special stylistic demands of his experiment, that his contraption is running better with practice. So, apart from the book's unforgettably ironic vibrations as a picture of waste, hypocrisy, debauchery, *1919* shows, as a good poem does, how much more a writer can accomplish by growing into his style. History now is not merely a happening but a bloody farce, is unspeakably wrong, is a complete abandoning of all the hopes associated with the beginning of the century. This is equally true for fictional characters like Joe Williams, Janey's brother, who will be dropped from one ship to another like a piece of cargo, and will eventually be killed in a barroom brawl on Armistice Day; historic personages like the writer and anti-war rebel Randolph Bourne, who died a pariah in 1918, and Paxton Hibben, "A Hoosier Quixote," who sided with the Russian Revolution when he represented the United States abroad. Wesley Everest, whose life is told as a biography under the title "Paul Bunyan," was a Wobbly leader who was castrated and lynched by a mob of businessmen in Centralia, Washington, in 1919. The fictional characters and the historic figures are equally the casualties of war. Just as Dos Passos' own creations are representative Americans, so the historic figures whom he has selected for his biographies become myths in the collective imagination of American history. One of the most brilliant things about Dos Passos' trilogy is the way in which the fictional and the historic characters come together on the same plane. One character in the book is both "fictional" and "historic": The Unknown Soldier. He is fictional because no one knows who *he* is; yet he was an actual soldier—picked at random from so many other dead soldiers. The symbolic corpse has become for Dos Passos the representative American, and his interment in Arlington Cemetery Dos Passos blazingly records in "The Body of an American," the prose poem that ends *1919* and is the most brilliant single piece of writing in the trilogy:

> they took to Châlons-sur-Marne
> and laid it out neat in a pine coffin
> and took it home to God's Country on a battleship
> and buried it in a sarcophagus in the Memorial
> Amphitheater   in the Arlington National Cemetery
> and draped the Old Glory over it
> and the bugler played taps

. . . .

> Woodrow Wilson brought a bouquet of poppies.

But on the other side of the representative American picture are those who made a good thing of war, like Theodore Roosevelt, "the happy warrior" who loved war and became Governor of New York by riding up San Juan Hill; J. P. Morgan,

> Wars and panics on the stock exchange,
> machinegun fire and arson,
> bankruptcies, warloans,
> starvation, lice, cholera and typhus:
> good growing weather for the House of Morgan;

"Meester Veelson," who despite his premonitions took the country into war; Richard Ellsworth Savage, who went back on his early idealism and profited from the corruption that war had encouraged.

What invests *1919* beyond all else is the contrast of the official and popular idealism with the hysterical hedonism of young gentlemen in the ambulance service. Ed Schuyler keeps saying, "Fellers, this ain't a war. It's a goddam whorehouse." The echoes of speech are now our last ties with the doomed. This monument to a whole generation sacrificed is built up out of those mythic quotations and slogans that make up the book in its shattering mimicry. "In Paris they were still haggling over the price of blood, squabbling over toy flags, the river-frontiers on relief maps"; "tarpaper barracks that stank of carbolic"; "the juggling mudspattered faces of the young French soldiers going up for the attack, drunk and desperate, and yelling *à bas la guerre, mort au vaches, à bas la guerre*"; "an establishment where they could *faire rigazig, une maison propre, convenable, et de haute moralité*"; "Did Meester Veelson know that in the peasants' wargrimed houses along the Brenta and the Piave they were burning candles in front of his picture cut out of the illustrated papers?"

The Versailles Peace Conference is cut to the style of Dos Passos' generation—"Three old men shuffling the pack, dealing out the cards."

Woodrow Wilson is caught forever when he says in Rome —". . . it is the greatest pride of Americans to have demonstrated the immense love of humanity which they bear in their hearts." But this mimicry is brought to a final pitch of brilliant indignation in the person of the Unknown Soldier, who *is* anybody and everybody. In "The Body of an American" we see that Dos Passos' book is not so much a novel of a few lives as an epic of democracy. Like other famous American books about democracy—*Representative Men, Leaves of Grass, Moby Dick*—its subject is that dearest of all American myths, the average man. But unlike these great romantic texts of what Whitehead called "the century of hope," *U.S.A.* does not raise the average man to hero. Dos Passos' subject is indeed democracy, but his belief—especially as he goes into the final volume of his trilogy, *The Big Money*—is that the force of circumstances that is twentieth-century life is too strong for the average man, who will probably never rise above mass culture, mass superstition, mass slogans.

The only heroes of *The Big Money* are in the "biographies"—Thorstein Veblen, who drank the "bitter drink" for analyzing predatory American society to its roots; the Wright Brothers, because

the fact remains
that a couple of young bicycle mechanics from Dayton, Ohio
had designed constructed and flown
for the first time ever a practical airplane

and the super-individualist architect, Frank Lloyd Wright,

whom Dos Passos thoroughly admires, though Wright never understood that architecture could serve the people and not the architect alone. The other biographies are of celebrities—Henry Ford, Rudolph Valentino, Isadora Duncan, William Randolph Hearst—whose lives ultimately fell victim to the power of the crowd. The mass, the popular idolatries of the time, have become the enemies of "our storybook democracy." (In the forties John Dos Passos will go back to "storybook democracy" in writing about Thomas Jefferson.) Charley Anderson, the garage mechanic who comes back from war a famous ace, gets so caught up in the dizzying profusion of drink, money and girls that his self-destructive ride through New York, Detroit and Miami resembles the mad gyrations of an airplane out of control. Margo Dowling, the movie actress, is a cold, utterly scheming trollop who in Hollywood turns her Cuban ex-husband into her chauffeur. But even she, like the Richard Ellsworth Savage who is now cynically writing advertising copy for "health foods," is just another victim rather than a villain. Society has gone mad with greed. The only fictional character in *The Big Money* who gets our respect is Mary French, the doctor's daughter and earnest social reformer who becomes a fanatical Communist in her rage over Sacco and Vanzetti. The emotions of the Sacco-Vanzetti case provide Dos Passos with his clearest and most powerful "Camera Eye" sections, but Mary French is futilely giving her life to the Communist Party. The chips are down; the only defense against the ravages of our century is personal integrity.

The particular artistic virtue of Dos Passos' book is its clarity, its strong-mindedness, the bold and sharp relief into which it puts all moral issues, all characterizations—indeed, all human destiny. There are no shadows in *U.S.A.*, no approximations, no fuzzy outlines. Everything is focused, set off from what is not itself, with that special clarity of presentation which Americans value above all else in the arts of communication. Yet in these last sections of *The Big Money*, Dos Passos makes it clear that though the subject of his book all along has been democracy itself, democracy can survive only through the superior man, the intellectual aristocrat, the poet who may not value what the crowd does. This is the political lesson of *U.S.A.* and may explain, for young people who come to the trilogy for the first time, why the book did not fertilize other books by Dos Passos equal to it. The philosophy behind *U.S.A.* is finally at variance with its natural interest, its subject matter, its greatest strength—the people and the people's speech. Like so many primary books in the American literary tradition, *U.S.A.* is a book at war with itself. It breathes

American confidence and is always so distinct in its effects as to seem simple. But its sense of America is complex, dark, and troubled. Perhaps this gives it the energy of disenchantment.

—Alfred Kazin

U.S.A.

The young man walks fast by himself through the crowd that thins into the night streets; feet are tired from hours of walking; eyes greedy for warm curve of faces, answering flicker of eyes, the set of a head, the lift of a shoulder, the way hands spread and clench; blood tingles with wants; mind is a beehive of hopes buzzing and stinging; muscles ache for the knowledge of jobs, for the roadmender's pick and shovel work, the fisherman's knack with a hook when he hauls on the slithery net from the rail of the lurching trawler, the swing of the bridgeman's arm as he slings down the whitehot rivet, the engineer's slow grip wise on the throttle, the dirtfarmer's use of his whole body when, whoaing the mules, he yanks the plow from the furrow. The young man walks by himself searching through the crowd with greedy eyes, greedy ears taut to hear, by himself, alone.

The streets are empty. People have packed into subways, climbed into streetcars and buses; in the stations they've scampered for suburban trains; they've filtered into lodgings and tenements, gone up in elevators into apartmenthouses. In a showwindow two sallow windowdressers in their shirtsleeves are bringing out a dummy girl in a red evening dress, at a corner welders in masks lean into sheets of blue flame repairing a cartrack, a few drunk bums shamble along, a sad streetwalker fidgets under an arclight. From the river comes the deep rumbling whistle of a steamboat leaving dock. A tug hoots far away.

The young man walks by himself, fast but not fast enough, far but not far enough (faces slide out of sight, talk trails into tattered scraps, footsteps tap fainter in alleys); he must catch the last subway, the streetcar, the bus, run up the gangplanks of all the steamboats, register at all the hotels, work in the cities, answer the wantads, learn the trades, take up the jobs, live in all the boardinghouses, sleep in all the beds. One bed is not enough, one job is not enough, one life is not enough. At night, head swimming with wants, he walks by himself alone.

No job, no woman, no house, no city.

Only the ears busy to catch the speech are not alone; the ears are caught tight, linked tight by the tendrils of phrased words, the turn of a joke, the singsong fade of a story, the gruff fall of a sentence; linking tendrils of speech twine through the city blocks, spread over pavements, grow out along broad parked avenues, speed with the trucks leaving on their long night runs over roaring highways, whisper down sandy byroads past wornout farms, joining up cities and fillingstations, roundhouses, steamboats, planes groping along airways; words call out on mountain pastures, drift slow down rivers widening to the sea and the hushed beaches.

It was not in the long walks through jostling crowds at night that he was less alone, or in the training camp at Allentown, or in the day on the docks at Seattle, or in the empty reek of Washington City hot boyhood summer nights, or in the meal on Market Street, or in the swim off the red rocks at San Diego, or in the bed full of fleas in New Orleans, or in the cold razorwind off the lake, or in the gray faces trembling in the grind of gears in the street under Michigan Avenue, or in the smokers of limited expresstrains, or walking across country, or riding up the dry mountain canyons, or the night without a sleepingbag among frozen beartracks in the Yellowstone, or canoeing Sundays on the Quinnipiac;

but in his mother's words telling about longago, in his father's telling about when I was a boy, in the kidding stories of uncles, in the lies the kids told at school, the hired man's yarns, the tall tales the doughboys told after taps;

it was the speech that clung to the ears, the link that tingled in the blood; U.S.A.

U.S.A. is the slice of a continent. U.S.A. is a group of holding companies, some aggregations of trade unions, a set of laws bound in calf, a radio network, a chain of moving picture theatres, a column of stockquotations rubbed out and written in by a Western Union boy on a blackboard, a publiclibrary full of old newspapers and dogeared historybooks with protests scrawled on the margins in pencil. U.S.A. is the world's greatest rivervalley fringed with mountains and hills. U.S.A. is a set of bigmouthed officials with too many bankaccounts. U.S.A. is a lot of men buried in their uniforms in Arlington Cemetery. U.S.A. is the letters at the end of an address when you are away from home. But mostly U.S.A. is the speech of the people.

Contents

THE 42ND PARALLEL

The 42nd Parallel

Newsreel I

It was that emancipated race
That was chargin' up the hill
Up to where them insurrectos
Was afightin' fit to kill

CAPITAL CITY'S CENTURY CLOSED

General Miles with his gaudy uniform and spirited charger was the center for all eyes, especially as his steed was extremely restless. Just as the band passed the Commanding General, his horse stood upon his hind legs and was almost erect. General Miles instantly reined in the frightened animal and dug in his spurs in an endeavor to control the horse which, to the horror of the spectators, fell over backwards and landed squarely on the Commanding General. Much to the gratification of the people, General Miles was not injured, but considerable skin was scraped off the flank of his horse. Almost every inch of General Miles's overcoat was covered with the dust of the street and between the shoulders a hole about an inch in diameter was punctured. Without waiting for anyone to brush the dust from his garments, General Miles remounted his horse and reviewed the parade as if it were an everyday occurrence.

The incident naturally attracted the attention of the crowd, and this brought to notice the fact that the Commanding General never permits a flag to be carried past him without uncovering and remaining so until the colors have passed

And the Captain bold of Company B
Was afightin' in the lead
Just like a trueborn soldier he
Of them bullets took no heed

OFFICIALS KNOW NOTHING OF VICE

Sanitary trustees turn water of Chicago River into drainage canal   LAKE MICHIGAN SHAKES HANDS WITH THE FATHER OF THE WATERS   German zuchterverein singing contest for canary-birds opens   the fight for bimetallism at the ratio of 16 to 1 has not been lost, says Bryan

BRITISH BEATEN AT MAFEKING

For there's many a man been murdered in Luzon

CLAIMS ISLANDS FOR ALL TIME

Hamilton Club listens to Oratory by ex-Congressman Posey of Indiana

NOISE GREETS NEW CENTURY

LABOR GREETS NEW CENTURY

CHURCHES GREET NEW CENTURY

Mr. McKinley is hard at work in his office when the new year begins.

NATION GREETS CENTURY'S DAWN

Responding to a toast, Hail Columbia! at the Columbia Club banquet in Indianapolis, Indiana, ex-President Benjamin Harrison said in part: I have no argument to make here or anywhere against territorial expansion; but I do not, as some do, look upon territorial expansion as the safest and most attractive avenue of national development. By the advantages of abundant and cheap coal and

28

iron, of an enormous overproduction of food products and of invention and economy in production, we are now leading by the nose the original and the greatest of the colonizing nations.

Society Girls Shocked: Danced with Detectives

For there's many a man been murdered in Luzon
and Mindanao

GAIETY GIRLS MOBBED IN NEW JERSEY

One of the lithographs of the leading lady represented her in less than Atlantic City bathing costume, sitting on a red-hot stove; in one hand she held a brimming glass of wine, in the other ribbons drawn over a pair of rampant lobsters.

For there's many a man been murdered in Luzon
and Mindanao
and in Samar

In responding to the toast, "The Twentieth Century," Senator Albert J. Beveridge said in part: *The twentieth century will be American. American thought will dominate it. American progress will give it color and direction. American deeds will make it illustrious.*
Civilization will never lose its hold on Shanghai. Civilization will never depart from Hongkong. The gates of Peking will never again be closed to the methods of modern man. The regeneration of the world, physical as well as moral, has begun, and revolutions never move backwards.

There's been many a good man murdered in the Philippines
Lies sleeping in some lonesome grave.

The Camera Eye (1)

when you walk along the street you have to step carefully always on the cobbles so as not to step on the bright

29

anxious grassblades   easier if you hold Mother's hand
and hang on it that way you can kick up your toes but
walking fast you have to tread on too many grassblades
the poor hurt green tongues shrink under your
feet   maybe that's why those people are so angry and
follow us shaking their fists   they're throwing stones
grownup people throwing stones   She's walking fast and
we're running her pointed toes sticking out sharp among
the poor trodden grassblades under the shaking folds of
the brown cloth dress   Englander   a pebble tinkles
along the cobbles

Quick darling quick in the postcard shop it's quiet the
angry people are outside and can't come in   non nein
nicht englander amerikanisch americain   Hoch Amerika
Vive l'Amérique She laughs My dear they had me right
frightened

war on the veldt Kruger Bloemfontein Ladysmith and
Queen Victoria an old lady in a pointed lace cap sent
chocolate to the soldiers at Christmas

under the counter it's dark and the lady the nice Dutch
lady who loves Americans and has relations in Trenton
shows you postcards that shine in the dark pretty hotels
and palaces   O que c'est beau schön prittie prittie
and the moonlight ripple ripple under a bridge and the little
reverbères are alight in the dark under the counter and
the little windows of hotels around the harbor   O que
c'est beau la lune

and the big moon

Mac

When the wind set from the silver factories across the river
the air of the gray fourfamily frame house where Fainy Mc-
Creary was born was choking all day with the smell of whaleoil soap. Other days it smelt of cabbage and babies and Mrs.
McCreary's washboilers. Fainy could never play at home because Pop, a lame cavechested man with a wispy blondgray
mustache, was nightwatchman at the Chadwick Mills and
slept all day. It was only round five o'clock that a curling
whiff of tobaccosmoke would seep through from the front

room into the kitchen. That was a sign that Pop was up and in good spirits, and would soon be wanting his supper.

Then Fainy would be sent running out to one of two corners of the short muddy street of identical frame houses where they lived.

To the right it was half a block to Finley's where he would have to wait at the bar in a forest of mudsplattered trouserlegs until all the rank brawling mouths of grownups had been stopped with beers and whiskies. Then he would walk home, making each step very carefully, with the handle of the pail of suds cutting into his hand.

To the left it was half a block to Maginnis's Fancy Groceries, Home and Imported Products. Fainy liked the cardboard Cream of Wheat darkey in the window, the glass case with different kinds of salami in it, the barrels of potatoes and cabbages, the brown smell of sugar, sawdust, ginger, kippered herring, ham, vinegar, bread, pepper, lard.

"A loaf of bread, please, Mister, a halfpound of butter, and a box of gingersnaps."

Some evenings, when Mom felt poorly, Fainy had to go further; round the corner past Maginnis's, down Riverside Avenue where the trolley ran, and across the red bridge over the little river that flowed black between icy undercut snowbanks in winter, yellow and spuming in the spring thaws, brown and oily in summer. Across the river all the way to the corner of Riverside and Main, where the drugstore was, lived Bohunks and Polaks. Their kids were always fighting with the kids of the Murphys and O'Haras and O'Flanagans who lived on Orchard Street.

Fainy would walk along with his knees quaking, the medicine bottle in its white paper tight in one mittened hand. At

31

the corner of Quince was a group of boys he'd have to pass. Passing wasn't so bad; it was when he was about twenty yards from them that the first snowball would hum by his ear. There was no comeback. If he broke into a run, they'd chase him. If he dropped the medicine bottle he'd be beaten up when he got home. A soft one would plunk on the back of his head and the snow began to trickle down his neck. When he was a half a block from the bridge he'd take a chance and run for it.

"Scared cat . . . Shanty Irish . . . Bowlegged Murphy . . . Running home to tell the cop" . . . would yell the Polak and Bohunk kids between snowballs. They made their snowballs hard by pouring water on them and leaving them to freeze overnight; if one of those hit him it drew blood.

The backyard was the only place you could really feel safe to play in. There were brokendown fences, dented garbage cans, old pots and pans too nearly sieves to mend, a vacant chickencoop that still had feathers and droppings on the floor, hogweed in summer, mud in winter; but the glory of the McCrearys' backyard was Tony Harriman's rabbit hutch, where he kept Belgian hares. Tony Harriman was a consumptive and lived with his mother on the groundfloor left. He wanted to raise all sorts of other small animals too, raccoons, otter, even silver fox, he'd get rich that way. The day he died nobody could find the key to the big padlock on the door of the rabbit hutch. Fainy fed the hares for several days by pushing in cabbage and lettuce leaves through the double thickness of chickenwire. Then came a week of sleet and rain when he didn't go out in the yard. The first day, when he went to look, one of the hares was dead. Fainy turned white; he tried to tell himself the hare was asleep, but it lay gawkily stiff, not asleep. The other hares were huddled in a corner looking about with twitching noses, their bag ears flopping helpless over their backs. Poor hares; Fainy wanted to cry. He ran upstairs to his mother's kitchen, ducked under the ironing board and got the hammer out of the drawer in the kitchen table. The first time he tried he mashed his finger, but the second time he managed to jump the padlock. Inside the cage there was a funny, sour smell. Fainy picked the dead hare up by its ears. Its soft white belly was beginning to puff up, one dead eye was scaringly open. Something suddenly got hold of Fainy and made him drop the hare in the nearest garbage can and run upstairs. Still cold and trembling, he tiptoed out onto the back porch and looked down. Breathlessly he watched the other hares. By cautious hops they were getting near the door of the hutch into the yard. One of them was out. It sat up on its hind legs, limp ears suddenly stiff. Mom called him to bring her a flatiron from the stove. When he got back to the porch the hares were all gone.

That winter there was a strike in the Chadwick Mills and Pop lost his job. He would sit all day in the front room smoking and cursing:

"Ablebodied man, by Jesus, if I couldn't lick any one of those damn Polaks with my crutch tied behind my back . . . I says so to Mr. Barry; I ain't goin' to join no strike. Mr. Barry, a sensible quiet man, a bit of an invalid, with a wife an' kiddies to think for. Eight years I've been watchman, an' now you give me the sack to take on a bunch of thugs from a detective agency. The dirty pugnosed sonofabitch."

"If those damn lousy furreners hadn't a-walked out," somebody would answer soothingly.

The strike was not popular on Orchard Street. It meant that Mom had to work harder and harder, doing bigger and bigger boilerfuls of wash, and that Fainy and his older sister Milly had to help when they came home from school. And then one day Mom got sick and had to go back to bed instead of starting in on the ironing, and lay with her round white creased face whiter than the pillow and her watercreased hands in a knot under her chin. The doctor came and the district nurse, and all three rooms of the flat smelt of doctors and nurses and drugs, and the only place Fainy and Milly could find to sit was on the stairs. There they sat and cried quietly together. Then Mom's face on the pillow shrank into a little creased white thing like a rumpled-up handkerchief and they said that she was dead and took her away.

The funeral was from the undertaking parlors on Riverside Avenue on the next block. Fainy felt very proud and important because everybody kissed him and patted his head and said he was behaving like a little man. He had a new black suit on, too, like a grownup suit with pockets and everything, except that it had short pants. There were all sorts of people at the undertaking parlors he had never been close to before, Mr. Russell the butcher, and Father O'Donnell and Uncle Tim O'Hara who'd come on from Chicago, and it smelt of whiskey and beer like at Finley's. Uncle Tim was a skinny man with a knobbed red face and blurry blue eyes. He wore a loose black silk tie that worried Fainy, and kept leaning down suddenly, bending from the waist as if he was going to close up like a jackknife, and whispering in a thick voice in Fainy's ear.

"Don't you mind 'em, old sport, they're a bunch o' bums, and hypocrytes, stewed to the ears most of 'em already. Look at Father O'Donnell the fat swine already figurin' up the burial fees. But don't you mind 'em, remember you're an O'Hara

33

on your mother's side. I don't mind 'em, old sport, and she was my own sister by birth and blood."

When they got home he was terribly sleepy and his feet were cold and wet. Nobody paid any attention to him. He sat whimpering on the edge of the bed in the dark. In the front room there were voices and a sound of knives and forks, but he didn't dare go in there. He curled up against the wall and went to sleep. Light in his eyes woke him up. Uncle Tim and Pop were standing over him talking loud. They looked funny and didn't seem to be standing very steady. Uncle Tim held the lamp.

"Well, Fainy, old sport," said Uncle Tim giving the lamp a perilous wave over Fainy's head. "Fenian O'Hara McCreary, sit up and take notice and tell us what you think of our proposed removal to the great and growing city of Chicago. Middletown's a terrible bitch of a dump if you ask me . . . Meanin' no offense, John . . . But Chicago . . . Jesus God, man, when you get there you'll think you've been dead and nailed up in a coffin all these years."

Fainy was scared. He drew his knees up to his chin and looked tremblingly at the two big swaying figures of men lit by the swaying lamp. He tried to speak but the words dried up on his lips.

"The kid's asleep, Tim, for all your speechifyin' . . . Take your clothes off, Fainy, and get into bed and get a good night's sleep. We're leavin' in the mornin'."

And late on a rainy morning, without any breakfast, with a big old swelltop trunk tied up with rope joggling perilously on the roof of the cab that Fainy had been sent to order from Hodgeson's Livery Stable, they set out. Milly was crying. Pop didn't say a word but sucked on an unlit pipe. Uncle Tim handled everything, making little jokes all the time that nobody laughed at, pulling a roll of bills out of his pocket at every juncture, or taking great gurgling sips out of the flask he had in his pocket. Milly cried and cried. Fainy looked out with big dry eyes at the familiar streets, all suddenly odd and lopsided, that rolled past the cab; the red bridge, the scabshingled houses where the Polaks lived, Smith's and Smith's corner drugstore . . . there was Billy Hogan just coming out with a package of chewing gum in his hand. Playing hookey again. Fainy had an impulse to yell at him, but something froze it . . . Main with its elms and streetcars, blocks of stores round the corner of Church, and then the fire department. Fainy looked for the last time into the dark cave where shone entrancingly the brass and copper curves of the engine, then past the cardboard fronts of the First Congregational Church, The Carmel Baptist Church, Saint Andrew's Episcopal Church built of brick and set catercornered on its lot instead of straight with a stern face to the street like the other churches, then the three castiron stags on the lawn in front of the Commercial House, and the residences, each with its lawn, each with its scrollsaw porch, each with its hydrangea bush. Then the houses got smaller, and the lawns disappeared; the cab trundled round past Simpson's Grain and Feed Warehouse, along a row of barbershops, saloons and lunchrooms, and they were all getting out at the station.

At the station lunchcounter Uncle Tim set everybody up at breakfast. He dried Milly's tears and blew Fainy's nose in a big new pockethandkerchief that still had the tag on the corner and set them to work on bacon and eggs and coffee. Fainy hadn't had coffee before, so the idea of sitting up like a man and drinking coffee made him feel pretty good. Milly didn't like hers, said it was bitter. They were left all alone in the lunchroom for some time with the empty plates and empty coffeecups under the beady eyes of a woman with the long neck and pointed face of a hen who looked at them disapprovingly from behind the counter. Then with an enormous, shattering rumble, sludgepuff sludge . . . puff, the train came into the station. They were scooped up and dragged across the platform and through a pipesmoky car and before they knew it the train was moving and the wintry russet Connecticut landscape was clattering by.

The Camera Eye (2)

we hurry wallowing like in a boat in the musty stably-smelling herdic cab.   He kept saying What would you do Lucy if I were to invite one of them to my table? They're very lovely people Lucy the colored people and He had cloves in a little silver box and a rye whiskey

36

smell on his breath hurrying to catch the cars to New York.

and She was saying Oh dolly I hope we won't be late and Scott was waiting with the tickets and we had to run up the platform of the Seventh Street Depot and all the little cannons kept falling out of the Olympia and everybody stooped to pick them up and the conductor Allaboard lady quick lady

they were little brass cannons and were bright in the sun on the platform of the Seventh Street Depot and Scott hoisted us all up and the train was moving and the engine bell was ringing and Scott put in your hand a little handful of brass tiny cannons just big enough to hold the smallest size red firecracker at the battle of Manila Bay and said Here's the artillery Jack

and He was holding forth in the parlor car Why Lucy if it were necessary for the cause of humanity I would walk out and be shot any day you would Jack wouldn't you? wouldn't you porter? who was bringing apollinaris and He had a flask in the brown grip where the silk initialed handkerchiefs always smelt of bay rum

and when we got to Havre de Grace He said Rememoer Lucy we used to have a ferry across the Susquehanna before the bridge was built

and across Gunpowder Creek too

Mac

Russet hills, patches of woods, farmhouses, cows, a red colt kicking up its heels in a pasture, rail fences, streaks of marsh.

"Well, Tim, I feel like a whipped cur . . . So long as I've lived, Tim, I've tried to do the right thing," Pop kept repeating in a rattling voice. "And now what can they be sayin' about me?"

"Jesus God, man, there was nothin' else you could do, was there? What the devil can you do if you haven't any money and haven't any job and a lot o' doctors and undertakers and landlords come round with their bills and you with two children to support?"

"But I've been a quiet and respectable man, steady and misfortunate ever since I married and settled down. And now

37

what'll they be thinkin' of me sneakin' out like a whipped cur?"

"John, take it from me that I'd be the last one to want to bring disrespect on the dead that was my own sister by birth and blood . . . But it ain't your fault and it ain't my fault . . . it's the fault of poverty, and poverty's the fault of the system . . . Fenian, you listen to Tim O'Hara for a minute and Milly, you listen too, cause a girl ought to know these things just as well as a man and for once in his life Tim O'Hara's tellin' the truth . . . It's the fault of the system that don't give a man the fruit of his labor . . . The only man that gets anything out of capitalism is a crook, an' he gets to be a millionaire in short order . . . But an honest workin'man like John or myself we can work a hundred years and not leave enough to bury us decent with."

Smoke rolled white in front of the window shaking out of its folds trees and telegraph poles and little square shingle-roofed houses and towns and trolleycars, and long rows of buggies with steaming horses standing in line.

"And who gets the fruit of our labor, the goddam business-men, agents, middlemen who never did a productive piece of work in their life."

Fainy's eyes are following the telegraph wires that sag and soar.

"Now, Chicago ain't no paradise, I can promise you that, John, but it's a better market for a workin'man's muscles and brains at present than the East is . . . And why, did you ask me why . . . ? Supply and demand, they need workers in Chicago."

"Tim, I tellyer I feel like a whipped cur."

"It's the system, John, it's the goddam lousy system."

A great bustle in the car woke Fainy up. It was dark. Milly was crying again. He didn't know where he was.

"Well, gentlemen," Uncle Tim was saying, "we're about to arrive in little old New York."

In the station it was light; that surprised Fainy, who thought it was already night. He and Milly were left a long time sitting on a suitcase in the waitingroom. The waiting-room was huge, full of unfamiliarlooking people, scary like people in picturebooks. Milly kept crying.

"Hey, Milly, I'll biff you one if you don't stop crying."

"Why?" whined Milly, crying all the more.

Fainy stood as far away from her as possible so that people wouldn't think they were together. When he was about ready to cry himself, Pop and Uncle Tim came and took them and the suitcase into the restaurant. A strong smell of fresh whiskey came from their breaths, and they seemed very bright around the eyes. They all sat at a table with a white cloth and

·a sympathetic colored man in a white coat handed them a large card full of printing.

"Let's eat a good supper," said Uncle Tim, "if it's the last thing we do on this earth."

"Damn the expense," said Pop, "it's the system that's to blame."

"To hell with the pope," said Uncle Tim. "We'll make a Social Democrat out of you yet."

They gave Fainy fried oysters and chicken and icecream and cake, and when they all had to run for the train he had a terrible stitch in his side. They got into a daycoach that smelt of coalgas and armpits. "When are we going to bed?" Milly began to whine. "We're not going to bed," said Uncle Tim airily. "We're going to sleep right here like little mice . . . like little mice in a cheese." "I doan like mice," yelled Milly with a new flood of tears as the train started.

Fainy's eyes smarted; in his ears was the continuous roar, the clatter clatter over crossings, the sudden snarl under bridges. It was a tunnel; all the way to Chicago it was a tunnel. Opposite him Pop's and Uncle Tim's faces looked red and snarling, he didn't like the way they looked, and the light was smoky and jiggly and outside it was all a tunnel and his eyes hurt and wheels and rails roared in his ears and he fell asleep.

When he woke up it was a town and the train was running right through the main street. It was a sunny morning. He could see people going about their business, stores, buggies and springwagons standing at the curb, newsboys selling newspapers, wooden Indians outside of cigarstores. At first he thought he was dreaming, but then he remembered and decided it must be Chicago. Pop and Uncle Tim were asleep on the seat opposite. Their mouths were open, their faces were splotched, and he didn't like the way they looked. Milly was curled up with a woolly shawl all over her. The train was slowing down, it was a station. If it was Chicago they ought to get off. At that moment the conductor passed, an old man who looked a little like Father O'Donnell.

"Please, Mister, is this Chicago?"

"Chicago's a long way off yet, son," said the conductor without smiling. "This is Syracuse."

And they all woke up, and for hours and hours the telephone poles went by, and towns, frame houses, brick factories with ranks and ranks of glittering windows, dumping grounds, trainyards, plowed land, pasture, and cows, and Milly got trainsick and Fainy's legs felt like they would drop off from sitting in the seat so long; some places it was snowing and some places it was sunny, and Milly kept getting sick and smelt dismally of vomit and it got dark and they all slept; and light again, and then the towns and the frame houses and the factories all started drawing together, humping into warehouses and elevators, and the trainyards spread out as far as you could see and it was Chicago.

But it was so cold and the wind blew the dust so hard in his face and his eyes were so stuck together by dust and tiredness that he couldn't look at anything. After they had waited round a long while, Milly and Fainy huddled together in the cold, they got on a streetcar and rode and rode. They were so sleepy they never knew exactly where the train ended and the streetcar began. Uncle Tim's voice went on talking proudly excitedly, Chicago, Chicago, Chicago. Pop sat with his chin on his crutch. "Tim, I feel like a whipped cur."

Fainy lived ten years in Chicago.

At first he went to school and played baseball on back lots on Saturday afternoons, but then came his last commencement, and all the children sang *My Country, 'Tis of Thee,* and school was over and he had to go to work. Uncle Tim at that time had his own jobprinting shop on a dusty side street off North Clark in the groundfloor of a cranky old brick building. It only occupied a small section of the building that was mostly used as a warehouse and was famous for its rats. It had a single wide plateglass window made resplendent by gold Old English lettering: TIMOTHY O'HARA, JOB PRINTER.

"Now, Fainy, old sport," said Uncle Tim, "you'll have a chance to learn the profession from the ground up." So he ran errands, delivered packages of circulars, throwaways, posters, was always dodging trolleycars, ducking from under the foamy bits of big truckhorses, bumming rides on deliverywagons. When there were no errands to run he swept out under the presses, cleaned type, emptied the office wastepaper basket, or, during rush times, ran round the corner for coffee and sandwiches for the typesetter, or for a small flask of bourbon for Uncle Tim.

Pop puttered round on his crutch for several years, always looking for a job. Evenings he smoked his pipe and cursed his luck on the back stoop of Uncle Tim's house and occasionally threatened to go back to Middletown. Then one day he got pneumonia and died quietly at the Sacred Heart Hospital. It was about the same time that Uncle Tim bought a linotype machine.

Uncle Tim was so excited he didn't take a drink for three days. The floorboards were so rotten they had to build a brick base for the linotype all the way up from the cellar. "Well, when we get another one we'll concrete the whole place," Uncle Tim told everybody. For a whole day there was no work done. Everybody stood around looking at the tall black intricate machine that stood there like an organ in a church. When the machine was working and the printshop filled with the hot smell of molten metal, everybody's eyes followed the quivering inquisitive arm that darted and flexed above the keyboard. When they handed round the warm shiny slugs of type the old German typesetter who for some reason they called Mike pushed back his glasses on his forehead and cried. "Fifty-five years a printer, and now when I'm old I'll have to carry hods to make a living."

The first print Uncle Tim set up on the new machine was the phrase: *Workers of the world unite; you have nothing to lose but your chains.*

When Fainy was seventeen and just beginning to worry about skirts and ankles and girls' underwear when he walked home from work in the evening and saw the lights of the city bright against the bright heady western sky, there was a strike in the Chicago printing trades. Tim O'Hara had always run a union shop and did all the union printing at cost. He even got up a handbill signed, "A Citizen," entitled "An Ernest Protest," which Fainy was allowed to set up on the linotype one evening after the operator had gone home. One phrase stuck in Fainy's mind, and he repeated it to himself after he had gone to bed that night: *It is time for all honest men to band together to resist the ravages of greedy privilege.*

The next day was Sunday, and Fainy went along Michigan Avenue with a package of the handbills to distribute. It was a day of premature spring. Across the rotting yellow ice on the lake came little breezes that smelt unexpectedly of flowers. The girls looked terribly pretty and their skirts blew in the wind and Fainy felt the spring blood pumping hot in him, he wanted to kiss and to roll on the ground and to run out across the icecakes and to make speeches from the tops of telegraph poles and to vault over trolleycars; but instead he distributed handbills and worried about his pants being frayed and wished he had a swell looking suit and a swell looking girl to walk with.

"Hey, young feller, where's your permit to distribute them handbills?" It was a cop's voice growling in his ear. Fainy gave the cop one look over his shoulders, dropped the handbills and ran. He ducked through between the shiny black cabs and carriages, ran down a side street and walked and walked and didn't look back until he managed to get across a bridge just before the draw opened. The cop wasn't following him anyway.

He stood on the curb a long time with the whistle of a peanutstand shrilling derisively in his ear.

That night at supper his uncle asked him about the handbills.

"Sure I gave 'em out all along the lakeshore . . . A cop

43

tried to stop me, but I told him right where to get off." Fainy turned burning red when a hoot went up from everybody at the table. He filled up his mouth with mashed potato and wouldn't say any more. His aunt and his uncle and their three daughters laughed and laughed.

"Well, it's a good thing you ran faster than the cop," said Uncle Tim, "else I should have had to bail you out and that would have cost money."

The next morning early Fainy was sweeping out the office, when a man with a face like a raw steak walked up the steps; he was smoking a thin black stogy of a sort Fainy had never seen before. He knocked on the groundglass door.

"I want to speak to Mr. O'Hara, Timothy O'Hara."

"He's not here yet, be here any minute now, sir. Will you wait?"

"You bet I'll wait." The man sat on the edge of a chair and spat, first taking the chewed end of the stogy out of his mouth and looking at it meditatively for a long time.

When Tim O'Hara came the office door closed with a bang. Fainy hovered nervously around, a little bit afraid the man might be a detective following up the affair of the handbills. Voices rose and fell, the stranger's voice in short rattling ti-

44

rades, O'Hara's voice in long expostulating clauses, now and then Fainy caught the word foreclose, until suddenly the door flew open and the stranger shot out, his face purpler than ever. On the iron stoop he turned and pulling a new stogy from his pocket, lit it from the old one; growling the words through the stogy and the blue puff of smoke, he said, "Mr. O'Hara, you have twentyfour hours to think it over . . . A word from you and proceedings stop immediately." Then he went off down the street leaving behind him a long trail of rancid smoke.

A minute later, Uncle Tim came out of the office, his face white as paper. "Fenian, old sport," he said, "you go get yourself a job. I'm going out of business . . . Keep a weather eye open. I'm going to have a drink." And he was drunk for six days. By the end of that time a number of meeklooking men appeared with summonses, and Uncle Tim had to sober up enough to go down to the court and put in a plea of bankruptcy.

Mrs. O'Hara scolded and stormed, "Didn't I tell you, Tim O'Hara, no good'll ever come with your fiddlin' round with these godless labor unions and social-democrats and knights of

labor, all of 'em drunk and loafin' bums like yourself, Tim O'Hara? Of course the master printers 'ud have to get together and buy up your outstandin' paper and squash you, and serve you right too, Tim O'Hara, you and your godless socialistic boozin' ways only they might have thought of your poor wife and her helpless wee babes, and now we'll starve all of us together, us and the dependents and hangerson you've brought into the house."

"Well, I declare," cried Fainy's sister Milly. "If I haven't slaved and worked my fingers to the bone for every piece of bread I've eaten in this house," and she got up from the breakfast table and flounced out of the room. Fainy sat there while the storm raged above his head; then he got up, slipping a corn muffin into his pocket as he went. In the hall he found the "help wanted" section of the *Chicago Tribune*, took his cap and went out into a raw Sunday morning full of churchbells jangling in his ears. He boarded a streetcar and went out to Lincoln Park. There he sat on a bench for a long time munching the muffin and looking down the columns of advertisements: Boy Wanted. But they none of them looked very inviting. One thing he was bound, he wouldn't get another job in a printing shop until the strike was over. Then his eye struck

Bright boy wanted with amb. and lit. taste, knowledge of print. and pub. business. Conf. sales and distrib. proposition $15 a week apply by letter P.O. Box 1256b

Fainy's head suddenly got very light. Bright boy, that's me, ambition and literary taste . . . Gee, I must finish *Looking Backward* . . . and jeez, I like reading fine, an' I could run a linotype or set up print if anybody'd let me. Fifteen bucks a week . . . pretty soft, ten dollars' raise. And he began to write a letter in his head, applying for the job.

Dear Sir (My dear sir)
or maybe Gentlemen,
In applying for the position you offer in today's Sunday *Tribune* I want to apply, (allow me to state) that I'm seventeen years old, no, nineteen, with several years' experience in the printing and publishing trades, ambitious and with excellent knowledge and taste in the printing and publishing trades,

No, I can't say that twice . . . And I'm very anxious for the job . . . As he went along it got more and more muddled in his head.

46

He found he was standing beside a peanut wagon. It was cold as blazes, a razor wind was shrieking across the broken ice and the black patches of water of the lake. He tore out the ad and let the rest of the paper go with the wind. Then he bought himself a warm package of peanuts.

Newsreel II

Come on and hear
Come on and hear
Come on and hear

In his address to the Michigan State Legislature the retiring governor, Hazen S. Pingree, said in part: I make the prediction that unless those in charge and in whose hands legislation is reposed do not change the present system of inequality, there will be a bloody revolution in less than a quarter of a century in this great country of ours.

CARNEGIE TALKS OF HIS EPITAPH

Alexander's Ragtime Band
It is the best
It is the best

the luncheon which was served in the physical laboratory was replete with novel features. A miniature blastfurnace four feet high was on the banquet table and a narrowgauge railroad forty feet long ran round the edge of the table. Instead of molten metal the blastfurnace poured hot punch into small cars on the railroad. Icecream was served in the shape of railroad ties and bread took the shape of locomotives.

Mr. Carnegie, while extolling the advantages of higher education in every branch of learning, came at last to this conclusion: Manual labor has been found to be the best foundation for the greatest work of the brain.

48

Come on and hear
Alexander's Ragtime Band
It is the best
It is the best

brother of Jesse James declares play picturing him as
bandit trainrobber and outlaw is demoralizing district battle ends with polygamy, according to an investigation by
Salt Lake ministers, still practiced by Mormons clubwomen gasp

It is the best band in the land

say circus animals only eat Chicago horsemeat Taxsale
of Indiana marks finale of World's Fair boom uses flag as
ragbag killed on cannibal isle keeper falls into water and
sealions attack him.

The launch then came alongside the halfdeflated bal-
loon of the aerostat which threatened at any moment to
smother Santos Dumont. The latter was half pulled and
half clambered over the gunwale into the boat.

The Prince of Monaco urged him to allow himself to
be taken on board the yacht to dry himself and change
his clothes. Santos Dumont would not leave the launch
until everything that could be saved had been taken
ashore, then, wet but smiling and unconcerned, he landed
amid the frenzied cheers of the crowd.

The Camera Eye (3)

O qu'il a des beaux yeux said the lady in the seat opposite but She said that was no way to talk to children
and the little boy felt all hot and sticky but it was dusk
and the lamp shaped like half a melon was coming on
dim red and the train rumbled and suddenly I've been
asleep and it's black dark and the blue tassel bobs on the
edge of the dark shade shaped like a melon and every-

49

where there are pointed curved shadows (the first time
He came He brought a melon and the sun was coming in
through the tall lace windowcurtains and when we cut it
the smell of melons filled the whole room) No don't eat
the seeds deary they give you appendicitis

but you're peeking out of the window into the black
rumbling dark suddenly ranked with squat chimneys and
you're scared of the black smoke and the puffs of flame
that flare and fade out of the squat chimneys   Potteries
dearie they work there all night Who works there all
night? Workingmen and people like that laborers travail-
leurs greasers

you were scared

but now the dark was all black again the lamp in the
train and the sky and everything had a blueback shade on
it and She was telling a story about

Longago Beforetheworldsfair Beforeyouwereborn and
they went to Mexico on a private car on the new international line and the men shot antelope off the back of the
train and big rabbits jackasses they called them and once
one night Longago Beforetheworldsfair Beforeyouwereborn one night Mother was so frightened on account of
all the rifleshots but it was allright turned out to be nothing but a little shooting they'd been only shooting a
greaser that was all

that was in the early days

Lover of Mankind

Debs was a railroadman, born in a weatherboarded shack
at Terre Haute.

He was one of ten children.

His father had come to America in a sailingship in '49,

an Alsatian from Colmar; not much of a moneymaker,
fond of music and reading,

he gave his children a chance to finish public school and
that was about all he could do.

At fifteen Gene Debs was already working as a machinist
on the Indianapolis and Terre Haute Railway.

He worked as a locomotive fireman,

clerked in a store

joined the local of the Brotherhood of Locomotive Firemen, was elected secretary, traveled all over the country as organizer.

He was a tall shamblefooted man, had a sort of gusty rhetoric that set on fire the railroad workers in their pineboarded halls

made them want the world he wanted,

a world brothers might own

where everybody would split even:

I am not a labor leader. I don't want you to follow me or anyone else. If you are looking for a Moses to lead you out of the capitalist wilderness you will stay right where you are. I would not lead you into this promised land if I could, because if I could lead you in, someone else would lead you out.

That was how he talked to freighthandlers and gandywalkers, to firemen and switchmen and engineers, telling them it wasn't enough to organize the railroadmen, that all workers must be organized, that all workers must be organized in the workers' co-operative commonwealth.

Locomotive fireman on many a long night's run,

under the smoke a fire burned him up, burned in gusty words that beat in pineboarded halls; he wanted his brothers to be free men.

That was what he saw in the crowd that met him at the old Wells Street Depot when he came out of jail after the Pullman strike,

those were the men that chalked up nine hundred thousand votes for him in nineteen-twelve and scared the frockcoats and the tophats and diamonded hostesses at Saratoga Springs, Bar Harbor, Lake Geneva with the bogy of a Socialist president.

But where were Gene Deb's brothers in nineteen eighteen when Woodrow Wilson had him locked up in Atlanta for speaking against war,

where were the big men fond of whiskey and fond of each other, gentle rambling tellers of stories over bars in small towns in the Middle West,

quiet men who wanted a house with a porch to putter around and a fat wife to cook for them, a few drinks and cigars, a garden to dig in, cronies to chew the rag with

and wanted to work for it

and others to work for it;

where were the locomotive firemen and engineers when they hustled him off to Atlanta Penitentiary?

And they brought him back to die in Terre Haute

to sit on his porch in a rocker with a cigar in his mouth,

beside him American Beauty roses his wife fixed in a bowl;

and the people of Terre Haute and the people in Indiana and the people of the Middle West were fond of him and afraid of him and thought of him as an old kindly uncle who loved them, and wanted to be with him and to have him give them candy,

but they were afraid of him as if he had contracted a social disease, syphilis or leprosy, and thought it was too bad,

but on account of the flag

and prosperity

and making the world safe for democracy,

they were afraid to be with him,

or to think much about him for fear they might believe him;

for he said:

While there is a lower class I am of it, while there is a criminal class I am of it, while there is a soul in prison I am not free.

The Camera Eye (4)

riding backwards through the rain in the rumbly cab looking at their two faces in the jiggly light of the four-wheeled cab and Her big trunks thumping on the roof and He reciting *Othello* in his lawyer's voice

Her father loved me, oft invited me
Still questioned me the story of my life
From year to year, the battles, sieges, fortunes
That I have past.
I ran it through, even from my boyish days,
To th' very moment that he bade me tell it
Wherein I spoke of the most disastrous chances
Of moving accidents by flood and field
Of hairbreadth 'scapes i' th' imminent deadly breach

why that's the Schuylkill   the horse's hoofs rattle sharp on smooth wet asphalt after cobbles   through the gray streaks of rain the river shimmers ruddy with winter mud   When I was your age Jack I dove off this bridge

through the rail of the bridge we can look way down into
the cold rainyshimmery water   Did you have any clothes
on?   Just my shirt

Mac

Fainy stood near the door in the crowded elevated train;
against the back of the fat man who held on to the strap in
front of him, he kept rereading a letter on crisp watermarked
stationery:

> The Truthseeker Literary Distributing Co., Inc.
>   General Offices 1104 S. Hamlin Avenue
>   Chicago, Ill. April 14, 1904
>
> Fenian O'H. McCreary
>   456 N. Wood Street
>   Chicago, Ill.
> DEAR SIR:
>   We take the pleasure to acknowledge yours of the 10th
> inst.
>   In reference to the matter in hand we feel that much
> could be gained by a personal interview. If you will be
> so good as to step around to the above address on Monday
> April 16th at nine o'clock, we feel that the matter of
> your adaptability for the position for which you have ap-
> plied can be thoroughly thrashed out.
>   Yours in search for Truth,
>
>   EMMANUEL R. BINGHAM, D.D.

Fainy was scared. The train got to his station too soon. He
had fifteen minutes to walk two blocks in. He loafed along
the street, looking in store windows. There was a golden
pheasant, stuffed, in a taxidermist's; above it hung a big flat
greenish fish with a sawtoothed bill from which dangled a
label:

> SAWFISH (pristis perrotetti)
> *Habitat Gulf and Florida waters. Frequents shallow bays
> and inlets.*

Maybe he wouldn't go at all. In the back of the window
was a lynx and on the other side a bobtailed cat, each on its
53

limb of a tree. Suddenly he caught his breath. He'd be late. He went tearing off down the block.

He was breathless and his heart was pounding to beat the cars when he reached the top of the fourth flight of stairs. He studied the groundglass doors on the landing:

THE UNIVERSAL CONTACT COMPANY
F. W. Perkins

Assurance

THE WINDY CITY MAGIC AND NOVELTY COMPANY

Dr. Noble
Hospital and Sickroom Supplies

The last one was a grimy door in the back beside the toilet. The gold leaf had come off the letters, but he was able to spell out from the outlines:

THE GENERAL OUTFITTING AND MERCHAN-DIZING CORPORATION.

Then he saw a card on the wall beside the door with a hand holding a torch drawn out on it and under it the words "Truthseeker Inc." He tapped gingerly on the glass. No answer. He tapped again.

"Come in . . . Don't knock," called out a deep voice. Fainy found himself stuttering as he opened the door and stepped into a dark, narrow room completely filled up by two huge rolltop desks:

"Please, I called to see Mr. Bingham, sir."

At the further desk, in front of the single window sat a big man with a big drooping jaw that gave him a little of the expression of a setter dog. His black hair was long and curled a little over each ear, on the back of his head was a broad black felt hat. He leaned back in his chair and looked Fainy up and down.

"How do you do, young man? What kind of books are you inclined to purchase this morning? What can I do for you this morning?" he boomed.

"Are you Mr. Bingham, sir, please?"

"This is Doc Bingham right here before you."

"Please, sir, I . . . I came about that job."

Doc Bingham's expression changed. He twisted his mouth as if he'd just tasted something sour. He spun around in his

54

swivelchair and spat into a brass spittoon in the corner of the room. Then he turned to Fainy again and leveled a fat finger at him, "Young man, how do you spell experience?"

"E . . . x . . . p . . . er . . . er . . . er . . . i . . . a . . . n . . ."

"That'll do . . . No education . . . I thought as much . . . No culture, none of those finer feelings that distinguish the civilized man from the savage aborigines of the wilds . . . No enthusiasm for truth, for bringing light into dark places . . . Do you realize, young man, that it is not a job I'm offering you, it is a great opportunity . . . a splendid opportunity for service and self-improvement. I'm offering you an education gratis."

Fainy shuffled his feet. He had a husk in his throat.

"If it's in the printin' line I guess I could do it."

"Well, young man, during the brief interrogatory through which I'm going to put you, remember that you stand on the threshold of opportunity."

Doc Bingham ferreted in the pigeonholes of his desk for a long time, found himself a cigar, bit off the end, lit it, and then turned again to Fainy, who was standing first on one foot and then on the other.

"Well, if you'll tell me your name."

"Fenian O'Hara McCreary . . ."

"Hum . . . Scotch and Irish . . . that's pretty good stock . . . that's the stock I come from."

"Religion?"

Fainy squirmed. "Pop was a Catholic but . . ." He turned red.

Dr. Bingham laughed, and rubbed his hands.

"Oh, religion, what crimes are committed in thy name. I'm an agnostic myself . . . caring nothing for class or creed when among friends; though sometimes, my boy, you have to bow with the wind . . . No, sir, my God is the truth, that rising ever higher in the hands of honest men will dispel the mists of ignorance and greed, and bring freedom and knowledge to mankind . . . Do you agree with me?"

"I've been working for my uncle. He's a social-democrat."

"Ah, hotheaded youth . . . Can you drive a horse?"

"Why, yessir, I guess I could."

"Well, I don't see why I shouldn't hire you."

"The advertisement in the *Tribune* said fifteen dollars a week."

Doc Bingham's voice assumed a particularly velvety tone.

"Why, Fenian, my boy, fifteen dollars a week will be the minimum you will make . . . Have you ever heard of the cooperative system? That is how I'm going to hire you . . .

55

As sole owner and representative of the Truthseeker Corporation, I have here a magnificent line of small books and pamphlets covering every phase of human knowledge and endeavor . . . I am embarking immediately on a sales campaign to cover the whole country. You will be one of my distributors. The books sell at from ten to fifty cents. On each ten-cent book you make a cent, on the fifty-cent books you make five cents . . ."

"And don't I get anything every week?" stammered Fainy.

"Would you be penny-wise and pound-foolish? Throwing away the most magnificent opportunity of a lifetime for the assurance of a paltry pittance. No, I can see by your flaming eye, by your rebellious name out of old Ireland's history, that you are a young man of spirit and determination . . . Are we on? Shake hands on it then and by gad, Fenian, you shall never regret it."

Doc Bingham jumped to his feet and seized Fainy's hand and shook it.

"Now, Fenian, come with me; we have an important preliminary errand to perform." Doc Bingham pulled his hat forward on his head and they walked down the stairs to the front door; he was a big man and the fat hung loosely on him as he walked. Anyway, it's a job, Fainy told himself.

First they went to a tailorshop where a longnosed yellow man whom Doc Bingham addressed as Lee shuffled out to meet them. The tailorshop smelt of steamed cloth and cleansing fluid. Lee talked as if he had no palate to his mouth.

" 'M pretty sick man," he said. "Spen' mor'n thou'an' dollarm on doctor, no get well."

"Well, I'll stand by you; you know that, Lee."

"Hure, Mannie, hure, only you owe me too much money."

Doctor Emmanuel Bingham glanced at Fainy out of the corner of his eye.

"I can assure you that the entire financial situation will be clarified within sixty days . . . But what I want you to do now is to lend me two of your big cartons, those cardboard boxes you send suits home in."

"What you wan' to do?"

"My young friend and I have a little project."

"Don't you do nothin' crooked with them cartons; my name's on them."

Doc Bingham laughed heartily as they walked out the door, carrying under each arm one of the big flat cartons that had LEVY AND GOLDSTEIN, RELIABLE TAILORING, written on them in florid lettering.

"He's a great joker, Fenian," he said. "But let that man's lamentable condition be a lesson to you . . . The poor unfortunate is suffering from the consequences of a horrible social disease, contracted through some youthful folly."

They were passing the taxidermist's store again. There were the wildcats and the golden pheasant and the big sawfish . . . *Frequents shallow bays and inlets.* Fainy had a temptation to drop the tailor's cartons and run for it. But anyhow, it was a job.

"Fenian," said Doc Bingham confidentially, "do you know the Mohawk House?"

"Yessir, we used to do their printing for them."

"They don't know you there, do they?"

"Naw, they wouldn't know me from Adam . . . I just delivered some writin' paper there once."

"That's superb . . . Now get this right; my room is 303. You wait and come in about five minutes. You're the boy from the tailor's, see, getting some suits to be cleaned. Then you come up to my room and get the suits and take 'em round to my office. If anybody asks you where you're goin' with 'em, you're goin' to Levy and Goldstein, see?"

Fainy drew a deep breath.

"Sure, I get you."

When he reached the small room in the top of the Mohawk House, Doc Bingham was pacing the floor.

"Levy and Goldstein, sir," said Fainy, keeping his face straight.

"My boy," said Doc Bingham, "you'll be an able assistant; I'm glad I picked you out. I'll give you a dollar in advance on your wages." While he talked he was taking clothes, papers, old books, out of a big trunk that stood in the middle of the floor. He packed them carefully in one of the cartons. In the other he put a furlined overcoat. "That coat cost two hundred dollars, Fenian, a remnant of former splendors . . . Ah, the autumn leaves at Vallombrosa . . . Et tu in Arcadia vixisti . . . That's Latin, a language of scholars."

"My Uncle Tim who ran the printing shop where I worked knew Latin fine."

"Do you think you can carry these, Fenian . . . they're not too heavy?"

"Sure I can carry 'em." Fainy wanted to ask about the dollar.

"All right, you'd better run along . . . Wait for me at the office."

In the office Fainy found a man sitting at the second rolltop desk. "Vell, what's your business?" he yelled out in a rasping voice. He was a sharpnosed waxyskinned young man with straight black hair standing straight up. Fainy was winded from running up the stairs. His arms were stiff from

57

carrying the heavy cartons. "I suppose this is some more of Mannie's tomfoolishness. Tell him he's got to clear out of here: I've rented the other desk."

"But Doctor Bingham has just hired me to work for the Truthseeker Literary Distributing Company."

"The hell he has."

"He'll be here in a minute."

"Well, sit down and shut up; can't you see I'm busy?"

Fainy sat down glumly in the swivelchair by the window, the only chair in the office not piled high with small paper-covered books. Outside the window he could see a few dusty roofs and fire escapes. Through grimy windows he could see other offices, other rolltop desks. On the desk in front of him were paperwrapped packages of books. Between them were masses of loose booklets. His eye caught a title:

THE QUEEN OF THE WHITE SLAVES

Scandalous revelations of Milly Meecham stolen from her parents at the age of sixteen, tricked by her vile seducer into a life of infamy and shame.

He started reading the book. His tongue got dry and he felt sticky all over.

"Nobody said anything to you, eh?" Doc Bingham's booming voice broke in on his reading.

Before he could answer, the voice of the man at the other desk snarled out: "Look here, Mannie, you've got to clear out of here . . . I've rented the desk."

"Shake not thy gory locks at me, Samuel Epstein. My young friend and I are just preparing an expedition among the aborigines of darkest Michigan. We are leaving for Saginaw tonight. Within sixty days I'll come back and take the office off your hands. This young man is coming with me to learn the business."

"Business, hell," growled the other man, and shoved his face back down among his papers again.

"Procrastination, Fenian, is the thief of time," said Doc Bingham, putting one fat hand Napoleonfashion into his doublebreasted vest. "There is a tide in the affairs of men that taken at its full . . ." And for two hours Fainy sweated under his direction, packing booklets into brown paper packages, tying them and addressing them to Truthseeker Inc., Saginaw, Mich.

He begged off for an hour to go home to see his folks. Milly kissed him on the forehead with thin tight lips. Then she burst out crying. "You're lucky; oh, I wish I was a boy," she spluttered and ran upstairs. Mrs. O'Hara said to be a good boy and always live at the Y.M.C.A.—that kept a boy out of temptation, and to let his Uncle Tim be a lesson to him, with his boozin' ways.

His throat was pretty tight when he went to look for his Uncle Tim. He found him in the back room at O'Grady's. His eyes were a flat bright blue and his lower lip trembled when he spoke, "Have one drink with me, son, you're on your own now." Fainy drank down a beer without tasting it.

"Fainy, you're a bright boy . . . I wish I could have helped you more; you're an O'Hara every inch of you. You read Marx . . . study all you can, remember that you're a rebel by birth and blood . . . Don't blame people for things . . . Look at that terrible forktongued virago I'm married to; do I blame her? No, I blame the system. And don't ever sell out to the sonsofbitches, son; it's women'll make you sell out every time. You know what I mean. All right, go on . . . better cut along or you'll miss your train."

"I'll write you from Saginaw, Uncle Tim, honest I will."

Uncle Tim's lanky red face in the empty cigarsmoky room, the bar and its glint of brass and the pinkarmed barkeep leaning across it, the bottles and the mirrors and the portrait of Lincoln gave a misty half turn in his head and he was out in the shiny rainy street under the shiny clouds, hurrying for the Elevated station with his suitcase in his hand.

At the Illinois Central station he found Doc Bingham waiting for him, in the middle of a ring of brown paper parcels. Fen felt a little funny inside when he saw him, the greasy sallow jowls, the doublebreasted vest, the baggy black ministerial coat, the dusty black felt hat that made the hair stick out in a sudden fuzzycurl over the beefy ears. Anyway, it was a job.

"It must be admitted, Fenian," began Doc Bingham as soon as Fainy had come up to him, "that confident as I am of my knowledge of human nature I was a little afraid you wouldn't turn up. Where is it that the poet says that difficult is the first fluttering course of the fledgeling from the nest. Put these packages on the train while I go purchase tickets, and be sure it's a smoker."

After the train had started and the conductor had punched the tickets, Doc Bingham leaned over and tapped Fainy on the knee with a chubby forefinger. "I'm glad you're a neat dresser, my boy; you must never forget the importance of putting up a fine front to the world. Though the heart be as dust and ashes, yet must the outer man be sprightly and of good cheer. We will go sit for a while in the Pullman smoker up ahead to get away from the yokels."

It was raining hard and the windows of the train were striped with transverse beaded streaks against the darkness. Fainy felt uneasy as he followed Doc Bingham lurching through the greenplush parlor car to the small leather upholstered smokingcompartment at the end. There Doc Bingham drew a large cigar from his pocket and began blowing a magnificent series of smoke rings. Fainy sat beside him with his feet under the seat trying to take up as little room as possible.

Gradually the compartment filled up with silent men and crinkly spiraling cigarsmoke. Outside the rain beat against the windows with a gravelly sound. For a long time nobody said anything. Occasionally a man cleared his throat and let fly to-

wards the cuspidor with a big gob of phlegm or a jet of tobaccojuice.

"Well, sir," a voice began, coming from nowhere in particular, addressed to nowhere in particular, "it was a great old
inauguration even if we did freeze to death."

"Were you in Washington?"

"Yessir, I was in Washington."

"Most of the trains didn't get in till the next day."

"I know it; I was lucky, there was some of them snowed
up for fortyeight hours."

"Some blizzard all right."

> All day the gusty northwind bore
> The lessening drift its breath before
> Low circling through its southern zone
> The sun through dazzling snowmist shone,

recited Doc Bingham coyly, with downcast eyes.

"You must have a good memory to be able to recite verses
right off the reel like that."

"Yessir, I have a memory that may I think, without undue
violation of modesty, be called compendious. Were it a natural gift I should be forced to blush and remain silent, but
since it is the result of forty years of study of what is best in
the world's epic lyric and dramatic literatures, I feel that to
call attention to it may sometimes encourage some other
whose feet are also bound on the paths of enlightenment and
selfeducation." He turned suddenly to Fainy. "Young man,
would you like to hear Othello's address to the Venetian Senate?"

"Sure I would," said Fainy, blushing.

"Well, at last Teddy has a chance to carry out his word
about fighting the trusts." "I'm telling you the insurgent
farmer vote of the great Northwest . . ." "Terrible thing the
wreck of those inauguration specials."

But Doc Bingham was off:

> Most potent grave and reverend signiors,
> My very noble and approved good masters,
> That I have ta'en away this old man's daughter
> It is most true; true, I have married her . . .

"They won't get away with those antitrust laws, believe me
they won't. You can't curtail the liberty of the individual liberty in that way." "It's the liberty of the individual business
man that the progressive wing of the Republican party is
trying to protect."

But Doc Bingham was on his feet, one hand was tucked into his doublebreasted vest, with the other he was making broad circular gestures:

> *Rude am I in speech*
> *And little blessed with the soft phrase of peace,*
> *For since these arms of mine had seven years' pith*
> *Till now some nine moons wasted they have used*
> *Their dearest action in the tented field.*

"The farmer vote," the other man began shrilly, but nobody was listening. Doc Bingham had the floor.

> *And little of the great world can I speak*
> *More than pertains to broils and battle*
> *And therefore little shall I grace my cause*
> *In speaking for myself.*

The train began to slacken speed. Doc Bingham's voice sounded oddly loud in the lessened noise. Fainy felt his back pushing into the back of the seat and then suddenly there was stillness and the sound of an engine bell in the distance and Doc Bingham's voice in a queasy whisper:

"Gentlemen, I have here in pamphlet form a complete and unexpurgated edition of one of the world's classics, the famous *Decameron* of Boccaccio, that for four centuries has been a byword for spicy wit and ribald humor . . ." He took a bundle of little books out of one of his sagging pockets and began dandling them in his hand. "Just as an act of friendship I would be willing to part with some if any of you gentlemen care for them . . . Here, Fenian, take these and see if anybody wants one; they're two dollars apiece. My young friend here will attend to distribution . . . Goodnight, gentlemen." And he went off and the train had started again and Fainy found himself standing with the little books in his hand in the middle of the lurching car with the suspicious eyes of all the smokers boring into him like so many gimlets.

"Let's see one," said a little man with protruding ears who sat in the corner. He opened the book and started reading greedily. Fainy stood in the center of the car, feeling pins and needles all over. He caught a white glint in the corner of an eyeball as the little man looked down the line of cigars through the crinkly smoke. A touch of pink came into the protruding ears.

"Hot stuff," said the little man, "but two dollars is too much."

Fainy found himself stuttering: "They're nnnot mmmine, sir; I don't know . . ."

"Oh, well, what the hell . . ." The little man dropped two dollar bills in Fainy's hand and went back to his reading. Fainy had six dollars in his pocket and two books left when he started back to the daycoach. Halfway down the car he met the conductor. His heart almost stopped beating. The conductor looked at him sharply but said nothing.

Doc Bingham was sitting in his seat with his head in his hand and his eyes closed as if he were dozing. Fainy slipped into the seat beside him.

"How many did they take?" asked Doc Bingham, talking out of the corner of his mouth without opening his eyes.

"I got six bucks . . . Golly, the conductor scared me, the way he looked at me."

"You leave the conductor to me, and remember that it's never a crime in the face of humanity and enlightenment to distribute the works of the great humanists among the merchants and moneychangers of this godforsaken country . . . You better slip me the dough."

Fainy wanted to ask about the dollar he'd been promised, but Doc Bingham was off on Othello again.

If after every tempest there come such calms as this
Then may the laboring bark climb hills of seas
Olympus high.

They slept late at the Commercial House in Saginaw, and ate a large breakfast, during which Doc Bingham discoursed on the theory and practice of book salesmanship. "I am very much afraid that through the hinterland to which we are about to penetrate," he said as he cut up three fried eggs and stuffed his mouth with bakingpowder biscuit, "that we will find the yokels still hankering after Maria Monk."

Fainy didn't know who Maria Monk was, but he didn't like to ask. He went with Doc Bingham round to Hummer's livery stable to hire a horse and wagon. There followed a long wrangle between the firm of Truthseeker Inc., and the management of Hummer's Livery Stable as to the rent of a springwagon and an elderly piebald horse with cruppers you could hang a hat on, so that it was late afternoon before they drove out of Saginaw with their packages of books piled behind them, bound for the road.

It was a chilly spring day. Sagging clouds moved in a gray blur over a bluish silvery sky. The piebald kept slackening to a walk; Fainy clacked the reins continually on his caving rump and clucked with his tongue until his mouth was dry.

At the first whack the piebald would go into a lope that would immediately degenerate into an irregular jogtrot and then into a walk. Fainy cursed and clucked, but he couldn't get the horse to stay in the lope or the jogtrot. Meanwhile Doc Bingham sat beside him with his broad hat on the back of his head, smoking a cigar and discoursing: "Let me say right now, Fenian, that the attitude of a man of enlightened ideas, is, *A plague on both your houses* . . . I myself am a pantheist . . . but even a pantheist . . . must eat, hence Maria Monk." A few drops of rain, icy and stinging as hail, had begun to drive in their faces. "I'll get pneumonia at this rate, and it'll be your fault, too; I thought you said you could drive a horse . . . Here, drive into that farmhouse on the left. Maybe they'll let us put the horse and wagon in their barn."

As they drove up the lane towards the gray house and the big gray barn that stood under a clump of pines a little off from the road, the piebald slowed to a walk and began reaching for the bright green clumps of grass at the edge of the ditch. Fainy beat at him with the ends of the reins, and even stuck his foot over the dashboard and kicked him, but he wouldn't budge.

"Goddam it, give me the reins."

Doc Bingham gave the horse's head a terrible yank, but all that happened was that he turned his head and looked at them, a green foam of partly chewed grass between his long yellow teeth. To Fainy it looked as if he were laughing. The rain had come on hard. They put their coat collars up. Fainy soon had a little icy trickle down the back of his neck.

"Get out and walk; goddam it to hell, lead it if you can't drive it," sputtered Doc Bingham. Fainy jumped out and led the horse up to the back door of the farmhouse; the rain ran down his sleeve from the hand he held the horse by.

"Good afternoon, ma'am." Doc Bingham was on his feet bowing to a little old woman who had come out of the door. He stood beside her on the stoop out of the rain. "Do you mind if I put my horse and wagon in your barn for a few moments? I have valuable perishable materials in the wagon and no waterproof covering . . ." The old woman nodded a stringy white head. "Well, that's very kind of you, I must say . . . all right, Fenian, put the horse in the barn and come here and bring in that little package under the seat . . . I was just saying to my young friend here that I was sure that some good samaritan lived in this house who would take in two weary wayfarers." "Come inside, mister . . . maybe you'd like to set beside the stove and dry yourself. Come inside, mister-

64

er?" "Doc Bingham's the name . . . the Reverend Doctor Bingham," Fainy heard him say as he went in the house.

He was soaked and shivering when he went into the house himself, carrying a package of books under his arm. Doc Bingham was sitting large as life in a rocking chair in front of the kitchen stove. Beside him on the well-scrubbed deal table was a piece of pie and a cup of coffee. The kitchen had a warm cosy smell of apples and bacon grease and lamps. The old woman was leaning over the kitchen table listening intently to what Doc Bingham was saying. Another woman, a big scrawny woman with her scant sandy hair done up in a screw on top of her head, stood in the background with her redknuckled hands on her hips. A black and white cat, back arched and tail in the air, was rubbing against Doc Bingham's legs.

"Ah, Fenian, just in time," he began in a voice that purred like the cat, "I was just telling . . . relating to your kind hostesses the contents of our very interesting and educational library, the prime of the world's devotional and inspirational literature. They have been so kind to us during our little misfortune with the weather that I thought it would be only fair to let them see a few of our titles."

The big woman was twisting her apron. "I like a mite o' readin' fine," she said, shyly, "but I don't git much chanct for it, not till wintertime."

Benignly smiling, Doc Bingham untied the string and pulled the package open on his knees. A booklet dropped to the floor. Fainy saw that it was *The Queen of the White Slaves*. A shade of sourness went over Doc Bingham's face. He put his foot on the dropped book. "These are Gospel Talks, my boy," he said. "I wanted *Doctor Spikenard's Short Sermons for All Occasions*." He handed the halfopen package to Fainy, who snatched it to him. Then he stooped and picked the book up from under his foot with a slow sweeping gesture of the hand and slipped it in his pocket. "I suppose I'll have to go and find them myself," he went on in his purringest voice. When the kitchen door closed behind them he snarled in Fainy's ear, "Under the seat, you little rat . . . If you play a trick like that again I'll break every goddam bone in your body." And he brought his knee up so hard into the seat of Fainy's pants that his teeth clacked together and he shot out into the rain towards the barn. "Honest, I didn't do it on purpose," Fainy whined. But Doc Bingham was already back in the house and his voice was burbling comfortably out into the rainy dusk with the first streak of lamplight.

This time Fainy was careful to open the package before he brought it in. Doc Bingham took the books out of his hand

65

without looking at him and Fainy went round behind the stovepipe. He stood there in the soggy steam of his clothes listening to Doc Bingham boom. He was hungry, but nobody seemed to think of offering him a piece of pie.

"Ah, my dear friends, how can I tell you with what gratitude to the Great Giver a lonely minister of the gospel of light, wandering among the tares and troubles of this world, finds ready listeners. I'm sure that these little books will be consoling, interesting and inspirational to all that undertake the slight effort of perusal. I feel this so strongly that I always carry a few extra copies with me to dispose of for a moderate sum. It breaks my heart that I can't yet give them away free gratis."

"How much are they?" asked the old woman, a sudden sharpness coming over her features. The scrawny woman let her arms drop to her side and shook her head.

"Do you remember, Fenian," asked Doc Bingham, leaning genially back in his chair, "what the cost price of these little booklets was?" Fainy was sore. He didn't answer. "Come here, Fenian," said Doc Bingham in honied tones, "allow me to remind you of the words of the immortal bard:

> Lowliness is your ambition's ladder
> Whereto the climber upward turns his face
> But when he once attains the topmost round
> He then unto the ladder turns his back

"You must be hungry. You can eat my pie."

"I reckon we can find the boy a piece of pie," said the old woman.

"Ain't they ten cents?" said Fainy, coming forward.

"Oh, if they're only ten cents I think I'd like one," said the old woman quickly. The scrawny woman started to say something, but it was too late.

The pie had hardly disappeared into Fainy's gullet and the bright dime out of the old tobaccobox in the cupboard into Doc Bingham's vest pocket when there was a sound of clinking harness and the glint of a buggylamp through the rainy dark outside the window. The old woman got to her feet and looked nervously at the door, which immediately opened. A heavyset grayhaired man with a small goatee sprouting out of a round red face came in, shaking the rain off the flaps of his coat. After him came a skinny lad about Fainy's age.

"How do you do, sir; how do you do, son?" boomed Doc Bingham through the last of his pie and coffee.

"They asked if they could put their horse in the barn until it should stop rainin'. It's all right, ain't it, James?" asked the old woman nervously. "I reckon so," said the older man, sitting down heavily in the free chair. The old woman had hidden the pamphlet in the drawer of the kitchen table. "Travelin' in books, I gather." He stared hard at the open package of pamphlets. "Well, we don't need any of that trash here, but you're welcome to stay the night in the barn. This is no night to throw a human being out inter."

So they unhitched the horse and made beds for themselves in the hay over the cowstable. Before they left the house the older man made them give up their matches. "Where there's matches there's danger of fire," he said. Doc Bingham's face was black as thunder as he wrapped himself in a horseblanket, muttering about "indignity to a wearer of the cloth." Fainy was excited and happy. He lay on his back listening to the beat of the rain on the roof and its gurgle in the gutters, and the muffled stirring and champing of the cattle and horse, under them; his nose was full of the smell of the hay and the warm meadowsweetness of the cows. He wasn't sleepy. He wished he had someone his own age to talk to. Anyway, it was a job and he was on the road.

He had barely got to sleep when a light woke him. The boy he'd seen in the kitchen was standing over him with a lantern. His shadow hovered over them enormous against the rafters.

"Say, I wanner buy a book."

"What kind of a book?" Fainy yawned and sat up.

"You know . . . one o' them books about chorusgirls an' white slaves an' stuff like that."

"How much do you want to pay, son?" came Doc Bingham's voice from under the horseblanket. "We have a number of very interesting books stating the facts of life frankly and freely, describing the deplorable licentiousness of life in the big cities, ranging from a dollar to five dollars. *The Complete Sexology of Doctor Burnside*, is six-fifty."

"I couldn't go higher'n a dollar . . . Say, you won't tell the old man on me?" the young man said, turning from one to another. "Seth Hardwick, he lives down the road, he went into Saginaw onct an' got a book from a man at the hotel. Gosh, it was a pippin." He tittered uneasily.

"Fenian, go down and get him *The Queen of the White Slaves* for a dollar," said Doc Bingham, and settled back to sleep.

Fainy and the farmer's boy went down the rickety ladder.

"Say, is she pretty spicy? . . . Gosh, if pop finds it he'll give me a whalin' . . . Gosh, I bet you've read all them books."

"Me?" said Fainy haughtily. "I don't need to read books. I

67

kin see life if I wanter. Here it is . . . it's about fallen women."

"Ain't that pretty short for a dollar? I thought you could get a big book for a dollar."

"This one's pretty spicy."

"Well, I guess I'll take it before dad ketches me snoopin' around . . . Goodnight." Fainy went back to his bed in the hay and fell fast asleep. He was dreaming that he was going up a rickety stair in a barn with his sister Milly who kept getting all the time bigger and white and fatter, and had on a big hat with ostrich plumes all round it and her dress began to split from the neck and lower and lower and Doc Bingham's voice was saying She's Maria Monk, the queen of the white slaves, and just as he was going to grab her, sunlight opened his eyes. Doc Bingham stood in front of him, his feet wide apart, combing his hair with a pocketcomb and reciting:

> Let us depart, the universal sun
> Confines not to one land his blessed beams
> Nor is man rooted like a tree . . .

"Come, Fenian," he boomed, when he saw that Fainy was awake, "let us shake the dust of this inhospitable farm, latcheting our shoes with a curse like philosophers of old . . . Hitch up the horse; we'll get breakfast down the road."

This went on for several weeks until one evening they found themselves driving up to a neat yellow house in a grove of feathery dark tamaracks. Fainy waited in the wagon while Doc Bingham interviewed the people in the house. After a while Doc Bingham appeared in the door, a broad smile creasing his cheeks. "We're going to be very handsomely treated, Fenian, as befits a wearer of the cloth and all that . . . You be careful how you talk, will you? Take the horse to the barn and unhitch."

"Say, Mr. Bingham, how about my money? It's three weeks now." Fainy jumped down and went to the horse's head.

An expression of gloom passed over Doc Bingham's face. "Oh, lucre, lucre . . .

> Examine well
> His milkwhite hand, the palm is hardly clean
> But here and there an ugly smutch appears,
> Foh, 'twas a bribe that left it. . . .

"I had great plans for a co-operative enterprise that you are spoiling by your youthful haste and greed . . . but if you

68

must I'll hand over to you this very night everything due you and more. All right, unhitch the horse and bring me that little package with *Maria Monk,* and *The Popish Plot.*"

It was a warm day. There were robins singing round the barn. Everything smelt of sweetgrass and flowers. The barn was red and the yard was full of white leghorns. After he had unhitched the spring wagon and put the horse in a stall, Fainy sat on a rail of the fence looking out over the silver-green field of oats out back, and smoked a cigarette. He wished there was a girl there he could put his arm round or a fellow to talk to.

A hand dropped onto his shoulder. Doc Bingham was standing beside him.

"Fenian, my young friend, we are in clover," he said. "She is alone in the house, and her husband has gone to town for two days with the hired man. There'll be nobody there but her two little children, sweet bairns. Perhaps I shall play Romeo. You've never seen me in love. It's my noblest role. Ah, some day I'll tell you about my headstrong youth. Come and meet the sweet charmer."

When they went in the kitchen door a dimplefaced pudgy woman in a lavender housecap greeted them coyly.

"This is my young assistant, ma'am," said Doc Bingham, with a noble gesture. "Fenian, this is Mrs. Kovach."

"You must be hungry. We're having supper right away."

The last of the sun lit up a kitchen range that was crowded with saucepans and stewpots. Fragrant steam rose in little jets from round wellpolished lids. As she spoke Mrs. Kovach leaned over so that her big blue behind with starched apronstrings tied in a bow above it stood up straight in the air, opened the oven door and pulled out a great pan of corn-muffins that she dumped into a dish on the dining table already set next the window. Their warm toasted smoke filled the kitchen. Fainy felt his mouth watering. Doc Bingham was rubbing his hands and rolling his eyes. They sat down, and the two blue-eyed smearyfaced children were sat down and started gobbling silently, and Mrs. Kovach heaped their plates with stewed tomatoes, mashed potatoes, beef stew and limabeans with pork. She poured them out coffee and then said with moist eyes, as she sat down herself:

"I love to see men eat."

Her face took on a crushed-pansy look that made Fainy turn away his eyes when he found himself looking at it. After supper she sat listening with a pleased, frightened expression while Doc Bingham talked and talked, now and then stopping to lean back and blow a smoke ring at the lamp.

"While not myself a Lutheran as you might say, ma'am, I

myself have always admired, nay, revered, the great figure of Martin Luther as one of the lightbringers of mankind. Were it not for him we would be still groveling under the dread domination of the Pope of Rome."

"They'll never get into this country; land sakes, it gives me the creeps to think of it."

"Not while there's a drop of red blood in the veins of free-born Protestants . . . but the way to fight darkness, ma'am, is with light. Light comes from education, reading of books and studies . . ."

"Land sakes, it gives me a headache to read most books, an' I don't get much time, to tell the truth. My husband, he reads books he gets from the Department of Agriculture. He tried to make me read one once, on raisin' poultry, but I couldn't make much sense out of it. His folks they come from the old country . . . I guess people feels different over there."

"It must be difficult being married to a foreigner like that."

"Sometimes I don't know how I stand it; 'course he was awful goodlookin' when I married him . . . I never could resist a goodlookin' man."

Doc Bingham leaned further across the table. His eyes rolled as if they were going to drop out.

"I never could resist a goodlooking lady."

Mrs. Kovach sighed deeply.

Fainy got up and went out. He'd been trying to get in a word about getting paid, but what was the use? Outside it was chilly; the stars were bright above the roofs of the barns and outhouses. From the chickencoop came an occasional sleepy cluck or the rustle of feathers as a hen lost her balance on her perch. He walked up and down the barnyard cursing Doc Bingham and kicking at an occasional clod of manure.

Later he looked into the lamplit kitchen. Doc Bingham had his arm around Mrs. Kovach's waist and was declaiming verses, making big gestures with his free hand:

> . . . These things to hear
> Would Desdemona seriously incline
> But still the house affairs would draw her hence
> Which ever as she could with haste dispatch
> She'd come again and with a greedy ear . . .

Fainy shook his fist at the window. "Goddam your hide, I want my money," he said aloud. Then he went for a walk down the road. When he came back he was sleepy and chilly. The kitchen was empty and the lamp was turned down low. He didn't know where to go to sleep, so he settled down

70

to warm himself in a chair beside the fire. His head began to
nod and he fell asleep.

A tremendous thump on the floor above and a woman's
shrieks woke him. His first thought was that Doc Bingham
was robbing and murdering the woman. But immediately he
heard another voice cursing and shouting in broken English.
He had half gotten up from the chair, when Doc Bingham
dashed past him. He had on only his flannel unionsuit. In one
hand were his shoes, in the other his clothes. His trousers
floated after him at the end of his suspenders like the tail of a
kite.

"Hey, what are we going to do?" Fainy called after him,
but got no answer. Instead he found himself face to face with
a tall dark man with a scraggly black beard who was coolly
fitting shells into a doublebarreled shotgun.

"Buckshot. I shoot the sonabitch."

"Hey, you can't do that," began Fainy. He got the butt of
the shotgun in the chest and went crashing down into the
chair again. The man strode out the door with a long elastic
stride, and there followed two shots that went rattling among
the farm buildings. Then the woman's shrieks started up
again, punctuating a longdrawnout hysterical tittering and
sobbing.

Fainy sat in the chair by the stove as if glued to it.

71

He noticed a fiftycent piece on the kitchen floor that must have dropped out of Doc Bingham's pants as he ran. He grabbed it and had just gotten it in his pocket when the tall man with the shotgun came back.

"No more shells," he said thickly. Then he sat down on the kitchen table among the uncleared supper dishes and began to cry like a child, the tears trickling through the knobbed fingers of his big dark hands. Fainy stole out of the door and went to the barn. "Doc Bingham," he called gently. The harness lay in a heap between the shafts of the wagon, but there was no trace of Doc Bingham or of the piebald horse. The frightened clucking of the hens disturbed in the hencoop mixed with the woman's shrieks that still came from upstairs in the farmhouse. "What the hell shall I do?" Fainy was asking himself when he caught sight of a tall figure outlined in the bright kitchen door and pointing the shotgun at him. Just as the shotgun blazed away he ducked into the barn and out through the back door. Buckshot whined over his head. "Gosh, he found shells." Fainy was off as fast as his legs could carry him across the oatfield. At last, without any breath in his body, he scrambled over a railfence full of briars that tore his face and hands and lay flat in a dry ditch to rest. There was nobody following him.

Newsreel III

"IT TAKES NERVE TO LIVE IN THIS WORLD" LAST WORDS OF GEORGE SMITH HANGED WITH HIS BROTHER BY MOB IN KANSAS   MARQUIS OF QUEENS-BERRY DEAD   FLAMES WRECK SPICE PLANT COURT SETS ZOLA FREE

a few years ago the anarchists of New Jersey, wearing the McKinley button and the red badge of anarchy on their coats and supplied with beer by the Republicans, plotted the death of one of the crowned heads of Europe and it is likely that the plan to assassinate the President was hatched at the same time or soon afterward.

It's moonlight fair tonight upon the Wabash
From the fields there comes the breath of newmown hay
Through the sycamores the candlelight is gleaming
On the banks of the Wabash far away

OUT FOR BULLY GOOD TIME

Six Thousand Workmen at Smolensk Parade with Placards Saying Death to Czar Assassin

Riots and Streetblockades Mark Opening of Teamsters Strike

WORLD'S GREATEST SEA BATTLE NEAR

Madrid Police Clash with Five Thousand Workmen Carrying Black Flag

The Camera Eye (5)

and we played the battle of Port Arthur in the bathtub
and the water leaked down through the drawingroom ceiling and it was altogether too bad but in Kew Gardens old
Mr. Garnet who was still hale and hearty although so
very old came to tea and we saw him first through the
window with his red face and John Bull whiskers and
aunty said it was a sailor's rolling gait and he was carrying a box under his arm and Vickie and Pompon
barked and here was Mr. Garnet come to tea and he took
a gramophone out of a black box and put a cylinder on
the gramophone and they pushed back the teathings off
the corner of the table. Be careful not to drop it now they
scratch rather heasy Why a hordinary sewin' needle
would do maam but I 'ave special needles

and we got to talking about Hadmiral Togo and the
Banyan and how the Roosians drank so much vodka and
killed all those poor fisherlads in the North Sea and he
wound it up very carefully so as not to break the spring
and the needle went rasp rasp Yes I was a bluejacket
miself miboy from the time I was a little shayver not
much bigger'n you rose to be bosun's mite on the first
British hironclad the *Warrior* and I can dance a 'ornpipe
yet maam and he had a mariner's compass in red and
blue on the back of his hand and his nails looked black
and thick as he fumbled with the needle and the needle
went rasp rasp and far away a band played and out of a
grindy noise in the little black horn came *God Save the
King* and the little dogs howled

74

Newsreel IV

I met my love in the Alamo
When the moon was on the rise
Her beauty quite bedimmed its light
So radiant were her eyes

during the forenoon union pickets turned back a wagon loaded with fifty campchairs on its way to the fire engine house at Michigan Avenue and Washington Street. The chairs, it is reported, were ordered for the convenience of policemen detailed on strike duty

FLEETS MAY MEET IN BATTLE TODAY
WEST OF LUZON

three big wolves were killed before the dinner.

A grand parade is proposed here in which President Roosevelt shall ride so that he can be seen by citizens. At the head will be a caged bear recently captured after killing a dozen dogs and injuring several men. The bear will be given an hour's start for the hills then the packs will be set on the trail and President Roosevelt and the guides will follow in pursuit.

Three Columbia Students Start Auto Trip to Chicago
on Wager

GENERAL STRIKE NOW THREATENS

It's moonlight fair tonight upon the Wa-abash

OIL KING'S HAPPYEST DAY

one cherub every five minutes   market for all classes of real-estate continues to be healthy with good demand for factory sites residence and business properties   court bills break labor lady angels are smashed   troops guard oilfields America tends to become empire like in the days of the Caesars five-dollar poem gets rich husband   eat less says Edison   rich pokerplayer falls dead when he draws royal flush   charges graft in Cicero

STRIKE MAY MEAN REVOLT IN RUSSIA

lake romance of two yachts   murder ends labor feud   Michigan runs all over Albion   red flags in St. Petersburg

CZAR YIELDS TO PEOPLE

holds dead baby forty hours   families evicted by bursting watermain

CZAR GRANTS CONSTITUTION

From the fields there comes the breath of newmown hay
Through the sycamores the candlelight is gleaming

The Camera Eye (6)

Go it go it said Mr. Linwood the headmaster when one was running up the field kicking the round ball footer they called it in Hampstead and afterwards it was time to walk home and one felt good because Mr. Linwood had said Go it

Taylor said There's another American come and he had teeth like Teddy in the newspapers and a turnedup nose and a Rough Rider suit and he said Who are you going to vote for? and one said I dunno and he stuck his chest out and said I mean who your folks for Roosevelt or Parker? and one said Judge Parker

the other American's hair was very black and he stuck his fists up and his nose turned up and he said I'm for Roosevelt wanto fight? all trembly one said I'm for Judge Parker but Taylor said Who's got tuppence for ginger beer? and there wasn't any fight that time

76

Newsreel V

BUGS DRIVE OUT BIOLOGIST

elopers bind and gag; is released by dog

**EMPEROR NICHOLAS II FACING REVOLT OF
EMPIRE GRANTS SUBJECTS LIBERTY**

paralysis stops surgeon's knife   by the stroke of a pen
the last absolute monarchy of Europe passes into
history   miner of Death Valley and freak advertiser of
Santa Fe Road may die   sent to bridewell for stealing
plaster angel

On the banks of the Wabash far away.

Mac

Next morning soon after daylight Fainy limped out of a
heavy shower into the railroad station at Gaylord. There was
a big swagbellied stove burning in the station waitingroom.
The ticket agent's window was closed. There was nobody in
sight. Fainy took off first one drenched shoe and then the
other and toasted his feet till his socks were dry. A blister had
formed and broken on each heel and the socks stuck to them
in a grimy scab. He put on his shoes again and stretched out
on the bench. Immediately he was asleep.

Somebody tall in blue was speaking to him. He tried to
raise his head but he was too sleepy.

"Hey, bo, you better not let the station agent find you,"
said a voice he'd been hearing before through his sleep. Fainy

opened his eyes and sat up. "Jeez, I thought you were a cop."

A squareshouldered young man in blue denim shirt and overalls was standing over him. "I thought I'd better wake you up, station agent's so friggin' tough in this dump."

"Thanks." Fainy stretched his legs. His feet were so swollen he could hardly stand on them. "Golly, I'm stiff."

"Say, if we each had a quarter I know a dump where we could get a bully breakfast."

"I gotta dollar an' a half," said Fainy slowly. He stood with his hands in his pockets, his back to the warm stove looking carefully at the other boy's square bulljawed face and blue eyes. "Where are you from?"

"I'm from Duluth . . . I'm on the bum more or less. Where are you from?"

"Golly, I wish I knew. I had a job till last night."

"Resigned?"

"Say, suppose we go eat that breakfast."

"That's slick. I didn't eat yesterday. . . . My name's George Hall . . . The fellers call me Ike. I ain't exactly on the bum, you know. I want to see the world."

"I guess I'm going to have to see the world now," said Fainy. "My name's McCreary. I'm from Chi. But I was born back east in Middletown, Connecticut."

As they opened the screen door of the railroadmen's

boardinghouse down the road they were met by a smell of ham and coffee and roach-powder. A horsetoothed blond woman with a rusty voice set places for them.

"Where do you boys work? I don't remember seein' you before."

"I worked down to the sawmill," said Ike.

"Sawmill shet down two weeks ago because the superintendent blew out his brains."

"Don't I know it?"

"Maybe you boys better pay in advance."

"I got the money," said Fainy, waving a dollar bill in her face.

"Well, if you got the money I guess you'll pay all right," said the waitress, showing her long yellow teeth in a smile.

"Sure, peaches and cream, we'll pay like millionaires," said Ike.

They filled up on coffee and hominy and ham and eggs and big heavy white bakingpowder biscuits, and by the end of breakfast they had gotten to laughing so hard over Fainy's stories of Doc Bingham's life and loves that the waitress asked them if they'd been drinking. Ike kidded her into bringing them each another cup of coffee without extra charge. Then he fished up two mashed cigarettes from the pocket of his overalls. "Have a coffin nail, Mac?"

"You can't smoke here," said the waitress. "The missus won't stand for smokin'."

"All right, bright eyes, we'll skidoo."

"How far are you goin'?"

"Well, I'm headed for Duluth myself. That's where my folks are . . ."

"So you're from Duluth, are you?"

"Well, what's the big joke about Duluth?"

"Its no joke, it's a misfortune."

"You don't think you can kid me, do you?"

" 'Taint worth my while, sweetheart." The waitress tittered as she cleared off the table. She had big red hands and thick nails white from kitchenwork.

"Hey, got any noospapers? I want somethin' to read waitin' for the train."

"I'll get you some. The missus takes the *American* from Chicago."

"Gee, I ain't seen a paper in three weeks."

"I like to read the paper, too," said Mac. "I like to know what's goin' on in the world."

"A lot of lies most of it . . . all owned by the interests."

"Hearst's on the side of the people."

"I don't trust him any more'n the rest of 'em."

"Ever read *The Appeal to Reason?*"

"Say, are you a Socialist?"

"Sure; I had a job in my uncle's printin' shop till the big interests put him outa business because he took the side of the strikers."

"Gee, that's swell . . . put it there . . . me, too. . . . Say, Mac, this is a big day for me . . . I don't often meet a guy thinks like I do."

They went out with a roll of newspapers and sat under a big pine a little way out of town. The sun had come out warm; big white marble clouds sailed through the sky. They lay on their backs with their heads on a piece of pinkish root with bark like an alligator. In spite of last night's rain the pineneedles were warm and dry under them. In front of them stretched the singletrack line through thickets and clearings of wrecked woodland where fireweed was beginning to thrust up here and there a palegreen spike of leaves. They read sheets of the weekold paper turn and turn about and talked.

"Maybe in Russia it'll start; that's the most backward country where the people are oppressed worst . . . There was a Russian feller workin' down to the sawmill, an educated feller who's fled from Siberia . . . I used to talk to him a lot . . . That's what he thought. He said the social revolution would start in Russia an' spread all over the world. He was a swell guy. I bet he was somebody."

"Uncle Tim thought it would start in Germany."

"Oughter start right here in America . . . We got free institutions here already . . . All we have to do is get out from under the interests."

"Uncle Tim says we're too well off in America . . . we don't know what oppression or poverty is. Him an' my other uncles was Fenians back in Ireland before they came to this country. That's what they named me Fenian . . . Pop didn't like it. I guess . . . he didn't have much spunk, I guess."

"Ever read Marx?"

"No . . . golly, I'd like to though."

"Me neither, I read Bellamy's *Looking Backward*, though; that's what made me a Socialist."

"Tell me about it; I'd just started readin' it when I left home."

"It's about a galoot that goes to sleep an' wakes up in the year two thousand and the social revolution's all happened and everything's socialistic an' there's no jails or poverty and nobody works for themselves an' there's no way anybody can get to be a rich bondholder or capitalist and life's pretty slick for the workingclass."

"That's what I always thought . . . It's the workers who create wealth and they ought to have it instead of a lot of drones."

"If you could do away with the capitalist system and the big trusts and Wall Street things 'ud be like that."

"Gee."

"All you'd need would be a general strike and have the workers refuse to work for a boss any longer . . . God damn it, if people only realized how friggin' easy it would be. The interests own all the press and keep knowledge and education from the workin' men."

"I know printin', pretty good, an' linotypin'. . . . golly, maybe some day I could do somethin'."

Mac got to his feet. He was tingling all over. A cloud had covered the sun, but down the railroad track the scrawny woods were full of the goldgreen blare of young birch leaves in the sun. His blood was like fire. He stood with his feet apart looking down the railroad track. Round the bend in the far distance a handcar appeared with a section gang on it, a tiny cluster of brown and dark blue. He watched it come nearer. A speck of red flag fluttered in the front of the handcar; it grew bigger, ducking into patches of shadow, larger and more distinct each time it came out into a patch of sun.

"Say, Mac, we better keep out of sight if we want to hop that freight. There's some friggin' mean yard detectives on this road."

"All right."

They walked off a hundred yards into the young growth of scrub pine and birch. Beside a big greenlichened stump Mac stopped to make water. His urine flowed bright yellow in the sun, disappearing at once into the porous loam of rotten leaves and wood. He was very happy. He gave the stump a kick. It was rotten. His foot went through it and a little powder like smoke went up from it as it crashed over into the alderbushes behind.

Ike had sat down on a log and was picking his teeth with a little birch-twig.

"Say, ever been to the coast, Mac?"

"No."

"Like to?"

"Sure."

"Well, let's you an' me beat our way out to Duluth . . . I want to stop by and say hello to the old woman, see. Haven't seen her in three months. Then we'll take in the wheat harvest and make Frisco or Seattle by fall. Tell me they have good free nightschools in Seattle. I want to do some studyin', see? I dunno a friggin' thing yet."

"That's slick."

"Ever hoppped a freight or ridden blind baggage, Mac?"

"Well, not exactly."

"You follow me and do what I do. You'll be all right."

Down the track they heard the hoot of a locomotive whistle.

"There is number three comin' round the bend now . . . We'll hop her right after she starts outa the station. She'll take us into Mackinaw City this afternoon."

Late that afternoon, stiff and cold, they went into a little shed on the steamboat wharf at Mackinaw City to get shelter. Everything was hidden in a driving rainstreaked mist off the lake. They had bought a ten-cent package of Sweet Caps, so that they only had ninety cents left between them. They were arguing about how much they ought to spend for supper when the steamboat agent, a thin man wearing a green eyeshade and a slicker, came out of his office.

"You boys lookin' for a job?" he asked. " 'Cause there's a guy here from the Lakeview House lookin' for a coupla pearldivers. Agency didn't send 'em enough help, I guess. They're openin' up tomorrer."

"How much do they pay ye?" asked Ike.

"I don't reckon it's much, but the grub's pretty good."

"How about it, Mac? We'll save up our fare an' then we'll go to Duluth like a coupla dudes on the boat."

So they went over that night on the steamboat to Mackinac Island. It was pretty dull on Mackinac Island. There was a lot of small scenery with signs on it reading "Devil's Cauldron," "Sugar Loaf," "Lover's Leap," and wives and children of mediumpriced business men from Detroit, Saginaw and Chicago. The grayfaced woman who ran the hotel, known as The Management, kept them working from six in the morning till way after sundown. It wasn't only dishwashing, it was sawing wood, running errands, cleaning toilets, scrubbing floors, smashing baggage and a lot of odd chores. The waitresses were all old maids or else brokendown farmers' wives whose husbands drank. The only other male in the place was the cook, a hypochondriac French-Canadian halfbreed who insisted on being called Mr. Chef. Evenings he sat in his little log shack back of the hotel drinking paregoric and mumbling about God.

When they got their first month's pay, they packed up their few belongings in a newspaper and sneaked on board the *Juniata* for Duluth. The fare took all their capital, but they were happy as they stood in the stern watching the spruce and balsamcovered hill of Mackinac disappear into the lake.

Duluth; girderwork along the waterfront, and the shackcovered hills and the tall thin chimneys and the huddle of hunchshouldered grain elevators under the smoke from the mills scrolled out dark against a huge salmoncolored sunset. Ike hated to leave the boat on account of a pretty darkhaired girl he'd meant all the time to speak to.

"Hell, she wouldn't pay attention to you, Ike, she's too swank for you," Mac kept saying.

"The old woman'll be glad to see us anyway," said Ike as they hurried off the gangplank. "I half expected to see her at the dock, though I didn't write we was coming. Boy, I bet she'll give us a swell feed."

"Where does she live?"

"Not far. I'll show you. Say, don't ask anythin' about my ole man, will ye; he don't amount to much. He's in jail, I guess. Ole woman's had pretty tough sleddin' bringin' up us kids . . . I got two brothers in Buffalo . . . I don't get along with 'em. She does fancy needlework and preservin' an' bakes cakes an' stuff like that. She used to work in a bakery but she's got the lumbago too bad now. She'd 'a' been a real bright woman if we hadn't always been so friggin' poor."

They turned up a muddy street on a hill. At the top of the hill was a little prim house like a schoolhouse.

"That's where we live . . . Gee, I wonder why there's no light."

They went in by a gate in the picket fence. There was sweetwilliam in bloom in the flowerbed in front of the house. They could smell it though they could hardly see, it was so dark. Ike knocked.

"Damn it, I wonder what's the matter." He knocked again. Then he struck a match. On the door was nailed a card "FOR SALE" and the name of a realestate agent. "Jesus Christ, that's funny, she musta moved. Now I think of it, I haven't

had a letter in a couple of months. I hope she ain't sick . . .
I'll ask at Bud Walker's next door."

Mac sat down on the wooden step and waited. Overhead in
a gash in the clouds that still had the faintest stain of red
from the afterglow his eye dropped into empty black full of
stars. The smell of the sweetwilliams tickled his nose. He felt
hungry.

A low whistle from Ike roused him. "Come along," he said
gruffly and started walking fast down the hill with his head
sunk between his shoulders.

"Hey, what's the matter?"

"Nothin'. The old woman's gone to Buffalo to live with my
brothers. The lousy bums got her to sell out so's they could
spend the dough, I reckon."

"Jesus, that's hell, Ike."

Ike didn't answer. They walked till they came to the corner
of a street with lighted stores and trolleycars. A tune from a
mechanical piano was tumbling out from a saloon. Ike turned
and slapped Mac on the back. "Let's go have a drink, kid
. . . What the hell."

There was only one other man at the long bar. He was a
very drunken tall elderly man in lumbermen's boots with a
sou'wester on his head who kept yelling in an inaudible voice,
"Whoop her up, boys," and making a pass at the air with a
long grimy hand. Mac and Ike drank down two whiskies
each, so strong and raw that it pretty near knocked the wind
out of them. Ike put the change from a dollar in his pocket
and said:

"What the hell, let's get out of here." In the cool air of the
street they began to feel lit. "Jesus, Mac, let's get outa here
tonight . . . It's terrible to come back to a town where you
was a kid . . . I'll be meetin' all the crazy galoots I ever
knew and girls I had crushes on . . . I guess I always get the
dirty end of the stick, all right."

In a lunchroom down by the freight depot they got hamburger and potatoes and bread and butter and coffee for fifteen cents each. When they'd bought some cigarettes
they still had eight-seventyfive between them.

"Golly, we're rich," said Mac. "Well, where do we go?"

"Wait a minute. I'll go scout round the freight depot. Used
to be a guy I knowed worked there."

Mac loafed round under a lamppost at the streetcorner and
smoked a cigarette and waited. It was warmer since the wind
had gone down. From a puddle somewhere in the freight
yards came the peep peep peep of toads. Up on the hill an
accordion was playing. From the yards came the heavy chug-

ging of a freight locomotive and the clank of shunted freight-cars and the singing rattle of the wheels.

After a while he heard Ike's whistle from the dark side of the street. He ran over.

"Say, Mac, we gotta hurry. I found the guy. He's goin' to open up a boxcar for us on the westbound freight. He says it'll carry us clear out to the coast if we stick to it."

"How the hell will we eat if we're locked up in a freight-car?"

"We'll eat fine. You leave the eatin' to me."

"But, Ike . . ."

"Keep your trap shut, can't you . . . do you want every-body in the friggin' town to know what we're tryin' to do?"

They walked along tiptoe in the dark between two tracks of boxcars. Then Ike found a door half open and darted in. Mac followed and they shut the sliding door very gently after them.

"Now all we got to do is go to sleep," whispered Ike, his lips touching Mac's ear. "This here galoot, see, said there wasn't any yard dicks on duty tonight."

In the end of the car they found hay from a broken bale. The whole car smelt of hay.

"Ain't this hunkydory?" whispered Ike.

"It's the cat's nuts, Ike."

Pretty soon the train started, and they lay down to sleep side by side in the sparse hay. The cold night wind streamed in through the cracks in the floor. They slept fitfully. The train started and stopped and started and shunted back and forth on sidings and the wheels rattled and rumbled in their ears and slambanged over crossings. Towards morning they fell into a warm sleep and the thin layer of hay on the boards was suddenly soft and warm. Neither of them had a watch and the day was overcast so they didn't know what time it was when they woke up. Ike slid open the door a little so that they could peek out; the train was running through a broad valley brimful-like with floodwater, with the green ripple of full-grown wheat. Now and then in the distance a clump of woodland stood up like an island. At each station was the hunched blind bulk of an elevator.

"Gee, this must be the Red River, but I wonder which way we're goin'," said Ike.

"Golly, I could drink a cup of coffee," said Mac.

"We'll have swell coffee in Seattle, damned if we won't, Mac."

They went to sleep again, and when they woke up they were thirsty and stiff. The train had stopped. There was no sound at all. They lay on their backs stretching and listening.

85

"Gee, I wonder where in hell we are." After a long while they heard the cinders crunching down the track and someone trying the fastenings of the boxcar doors down the train. They lay so still they could hear both their hearts beating. The steps on the cinders crunched nearer and nearer. The sliding door slammed open, and their car was suddenly full of sunlight. They lay still. Mac felt the rap of a stick on his chest and sat up blinking. A Scotch voice was burring in his ears:

"I thought I'd find some Pullman passengerrs . . . All right, byes, stand and deliver, or else you'll go to the constabulary."

"Aw, hell," said Ike, crawling forward.

"Currsin' and swearin' won't help ye . . . If you got a couple o' quid you can ride on to Winnipeg an' take your chances there . . . If not you'll be doin' a tidy bit on the roads before you can say Jack Robinson."

The brakeman was a small blackhaired man with a mean quiet manner.

"Where are we, guv'ner?" asked Ike, trying to talk like an Englishman.

"Gretna . . . You're in the Dominion of Canada. You can be had up, too, for illegally crossin' Her Majesty's frontier as well as for bein' vags."

"Well, I guess we'd better shell out . . . You see we're a couple of noblemen's sons out for a bit of a bloody lark, guv'-ner."

"No use currsin and prevarricatin'. How much have you?"

"Coupla dollars."

"Let's see it quick."

Ike pulled first one dollar, then another, out of his pocket; folded in the second dollar was a five. The Scotchman swept the three bills up with one gesture and slammed the sliding door to. They heard him slip down the catch on the outside. For a long time they sat there quiet in the dark.

Finally Ike said, "Hey, Mac, gimme a sock in the jaw. That was a damn fool thing to do . . . Never oughta had that in my jeans anyway . . . oughta had it inside my belt. That leaves us with about seventyfive cents. We're up shit creek now for fair . . . He'll probably wire ahead to take us outa here at the next big town."

"Do they have mounted police on the railroad, too?" asked Mac in a hollow whisper.

"Jeez, I don't know any more about it than you do."

The train started again and Ike rolled over on his face and went glumly to sleep. Mac lay on his back behind him looking at the slit of sunlight that made its way in through the

86

crack in the door and wondered what the inside of a Canadian jail would be like.

That night, after the train had lain still for some time in the middle of the hissing and clatter of a big freightyard, they heard the catch slipped off the door. After a while Ike got up his nerve to slide the door open and they dropped, stiff and terribly hungry, down to the cinders. There was another freight on the next track, so all they could see was a bright path of stars overhead. They got out of the freightyards without any trouble and found themselves walking through the deserted streets of a large widescattered city.

"Winnipeg's a pretty friggin' lonelylookin' place, take it from me," said Ike.

"It must be after midnight."

They tramped and tramped and at last found a little lunchroom kept by a Chink who was just closing up. They spent forty cents on some stew and potatoes and coffee. They asked the Chink if he'd let them sleep on the floor behind the counter, but he threw them out and they found themselves dogtired tramping through the broad deserted streets of Winnipeg again. It was too cold to sit down anywhere, and they couldn't find anyplace that looked as if it would give them a flop for thirtyfive cents, so they walked and walked, and anyway the sky was beginning to pale into a slow northern summer dawn. When it was fully day they went back to the Chink's and spent the thirtyfive cents on oatmeal and coffee. Then they went to the Canadian Pacific employment office and signed up for work in a construction camp at Banff. The hours they had to wait till traintime they spent in the public library. Mac read part of Bellamy's *Looking Backward*, and Ike, not being able to find a volume of Karl Marx, read an installment of "When the Sleeper Wakes" in the *Strand Maga-*

87

zine. So when they got on the train they were full of the coming Socialist revolution and started talking it up to two lanky redfaced lumberjacks who sat opposite them.

One of them chewed tobacco silently all the while, but the other spat his quid out of the window and said, "You blokes'll keep quiet with that kinder talk if you knows what's 'ealthy for ye."

"Hell, this is a free country, ain't it? A guy's free to talk, ain't he?" said Ike.

"A bloke kin talk so long as his betters don't tell him to keep his mouth shut."

"Hell, I'm not tryin' to pick a fight," said Ike.

"Better not," said the other man, and didn't speak again.

They worked for the C.P.R. all summer and by the first of October they were in Vancouver. They had new suitcases and new suits. Ike had fortynine dollars and fifty cents and Mac had eightythree fifteen in a brandnew pigskin wallet. Mac had more because he didn't play poker. They took a dollar and a half room between them and lay in bed like princes their first free morning. They were tanned and toughened and their hands were horny. After the smell of rank pipes and unwashed feet and the bedbugs in the railroad bunkhouses the small cleanboarded hotel room with its clean beds seemed like a palace.

When he was fully awake Mac sat up and reached for his Ingersoll. Eleven o'clock. The sunlight on the windowledge was ruddy from the smoke of forestfires up the coast. He got up and washed in cold water at the washbasin. He walked up and down the room wiping his face and arms in the towel. It made him feel good to follow the contours of his neck and the hollow between his shoulderblades and the muscles of his arms as he dried himself with the fresh coarse towel.

"Say, Ike, what do you think we oughta do? I think we oughta go down on the boat to Seattle, Washington, like a coupla dude passengers. I wanta settle down an' get a printin' job; there's good money in that. I'm goin' to study to beat hell this winter. What do you think, Ike? I want to get out of this limejuicy hole an' get back to God's country. What do you think, Ike?"

Ike groaned and rolled over in bed.

"Say, wake up, Ike, for crissake. We want to take a look at this burg an' then twentythree."

Ike sat up in bed. "God damn it, I need a woman."

"I've heard tell there's swell broads in Seattle, honest, Ike."

Ike jumped out of bed and began splattering himself from head to foot with cold water. Then he dashed into his clothes and stood looking out the window combing the water out of his hair.

"When does the friggin' boat go? Jeez, I had two wet dreams last night, did you?"

Mac blushed. He nodded his head.

"Jeez, we got to get us women. Wet dreams weakens a guy."

"I wouldn't want to get sick."

"Aw, hell, a man's not a man until he's had his three doses."

"Aw, come ahead, let's go see the town."

"Well, ain't I been waitin' for ye this half-hour?"

They ran down the stairs and out into the street. They walked round Vancouver, sniffing the winey smell of lumbermills along the waterfront, loafing under the big trees in the park. Then they got their tickets at the steamboat office and went to a haberdashery store and bought themselves striped neckties, colored socks and fourdollar silk shirts. They felt like millionaires when they walked up the gangplank of the boat for Victoria and Seattle, with their new suits and their new suitcases and their silk shirts. They strolled round the deck smoking cigarettes and looking at the girls. "Gee, there's a couple looks kinda easy . . . I bet they're hookers at that," Ike whispered in Mac's ear and gave him a dig in the ribs with his elbow as they passed two girls in Spring Maid hats who were walking round the deck the other way. "Shit, let's try pick 'em up."

They had a couple of beers at the bar, then they went on deck. The girls had gone. Mac and Ike walked disconsolately round the deck for a while, then they found the girls leaning over the rail in the stern. It was a cloudy moonlight night.

The sea and the dark islands covered with spiring evergreens shone light and dark in a mottling silvery green. Both girls had frizzy hair and dark circles under their eyes. Mac thought they looked too old, but as Ike had gone sailing ahead it was too late to say anything. The girl he talked to was named Gladys. He liked the looks of the other one, whose name was Olive, better, but Ike got next to her first. They stayed on deck kidding and giggling until the girls said they were cold, then they went in the saloon and sat on a sofa and Ike went and bought a box of candy.

"We ate onions for dinner today," said Olive. "Hope you fellers don't mind. Gladys, I told you we oughtn't to of eaten them onions, not before comin' on the boat."

"Gimme a kiss an' I'll tell ye if I mind or not," said Ike.

"Kiddo, you can't talk fresh like that to us, not on this boat," snapped Olive, two mean lines appearing on either side of her mouth.

"We have to be awful careful what we do on the boat," explained Gladys. "They're terrible suspicious of two girls travelin' alone nowadays. Ain't it a crime?"

"It sure is." Ike moved up a little closer on the seat.

"Quit that . . . make a noise like a hoop an' roll away. I mean it." Olive went and sat on the opposite bench. Ike followed her.

"In the old days it was liberty hall on these boats, but not so any more," Gladys said, talking to Mac in a low intimate voice. "You fellers been workin' up in the canneries?"

"No, we been workin' for the C.P.R. all summer."

"You must have made big money." As she talked to him, Mac noticed that she kept looking out of the corner of her eye at her friend.

"Yare . . . not so big . . . I saved up pretty near a century."

"An' now you're going to Seattle."

"I want to get a job linotypist."

"That's where we live, Seattle. Olive an' I've got an apartment . . . Let's go out on deck, it's too hot in here."

As they passed Olive and Ike, Gladys leaned over and whispered something in Olive's ear. Then she turned to Mac with a melting smile. The deck was deserted. She let him put his arm around her waist. His fingers felt the bones of some sort of corset. He squeezed. "Oh, don't be too rough, kiddo," she whined in a funny little voice. He laughed. As he took his hand away he felt the contour of her breast. Walking, his leg brushed against her leg. It was the first time he'd been so close to a girl.

After a while she said she had to go to bed. "How about me goin' down with ye?"

She shook her head. "Not on this boat. See you tomorrow; maybe you and your pal'll come and see us at our apartment. We'll show you the town."

"Sure," said Mac. He walked on round the deck, his heart beating hard. He could feel the pound of the steamboat's engines and the arrowshaped surge of broken water from the bow and he felt like that. He met Ike.

"My girl said she had to go to bed."

"So did mine."

"Get anywheres, Mac?"

"They got an apartment in Seattle."

"I got a kiss off mine. She's awful hot. Jeez, I thought she was going to feel me up."

"We'll get it tomorrow all right."

The next day was sunny; the Seattle waterfront was sparkling, smelt of lumberyards, was noisy with rattle of carts and yells of drivers when they got off the boat. They went to the Y.M.C.A. for a room. They were through with being laborers and hobos. They were going to get clean jobs, live decently and go to school nights. They walked round the city all day, and in the evening met Olive and Gladys in front of the totempole on Pioneer Square.

Things happened fast. They went to a restaurant and had wine with a big feed and afterwards they went to a beergarden where there was a band, and drank whiskey-sours. When they went to the girls' apartment they took a quart of whiskey with them and Mac almost dropped it on the steps and the girls said, "For crissake don't make so much noise or you'll have the cops on us," and the apartment smelt of musk and facepowder and there was women's underwear around on all the chairs and the girls got fifteen bucks out of each of them first thing. Mac was in the bathroom with his girl and she smeared liprouge on his nose and they laughed and laughed until he got rough and she slapped his face. Then they all sat together round the table and drank some more and Ike danced a Salomeydance in his bare feet. Mac laughed, it was so very funny, but he was sitting on the floor and when he tried to get up he fell on his face and all of a sudden he was being sick in the bathtub and Gladys was cursing hell out of him. She got him dressed, only he couldn't find his necktie, and everybody said he was too drunk and pushed him out and he was walking down the street singing

and asked a cop where the Y.M.C.A. was and the cop pushed
him into a cell at the stationhouse and locked him up.

He woke up with his head like a big split millstone. There
was vomit on his shirt and a rip in his pants. He went over
all his pockets and couldn't find his pocketbook. A cop
opened the cell door and told him to make himself scarce
and he walked out into the dazzling sun that cut into his eyes
like a knife. The man at the desk at the Y looked at him
queerly when he went in, but he got up to his room and fell
into bed without anybody saying anything to him. Ike wasn't
back yet. He dozed off feeling his headache all through his
sleep.

When he woke up Ike was sitting on the bed. Ike's eyes
were bright and his cheeks were red. He was still a little
drunk. "Say, Mac, did they roll yer? I can't find my pocketbook an' I tried to go back, but I couldn't find the apartment.
God, I'd have beat up the goddam flousies . . . Shit, I'm
drunk as a pissant still. Say, the galoot at the desk said we'd
have to clear out. Can't have no drunks in the Y.M.C.A."

"But jeez, we paid for a week."

"He'll give us part of it back . . . Aw, what the hell, Mac
. . . We're flat, but I feel swell . . . Say, I had a rough time
with your Jane after they'd thrown you out."

93

"Hell, I feel sick as a dog."

"I'm afraid to go to sleep for fear of getting a hangover.
Come on out, it'll do you good."

It was three in the afternoon. They went into a little
Chinese restaurant on the waterfront and drank coffee. They
had two dollars they got from hocking their suitcases. The
pawnbroker wouldn't take the silk shirts because they were
dirty. Outside it was raining pitchforks.

"Jesus, why the hell didn't we have the sense to keep
sober? God, we're a coupla big stiffs, Ike."

"We had a good party . . . Jeez, you looked funny with
that liprouge all over your face."

"I feel like hell . . . I wanta study an' work for things; you
know what I mean, not to get to be a goddam slavedriver,
but for socialism and the revolution an' like that, not work
an' go on a bat an' work an' go on a bat like those damn
yaps on the railroad."

"Hell, another time we'll have more sense an' leave our
wads somewhere safe . . . Gee, I'm beginning to sink by the
bows myself."

"If the damn house caught fire I wouldn't have the
strength to walk out."

They sat in the Chink place as long as they could and then
they went out in the rain to find a thirtycent flophouse where
they spent the night, and the bedbugs ate them up. In the
morning they went around looking for jobs, Mac in the print-

ROOMS
30¢
PER NIGHT

ing trades and Ike at the shipping agencies. They met in the evening without having had any luck and slept in the park, as it was a fine night. Eventually they both signed up to go to a lumbercamp up the Snake River. They were sent up by the agency on a car full of Swedes and Finns. Mac and Ike were the only ones who spoke English. When they got there they found the foreman so hardboiled and the grub so rotten and the bunkhouse so filthy that they lit out at the end of a couple of days, on the bum again. It was already cold in the Blue Mountains and they would have starved to death if they hadn't been able to beg food in the cookhouses of lumber-camps along the way. They hit the railroad at Baker City, managed to beat their way back to Portland on freights. In Portland, they couldn't find jobs because their clothes were so dirty, so they hiked southward along a big endless Oregon valley full of fruitranches, sleeping in barns and getting an occasional meal by cutting wood or doing chores around a ranchhouse.

In Salem, Ike found that he had a dose and Mac couldn't sleep nights worrying for fear he might have it too. They tried to go to a doctor in Salem. He was a big roundfaced man with a hearty laugh. When they said they didn't have any money, he guessed it was all right and that they could do some chores to pay for the consultation, but when he heard it was a venereal disease he threw them out with a hot lecture on the wages of sin.

They trudged along the road, hungry and footsore; Ike had fever and it hurt him to walk. Neither of them said anything. Finally they got to a small fruitshipping station where there were watertanks, on the main line of the Southern Pacific.

There Ike said he couldn't walk any further, that they'd have to wait for a freight. "Jesus Christ, jail 'ud be better than this."

"When you're outa luck in this man's country, you certainly are outa luck," said Mac and for some reason they both laughed.

Among the bushes back of the station they found an old tramp boiling coffee in a tin can. He gave them some coffee

96

and bread and baconrind and they told him their troubles. He said he was headed south for the winter and that the thing to cure it up was tea made out of cherry pits and stems. "But where the hell am I going to get cherry pits and stems?" Anyway he said not to worry, it was no worse than a bad cold. He was a cheerful old man with a face so grimed with dirt it looked like a brown leather mask. He was going to take a chance on a freight that stopped there to water a little after sundown. Mac dozed off to sleep while Ike and the old man talked. When he woke up Ike was yelling at him and they were all running for the freight that had already started. In

the dark Mac missed his footing and fell flat on the ties. He wrenched his knee and ground cinders into his nose and by the time he had got to his feet all he could see were the two lights on the end of the train fading into November haze.

That was the last he saw of Ike Hall.

He got himself back on the road and limped along until he came to a ranchhouse. A dog barked at him and worried his ankles, but he was too down and out to care. Finally a stout woman came to the door and gave him some cold biscuits and applesauce and told him he could sleep in the barn if he gave her all his matches. He limped to the barn and snuggled into a pile of dry sweetgrass and went to sleep.

In the morning the rancher, a tall ruddy man named Thomas, with a resonant voice, went over to the barn and offered him work for a few days at the price of his board and lodging. They were kind to him, and had a pretty daughter named Mona that he kinder fell in love with. She was a plump rosycheeked girl, strong as a boy and afraid of nothing. She punched him and wrestled with him; and, particularly after he'd gotten fattened up a little and rested, he could hardly sleep nights for thinking of her. He lay in his bed of sweetgrass telling over the touch of her bare arm that rubbed along his when she handed him back the nozzle of the sprayer for the fruittrees, or was helping him pile up the pruned twigs to burn, and the roundness of her breasts and her breath sweet as a cow's on his neck when they romped and played tricks on each other evenings after supper. But the Thomases had other ideas for their daughter and told Mac that they didn't need him any more. They sent him off kindly with a lot of good advice, some old clothes and a cold lunch done up in newspaper, but no money. Mona ran after him as he walked off down the dustyrutted wagonroad and kissed him right in front of her parents. "I'm stuck on you,"

she said. "You make a lot of money and come back and marry me." "By gum, I'll do that," said Mac, and he walked off with tears in his eyes and feeling very good. He was particularly glad he hadn't got the clap off that girl in Seattle.

Newsreel VI

PARIS SHOCKED AT LAST

HARRIMAN SHOWN AS RAIL COLOSSUS

NOTED SWINDLER RUN TO EARTH

TEDDY WIELDS BIG STICK

STRAPHANGERS DEMAND RELIEF

We were sailing along
On moonlight bay
You can hear the voices ringing
They seem to say
You have stolen my heart, now don't go away
Just as we sang
love's
old
sweet
songs
On moonlight bay

MOB LYNCHES AFTER PRAYER

when the metal poured out of the furnace I saw the men running to a place of safety. To the right of the furnace I saw a party of ten men all of them running wildly and their clothes a mass of flames. Apparently some of them had been injured when the explosion occurred and several of them tripped and fell. The hot metal ran over the poor men in a moment.

PRAISE MONOPOLY AS BOON TO ALL

industrial foes work for peace at Mrs. Potter Palmer's

love's

old

sweet

song

We were sailing along

on moonlight bay

The Camera Eye (7)

skating on the pond next the silver company's mills where there was a funny fuzzy smell from the dump whaleoil soap somebody said it was that they used in cleaning the silver knives and spoons and forks putting shine on them for sale   there was shine on the ice early black ice that rang like a sawblade just scratched white by the first skaters   I couldn't learn to skate and kept falling down   look out for the muckers everybody said   Bohunk and Polak kids put stones in their snowballs write dirty words up on walls do dirty things up alleys their folks work in the mills

we clean young American Rover Boys handy with tools Deerslayers played hockey Boy Scouts and cut figure eights on the ice Achilles Ajax Agamemnon I couldn't learn to skate and kept falling down.

The Plant Wizard

Luther Burbank was born in a brick farmhouse in Lancaster Mass.
he walked round the woods one winter
crunching through the shinycrusted snow
stumbled into a little dell where a warm spring was
and found the grass green and weeds sprouting
and skunk cabbage pushing up a potent thumb,
He went home and sat by the stove and read Darwin
Struggle for Existence Origin of Species Natural
Selection that wasn't what they taught in church,
so Luther Burbank ceased to believe moved to Lunenburg,
found a seedball in a potato plant
sowed the seed and cashed in on Mr. Darwin's Natural
Selection

on Spencer and Huxley
with the Burbank potato.

Young man go west;
Luther Burbank went to Santa Rosa
full of his dream of green grass in winter everblooming flowers ever-
bearing berries; Luther Burbank
could cash in on Natural Selection Luther Burbank
carried his apocalyptic dream of green grass in winter
and seedless berries and stoneless plums and thornless
roses brambles cactus—
      winters were bleak in that bleak
      brick farmhouse in bleak Massachusetts—
out to sunny Santa Rosa;
and he was a sunny old man
where roses bloomed all year
everblooming everbearing
hybrids.

America was hybrid
America should cash in on Natural Selection.
He was an infidel he believed in Darwin and Natural
Selection and the influence of the mighty dead
and a good firm shipper's fruit
suitable for canning.
He was one of the grand old men until the churches
and the congregations
got wind that he was an infidel and believed
in Darwin.
Luther Burbank had never a thought of evil,
selecting improved hybrids for America
those sunny years in Santa Rosa.
But he brushed down a wasp's nest that time;
he wouldn't give up Darwin and Natural Selection
and they stung him and he died
puzzled.

They buried him under a cedartree.
His favorite photograph
was of a little tot
standing beside a bed of hybrid
everblooming double Shasta daisies
with never a thought of evil
And Mount Shasta
in the background, used to be a volcano
but they don't have volcanos
any more.

Newsreel VII

SAYS THIS IS CENTURY WHERE BILLIONS AND
BRAINS ARE TO RULE

INFANT BORN IN MINNEAPOLIS COMES HERE
IN INCUBATOR

Cheyenne Cheyenne
Hop on my pony

SAYS JIM HILL HITS OIL TRUST ON 939 COUNTS
BIG FOUR TRAIN BLOWN TO PIECES

woman and children blotted out   admits he saw flog-
gings and even mutilations but no frightful outrages

TRUTH ABOUT THE CONGO FREE STATE

Find bad fault in Dreadnaught   Santos Dumont tells
of rival of bird of prey   wives, prime aim of Congo natives extraordinary letter ordering away U.S. marines

WHITES IN CONGO LOSE MORAL SENSE

WOMAN HELD A CAPTIVE BY AMBULANCE CHASERS

THAW FACES JUDGE IN FATEFUL FIGHT

LABOR MENACE IN POLITICS

last of Salome seen in New York   heroism of mother
unavailing

There's room here for two, dear
    But after the ceremony
Two, dear, as one, dear, will ride back on my pony
From old Cheyenne

The Camera Eye (8)

you sat on the bed unlacing your shoes Hey Frenchie
yelled Tylor in the door you've got to fight the
Kid   doan wanna fight him   gotto fight him hasn't he
got to fight him fellers? Freddie pushed his face through
the crack in the door and made a long nose   Gotta fight
him umpyaya and all the fellows on the top floor were
there if not you're a girlboy and I had on my pyjamas
and they pushed in the Kid and the Kid hit Frenchie and
Frenchie hit the Kid and your mouth tasted bloody and
everybody yelled Go it Kid except Gummer and he yelled
Bust his jaw Jack and Frenchie had the Kid down on the
bed and everybody pulled him off and they all had Frenchie against the door and he was slamming right an' left
and he couldn't see who was hitting and Tylor and
Freddy held his arms and told the Kid to come and hit
him but the Kid wouldn't and the Kid was crying

the bloody sweet puky taste and then the bell rang for
lights and everybody ran to their rooms and you got into
bed with your head throbbing and you were crying when
Gummer tiptoed in an' said you had him licked Jack it was
a fucking shame it was Freddy hit you that time, but
Hoppy was tiptoeing round the hall and caught Gummer
trying to get back to his room and he got his

Mac

By Thanksgiving Mac had beaten his way to Sacramento,
where he got a job smashing crates in a driedfruit warehouse.
By the first of the year he'd saved up enough to buy a suit of
dark clothes and take the steamboat down the river to San
Francisco.

It was around eight in the evening when he got in. With

his suitcase in his hand, he walked up Market Street from the dock. The streets were full of lights. Young men and pretty girls in brightcolored dresses were walking fast through a big yanking wind that fluttered dresses and scarfs, slapped color into cheeks, blew grit and papers into the air. There were Chinamen, Wops, Portuguese, Japs in the streets. People were hustling to shows and restaurants. Music came out of the doors of bars, frying, buttery foodsmells from restaurants, smells of winecasks and beer. Mac wanted to go on a party but he only had four dollars so he went and got a room at the Y and ate some soggy pie and coffee in the deserted cafeteria downstairs.

When he got up in the bare bedroom like something in a hospital he opened the window, but it only gave on an airshaft. The room smelt of some sort of cleaning fluid and when he lay down on the bed the blanket smelt of formaldehyde. He felt too well. He could feel the prancing blood steam all through him. He wanted to talk to somebody, to go to a dance or have a drink with a fellow he knew or kid a girl somewhere. The smell of rouge and musky facepowder in the room of those girls in Seattle came back to him. He got up and sat on the edge of the bed swinging his legs. Then he decided to go out, but before he went he put his money in his suitcase and locked it up. Lonely as a ghost he walked up and down the streets until he was deadtired; he walked fast not looking to the right or left, brushing past painted girls at streetcorners, touts that tried to put addresscards into his hand, drunks that tried to pick fights with him, panhandlers whining for a handout. Then, bitter and cold and tired, he went back to his room and fell into bed.

Next day he went out and got a job in a small printshop run and owned by a baldheaded Italian with big whiskers and a flowing black tie, named Bonello. Bonello told him he had been a redshirt with Garibaldi and was now an anarchist. Ferrer was his great hero; he hired Mac because he thought he might make a convert out of him. All that winter Mac

105

worked at Bonello's, ate spaghetti and drank red wine and talked revolution with him and his friends in the evening, went to Socialist picnics or libertarian meetings on Sundays. Saturday nights he went round to whorehouses with a fellow named Miller, whom he'd met at the Y. Miller was studying to be a dentist. He got to be friends with a girl named Maisie Spencer who worked in the millinery department at the Emporium. Sundays she used to try to get him to go to church. She was a quiet girl with big blue eyes that she turned up to him with an unbelieving smile when he talked revolution to her. She had tiny regular pearly teeth and dressed prettily. After a while she got so that she did not bother him so much about church. She liked to have him take her to hear the band play at the Presidio or to look at the statuary in Sutro Park.

The morning of the earthquake Mac's first thought, when he got over his own terrible scare, was for Maisie. The house where her folks lived on Mariposa Street was still standing when he got there, but everyone had cleared out. It was not till the third day, three days of smoke and crashing timbers and dynamiting he spent working in firefighting squad, that he found her in a provision line at the entrance to Golden Gate Park. The Spencers were living in a tent near the shattered greenhouses.

She didn't recognize him because his hair and eyebrows were singed and his clothes were in tatters and he was soot from head to foot. He'd never kissed her before, but he took her in his arms before everybody and kissed her. When he let her go her face was all sooty from his. Some of the people in the line laughed and clapped, but the old woman right behind, who had her hair done in a pompadour askew so that the rat showed through and who wore two padded pink silk dressing gowns one above the other said spitefully, "Now you'll have to go and wash your face."

After that they considered themselves engaged, but they couldn't get married, because Bonello's printshop had been gutted with the rest of the block it stood in, and Mac was out of a job. Maisie used to let him kiss her and hug her in dark doorways when he took her home at night, but further than that he gave up trying to go.

In the fall he got a job on the *Bulletin*. That was night work and he hardly ever saw Maisie except Sundays, but they began to talk about getting married after Christmas. When he was away from her he felt somehow sore at Maisie most of the time, but when he was with her he melted absolutely. He tried to get her to read pamphlets on socialism, but she laughed and looked up at him with her big intimate blue eyes and said it was too deep for her. She liked to go to the theater and eat in restaurants where the linen was starched and there were waiters in dress suits.

About that time he went one night to hear Upton Sinclair speak about the Chicago stockyards. Next to him was a young man in dungarees. He had a nose like a hawk and gray eyes and deep creases under his cheekbones and talked in a slow drawl. His name was Fred Hoff. After the lecture they went and had a beer together and talked. Fred Hoff belonged to the new revolutionary organization called The Industrial Workers of the World. He read Mac the preamble over a second glass of beer. Fred Hoff had just hit town as donkeyengine man on a freighter. He was sick of the bum grub and hard life on the sea. He still had his pay in his pocket and he was bound he wouldn't blow it in on a bust. He'd heard that there was a miners' strike in Goldfield and he thought he'd go up there and see what he could do. He made Mac feel that he was leading a pretty stodgy life helping print lies against the workingclass. "Godalmighty, man, you're just the kind o' stuff we need out there. We're goin' to publish a paper in Goldfield, Nevada."

That night Mac went round to the local and filled out a card, and went home to his boardinghouse with his head swimming. I was just on the point of selling out to the sonsofbitches, he said to himself.

The next Sunday he and Maisie had been planning to go up the Scenic Railway to the top of Mount Tamalpais. Mac was terribly sleepy when his alarmclock got him out of bed. They had to start early because he had to be on the job again that night. As he walked to the ferry station where he was going to meet her at nine the clank of the presses was still in his head, and the sour smell of ink and paper bruised under the presses, and on top of that the smell of the hall of the house he'd been in with a couple of the fellows, the smell of moldy rooms and sloppails and the smell of armpits and the dressingtable of the frizzyhaired girl he'd had on the clammy bed and the taste of the stale beer they'd drunk and the cooing mechanical voice, "Goodnight, dearie, come round soon."

"God, I'm a swine," he said to himself.

For once it was a clear morning, all the colors in the street shone like bits of glass. God, he was sick of whoring round. If Maisie would only be a sport, if Maisie was only a rebel you could talk to like you could to a friend. And how the hell was he going to tell her he was throwing up his job?

She was waiting for him at the ferry looking like a Gibson girl with her neat sailorblue dress and picture hat. They didn't have time to say anything as they had to run for the ferry. Once on the ferryboat she lifted up her face to be kissed. Her lips were cool and her gloved hand rested so lightly on his. At Sausalito they took the trolleycar and

changed and she kept smiling at him when they ran to get good places in the scenic car and they felt so alone in the roaring immensity of tawny mountain and blue sky and sea. They'd never been so happy together. She ran ahead of him all the way to the top. At the observatory they were both breathless. They stood against a wall out of sight of the other people and she let him kiss her all over her face, all over her face and neck.

Scraps of mist flew past cutting patches out of their view of the bay and the valleys and the shadowed mountains. When they went round to the seaward side an icy wind was shrilling through everything. A churning mass of fog was welling up from the sea like a tidal wave. She gripped his arm. "Oh, this scares me, Fainy!" Then suddenly he told her that he'd given up his job. She looked up at him frightened and shivering in the cold wind and little and helpless; tears began to run down either side of her nose. "But I thought you loved me, Fenian . . . Do you think it's been easy for me waitin' for you all this time, wantin' you and lovin' you? Oh, I thought you loved me!"

He put his arm round her. He couldn't say anything. They started walking towards the gravity car.

"I don't want all those people to see I've been crying. We were so happy before. Let's walk down to Muir Woods."

"It's pretty far, Maisie."

"I don't care; I want to."

"Gee, you're a good sport, Maisie."

They started down the footpath and the mist blotted out everything.

After a couple of hours they stopped to rest. They left the path and found a patch of grass in the middle of a big thicket of cistus. The mist was all around, but it was bright overhead and they could feel the warmth of the sun through it. "Ouch,

I've got blisters," she said and made a funny face that made him laugh. "It can't be so awful far now," he said; "honest, Maisie." He wanted to explain to her about the strike and the wobblies and why he was going to Goldfield, but he couldn't. All he could do was kiss her. Her mouth clung to his lips and her arms were tight round his neck.

"Honest, it won't make any difference about our gettin' married; honest, it won't . . . Maisie, I'm crazy about you

. . . Maisie, do let me . . . You must let me . . . Honest, you don't know how terrible it is for me, lovin' you like this and you never lettin' me."

He got up and smoothed down her dress. She lay there with her eyes closed and her face white; he was afraid she had fainted. He kneeled down and kissed her gently on the cheek. She smiled ever so little and pulled his head down and ruffled his hair. "Little husband," she said. After a while they got to their feet and walked through the redwood grove, without seeing it, to the trolley station. Going home on the ferry they decided they'd get married inside of the week. Mac promised not to go to Nevada.

Next morning he got up feeling depressed. He was selling out. When he was shaving in the bathroom he looked at himself in the mirror and said, half aloud: "You bastard, you're selling out to the sonsofbitches."

He went back to his room and wrote Maisie a letter.

DEAR MAISIE:

Honestly you mustn't think for one minute I don't love you ever so much, but I promised to go to Goldfield to help the gang run that paper and I've got to do it. I'll send you my address as soon as I get there and if you really need me on account of anything, I'll come right back, honestly I will.

A whole lot of kisses and love
FAINY

He went down to the *Bulletin* office and drew his pay, packed his bag and went down to the station to see when he could get a train for Goldfield, Nevada.

The Camera Eye (9)

all day the fertilizer factories smelt something awful and at night the cabin was full of mosquitoes fit to carry you away but it was Crisfield on the Eastern Shore and if we had a gasoline boat to carry them across the bay here we could ship our tomatoes and corn and early peaches ship 'em clear to New York instead of being gypped by the commission merchants in Baltimore we'd run a truck farm ship early vegetables irrigate fertilize enrich the tobacco-exhausted land of the Northern Neck if we had a gasoline boat we'd run oysters in her in winter raise terrapin for the market

but up on the freight siding I got talking to a young guy couldn't have been much older 'n me was asleep in one of the boxcars asleep right there in the sun and the smell of cornstalks and the reek of rotting menhaden from the fertilizer factories   he had curly hair and wisps of hay in it and through his open shirt you could see his body was burned brown to the waist I guess he wasn't much account but he'd bummed all way from Minnesota he was going south and when I told him about Chesapeake Bay he wasn't surprised but said I guess it's too fur to swim it I'll git a job in a menhaden boat

Big Bill

Big Bill Haywood was born in sixtynine in a boarding-house in Salt Lake City.

He was raised in Utah, got his schooling in Ophir, a mining camp with shooting scrapes, faro Saturday nights, whiskey spilled on pokertables piled with new silver dollars.

When he was eleven his mother bound him out to a farmer, he ran away because the farmer lashed him with a whip. That was his first strike.

He lost an eye whittling a slingshot out of scruboak.

He worked for storekeepers, ran a fruitstand, ushered in the Salt Lake Theater, was a messengerboy, bellhop at the Continental Hotel.

When he was fifteen
he went out to the mines in Humboldt County, Nevada, his outfit was overalls, a jumper, a blue shirt, miningboots, two pair of blankets, a set of chessmen, boxinggloves and a big lunch of plum pudding his mother fixed for him.

When he married he went to live in Fort McDermitt built in the old days against the Indians, abandoned now that there was no more frontier;

there his wife bore their first baby without doctor or mid-wife. Bill cut the navelstring, Bill buried the afterbirth;

the child lived. Bill earned money as he could surveying, haying in Paradise Valley, breaking colts, riding a wide rangy country.

One night at Thompson's Mill, he was one of five men who met by chance and stopped the night in the abandoned ranch. Each of them had lost an eye, they were the only oneeyed men in the county.

They lost the homestead, things went to pieces, his wife was sick, he had children to support. He went to work as a miner at Silver City.

At Silver City, Idaho, he joined the W.F.M., there he held his first union office; he was delegate to the Silver City miners to the convention of the Western Federation of Miners held in Salt Lake City in '98.

From then on he was an organizer, a speaker, an exhorter, the wants of all the miners were his wants; he fought Coeur D'Alenes, Telluride, Cripple Creek,

joined the Socialist Party, wrote and spoke through Idaho, Utah, Nevada, Montana, Colorado to miners striking for an eighthour day, better living, a share of the wealth they hacked out of the hills.

In Chicago in January 1905 a conference was called that met at the same hall in Lake Street where the Chicago anarchists had addressed meetings twenty years before.

William D. Haywood was permanent chairman. It was this conference that wrote the manifesto that brought into being the I.W.W.

When he got back to Denver he was kidnapped to Idaho and tried with Moyer and Pettibone for the murder of the sheepherder Steunenberg, ex-Governor of Idaho, blown up by a bomb in his own home.

When they were acquitted at Boise (Darrow was their law-yer), Big Bill Haywood was known as a workingclass leader from coast to coast.

Now the wants of all the workers were his wants, he was the spokesman of the West, of the cowboys and the lumber-jacks and the harvesthands and the miners.

(The steamdrill had thrown thousands of miners out of work; the steamdrill had thrown a scare into all the miners of the West.)

The W.F.M. was going conservative. Haywood worked with the I.W.W. *building a new society in the shell of the old,* campaigned for Debs for President in 1908 on the Red Special. He was in on all the big strikes in the East where revolutionary spirit was growing, Lawrence, Paterson, the strike of the Minnesota ironworkers.

They went over with the A.E.F. to save the Morgan loans, to save Wilsonian Democracy, they stood at Napoleon's tomb and dreamed empire, they had champagne cocktails at the Ritz bar and slept with Russian countesses in Montmartre and dreamed empire, all over the country at American legion posts and businessmen's luncheons it was worth money to make the eagle scream;

they lynched the pacifists and the pro-Germans and the wobblies and the reds and the bolsheviks.

Bill Haywood stood trial with the hundred and one at Chicago where Judge Landis the baseball czar

with the lack of formality of a traffic court

handed out his twenty-year sentences and thirty-thousand dollar fines.

After two years in Leavenworth they let them bail out Big Bill (he was fifty years old a heavy broken man), the war was over, but they'd learned empire in the Hall of the Mirrors at Versailles;

the courts refused a new trial.

It was up to Haywood to jump his bail or to go back to prison for twenty years.

He was sick with diabetes, he had had a rough life, prison had broken down his health. Russia was a workers' republic; he went to Russia and was in Moscow a couple of years but he wasn't happy there, that world was too strange for him. He died there and they burned his big broken hulk of a body and buried the ashes under the Kremlin wall.

The Camera Eye (10)

the old major who used to take me to the Capitol when the Senate and the House of Representatives were in session had been in the commissary of the Confederate Army and had very beautiful manners so the attendants bowed to the old major except for the pages who were little boys not much older than your brother was a page in the Senate once and occasionally a Representative or a Senator would look at him with slit eyes may be somebody and bow or shake hearty or raise a hand

the old major dressed very well in a morningcoat and had muttonchop whiskers and we would walk very slowly through the flat sunlight in the Botanical Gardens and look at the little labels on the trees and shrubs and see the fat robins and the starlings hop across the grass and walk up the steps and through the flat air of the rotunda with the dead statues of different sizes and the Senate Chamber flat red and the committee room and the House flat green and the committee rooms and the Supreme Court I've forgotten what color the Supreme Court was and the committee rooms

and whispering behind the door of the visitors' gallery and the dead air and a voice rattling under the glass skylights and desks slammed and the long corridors full of the dead air and our legs would get very tired and I thought of the starlings on the grass and the long streets full of dead air and my legs were tired and I had a pain between the eyes and the old men bowing with quick slit eyes

may be somebody and big slit unkind mouths and the dusty black felt and the smell of coatclosets and dead air and I wonder what the old major thought about and what I thought about maybe about that big picture at the Corcoran Art Gallery full of columns and steps and conspirators and Caesar in purple fallen flat called Caesar dead

Mac

Mac had hardly gotten off the train at Goldfield when a lanky man in khaki shirt and breeches, wearing canvas army leggins, went up to him. "If you don't mind, what's your business in this town, brother?"

"I'm travelin' in books."

"What kinda books?"

"Schoolbooks and the like, for Truthseeker, Inc., of Chicago." Mac rattled it off very fast, and the man seemed impressed.

115

"I guess you're all right," he said. "Going up to the Eagle?" Mac nodded. "Plug'll take ye up, the feller with the team . . . You see we're looking out for these goddam agitators, the I Won't Work outfit."

Outside the Golden Eagle Hotel there were two soldiers on guard, toughlooking sawedoff men with their hats over their eyes. When Mac went in everybody at the bar turned and looked at him. He said "Good evening, gents," as snappily as possible and went up to the proprietor to ask for a room. All the while he was wondering who the hell he dared ask where the office of the *Nevada Workman* was.

"I guess I can fix you up with a bed. Travelin' man?"

"Yes," said Mac. "In books."

Down at the end a big man with walrus whiskers was standing at the bar talking fast in a drunken whining voice, "If they'd only give me my head I'd run the bastards outa town soon enough. Too goddam many lawyers mixed up in this. Run the sonsobitches out. If they resists shoot 'em, that's what I says to the Governor, but they're all these sonsobitches a lawyers fussin' everythin' up all the time with warrants and habeas corpus and longwinded rigmarole. My ass to habeas corpus."

"All right, Joe, you tell 'em," said the proprietor soothingly.

Mac bought a cigar and sauntered out. As the door closed behind him the big man was yelling out again, "I said, My ass to habeas corpus."

It was nearly dark. An icy wind blew through the ramshackle clapboard streets. His feet stumbling in the mud of the deep ruts, Mac walked round several blocks looking up at dark windows. He walked all over the town, but no sign of a newspaper office. When he found himself passing the same Chink hashjoint for the third time, he slackened his steps and stood irresolutely on the curb. At the end of the street the great jagged shank of a hill hung over the town. Across the street a young man, his head and ears huddled into the collar of a mackinaw, was loafing against the dark window of a hardware store. Mac decided he was a squarelooking stiff and went over to speak to him.

"Say, bo, where's the office of the *Nevada Workman?*"

"What the hell d'you wanter know for?"

Mac and the other man looked at each other. "I want to see Fred Hoff . . . I came on from San Fran to help in the printin'."

"Got a red card?"

Mac pulled out his I.W.W. membership card. "I've got my union card, too, if you want to see that."

"Hell, no . . . I guess you're all right, but, as the feller said, suppose I'd been a dick, you'd be in the bullpen now, bo."

"I told 'em I was a friggin' bookagent to get into the damn town. Spent my last quarter on a cigar to keep up the burjwa look."

The other man laughed. "All right, fellowworker. I'll take you round."

"What they got here, martial law?" asked Mac as he followed the man down an alley between two overgrown shanties.

"Every sonofabitchin' yellerleg in the State of Nevada right here in town . . . Lucky if you don't get run outa town with a bayonet in yer crotch, as the feller said."

At the end of the alley was a small house like a shoebox with brightly lit windows. Young fellows in miners' clothes or overalls filled up the end of the alley and sat three deep on the rickety steps.

"What's this, a poolroom?" asked Mac.

"This is the *Nevada Workman* . . . Say, my name's Ben Evans; I'll introjuce you to the gang . . . Say, yous guys, this is fellowworker McCreary . . . he's come on from Frisco to set up type."

"Put it there, Mac," said a sixfooter who looked like a

117

Swede lumberman, and gave Mac's hand a wrench that made the bones crack.

Fred Hoff had on a green eyeshade and sat behind a desk piled with galleys. He got up and shook hands. "Oh, boy, you're just in time. There's hell to pay. They got the printer in the bullpen and we've got to get this sheet out."

Mac took off his coat and went back to look over the press. He was leaning over the typesetter's "stone" when Fred Hoff came back and beckoned him into a corner.

"Say, Mac, I want to explain the layout here . . . It's kind of a funny situation . . . The W.F.M.'s goin' yellow on us . . . It's a hell of a scrap. The Saint was here the other day and that bastard Mullany shot him through both arms and he's in hospital now . . . They're sore as a boil because we're instillin' ideas of revolutionary solidarity, see? We got the restaurant workers out and we got some of the minin' stiffs. Now the A.F. of L.'s gettin' wise and they've got a bonehead scab organizer in hobnobbin' with the mineowners at the Montezuma Club."

"Hey, Fred, let me take this on gradually," said Mac.

"Then there was a little shootin' the other day out in front of a restaurant down the line an' the stiff that owned the joint got plugged an' now they've got a couple of the boys in jail for that."

"The hell you say."

"And Big Bill Haywood's comin' to speak next week . . . That's about the way the situation is, Mac. I've got to tear off an article . . . You're boss printer an' we'll pay you seventeen-fifty like we all get. Ever written any?"

"No."

"It's a time like this a feller regrets he didn't work harder in school. Gosh, I wish I could write decent."

"I'll take a swing at an article if I get a chance."

"Big Bill'll write us some stuff. He writes swell."

They set up a cot for Mac back of the press. It was a week before he could get time to go round to the Eagle to get his suitcase. Over the office and the presses was a long attic, with a stove in it, where most of the boys slept. Those that had blankets rolled up in their blankets, those that hadn't put their jackets over their heads, those that didn't have jackets slept as best they could. At the end of the room was a long sheet of paper where someone had printed out the Preamble in shaded block letters. On the plaster wall of the office someone had drawn a cartoon of a workingstiff labeled "I.W.W." giving a fat man in a stovepipe hat labeled "mineowner" a kick in the seat of the pants. Above it they had started to letter "solidarity" but had only gotten as far as "S O L I D A."

118

One November night Big Bill Haywood spoke at the miners' union. Mac and Fred Hoff went to report the speech for the paper. The town looked lonely as an old trashdump in the huge valley full of shrill wind and driving snow. The hall was hot and steamy with the steam of big bodies and plug tobacco and thick mountaineer clothes that gave off the shanty smell of oil lamps and charred firewood and greasy fryingpans and raw whiskey. At the beginning of the meeting men moved round uneasily, shuffling their feet and clearing the phlegm out of their throats. Mac was uncomfortable himself. In his pocket was a letter from Maisie. He knew it by heart:

DEAREST FAINY:
   Everything has happened just as I was afraid of. You know what I mean, dearest little husband. It's two months already and I'm so frightened and there's nobody I can tell. Darling, you must come right back. I'll die if you don't. Honestly I'll die and I'm so lonely for you anyways and so afraid somebody'll notice. As it is we'll have to go away somewheres when we're married and not come back until plenty of time has elapsed. If I thought I could get work there I'd come to you to Goldfield. I think it would be nice if we went to San Diego. I

119

have friends there and they say it's lovely and there we could tell people we'd been married a long time. Please come sweetest little husband. I'm so lonely for you and it's so terrible to stand this all alone. The crosses are kisses. Your loving wife,

MAISIE
XXXXXXXXXXXXXXXX

Big Bill talked about solidarity and sticking together in the face of the masterclass and Mac kept wondering what Big Bill would do if he'd got a girl in trouble like that. Big Bill was saying the day had come to start building a new society in the shell of the old and for the workers to get ready to assume control of the industries they'd created out of their sweat and blood. When he said, "We stand for the one big union," there was a burst of cheering and clapping from all the wobblies in the hall. Fred Hoff nudged Mac as he clapped. "Let's raise the roof, Mac." The exploiting classes would be helpless against the solidarity of the whole workingclass. The militia and the yellowlegs were workingstiffs too. Once they realized the historic mission of solidarity the masterclass couldn't use them to shoot down their brothers any more. The workers must realize that every small fight, for higher wages, for free speech, for decent living conditions, was only significant as part of the big fight for the revolution and the co-operative commonwealth. Mac forgot about Maisie. By the time Big Bill had finished speaking his mind had run ahead of the speech so that he'd forgotten just what he said, but Mac was in a glow all over and was cheering to beat hell. He and Fred Hoff were cheering and the stocky Bohemian miner that smelt so bad next them was clapping and the oneeyed Pole on the other side was clapping and the bunch of Wops were clapping and the little Jap who was waiter at the Montezuma Club was clapping and the sixfoot ranchman who'd come in in hopes of seeing a fight was clapping. "Ain't the sonofabitch some orator," he was saying again and again. "I tellyer, Utah's the state for mansized men. I'm from Ogden myself."

After the meeting Big Bill was round at the office and he joked everybody and sat down and wrote an article right there for the paper. He pulled out a flask and everybody had a drink, except Fred Hoff who didn't like Big Bill's drinking, or any drinking, and they all went to bed with the next issue on the press, feeling tired and flushed and fine.

Next morning when Mac woke up he suddenly thought of Maisie and reread her letter, and tears came to his eyes sitting on the edge of the cot before anybody was up yet. He stuck his head in a pail of icy water from the pump, that was frozen

120

so hard he had to pour a kettleful of hot water off the stove into it to thaw it, but he couldn't get the worried stiff feeling out of his forehead. When he went over with Fred Hoff to the Chink joint for breakfast he tried to tell him he was going back to San Francisco to get married.

"Mac, you can't do it; we need you here."

"But I'll come back, honest I will, Fred."

"A man's first duty's to the workin'class," said Fred Hoff.

"As soon as the kid's born an' she can go back to work I'll come back. But you know how it is, Fred. I can't pay the hospital expenses on seventeen-fifty a week."

"You oughta been more careful."

"But hell, Fred, I'm made of flesh and blood like everybody else. For crissake, what do you want us to be, tin saints?"

"A wobbly oughtn't to have any wife or children, not till after the revolution."

"I'm not giving up the fight, Fred . . . I'm not sellin' out; I swear to God I'm not."

Fred Hoff had gotten very pale. Sucking his lips in between his teeth he got up from the table and left the restaurant. Mac sat there a long time feeling gloomy as hell. Then he went back to the office of the *Workman*. Fred Hoff was at the desk writing hard. "Say, Fred," said Mac, "I'll stay another month. I'll write Maisie right now."

"I knew you'd stay, Mac; you're no quitter."

"But Jesus God, man, you expect too much of a feller."

"Too much is too damn little," said Fred Hoff.

Mac started running the paper through the press.

For the next few weeks, when Maisie's letters came he put them in his pocket without reading them. He wrote her as reassuringly as he could, that he'd come as soon as the boys could get someone to take his place.

Then Christmas night he read all Maisie's letters. They were all the same; they made him cry. He didn't want to get married, but it was hell living up here in Nevada all winter without a girl, and he was sick of whoring around. He didn't want the boys to see him looking so glum, so he went down to have a drink at the saloon the restaurant workers went to. A great roaring stream of drunken singing came out of the saloon.

Going in the door he met Ben Evans. "Hello, Ben, where you goin'?"

"I'm goin' to have a drink as the feller said."

"Well, so am I."

"What's the matter?"

"I'm blue as hell."

Ben Evans laughed. "Jesus, so am I . . . and it's Christmas, ain't it?"

They had three drinks each, but the bar was crowded and they didn't feel like celebrating; so they took a pint flask, which was all they could afford, up to Ben Evans's room. Ben Evans was a dark thickset young man with very black eyes and hair. He hailed from Louisville, Kentucky. He'd had considerable schooling and was an automobile mechanic. The room was icy cold. They sat on the bed, each of them wrapped in one of his blankets.

"Well, ain't this a way to spend Christmas?" said Mac.

"Holy Jesus, it's a good thing Fred Hoff didn't ketch us," Mac snickered.

"Fred's a hell of a good guy, honest as the day an' all that, but he won't let a feller live."

"I guess if the rest of us were more like Fred we'd get somewheres sooner."

"We would at that . . . Say, Mac, I'm blue as hell about all this business, this shootin' an' these fellers from the W.F.M. goin' up to the Montezuma Club and playin' round with that damn scab delegate from Washington."

"Well, none of the wobbly crowd's done anything like that."

"No, but there's not enough of us . . ."

"What you need's a drink, Ben."

"It's just like this goddam pint, as the feller said, if we had enough of 'em, we'd get fried, but we haven't. If we had enough boys like Fred Hoff, we'd have a revolution, but we haven't."

They each had a drink from the pint and then Mac said: "Say, Ben, did you ever get a girl in trouble, a girl you liked a hellova lot?"

"Sure, hundreds of 'em."

"Didn't it worry you?"

"For chrissake, Mac, if a girl wasn't a goddam whore she wouldn't let you, would she?"

"Jeez, I don't see it like that, Ben . . . But hell, I don't know what to do about it . . . She's a good kid, anyways, gee . . ."

"I don't trust none of 'em . . . I know a guy onct married a girl like that, carried on and bawled an' made out he'd knocked her up. He married her all right an' she turned out to be a goddam whore and he got the siph off'n her . . . You take it from me, boy. . . . Love 'em and leave 'em, that's the only way for stiffs like us."

They finished up the pint. Mac went back to the *Workman* office and went to sleep with the whiskey burning in his stomach. He dreamed he was walking across a field with a girl on

122

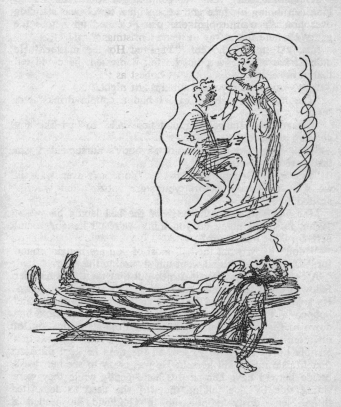

a warm day. The whiskey was hotsweet in his mouth, buzzed like bees in his ears. He wasn't sure if the girl was Maisie or just a goddam whore, but he felt very warm and tender, and she was saying in a little hotsweet voice, "Love me up, kid," and he could see her body through her thin gauze dress as he leaned over her and she kept crooning, "Love me up, kid," in a hotsweet buzzing.

"Hey, Mac, ain't you ever goin' to get waked up?" Fred Hoff, scrubbing his face and neck with a towel, was standing over him. "I want to get this place cleaned up before the gang gets here."

Mac sat up on the cot. "Yare, what's the matter?" He didn't have a hangover, but he felt depressed, he could tell that at once.

"Say, you certainly were stinkin' last night."

"The hell I was, Fred . . . I had a coupla drinks, but, Jesus . . ."

"I heard you staggerin' round here goin' to bed like any goddam scissorbill."

"Look here, Fred, you're not anybody's nursemaid. I can take care of myself."

"You guys need nursemaids . . . You can't even wait till we won the strike before you start boozin' and whorin' around."

Mac was sitting on the edge of the bed lacing his boots. "What in God's name do you think we're all hangin' round here for . . . our health?"

"I don't know what the hell most of you are hangin' round for," said Fred Hoff and went out slamming the door.

A couple of days later it turned out that there was another fellow around who could run a linotype and Mac left town. He sold his suitcase and his good clothes for five dollars and hopped a train of flatcars loaded with ore that took him down to Ludlow. In Ludlow he washed the alkali dust out of his mouth, got a meal and got cleaned up a little. He was in a terrible hurry to get to Frisco, all the time he kept thinking that Maisie might kill herself. He was crazy to see her, to sit beside her, to have her pat his hand gently while they were sitting side by side talking the way she used to do. After those bleak dusty months up in Goldfield he needed a woman. The fare to Frisco was $11.15 and he had only four dollars and some pennies left. He tried risking a dollar in a crapgame in the back of a saloon, but he lost it right away and got cold feet and left.

Newsreel VIII

Professor Ferrer, former director of the Modern School in Barcelona who has been on trial there on the charge of having been the principal instigator of the recent revolutionary movement has been sentenced to death and will be shot Wednesday unless

Cook still pins faith on Esquimaux says interior of the Island of Luzon most beautiful place on earth

QUIZZES WARM UP POLE TALK

Oh bury me not on the lone prairie
Where the wild kiyotes will howl over me
Where the rattlesnakes hiss and the wind blows free

GYPSY'S MARCHERS STORM SIN'S FORT

Nation's big men await trip   Englewood clubwomen move to uplift drama   Evangelist's host thousand strong pierces heart of crowded hushed levee has $3018 and is arrested

GIVE MILLION IN HOOKWORM WAR

gypsy smith's spectral parade through south side redlight region

with a bravery that brought tears to the eyes of the squad of twelve men who were detailed to shoot him Francisco Ferrer marched this morning to the trench that had been prepared to receive his body after the fatal volley

PLUNGE BY AUTO; DEATH IN RIVER

The Camera Eye (11)

the Pennypackers went to the Presbyterian Church and the Pennypacker girls sang chilly shrill soprano in the choir and everybody was greeted when they went into church and outside the summer leaves on the trees wigwagged greenblueyellow through the windows and we all filed into the pew and I'd asked Mr. Pennypacker he was a deacon in the church who were the Molly Maguires?

a squirrel was scolding in the whiteoak but the Pennypacker girls all the young ladies in their best hats singing the anthem who were the Molly Maguires? thoughts, bulletholes in an old barn abandoned mine pits black skeleton tipples weedgrown dumps who were the Molly Maguires? but it was too late you couldn't talk in church and all the young ladies best hats and pretty pink green blue yellow dresses and the squirrel scolding who were the Molly Maguires?

and before I knew it it was communion and I wanted to say I hadn't been baptized but all eyes looked shut up when I started to whisper to Con

communion was grapejuice in little glasses and little squares of stale bread and you had to gulp the bread and put your handkerchief over your mouth and look holy and the little glasses made a funny sucking noise and all the quiet church in the middle of the sunny brightblue Sunday in the middle of whiteoaks wigwagging and the smell of fries from the white house and the blue quiet Sunday smoke of chimneys from stoves where fried chicken sizzled and fritters and brown gravy set back to keep hot

in the middle of squirrels and minetipples in the middle of the blue Pennsylvania summer Sunday the little glasses sucking to get the last drop of communion

and I felt itchy in the back of my neck would I be struck by lightning eating the bread drinking the communion me not believing or baptized or Presbyterian and who were the Molly Maguires? masked men riding at night shooting bullets into barns at night what were they after in the oldtime night?

church was over and everybody was filing out and being greeted as they went out and everybody had a good appetite after communion but I couldn't eat much itchy in the back of the neck scary with masked men riding Molly Maguires

Newsreel IX

FORFEIT STARS BY DRINKING

"Oh bury me not
*   on the lone prairie"*

They heeded not his dying prayer
They buried him there on the lone prairie

COLLEGE HEAD DENIES KISSES

then our courage returned, for we knew that rescue was near at hand, we shouted and yelled again but did not know whether we were heard. Then came the unsealing and I lost consciousness. All the days and nights fell back and I dropped into a sleep

VOTE AT MIDNIGHT ON ALTMAN'S FATE

This is the fourth day we have been down here. That is what I think, but our watches stopped. I have been waiting in the dark because we have been eating the wax from our safety lamps. I have also eaten a plug of tobacco, some bark and some of my shoe. I could only chew it. I hope you can read this. I am not afraid to die. O holy Virgin have mercy on me. I think my time has come. You know what my property is. We worked for it together and it is all yours. This is my will and you must keep it. You have been a good wife. May the Holy Virgin guard you. I hope this reaches you sometime and you can read it. It has been very quiet down here and I wonder what has become of our comrades. Goodbye until heaven shall bring us together.

GIRLS' ANNOYER LASHED IN PUBLIC
COVETS OSTRICHES

In a little box just six by three
And his bones now rot on the lone prairie

Mac

Mac went down to the watertank beyond the yards to wait for a chance to hop a freight. The old man's hat and his ruptured shoes were ashen gray with dust; he was sitting all hunched up with his head between his knees and didn't make a move until Mac was right up to him. Mac sat down beside him. A rank smell of feverish sweat came from the old man. "What's the trouble, daddy?"

"I'm through, that's all . . . I been a lunger all my life an' I guess it's got me now." His mouth twisted in a spasm of pain. He let his head droop between his knees. After a minute he raised his head again, making little feeble gasps with his mouth like a dying fish. When he got his breath he said, "It's a razor a-slicin' off my lungs every time. Stand by, will you, kid?"

"Sure I will," said Mac.

"Listen, kid, I wanna go West to where there's trees an' stuff . . . You got to help me into one o' them cars. I'm too weak for the rods . . . Don't let me lay down . . . I'll start bleedin' if I lay down, see." He choked again.

"I got a coupla bucks. I'll square it with the brakeman, maybe."

"You don't talk like no vag."

"I'm a printer. I wanta make San Francisco soon as I can."

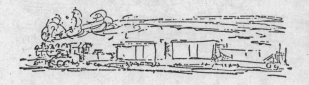

"A workingman; I'll be a sonofabitch. Listen here, kid . . . I ain't worked in seventeen years."

The train came in and the engine stood hissing by the watertank.

Mac helped the old man to his feet and got him propped in the corner of a flatcar that was loaded with machine parts covered with a tarpaulin. He saw the fireman and the engineer looking at them out of the cab, but they didn't say anything.

When the train started the wind was cold. Mac took off his coat and put it behind the old man's head to keep it from jiggling with the rattling of the car. The old man sat with his eyes closed and his head thrown back. Mac didn't know whether he was dead or not. It got to be night. Mac was terribly cold and huddled shivering in a fold of tarpaulin in the other end of the car.

In the gray of dawn Mac woke up from a doze with his teeth chattering. The train had stopped on a siding. His legs were so numb it was some time before he could stand on them. He went to look at the old man, but he couldn't tell whether he was dead or not. It got a little lighter and the east began to glow like the edge of a piece of iron in a forge. Mac jumped to the ground and walked back along the train to the caboose.

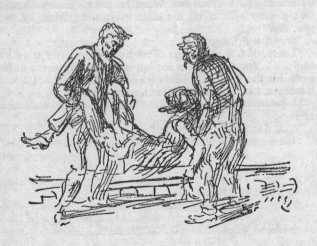

The brakeman was drowsing beside his lantern. Mac told him that an old tramp was dying in one of the flatcars. The brakeman had a small flask of whiskey in his good coat that hung on a nail in the caboose. They walked together up the track again. When they got to the flatcar it was almost day. The old man had flopped over on his side. His face looked white and grave like the face of a statue of a Civil War general. Mac opened his coat and the filthy torn shirts and underclothes and put his hand on the old man's chest. It was cold and lifeless as a board. When he took his hand away there was sticky blood on it.

"Hemorrhage," said the brakeman, making a perfunctory clucking noise in his mouth.

The brakeman said they'd have to get the body off the train. They laid him down flat in the ditch beside the ballast with his hat over his face. Mac asked the brakeman if he had a spade so that they could bury him, so that the buzzards wouldn't get him, but he said no, the gandywalkers would find him and bury him. He took Mac back to the caboose and gave him a drink and asked him all about how the old man had died.

Mac beat his way to San Francisco.

Maisie was cold and bitter at first, but after they'd talked a little while she said he looked thin and ragged as a bum and burst into tears and kissed him. They went to get her savings out of the bank and bought Mac a suit and went down to City Hall and got married without saying anything to her folks. They were both very happy going down on the train to San Diego, and they got a furnished room there with kitchen privileges and told the landlady they'd been married a year. They wired Maisie's folks that they were down there on their honeymoon and would be back soon.

Mac got work there at a job printer's and they started payments on a bungalow at Pacific Beach. The work wasn't bad and he was pretty happy in his quiet life with Maisie. After all, he'd had enough bumming for a while. When Maisie went to the hospital to have the baby, Mac had to beg a two months' advance of pay from Ed Balderston, his boss. Even at that they had to take out a second mortgage on the bungalow to pay the doctor's bill. The baby was a girl and had blue eyes and they named her Rose.

Life in San Diego was sunny and quiet. Mac went to work mornings on the steamcar and came back evenings on the steamcar and Sundays he puttered round the house or sometimes sat on one of the beaches with Maisie and the kid. It was understood between them now that he had to do everything that Maisie wanted because he'd given her such a tough

131

time before they were married. The next year they had another kid and Maisie was sick and in hospital a long time after, so that now all that he could do with his pay each week was cover the interest on his debts, and he was always having to kid the grocerystore along and the milkman and the bakery to keep their charge-accounts going from week to week. Maisie read a lot of magazines and always wanted new things for the house, a pianola, or a new icebox, or a fireless cooker. Her brothers were making good money in the realestate business in Los Angeles and her folks were coming up in the world. Whenever she got a letter from them she'd worry Mac about striking his boss for more pay or moving to a better job.

When there was anybody of the wobbly crowd in town down on his uppers or when they were raising money for strike funds or anything like that, he'd help them out with a couple of dollars, but he never could do much for fear Maisie would find out about it. Whenever she found *The Appeal to Reason* or any other radical paper round the house she'd burn it up, and then they'd quarrel and be sulky and make each other's lives miserable for a few days, until Mac decided what was the use, and never spoke to her about it. But it kept them apart almost as if she thought he was going out with some other woman.

One Saturday afternoon Mac and Maisie had managed to get a neighbor to take care of the kids and were going into a vaudeville theater when they noticed a crowd at the corner in front of Marshall's drugstore. Mac elbowed his way through. A thin young man in blue denim was standing close to the corner lamppost where the firealarm was, reading the Declaration of Independence: *When in the course of human events* . . . A cop came up and told him to move on . . . *inalienable right . . . life, liberty, and the pursuit of happiness.*

Now there were two cops. One of them had the young man by the shoulders and was trying to pull him loose from the lamppost.

"Come on, Fainy, we'll be late for the show," Maisie kept saying.

"Hey, get a file; the bastard's locked himself to the post," he heard one cop say to the other. By that time Maisie had managed to hustle him to the theater boxoffice. After all, he'd promised to take her to the show and she hadn't been out all winter. The last thing he saw the cop had hauled off and hit the young guy in the corner of the jaw.

Mac sat there in the dark stuffy theater all afternoon. He didn't see the acts or the pictures between the acts. He didn't speak to Maisie. He sat there feeling sick in the pit of his

133

DECLARATION
OF
INDEPENDENCE

stomach. The boys must be staging a free-speech fight right here in town. Now and then he glanced at Maisie's face in the dim glow from the stage. It had puffed out a little in well-satisfied curves like a cat sitting by a warm stove, but she was still a good looker. She'd already forgotten everything and was completely happy looking at the show, her lips parted, her eyes bright, like a little girl at a party. "I guess I've sold out to the sonsobitches all right, all right," he kept saying to himself.

The last number on the programme was Eva Tanguay. The nasal voice singing *I'm Eva Tanguay, I don't care* brought Mac out of his sullen trance. Everything suddenly looked bright and clear to him, the proscenium with its heavy gold fluting, the people's faces in the boxes, the heads in front of him, the tawdry powdery mingling of amber and blue lights on the stage, the scrawny woman flinging herself around inside the rainbow hoop of the spotlight.

> *The papers say that I'm insane*
> *But . . . I . . . don't . . . care.*

Mac got up. "Maisie, I'll meet you at the house. You see the rest of the show. I feel kind of bum." Before she could answer, he'd slipped out past the other people in the row, down the aisle and out. On the street there was nothing but the ordinary Saturday afternoon crowd. Mac walked round and round the downtown district. He didn't even know where I.W.W. headquarters was. He had to talk to somebody. As he passed the Hotel Brewster he caught a whiff of beer. What he needed was a drink. This way he was going nuts.

At the next corner he went into a saloon and drank four rye whiskies straight. The bar was lined with men drinking, treating each other, talking loud about baseball, prizefights, Eva Tanguay and her Salome dance.

Beside Mac was a big redfaced man with a widebrimmed felt hat on the back of his head. When Mac reached for his fifth drink this man put his hand on his arm and said, "Pard, have that on me if you don't mind . . . I'm celebratin' today."

"Thanks; here's lookin' at you," said Mac.

"Pard, if you don't mind my sayin' so, you're drinkin' like you wanted to drink the whole barrel up at once and not leave any for the rest of us . . . Have a chaser."

"All right, bo," said Mac. "Make it a beer chaser."

"My name's McCreary," said the big man. "I just sold my fruit crop. I'm from up San Jacinto way."

"So's my name McCreary, too," said Mac.

135

They shook hands heartily.

"By the living jumbo, that's a coincidence . . . We must be kin or pretty near it . . . Where you from, pard?"

"I'm from Chicago, but my folks was Irish."

"Mine was from East, Delaware . . . but it's the good old Scotch-Irish stock."

They had more drinks on that. Then they went to another saloon where they sat in a corner at a table and talked. The big man talked about his ranch and his apricot crop and how his wife was bedridden since his last child came. "I'm awful fond of the old gal, but what can a feller do? Can't get gelded just to be true to your wife."

"I like my wife swell," said Mac, "and I've got swell kids. Rose is four and she's beginning to read already, and Ed's about learnin' to walk. . . . But hell, before I was married I used to think I might amount to somethin' in the world . . . I don't mean I thought I was anythin' in particular . . . You know how it is."

"Sure, pard, I used to feel that way when I was a young feller."

"Maisie's a fine girl, too, and I like her better all the time," said Mac, feeling a warm tearing wave of affection go over him, like sometimes a Saturday evening when he'd helped her bathe the kids and put them to bed and the room was still steamy from their baths and his eyes suddenly met Maisie's eyes and there was nowhere they had to go and they were just both of them there together.

The man from up San Jacinto way began to sing:

Oh my wife has gone to the country,
    Hooray, hooray.
I love my wife, but oh you kid,
    My wife's gone away.

"But God damn it to hell," said Mac, "a man's got to work for more than himself and his kids to feel right."

"I agree with you absholootely, pard; every man for himself, and the devil take the hindmost."

"Oh, hell," said Mac, "I wish I was on the bum again or up at Goldfield with the bunch."

They drank and drank and ate free lunch and drank some more, all the time rye with beer chasers, and the man from up San Jacinto way had a telephone number and called up some girls and they bought a bottle of whiskey and went out to their apartment, and the rancher from up San Jacinto way sat with a girl on each knee singing *My wife has gone to the country*. Mac just sat belching in a corner with his head dan-

136

gling over his chest; then suddenly he felt bitterly angry and
got to his feet upsetting a table with a glass vase on it.

"McCreary," he said, "this is no place for a classconscious
rebel . . . I'm a wobbly, damn you . . . I'm goin' out and
get in this free-speech fight."

The other McCreary went on singing and paid no attention. Mac went out and slammed the door. One of the girls
followed him out jabbering about the broken vase, but he
pushed her in the face and went out into the quiet street. It
was moonlight. He'd lost the last steamcar and would have to
walk home.

When he got to the house he found Maisie sitting on the
porch in her kimono. She was crying. "And I had such a nice
supper for you," she kept saying, and her eyes looked into
him cold and bitter the way they'd been when he'd gotten
back from Goldfield before they were married.

The next day he had a hammering headache and his stomach was upset. He figured up he'd spent fifteen dollars that
he couldn't afford to waste. Maisie wouldn't speak to him. He

stayed on in bed, rolling round, feeling miserable, wishing he could go to sleep and stay asleep forever. That Sunday evening Maisie's brother Bill came to supper. As soon as he got into the house Maisie started talking to Mac as if nothing had happened. It made him sore to feel that this was just in order to keep Bill from knowing they had quarreled.

Bill was a powerfullybuilt towhaired man with a red neck, just beginning to go fat. He sat at the table, eating the potroast and cornbread Maisie had made, talking big about the real estate boom up in Los Angeles. He'd been a locomotive engineer and had been hurt in a wreck and had had the lucky breaks with a couple of options on lots he'd bought with his compensation money. He tried to argue Mac into giving up his job in San Diego and coming in with him. "I'll get you in on the ground floor, just for Maisie's sake," he said over and over again. "And in ten years you'll be a rich man, like I'm goin' to be in less time than that . . . Now's the time, Maisie, for you folks to make a break, while you're young, or it'll be too late and Mac'll just be a workingman all his life."

Maisie's eyes shone. She brought out a chocolate layer cake and a bottle of sweet wine. Her cheeks flushed and she kept laughing showing all her pearly teeth. She hadn't looked so pretty since she'd had her first baby. Bill's talk about money made her drunk.

"Suppose a feller didn't want to get rich . . . you know what Gene Debs said, 'I want to rise with the ranks, not from the ranks,' " said Mac.

Maisie and Bill laughed. "When a guy talks like that he's ripe for the nuthouse, take it from me," said Bill.

Mac flushed and said nothing.

Bill pushed back his chair and cleared his throat in a serious tone: "Look here, Mac . . . I'm goin' to be around this town for a few days lookin' over the situation, but looks to me like things was pretty dead. Now what I propose is this . . . You know what I think of Maisie . . . I think she's about the sweetest little girl in the world. I wish my wife had half what Maisie's got . . . Well, anyway, here's my proposition: Out on Ocean View Avenue I've got several magnificent missionstyle bungalows I haven't disposed of yet, twentyfivefoot frontage on a refined residential street by a hundred foot depth. Why, I've gotten as high as five grand in cold cash for 'em. In a year or two none of us fellers'll be able to stick our noses in there. It'll be millionaires' row . . . Now if you're willing to have the house in Maisie's name I'll tell you what I'll do . . . I'll swap properties with you, paying all the expenses of searching title and transfer and balance up the mortgages, that I'll hold so's to keep 'em in the

138

family, so that you won't have to make substantially bigger payments than you do here, and will be launched on the road to success."

"Oh, Bill, you darling!" cried Maisie. She ran over and kissed him on the top of the head and sat swinging her legs on the arm of the chair.

"Gee, I'll have to sleep on that," said Mac; "it's mighty white of you to make the offer."

"Fainy, I'd think you'd be more grateful to Bill," snapped Maisie. "Of course we'll do it."

"No, you're quite right," said Bill. "A man's got to think a proposition like that over. But don't forget the advantages offered, better schools for the kids, more refined surroundings, an upandcoming boom town instead of a dead one, chance to get ahead in the world instead of being a goddam wageslave."

So a month later the McCrearys moved up to Los Angeles. The expenses of moving and getting the furniture installed put Mac five hundred dollars in debt. On top of that little Rose caught the measles and the doctor's bill started mounting. Mac couldn't get a job on any of the papers. Up at the union local that he transferred to they had ten men out of work as it was.

He spent a lot of time walking about town worrying. He didn't like to be at home any more. He and Maisie never got on now. Maisie was always thinking about what went on at brother Bill's house, what kind of clothes Mary Virginia, his wife, wore, how they brought up their children, the fine new victrola they'd bought. Mac sat on benches in parks round town, reading *The Appeal to Reason* and *The Industrial Worker* and the local papers.

One day he noticed *The Industrial Worker* sticking out of the pocket of the man beside him. They had both sat on the bench a long time when something made him turn to look at the man. "Say, aren't you Ben Evans?"

"Well, Mac, I'll be goddamned . . . What's the matter, boy, you're lookin' thin?"

"Aw, nothin', I'm lookin for a master, that's all."

They talked for a long time. Then they went to have a cup of coffee in a Mexican restaurant where some of the boys hung out. A young blond fellow with blue eyes joined them there who talked English with an accent. Mac was surprised to find out that he was a Mexican. Everybody talked Mexico. Madero had started his revolution. The fall of Diaz was expected any day. All over the peons were taking to the hills, driving the rich cientificos off their ranches. Anarchist propaganda was spreading among the town workers. The restaurant had a warm smell of chiles and overroasted coffee. On each table there were nigger-pink and vermilion paper flowers, an occasional flash of white teeth in bronze and brown faces talking low. Some of the Mexicans there belonged to the I.W.W., but most of them were anarchists. The talk of revolution and foreign places made him feel happy and adventurous again, as if he had a purpose in life, like when he'd been on the bum with Ike Hall.

"Say, Mac, let's go to Mexico and see if there's anything in this revoloossione talk," Ben kept saying.

"If it wasn't for the kids . . . Hell, Fred Hoff was right when he bawled me out and said a revolutionist oughtn't to marry."

Eventually Mac got a job as linotype operator on *The Times,* and things at the house were a little better, but he never had any spare money, as everything had to go into paying debts and interest on mortgages. It was night work again, and he hardly ever saw Maisie and the kids any more. Sundays Maisie would take little Ed to brother Bill's and he and Rose would go for walks or take trolleytrips. That was the best part of the week. Saturday nights he'd sometimes get to a lecture or go down to chat with the boys at the I.W.W. local, but he was scared to be seen round in radical company too much for fear of losing his job. The boys thought he was pretty yellow but put up with him because they thought of him as an oldtimer.

He got occasional letters from Milly telling him about Uncle Tim's health. She had married a man named Cohen who was a registered accountant and worked in one of the offices at the stockyards. Uncle Tim lived with them. Mac would have liked to bring him down to live with him in Los Angeles, but he knew that it would only mean squabbling with Maisie. Milly's letters were pretty depressing. She felt funny, she said, to be married to a Jew. Uncle Tim was always poorly. The doctor said it was the drink, but whenever they gave him any money he drank it right up. She wished she could have children. Fainy was lucky, she thought, to have such nice children. She was afraid that poor Uncle Tim wasn't long for this world.

The same day that the papers carried the murder of Madero in Mexico City, Mac got a wire from Milly that Uncle Tim was dead and please to wire money for the funeral. Mac went to the savingsbank and drew out $53.75 he had in an account for the children's schooling and took it down to the Western Union and wired fifty to her. Maisie didn't find out until the baby's birthday came around, when

140

she went down to deposit five dollars birthday money from brother Bill.

That night when Mac let himself in by the latchkey he was surprised to find the light on in the hall. Maisie was sitting half asleep on the hall settee with a blanket wrapped round her waiting for him. He was pleased to see her and went up to kiss her. "What's the matter, baby?" he said. She pushed him away from her and jumped to her feet.

"You thief," she said. "I couldn't sleep till I told you what I thought of you. I suppose you've been spending it on drink or on some other woman. That's why I never see you any more."

"Maisie, calm down, old girl . . . What's the matter; let's talk about it quietly."

"I'll get a divorce, that's what I'll do. Stealing money from your own children to make yourself a bum with . . . your own poor little . . ."

Mac drew himself up and clenched his fists. He spoke very quietly, although his lips were trembling.

"Maisie, I had an absolute right to take out that money. I'll deposit some more in a week or two, and it's none of your damn business."

"A fat chance you saving up fifty dollars; you aren't man enough to make a decent living for your wife and children so you have to take it out of your poor little innocent children's bank account." Maisie broke out into dry sobbing.

"Maisie, that's enough of that . . . I'm about through."

"I'm the one that's through with you and your ungodly socialistic talk. That never got nobody anywheres, and the lowdown bums you go around with . . . I wish to God I'd never married you. I never would have, you can be damn well sure of that if I hadn't got caught the way I did."

"Maisie, don't talk like that."

Maisie walked straight up to him, her eyes wide and feverish.

"This house is in my name; don't forget that."

"All right, I'm through."

Before he knew it he had slammed the door behind him and was walking down the block. It began to rain. Each raindrop made a splatter the size of a silver dollar in the dust of the street. It looked like stage rain round the arclight. Mac couldn't think where to go. Drenched, he walked and walked. At one corner there was a clump of palms in a yard that gave a certain amount of shelter. He stood there a long time shivering. He was almost crying thinking of the warm gentleness of Maisie when he used to pull the cover a little way back and slip into bed beside her asleep when he got home from

141

work in the clanking sour printing plant, her breasts, the feel of the nipples through the thin nightgown; the kids in their cots out on the sleepingporch, him leaning over to kiss each of the little warm foreheads. "Well, I'm through," he said aloud as if he were speaking to somebody else. Then only did the thought come to him, "I'm free to see the country now, to work for the movement, to go on the bum again."

Finally he went to Ben Evans's boardinghouse. It was a long time before he could get anybody to come to the door. When he finally got in Ben sat up in bed and looked at him stupid with sleep. "What the hell?"

"Say, Ben, I've just broken up housekeepin' . . . I'm goin' to Mexico."

"Are the cops after you? For crissake, this wasn't any place to come."

"No, it's just my wife."

Ben laughed. "Oh, for the love of Mike!"

"Say, Ben, do you want to come to Mexico and see the revolution?"

"What the hell could you do in Mexico? . . . Anyway, the boys elected me secretary of local 257 . . . I got to stay here an' earn my seventeen-fifty. Say, you're soaked; take your clothes off and put on my workclothes hangin' on the back of the door . . . You better get some sleep. I'll move over."

Mac stayed in town two weeks until they could get a man to take his place at the linotype. He wrote Maisie that he was going away and that he'd send her money to help support the kids as soon as he was in a position to. Then one morning he got on the train with twentyfive dollars in his pocket and a ticket to Yuma, Arizona. Yuma turned out to be hotter'n the hinges of hell. A guy at the railroadmen's boardinghouse told him he'd sure die of thirst if he tried going into Mexico there, and nobody knew anything about the revolution, anyway. So he beat his way along the Southern Pacific to El Paso. Hell had broken loose across the border, everybody said. The bandits were likely to take Juarez at any moment. They shot Americans on sight. The bars of El Paso were full of ranchers and miningmen bemoaning the good old days when Porfirio Diaz was in power and a white man could make money in Mexico. So it was with beating heart that Mac walked across the international bridge into the dusty bustling adobe streets of Juarez.

Mac walked around looking at the small trolleycars and the mules and the walls daubed with seablue and the peon women squatting behind piles of fruit in the marketplace and the crumbling scrollface churches and the deep bars open to the street. Everything was strange and the air was peppery to his nostrils and he was wondering what he was going to do next. It was late afternoon of an April day. Mac was sweating in his blue flannel shirt. His body felt gritty and itchy and he wanted a bath. "Gettin' too old for this kinda stuff," he told himself. At last he found the house of a man named Ricardo Perez whom one of the Mexican anarchists in Los Angeles had told him to look up. He had trouble finding him in the big house with an untidy courtyard, on the edge of town. None of the women hanging out clothes seemed to understand Mac's lingo. At last Mac heard a voice from above in carefully modulated English. "Come up if you are looking for Ricardo Perez . . . please . . . I am Ricardo Perez." Mac looked up and saw a tall bronzecolored grayhaired man in an old tan duster leaning from the top gallery of the courtyard. He went up the iron steps. The tall man shook hands with him.

"Fellowworker McCreary . . . My comrades wrote me you were coming."

"That's me, all right . . . I'm glad you talk English."

"I lived in Santa Fe many years and in Brockton, Massachusetts. Sit down . . . please . . . I am very happy to welcome an American revolutionary worker . . . Though our ideas probably do not entirely agree we have much in common. We are comrades in the big battle." He patted Mac on the shoulder and pressed him into a chair. "Please." There were several little yellow children in torn shirts running round barefoot. Ricardo Perez sat down and took the smallest on his knee, a little girl with kinky pigtails and a smudged face. The place smelt of chile and scorched olive oil and children and washing. "What are you going to do in Mexico, fellowworker?"

Mac blushed. "Oh, I want to kinda get into things, into the revolution."

"The situation is very confusing here . . . Our townworkers are organizing and are classconscious, but the peons, the peasants, are easily misled by unscrupulous leaders."

"I want to see some action, Perez . . . I was living in Los Angeles an' gettin' to be a goddam booster like the rest of 'em. I can earn my keep in the printin' line, I guess."

"I must introduce you to the comrades . . . Please . . . We will go now."

Blue dusk was swooping down on the streets when they went out. Lights were coming out yellow. Mechanical pianos jinglejangled in bars. In a gateway a little outoftune orchestra was playing. The market was all lit up by flares, all kinds of shiny brightcolored stuff was for sale at booths. At a corner an old Indian and an old broadfaced woman, both of them

143

blind and heavily pockmarked, were singing a shrill endless song in the middle of a dense group of short thickset country people, the women with black shawls over their heads, the men in white cotton suits like pajamas.

"They sing about the murder of Madero . . . It is very good for the education of the people . . . You see they cannot read the papers so they get their news in songs . . . It was your ambassador murdered Madero. He was a bourgeois idealist but a great man . . . Please . . . Here is the hall. . . . You see that sign says 'Viva the Revindicating Revolution prelude to the Social Revolution.' This is the hall of the Anarchist Union of Industry and Agriculture. Huerta has a few federales here but they are so weak they dare not attack us. Ciudad Juarez is heart and soul with the revolution . . . Please . . . you will greet the comrades with a few words."

The smoky hall and the platform were filled with swarthy men in blue denim workclothes; in the back were a few peons in white. Many hands shook Mac's, black eyes looked sharp into his, several men hugged him. He was given a campchair in the front row on the platform. Evidently Ricardo Perez was chairman. Applause followed in every pause in his speech. A feeling of big events hovered in the hall. When Mac got on his feet, somebody yelled "Solidarity forever" in English. Mac stammered a few words about how he wasn't an official representative of the I.W.W., but that all the same classconscious American workers were watching the Mexican revolution with big hopes, and ended up with the wobbly catchword about building the new society in the shell of the old. The speech went big when Perez translated it and Mac felt pretty good. Then the meeting went on and on, more and more speeches and occasional songs. Mac found himself nodding several times. The sound of the strange language made him sleepy. He barely managed to keep awake until a small band in the open door of the hall broke into a tune and everybody sang and the meeting broke up.

"That's *Cuatro Milpas* . . . that means four cornfields . . . that's a song of the peons everybody's singin' now," said Perez.

"I'm pretty hungry . . . I'd like to get a little something to eat somewheres," said Mac. "I haven't eaten since morning when I had a cup of coffee and a doughnut in El Paso."

"We will eat at the house of our comrade," said Perez. "Please . . . this way."

They went in off the street, now black and empty, through a tail door hung with a bead curtain, into a whitewashed room brightly lit by an acetylene flare that smelt strong of carbide. They sat down at the end of a long table with a spotted cloth on it. The table gradually filled with people from the meeting, mostly young men in blue workclothes, with thin sharp faces. At the other end sat an old dark man with the big nose and broad flat cheekbones of an Indian. Perez poured Mac out two glasses of a funnytasting white drink that made his head spin. The food was very hot with pepper and chile and he choked on it a little bit. The Mexicans petted Mac like a child at his birthday party. He had to drink many glasses of beer and cognac. Perez went home early and left him in charge of a young fellow named Pablo. Pablo had a Colt automatic on a shoulder strap that he was very proud of. He spoke a little pidginenglish and sat with one hand round Mac's neck and the other on the buckle of his holster. "Gringo bad . . . Kill him quick . . . Fellowworker good . . . internacional . . . hurray," he kept saying. They sang the *International* several times and then the *Marseillaise* and the *Carmagnole*. Mac was carried along in a peppery haze. He sang and drank and ate and everything began to lose outline.

"Fellowworker marry nice girl," said Pablo. They were standing at a bar somewhere. He made a gesture of sleeping with his two hands against his face. "Come."

They went to a dancehall. At the entrance everybody had to leave his gun on a table guarded by a soldier in a visored cap. Mac noticed that the men and girls drew away from him a little. Pablo laughed. "They think you gringo . . . I tell them revolucionario internacional. There she, nice girl . . . No goddam whore . . . not pay, she nice workinggirl . . . comrade."

Mac found himself being introduced to a brown broadfaced girl named Encarnacion. She was neatly dressed and her hair was very shinyblack. She gave him a bright flash of a smile. He patted her on the cheek. They drank some beer at the bar and left. Pablo had a girl with him too. The others stayed on at the dancehall. Pablo and his girl walked round to Encarnacion's house with them. It was a room in a little courtyard. Beyond it was a great expanse of lightcolored desert land stretching as far as you could see under a waning moon. In the distance were some tiny specks of fires. Pablo pointed at them with his full hand and whispered, "Revolucion."

Then they said goodnight at the door of Encarnacion's little room that had a bed, a picture of the Virgin and a new photograph of Madero stuck up by a pin. Encarnacion closed the door, bolted it and sat down on the bed looking up at Mac with a smile.

The Camera Eye (12)

when everybody went away for a trip Jeanne took us out to play every day in Farragut Square and told you about how in the Jura in winter the wolves come down and howl through the streets of the villages

and sometimes we'd see President Roosevelt ride by all alone on a bay horse and once we were very proud because when we took off our hats we were very proud because he smiled and showed his teeth like in the newspaper and touched his hat and we were very proud and he had an aide de camp

but we had a cloth duck that we used to play with on the steps until it began to get dark and the wolves howled ran with little children's blood dripping from their snout through the streets of the villages only it was summer and between dog and wolf we'd be put to bed and Jeanne was a young French girl from the Jura where the wolves howled ran through the streets and when everybody had gone to bed she would take you into her bed

and it was a very long scary story and the worst of the wolves howled through the streets gloaming to freeze little children's blood was the Loup Garou howling in the Jura and we were scared and she had breasts under her nightgown and the Loup Garou was terrible scary and black hair and rub against her and outside the wolves howled in the streets and it was wet there and she said it was nothing she had just washed herself

but the Loup Garou was really a man hold me close cheri a man howled through streets with a bloody snout that tore up the bellies of girls and little children Loup Garou

and afterwards you knew what girls were made like and she was very silly and made you promise not to tell but you wouldn't have anyway

147

Newsreel X

MOON'S PATENT IS FIZZLE

insurgents win at Kansas polls.   Oak Park soulmates part   Eight thousand to take autoride   says girl begged for her husband

PIT SENTIMENT FAVORS UPTURN

Oh you be-eautiful doll
You great big beautiful doll

the world cannot understand all that is involved in this, she said. It appears like an ordinary worldly affair with the trappings of what is low and vulgar but there is nothing of the sort. He is honest and sincere. I know him. I have fought side by side with him. My heart is with him now.

Let me throw my arms around you
Honey ain't I glad I found you

ALMOST MOTIONLESS IN MIDSUMMER LANGUOR
ON BUSINESS SEAS ONE MILLION SEE
DRUNKARDS BOUNCED

JURORS AT GATES OF BEEF BARONS

compare love with Vesuvius   emblazoned streets await
tramp of paladins

Honey ain't I glad I found you
Oh you beautiful doll
You great big beautiful doll

TRADES WHITE HORSE FOR RED

Madero's troops defeat rebels in battle at Parral
Roosevelt carries Illinois oratory closes eyelids Chicago pleads for more water

CONFESSED ANARCHISTS ON BENDED KNEES KISS
U.S. FLAG

THE SUNBEAM MOVEMENT IS SPREADING
BOMB NO. 4 IN LEVEE WAR SPLINTERS
WEST SIDE SALOON

a report printed Wednesday that a patient in a private
pavilion in St. Luke's Hospital undergoing an operation
for the extirpation of a cancerous growth at the base of
the tongue was General Grant was denied by both the
hospital authorities and Lieut. Howzes who characterized
the story as a deliberate fabrication

The Camera Eye (13)

he was a towboat captain and he knew the river blind-
fold from Indian Head to the Virginia Capes and the bay
and the Eastan Shoa up to Baltima' for that matter and
he lived in a redbrick house in Alexandria the pilothouse
smelt of a hundred burntout pipes

that's the *Mayflower* the President's yacht and that
there's the *Dolphin* and that's the ole monitor *Tippecanoe*
and that there's the ravenoo cutter and we're just passin'
the po-lice boat

when Cap'n Keen reaches up to pull the whistle on the
ceiling of the pilothouse you can see the red and green
bracelet tattooed under the black hairs on his wrist

Ma soul an' body ole Cap'n Gifford used ter be a frien'
o' mahne many's the time we been oysterin' together on

149

the Eastan Shoa an' oysterpirates used to shanghai young
fellers in those days an' make 'em work all winter you
couldn't git away less you swam ashoa and the water was
too damnation cole an' the ole man used to take the fellers'
clothes away so's they couldn't git ashoa when they was
anchored up in a crik or near a house or somethin' boy
they was mean customers the oysterpirates ma soul and
body onct there was a young feller they worked till he
dropped and then they'd just sling him overboard tongin'
for oysters or dredgin' like them oysterpirates did's the
meanest kinda work in winter with the spray freezin' on
the lines an' cuttin' your hands to shreds an' the dredge
foulin' every minute an' us havin' to haul it up an' fix
it with our hands in the icy water hauled up a stiff
onct   What's a stiff?   Ma soul an' body a stiff's a dead
man ma boy a young feller it was too without a stitch on
him an' the body looked like it had been beat with a be-
layin' pin somethin' terrible or an' oar mebbe reckon he
wouldn't work or was sick or somethin' an' the ole man
jus' beat him till he died sure couldn't a been nothin' but
an oysterpirate

Janey

When Janey was little she lived in an old flatface brick
house a couple of doors up the hill from M Street in Georgetown. The front part of the house was always dark because
Mommer kept the heavy lace curtains drawn to and the yellow linen shades with lace inset bands down. Sunday afternoons Janey and Joe and Ellen and Francie had to sit in the
front room and look at pictures or read books. Janey and Joe
read the funnypaper together because they were the oldest
and the other two were just babies and not old enough to
know what was funny anyway. They couldn't laugh out loud
because Popper sat with the rest of *The Sunday Star* on his
lap and usually went to sleep after dinner with the editorial
section crumpled in one big blueveined hand. Tiny curds of
sunlight flickering through the lace insets in the windowshade
would lie on his bald head and on one big red flange on his
nose and on the droop of one mustache and on his speckled
Sundayvest and on the white starched shirtsleeves with shiny
cuffs, held up above the elbow by a rubber band. Janey and

Joe would sit on the same chair feeling each other's ribs jiggle when they laughed about the Katzenjammer kids setting off a cannoncracker under the captain's stool. The little ones would see them laughing and start laughing too, "Shut up, can't you," Joe would hiss at them out of the corner of his mouth. "You don't know what we're laughing at." Once in a while, if there was no sound from Mommer who was taking her Sunday afternoon nap upstairs stretched out in the back bedroom in a faded lilac sack with frills on it, after they'd listened for a long time to the drawnout snort that ended in a little hiss of Popper's snores, Joe would slip off his chair and Janey would follow him without breathing into the front hall and out the front door. Once they'd closed it very carefully so that the knocker wouldn't bang, Joe would give her a slap, yell "You're it" and run down the hill towards M Street, and she'd have to run after him, her heart pounding, her hands cold for fear he'd run away and leave her.

Winters the brick sidewalks were icy and there were colored women out spreading cinders outside their doors when the children went to school mornings. Joe never would walk with the rest of them because they were girls, he lagged behind or ran ahead. Janey wished she could walk with him, but she couldn't leave her little sisters who held tight onto her hands. One winter they got in the habit of walking up the hill with a little yaller girl who lived directly across the street and whose name was Pearl. Afternoons Janey and Pearl walked home together. Pearl usually had a couple of pennies to buy bullseyes or candy bananas with at a little store on Wisconsin Avenue, and she always gave Janey half, so Janey was very fond of her. One afternoon she asked Pearl to come in and they played dolls together under the big rose of sharon bush in the back yard. When Pearl had gone Mommer's voice called from the kitchen. Mommer had her sleeves rolled up on her faded pale arms and a checked apron on and was rolling piecrust for supper so that her hands were covered with flour.

"Janey, come here," she said. Janey knew from the cold quaver in her voice that something was wrong.

"Yes, Mommer." Janey stood in front of her mother shaking her head about so that the two stiff sandy pigtails lashed from side to side.

"Stand still, child, for gracious sake . . . Jane, I want to talk to you about something. That little colored girl you brought in this afternoon . . ." Janey's heart was dropping. She had a sick feeling and felt herself blushing, she hardly knew why. "Now, don't misunderstand me; I like and respect the colored people; some of them are fine selfrespecting people in their place . . . But you mustn't bring that little colored girl in the house again. Treating colored people kindly and with respect is one of the signs of good breeding . . . You mustn't forget that your mother's people were wellborn every inch of them . . . Georgetown was very different in those days. We lived in a big house with most lovely lawns . . . but you must never associate with colored people on an equal basis. Living in this neighborhood it's all the more important to be careful about those things . . . Neither the whites nor the blacks respect those who do . . . That's all, Janey, you understand; now run out and play, it'll soon be time for your supper."

Janey tried to speak, but she couldn't. She stood stiff in the middle of the yard on the grating that covered the drainpipe, staring at the back fence. "Niggerlover," yelled Joe in her ear. "Niggerlover ump-mya-mya . . . Niggerlover niggerlover ump-mya-mya." Janey began to cry.

Joe was an untalkative sandyhaired boy who could pitch a mean outcurve when he was still little. He learned to swim and dive in Rock Creek and used to say he wanted to be motorman on a streetcar when he grew up. For several years his best friend was Alec McPherson whose father was a locomotive engineer on the B. and O. After that Joe wanted to be a locomotive engineer. Janey used to tag around after the two boys whenever they'd let her, to the carbarns at the head of Pennsylvania Avenue where they made friends with some of the conductors and motormen who used to let them ride on the platform a couple of blocks sometimes if there wasn't any inspector around, down along the canal or up Rock Creek where they caught tadpoles and fell in the water and splashed each other with mud.

Summer evenings when the twilight was long after supper they played lions and tigers with other kids from the neighborhood in the long grass of some empty lots near Oak Hill Cemetery. There were long periods when there was measles or scarlet fever around and Mommer wouldn't let them out. Then Alec would come down and they'd play three-o-cat in the back yard. Those were the times Janey liked best. Then the boys treated her as one of them. Summer dusk would come down on them sultry and full of lightningbugs. If Popper was feeling in a good mood he'd send them up the hill to the drugstore on N Street to buy icecream, there'd be young men in their shirtsleeves and straw hats strolling with girls who wore a stick of punk in their hair to keep off the mosquitoes, a rankness and a smell of cheap perfume from the colored families crowded on their doorsteps, laughing, talking softly with an occasional flash of teeth, rolling of a white eyeball. The dense sweaty night was scary, hummed, rumbled with distant thunder, with junebugs, with the clatter of traffic from M Street, the air of the street dense and breathless under the thick trees; but when she was with Alec and Joe she wasn't scared, not even of drunks or big shamblefooted coloredmen. When they got back Popper would smoke a cigar and they'd sit out in the back yard and the mosquitoes 'ud eat them up and Mommer and Aunt Francine and the kids 'ud eat the icecream and Popper would just smoke a cigar and tell them stories of when he'd been a towboat captain down on the Chesapeake in his younger days and he'd saved the barkentine *Nancy Q* in distress on the Kettlebottoms in a sou'west gale. Then it'd get time to go to bed and Alec 'ud be sent home and Janey'd have to go to bed in the stuffy little back room on the top floor with her two little sisters in their cribs against the opposite wall. Maybe a thunderstorm would come up and she'd lie awake staring up at the ceiling cold with fright, listening to her little sisters whimper as they slept until she heard the reassuring sound of Mommer scurrying about the house closing windows, the slam of a door, the whine of wind and rattle of rain and the thunder rolling terribly loud and near overhead like a thousand beertrucks roaring over the bridge. Times like that she thought of going down to Joe's room and crawling into bed with him, but for some reason she was afraid to, though sometimes she got as far as the landing. He'd laugh at her and call her a softie.

About once a week Joe would get spanked. Popper would come home from the Patent Office where he worked, angry and out of sorts, and the girls would be scared of him and go about the house quiet as mice; but Joe seemed to like to provoke him, he'd run whistling through the back hall or clatter up and down stairs making a tremendous racket with his stubtoed ironplated shoes. Then Popper would start scolding him and Joe would stand in front of him without saying a word glaring at the floor with bitter blue eyes. Janey's insides knotted up and froze when Popper would start up the stairs to the bathroom pushing Joe in front of him. She knew what would happen. He'd take down the razorstrop from behind the door and put the boy's head and shoulders under his arm and beat him. Joe would clench his teeth and flush and not say a word and when Popper was tired of beating him they'd look at each other and Joe would be sent up to his room and Popper would come down stairs trembling all over and pretend nothing had happened, and Janey would slip out into the yard with her fists clenched, whispering to herself, "I hate him . . . I hate him . . . I hate him."

Once a drizzly Saturday night she stood against the fence in the dark looking up at the lighted window. She could hear Popper's voice and Joe's in an argument. She thought maybe she'd fall down dead at the first thwack of the razorstrop. She couldn't hear what they were saying. Then suddenly it came, the leather sound of blows and Joe stifling a gasp. She was eleven years old. Something broke loose. She rushed into the kitchen with her hair all wet from the rain, "Mommer, he's killing Joe. Stop it." Her mother turned up a withered helpless drooping face from a pan she was scouring. "Oh, you can't do anything." Janey ran upstairs and started beating on the bathroom door. "Stop it, stop it," her voice kept yelling. She was scared, but something stronger than she was had hold of her. The door opened; there was Joe looking sheepish and Popper with his face all flushed and the razorstrop in his hand.

"Beat me . . . it's me that's bad . . . I won't have you beating Joe like that." She was scared. She didn't know what to do, tears stung in her eyes.

Popper's voice was unexpectedly kind:

"You go straight up to bed without any supper and re-

154

member that you have enough to do to fight your own battles, Janey."

She ran up to her room and lay on the bed shaking. When she'd gone to sleep, Joe's voice woke her up with a start.

He was standing in his nightgown in the door. "Say, Janey," he whispered. "Don't you do that again, see. I can take care of myself, see. A girl can't butt in between men like that. When I get a job and make enough dough I'll get me a gun and if Popper tries to beat me up I'll shoot him dead." Janey began to sniffle. "What you wanna cry for; this ain't no Johnstown flood."

She could hear him tiptoe down the stairs again in his bare feet.

At highschool she took the commercial course and learned stenography and typewriting. She was a plain thinfaced sandyhaired girl, quiet and popular with the teachers. Her fingers were quick and she picked up typing and shorthand easily. She liked to read and used to get books like *The Inside of the Cup, The Battle of the Strong, The Winning of Barbara Worth* out of the library. Her mother kept telling her that she'd spoil her eyes if she read so much. When she read she used to imagine she was the heroine, that the weak brother who went to the bad but was a gentleman at core and capable of every sacrifice, like Sidney Carton in *A Tale of Two Cities*, was Joe and that the hero was Alec.

She thought Alec was the bestlooking boy in Georgetown and the strongest. He had black closecropped hair and a very white skin with a few freckles and a strong squareshouldered way of walking. After him Joe was the bestlooking and strongest and the best baseball player anyway. Everybody said he ought to go on through highschool on account of being such a good baseball player, but at the end of his first year Popper said he had three girls to support and that Joe would have to get to work; so he got a job as a Western Union messenger. Janey was pretty proud of him in his uniform until the girls at highschool kidded her about it. Alec's folks had promised to put him through college if he made good in highschool, so Alec worked hard. He wasn't tough and dirtytalking like most of the boys Joe knew. He was always nice to Janey, though he never seemed to want to be left alone with her. She pretty well admitted to herself that she had a terrible crush on Alec.

The best day of her life was the sweltering summer Sunday they all went canoeing up to Great Falls. She had put up the lunch the night before. In the morning she added a steak she found in the icebox. There was blue haze at the end of every street of brick houses and dark summergreen trees when be-

155

fore anybody else was awake she and Joe crept out of the house round seven that morning.

They met Alec at the corner in front of the depot. He stood waiting for them with his feet wide apart and a skillet in his hand.

They all ran and caught the car that was just leaving for Cabin John's Bridge. They had the car all to themselves like it was a private car. The car hummed over the rails past whitewashed shanties and nigger cabins along the canal, skirting hillsides where the sixfoot tall waving corn marched in ranks like soldiers. The sunlight lanced in bluewhite glare on the wavingdrooping leaves of the tasseling corn; glare, and a whirring and tinkling of grasshoppers and dryflies rose in hot smoke into the pale sky round the clattering shaking electric car. They ate sweet summerapples Joe had bought off a colored woman in the station and chased each other round the car and flopped down on top of each other in the cornerseats; and they laughed and giggled till they were weak. Then the car was running through woods; they could see the trestlework of the rollercoasters of Glen Echo through the trees and they piled off the car at Cabin John's having more fun than a barrel of monkeys.

They ran down to the bridge to look up and down the river brown and dark in the white glary morning between fo-

liagesodden banks; then they found the canoe that belonged to
a friend of Alec's and some packages of neccos and started
out. Alec and Joe paddled and Janey sat in the bottom with
her sweater rolled round a thwart for a pillow. Alec was pad-
dling in the bow. It was sweltering hot. The seat made the
shirt cling to the hollow of his chunky back that curved with
every stroke of the paddle. After a while the boys stripped to
their bathingsuits that they wore under their clothes. It made
Janey's throat tremble to watch Alec's back and the bulging
muscles of his arm as he paddled, made her feel happy and
scared. She sat there in her white dimity dress, trailing her
hand in the weedy browngreen water. They stopped to pick
waterlilies and the white flowers of arrowhead that glistened
like ice and everything smelt wet rank of the muddy roots of
waterlilies. The cream soda got warm and they drank it that
way and kidded each other back and forth and Alec caught a
crab and covered Janey's dress with greenslimy splashes and
Janey didn't care a bit and they called Joe skipper and he
loosened up and said he was going to join the navy and Alec
said he'd be a civil engineer and build a motorboat and take
them all cruising and Janey was happy because they included
her when they talked just like she was a boy too. At a place
below the Falls where there were locks in the canal they had
a long portage down to the river. Janey carried the grub and
the paddles and the frying pan and the boys sweated and
cussed under the canoe. Then they paddled across to the Virginia side and made a fire in a little hollow among gray rusty
bowlders. Joe cooked the steak and Janey unpacked the sandwiches and cookies she'd made and nursed some murphies
baking in the ashes. They roasted ears of corn too that they
had swiped out of a field beside the canal. Everything turned

out fine except that they hadn't brought enough butter. Afterwards they sat eating cookies and drinking rootbeer quietly talking round the embers. Alec and Joe brought out pipes and she felt pretty good sitting there at the Great Falls of the Potomac with two men smoking pipes.

"Geewhiz, Janey, Joe cooked that steak fine."

"When we was kids we used to ketch frogs and broil 'em up in Rock Creek . . . Remember, Alec?"

"Damned if I don't, and Janey she was along once; gee-whiz, the fuss you kicked up then, Janey."

"I don't like seeing you skin them."

"We thought we was regular wildwest hunters then. We had packs of fun then."

"I like this better, Alec," said Janey hesitatingly.

"So do I . . ." said Alec. "Dod gast it, I wisht we had a watermelon."

"Maybe we'll see some along the riverbank somewhere goin' home."

"Jiminy crickets, what I couldn't do to a watermelon, Joe."

"Mommer had a watermelon on ice," said Janey; "maybe there'll be some yet when we get home."

"I don't never want to go home," said Joe, suddenly bitter serious.

"Joe, you oughtn't to talk like that." She felt girlish and frightened.

"I'll talk how I goddam please . . . Kerist, I hate the scrimpy dump."

"Joe, you oughtn't to talk like that." Janey felt she was going to cry.

"Dod gast it," said Alec. "It's time we shoved . . . What you say, bo. . . ? We'll take one more dip and then make tracks for home."

When the boys were through swimming they all went up to look at the Falls and then they started off. They went along fast in the swift stream under the steep treehung bank. The afternoon was very sultry, they went through layers of hot steamy air. Big cloudheads were piling up in the north. It wasn't fun any more for Janey. She was afraid it was going to rain. Inside she felt sick and drained out. She was afraid her period was coming on. She'd only had the curse a few times yet and the thought of it scared her and took all the strength out of her, made her want to crawl away out of sight like an old sick mangy cat. She didn't want Joe and Alec to notice how she felt. She thought how would it be if she turned the canoe over. The boys could swim ashore all right, and she'd drown and they'd drag the river for her body and everybody'd cry and feel so sorry about it.

158

Purplegray murk rose steadily and drowned the white summits of the cloudheads. Everything got to be livid white and purple. The boys paddled as hard as they could. They could hear the advancing rumble of thunder. The bridge was well in sight when the wind hit them, a hot stormwind full of dust and dead leaves and bits of chaff and straw, churning the riverwater.

They made the shore just in time. "Dod gast it, this is goin' to be some storm," said Alec; "Janey, get under the boat." They turned the canoe over on the pebbly shore in the lee of a big bowlder and huddled up under it. Janey sat in the middle with the waterlilies they had picked that morning all shriveled and clammy from the heat in her hand. The boys lay in their damp bathingsuits on either side of her. Alec's towsled black hair was against her cheek. The other side of her Joe lay with his head in the end of the canoe and his lean brown feet and legs in their rolledup pants tucked under her dress. The smell of sweat and riverwater and the warm boysmell of Alec's hair and shoulders made her dizzy. When the rain came drumming on the bottom of the canoe curtaining them in with lashing white spray, she slipped her arm round Alec's neck and let her hand rest timidly on his bare shoulder. He didn't move.

The rain passed after a while. "Gee, that wasn't as bad as I thought it would be," said Alec. They were pretty wet and chilly, but they felt good in the fresh rainwashed air. They put the canoe back in the water and went on down as far as the bridge. Then they carried it back to the house they'd gotten it from, and went to the little shelter to wait for the electric car. They were tired and sunburned and sticky. The car was packed with a damp Sunday afternoon crowd, picnickers caught by the shower at Great Falls and Glen Echo. Janey thought she'd never stand it till she got home. Her belly was all knotted up with a cramp. When they got to Georgetown the boys still had fifty cents between them and wanted to go to a movie, but Janey ran off and left them. Her only thought was to get to bed so that she could put her face into the pillow and cry.

After that Janey never cried much; things upset her, but she got a cold hard feeling all over instead. Highschool went by fast, with hot thunderstormy Washington summers in between terms, punctuated by an occasional picnic at Marshall Hall or a party at some house in the neighborhood. Joe got a job at the Adams Express. She didn't see him much, as he didn't eat home any more. Alec had bought a motorcycle and although he was still in highschool Janey heard little about him. Sometimes she sat up to get a word with Joe when he came home at night. He smelt of tobacco and liquor, though he never seemed to be drunk. He went to his job at seven and when he got out in the evenings he went out with the bunch hanging round poolrooms on 4½ Street or playing craps or bowling. Sundays he played baseball in Maryland. Janey would sit up for him, but when he came she'd ask how things were going where he worked and he'd say "Fine" and he'd ask her how things were going at school and she'd say "Fine" and then they'd both go off to bed. Once in a while she'd ask if he'd seen Alec and he'd say "Yes" with a scrap of a smile and she'd ask how Alec was and he'd say "Fine."

She had one friend, Alice Dick, a dark stubby girl with glasses who took all the same classes with her in highschool. Saturday afternoons they'd dress up in their best and go window-shopping down F Street way. They'd buy a few little things, stop in for a soda and come home on the streetcar feeling they'd had a busy afternoon. Once in a very long while they went to a matinee at Poli's and Janey would take Alice Dick home to supper. Alice Dick liked the Williamses and they liked her. She said it made her feel freer to spend a few hours with broadminded people. Her own folks were Southern Methodists and very narrow. Her father was a clerk in the Government Printing Office and was in daily dread that his job would come under the civil service regulations. He was a stout shortwinded man, fond of playing practical jokes

160

on his wife and daughter, and suffered from chronic dyspepsia.

Alice Dick and Janey planned that as soon as they got through highschool they'd get jobs and leave home. They even picked out the house where they'd board, a greenstone house near Thomas Circle, run by Mrs. Jenks, widow of a naval officer, who was very refined and had Southern cooking and charged moderately for table-board.

One Sunday night during the spring of her last term in highschool Janey was in her room getting undressed. Francie and Ellen were still playing in the backyard. Their voices came in through the open window with a spicy waft of lilacs from the lilacbushes in the next yard. She had just let down her hair and was looking in the mirror imagining how she'd look if she was a peach and had auburn hair, when there was a knock at the door and Joe's voice outside. There was something funny about his voice.

"Come in," she called. "I'm just fixin' my hair."

She first saw his face in the mirror. It was very white and the skin was drawn back tight over the cheekbones and round the mouth.

"Why, what's the matter, Joe?" She jumped up and faced him.

"It's like this, Janey," said Joe, drawling his words out painfully. "Alec was killed. He smashed up on his motorbike. I've just come from the hospital. He's dead, all right."

Janey seemed to be writing the words on a white pad in her mind. She couldn't say anything.

"He smashed up comin' home from Chevy Chase . . . He'd gone out to the ballgame to see me pitch. You oughter seen him all smashed to hell."

Janey kept trying to say something.

"He was your best . . ."

"He was the best guy I'll ever know," Joe went on gently. "Well, that's that, Janey . . . But I wanted to tell you I don't

161

want to hang round this lousy dump now that Alec's gone. I'm goin' to enlist in the navy. You tell the folks, see . . . I don't wanna talk to 'em. That's it; I'll join the navy and see the world."

"But, Joe . . ."

"I'll write you, Janey; honestly, I will . . . I'll write you a hell of a lot. You an' me . . . Well, goodbye, Janey." He grabbed her by the shoulders and kissed her awkwardly on the nose and cheek. All she could do was whisper "Do be careful, Joe," and stand there in front of the bureau in the gust of lilacs and the yelling of the kids that came through the open window. She heard Joe's steps light quick down the stairs and heard the frontdoor shut. She turned out the light, took off her clothes in the dark, and got into bed. She lay there without crying.

Graduation came and commencement and she and Alice went out to parties and even once with a big crowd on one of the moonlight trips down the river to Indian Head on the steamboat *Charles McAlister*. The crowd was rougher than Janey and Alice liked. Some of the boys were drinking a good deal and there were couples kissing and hugging in every shadow; still the moonlight was beautiful rippling on the river and she and Janey put two chairs together and talked. There was a band and dancing, but they didn't dance on account of the rough men who stood round the dancefloor making remarks. They talked and on the way home up the river, Janey, talking very low and standing by the rail very close to Alice, told her about Alec. Alice had read about it in the paper, but hadn't dreamed that Janey had known him so well or felt that way about him. She began to cry and Janey felt very strong comforting her and they felt that they'd be very close friends after that. Janey whispered that she'd never be able to love anybody else and Alice said she didn't think she could ever love a man anyway, they all drank and smoked and talked dirty among themselves and had only one idea.

In July Alice and Janey got jobs in the office of Mrs. Robinson, public stenographer in the Riggs Building, to replace girls away on their vacations. Mrs. Robinson was a small grayhaired pigeonbreasted woman with a Kentucky shriek in her voice, that made Janey think of a parrot's. She was very precise and all the proprieties were observed in her office. "Miss Williams," she would chirp, leaning back from her desk, "that em ess of Judge Roberts's has absolutely got to be finished today . . . My dear, we've given our word and we'll deliver if we have to stay till midnight. Noblesse oblige, my dear," and the typewriters would trill and jingle and all the girls' fingers would go like mad typing briefs, manuscripts of undelivered speeches by lobbyists, occasional overflow from a newspaperman or a scientist, or prospectuses from realestate offices or patent promoters, dunning letters for dentists and doctors.

The Camera Eye (14)

Sunday nights when we had fishballs and baked beans and Mr. Garfield read to us in a very beautiful reading voice and everybody was so quiet you could have heard a pin drop because he was reading *The Man Without a Country* and it was a very terrible story and Aaron Burr had been a very dangerous man and this poor young man had said "Damn the United States; I never hope to hear her name again" and it was a very terrible thing to say and the grayhaired judge was so kind and good

and the judge sentenced me and they took me far away to foreign lands on a frigate and the officers were kind and good and spoke in kind grave very sorry reading voices like Mr. Garfield and everything was very kind and grave and very sorry and frigates and the blue Mediterranean and islands and when I was dead I began to cry and I was afraid the other boys would see I had tears in my eyes

American shouldn't cry he should look kind and grave and very sorry when they wrapped me in the stars and stripes and brought me home on a frigate to be buried I was so sorry I never remembered whether they brought me home or buried me at sea but anyway I was wrapped in Old Glory

Newsreel XI

the government of the United States must insist and demand that American citizens who may be taken prisoner whether by one party or the other as participants in the present insurrectionary disturbances shall be dealt with in accordance with the broad principles of international law

SOLDIERS GUARD CONVENTION

the *Titanic* left Southampton on April 10th on its maiden   operation is to be performed against the wishes of the New York Life according to "Kimmel" Why they know I'm Kimmel in Niles I'm George to everyone even mother and sister when we meet on the streets

> *I'm going to Maxim's*
> *Where fun and frolic beams*
> *With all the girls I'll chatter*
> *I'll laugh and kiss and flatter*
> *Lolo, Dodo, Joujou.*
> *Cloclo, Margot, Froufrou*

TITANIC LARGEST SHIP IN THE WORLD SINKING

personally I am not sure that the twelvehour day is bad for employees especially when they insist on working that long in order to make more money

> *Still all my song shall be*
> *Nearer My God to thee*
> *Nearer to thee*

it was now about 1 A.M., a beautiful starlight night with no moon. The sea was as calm as a pond, just a gentle heave as the boat dipped up and down in the swell, an ideal night except for the bitter cold. In the distance the *Titanic* looked an enormous length, its great hulk outlined in black against the starry sky, every porthole and saloon blazing with light

ASK METHODISM TO OUST TRINITY

the bride's gown is of charmeuse satin with a chiffon veiled lace waist. The veil is of crepe lisse edged with point de venise a departure from the conventional bridal veil and the bouquet is to be lilies of the valley and gardenias

> Lolo, Dodo, Joujou,
> Cloclo, Margot, Froufrou
> I'm going to Maxim's
> And you can go to . . .

the *Titanic* slowly tilted straight on end with the stern vertically upward and as it did so the lights in the cabins and saloons which had not flickered for a moment since we left, died out, came on again for a single flash and finally went out altogether. Meanwhile the machinery rattled through the vessel with a rattle and a groaning that could be heard for miles. Then with a quiet slanting dive

Janey

"But it's so interesting, Mommer," Janey would say when her mother bewailed the fact that she had to work.

"In my day it wasn't considered ladylike, it was thought to be demeaning."

"But it isn't now," Janey would say, getting into a temper.

Then it would be a great relief to get out of the stuffy house and the stuffy treeshaded streets of Georgetown and to stop by for Alice Dick and go downtown to the moving pictures and to see the pictures of foreign countries, and the crowds on F Street and to stop in at a drugstore for a soda

165

afterwards, before getting on the Georgetown car, and to sit up at the fountain talking about the picture they'd seen and Olive Thomas and Charley Chaplin and John Bunny. She began to read the paper every day and to take an interest in politics. She began to feel that there was a great throbbing arclighted world somewhere outside and that only living in Georgetown where everything was so poky and oldfashioned, and Mommer and Popper were so poky and oldfashioned, kept her from breaking into it.

Postcards from Joe made her feel like that too. He was a sailor on the battleship *Connecticut*. There'd be a picture of the waterfront at Havana or the harbor of Marseille or Villefranche or a photograph of a girl in peasant costume inside a tinsel horseshoe and a few lines hoping she was well and liked her job, never a word about himself. She wrote him long letters full of questions about himself and foreign countries, but he never answered them. Still it gave her a sort of feeling of adventure to get the postcards. Whenever she saw a navy man on the street or marines from Quantico she thought of Joe and wondered how he was getting on. The sight of a gob lurching along in blue with his cap on one side took a funny twist at her heart.

Sundays Alice almost always came out to Georgetown. The house was different now, Joe gone, her mother and father older and quieter, Francie and Ellen blooming out into pretty giggly highschool girls, popular with the boys in the neighborhood, going out to parties, all the time complaining because they didn't have any money to spend. Sitting at the table with them, helping Mommer with the gravy, bringing in the potatoes or the Brussels sprouts for Sunday dinner, Janey felt grownup, almost an old maid. She was on the side of her father and mother now against the sisters. Popper began to look old and shrunk-up. He talked often about retiring, and was looking forward to his pension.

When she'd been eight months with Mrs. Robinson she got an offer from Dreyfus and Carroll, the patent lawyers up on the top floor of the Riggs Building to work for them for seventeen a week, which was five dollars more than she was getting from Mrs. Robinson. It made her feel fine. She realized now that she was good at her work and that she could support herself whatever happened. On the strength of it she went down to Woodward and Lothrop's with Alice Dick to buy a dress. She wanted a silk grownup dress with embroidery on it. She was twentyone and was going to make seventeen dollars a week and thought she had a right to one nice dress. Alice said it ought to be a bronzy gold color to match her hair. They went in all the stores down F Street, but they

166

couldn't find anything that suited that wasn't too expensive, so all they could do was buy some materials and some fashion magazines and take it home to Janey's mother to make up. It galled Janey still being dependent on her mother this way, but there was nothing for it; so Mrs. Williams had to make up Janey's new dress the way she had made all her children's dresses since they were born. Janey had never had the patience to learn to sew the way Mommer could. They bought enough material so that Alice could have one too, so Mrs. Williams had to make up two dresses.

Working at Dreyfus and Carroll's was quite different from working at Mrs. Robinson's. There were mostly men in the office. Mr. Dreyfus was a small thinfaced man with a small

black mustache and small black twinkly eyes and a touch of
accent that gave him a distinguished foreign diplomat manner. He carried yellow wash gloves and a yellow cane and
had a great variety of very much-tailored overcoats. He was
the brains of the firm, Jerry Burnham said. Mr. Carroll was a
stout redfaced man who smoked many cigars and cleared his
throat a great deal and had a very oldtimey Southern God-
blessmysoul way of talking. Jerry Burnham said he was the
firm's bay window. Jerry Burnham was a wrinkledfaced
young man with dissipated eyes who was the firm's adviser in
technical and engineering matters. He laughed a great deal,
always got into the office late, and for some reason took a
fancy to Janey and used to joke about things to her while he

was dictating. She liked him, though the dissipated look under his eyes scared her off a little. She'd have liked to have talked to him like a sister, and gotten him to stop burning the candle at both ends. Then there was an elderly accountant, Mr. Sills, a shriveled man who lived in Anacostia and never said a word to anybody. At noon he didn't go out for lunch, but sat at his desk eating a sandwich and an apple wrapped in waxed paper which he carefully folded afterwards and put back in his pocket. Then there were two fresh errandboys and a little plainfaced typist named Miss Simonds who only got twelve a week. All sorts of people in every sort of seedy-respectable or Peacock Alley clothes came in during the day and stood round in the outer office listening to Mr. Carroll's rich bloom from behind the groundglass door. Mr. Dreyfus slipped in and out without a word, smiling faintly at his acquaintances, always in a great mysterious hurry. At lunch in the little cafeteria or at a sodafountain Janey 'ud tell Alice all about it and Alice would look up at her admiringly. Alice always waited for her in the vestibule at one. They'd arranged to go out then because there was less of a crowd. Neither of them ever spent more than twenty cents, so lunch didn't take them very long and they'd have time to take a turn round Lafayette Square or sometimes round the White House grounds before going back to the office.

There was one Saturday night when she had to work late to finish up typing the description of an outboard motor that had to be in at the Patent Office first thing Monday morning. Everybody else had left the office. She was making out the complicated technical wording as best she could, but her mind was on a postcard showing the Christ of the Andes she'd gotten from Joe that day. All it said was:

"To hell with Uncle Sam's tin ships. Coming home soon."

It wasn't signed but she knew the writing. It worried her. Burnham sat at the telephone switchboard going over the pages as she finished them. Now and then he went out to the washroom; when he came back each time a hot breath of whiskey wafted across the office. Janey was nervous. She typed till the little black letters squirmed before her eyes. She was worried about Joe. How could he be coming home before his enlistment was up? Something must be the matter. And Jerry Burnham moving restlessly round on the telephone girl's seat made her uncomfortable. She and Alice had talked about the danger of staying in an office alone with a man like this. Late like this and drinking, a man had just one idea.

When she handed him the next to the last sheet, his eye, bright and moist, caught hers. "I bet you're tired, Miss Wil-
171

liams," he said. "It's a darned shame to keep you in like this and Saturday night too."

"It's quite all right, Mr. Burnham," she said icily and her fingers chirruped.

"It's the damned old baywindow's fault. He chewed the rag so much about politics all day, nobody could get any work done."

"Well, it doesn't matter now," said Janey.

"Nothing matters any more. . . . It's almost eight o'clock. I had to pass up a date with my best girl . . . or thereabouts. I bet you passed up a date too, Miss Williams."

"I was going to meet another girl, that's all."

"Now I'll tell one . . ." He laughed so easily that she found herself laughing too.

When the last page was done and in the envelope, Janey got up to get her hat. "Look, Miss Williams, we'll drop this in the mail and then you'd better come and have a bite with me."

Going down in the elevator Janey intended to excuse her-

self and go home, but somehow she didn't and found herself, everything aflutter inside of her, sitting coolly down with him in a French restaurant on H Street.

"Well, what do you think of the New Freedom, Miss Williams?" asked Jerry Burnham with a laugh after he'd sat down. He handed her the menu. "Here's the scorecard . . . Let your conscience be your guide."

172

"Why, I hardly know, Mr. Burnham."

"Well, I'm for it, frankly. I think Wilson's a big man . . . Nothing like change anyway, the best thing in the world, don't you think so? Bryan's a big bellowing blatherskite, but even he represents something, and even Josephus Daniels filling the navy with grapejuice. I think there's a chance we may get back to being a democracy . . . Maybe there won't have to be a revolution; what do you think?"

He never waited for her to answer a question, he just talked and laughed all by himself.

When Janey tried to tell Alice about it afterwards the things Jerry Burnham said didn't seem so funny, nor the food so good nor everything so jolly. Alice was pretty bitter about it. "Oh, Janey, how could you go out late at night with a drunken man and to a place like that, and here I was crazy anxious . . . You know a man like that has only one idea . . . I declare I think it was heartless and light . . . I wouldn't have thought you capable of such a thing." "But, Alice, it wasn't like that at all," Janey kept saying, but Alice cried and went round looking hurt for a whole week; so that after that Janey kept off the subject of Jerry Burnham. It was the first disagreement she'd ever had with Alice and it made her feel bad.

Still she got to be friends with Jerry Burnham. He seemed to like taking her out and having her listen to him talk. Even after he'd thrown up his job at Dreyfus and Carroll, he sometimes called for her Saturday afternoons to take her to Keith's. Janey arranged a meeting with Alice out in Rock Creek Park, but it wasn't much of a success. Jerry set the girls up to tea at the old stone mill. He was working for an engineering paper and writing a weekly letter for the *New York Sun*. He upset Alice by calling Washington a cesspool and a sink of boredom and saying he was rotting there and that most of the inhabitants were dead from the neck up anyway. When he put them on the car to go back to Georgetown, Alice said emphatically that young Burnham was not the sort of boy a respectable girl ought to know. Janey sat back happily in the seat of the open car, looking out at trees, girls in summer dresses, men in straw hats, mailboxes, storefronts sliding by and said, "But, Alice, he's smart as a whip. . . . Gosh, I like brainy people, don't you?" Alice looked at her and shook her head sadly and said nothing.

That same afternoon they went to the Georgetown hospital to see Popper. It was pretty horrible. Mommer and Janey and the doctor and the wardnurse knew that he had cancer of the bladder and couldn't live very long, but they didn't admit it even to themselves. They had just moved him into a private room where he would be more comfortable. It was costing lots of money and they'd had to put a second mortgage on the house. They'd already spent all Janey's savings that she had in a bankaccount of her own against a rainy day. That afternoon they had to wait quite a while. When the nurse came out with a glass urinal under a towel Janey went in alone.

"Hello, Popper," she said with a forced smile. The smell of disinfectant in the room sickened her. Through the open window came warm air of sunwilted trees, drowsy Sundayafternoon noises, the caw of a crow, a distant sound of traffic. Popper's face was drawn in and twisted to one side. His big mustaches looked pathetically silky and white. Janey knew that she loved him better than anybody else in the world . . .

His voice was feeble but fairly firm. "Janey, I'm in drydock, girl, and I guess I'll never . . . you know better'n I do, the sonsobitches won't tell me . . . Say, tell me about Joe. You hear from him, don't you? I wish he hadn't joined the navy; no future for a boy there without pull higher up; but I'm glad he went to sea, takes after me . . . I'd been three times round the Horn in the old days before I was twenty. That was before I settled down in the towboat business, you understand . . . But I been thinkin' here lyin' in bed that Joe done just what I'd 'a' done, a chip of the old block, and I'm glad of it. I don't worry about him, but I wish you girls was married an' off my hands. I'd feel easier. I don't trust girls nowadays with these here anklelength skirts an' all that." Popper's eyes traveled all over her with a chilly feeble gleam that made her throat stiffen when she tried to speak.

"I guess I can take care of myself," she said.

"You got to take care of me now. I done my best by you kids. You don't know what life is, none of you, been sheltered and now you ship me off to die in the hospital."

"But, Popper, you said yourself you thought it would be best to go where you'd get better care."

"I don't like that night nurse, Janey, she handles me too rough . . : You tell 'em down at the office."

It was a relief when it was time to go. She and Alice walked along the street without saying anything. Finally Janey said, "For goodness' sake, Alice, don't get sulky. If you only knew how I hate it all too . . . oh, goodness, I wish . . ."

"What do you wish, Janey?"

"Oh, I dunno."

July was hot that summer, in the office they worked in a continual whir of electric fans, the men's collars wilted and the girls kept themselves overplastered with powder; only Mr.

174

Dreyfus still looked cool and crisply tailored as if he'd just stepped out of a bandbox. The last day of the month Janey was sitting a minute at her desk getting up energy to go home along the simmering streets when Jerry Burnham came in. He had his shirtsleeves rolled above the elbow and white duck pants on and carried his coat. He asked her how her father was and said he was all excited about the European news and would have to take her out to supper to talk to somebody soothing. "I've got a car belongs to Bugs Dolan and I haven't any driver's license, but I guess we can sneak round the Speedway and get cooled off all the same." She tried to refuse because she ought to go home to supper and Alice was always sulky when she went out with Jerry, but he could see that she really wanted to come and insisted.

They both sat in the front seat of the Ford and dropped their coats in the back. They went once round the Speedway, but the asphalt was like a griddle. The trees and the brown stagnant river stewed in late afternoon murk like meat and vegetables in a pot. The heat from the engine suffocated them. Jerry, his face red, talked incessantly about war brewing in Europe and how it would be the end of civilization and the signal for a general workingclass revolution and how he didn't care and anything that got him out of Washington, where he was drinking himself silly with his brains addled by the heat and the *Congressional Record*, would be gravy to him, and how tired he was of women who didn't want anything but to get money out of him or parties or marriage or some goddam thing or other and how cool and soothing it was to talk to Janey who wasn't like that.

It was too hot, so they put off driving till later and went to the Willard to get something to eat. He insisted on going to the Willard because he said he had his pockets full of money and would just spend it anyhow and Janey was very much awed because she'd never been in a big hotel before and felt she wasn't dressed for it and said she was afraid she'd disgrace him and he laughed and said it couldn't be done. They sat in the big long gilt dining room and Jerry said it looked like a millionaire morgue and the waiter was very polite and Janey couldn't find what she wanted to eat on the big bill-of-fare and took a salad. Jerry made her take a gin fizz because he said it was cooling; it made her feel lightheaded and tall and gawky. She followed his talk breathless the way she used to tag along after Joe and Alec down to the carbarns when she was little.

After supper they drove round some more and Jerry got quiet and she felt constrained and couldn't think of what to say. They went way out Rhode Island Avenue and circled

175

round back by the Old Soldiers' Home. There was no air anywhere and staring identical streetlights went by on either side, lighting segments of monotonous unrustling trees. Even out on the hills there was not a breath stirring.

Out in the dark roads beyond the streetlamps it was better. Janey lost all sense of direction and lay back breathing in an occasional patch of freshness from a cornfield or a copse of woods. In a spot where a faint marshy dampness almost cool drifted across the road Jerry suddenly stopped the car and leaned over and kissed her. Her heart began to beat very fast. She wanted to tell him not to, but she couldn't.

"I didn't mean to, but I can't help it," he whispered. "It's living in Washington undermines the will . . . Or maybe I'm in love with you, Janey. I don't know . . . Let's sit in the back seat where it's cooler."

Weakness started in the pit of her stomach and welled up through her. As she stepped out he caught her in his arms. She let her head droop on his shoulder, her lips against his neck. His arms were burning hot round her shoulders, she could feel his ribs through his shirt pressing against her. Her head started going round in a reek of tobacco and liquor and male sweat. His legs began pressing up to hers. She yanked herself away and got into the back seat. She was trembling. He was right after her. "No, no," she said. He sat down be-

176

side her with his arm round her waist. "Lez have a cigarette," he said in a shaky voice.

Smoking gave her something to do, made her feel even with him. The two granulated red ends of the cigarettes glowed side by side.

"Do you mean you like me, Jerry?"

"I'm crazy about you, kid."

"Do you mean you . . . ?"

"Want to marry you . . . Why the hell not? I dunno . . . Suppose we were engaged?"

"You mean you want me to marry you?"

"If you like . . . But don't you understand the way a feller feels . . . a night like this . . . the smell of the swamp . . . God, I'd give anything to have you."

They'd smoked out their cigarettes. They sat a long time without saying a word. She could feel the hairs on his bare arm against her bare arm.

"I'm worried about my brother Joe . . . He's in the navy, Jerry, and I'm afraid he's going to desert or something . . . I think you'd like him. He's a wonderful baseball player."

"What made you think of him? Do you feel that way towards me? Love's a swell thing; goddam it, don't you realize it's not the way you feel towards your brother?"

He put his hand on her knee. She could feel him looking at her in the dark. He leaned over and kissed her very gently. She liked his lips gentle against hers that way. She was kissing them. She was falling through centuries of swampy night. His hot chest was against her breasts bearing her down. She would cling to him bearing her down through centuries of swampy night. Then all at once in a cold spasm she felt sick, choking for breath like drowning. She began to fight him. She got her leg up and pushed him hard in the groin with her knee.

He let go of her and got out of the car. She could hear him walking up and down the road in the dark behind her. She was trembling and scared and sick. After a while he got in, switched on the light and drove on without looking at her. He was smoking a cigarette and little sparks came from it as he drove.

When he got to the corner of M Street below the Williams house in Georgetown he stopped and got out and opened the door for her. She got out, not knowing what to say, afraid to look at him.

"I suppose you think I ought to apologize to you for being a swine," he said.

"Jerry, I'm sorry," she said.

"I'll be damned if I will . . . I thought we were friends. I might have known there wouldn't be a woman in this muck hole with a human spark in her . . . I suppose you think you ought to hold out for the wedding bells. Go ahead; that's your business. I can get what I want with any nigger prostitute down the street here . . . Goodnight." Janey didn't say anything. He drove off. She went home and went to bed.

All that August her father was dying, full of morphine, in the Georgetown hospital. The papers came out every day with big headlines about war in Europe, Liège, Louvain, Mons. Dreyfus and Carroll's was in a fever. Big lawsuits over munitions patents were on. It began to be whispered about that the immaculate Mr. Dreyfus was an agent of the German government. Jerry came to see Janey one noon to apologize for having been so rude that night and to tell her that he had a job as a war correspondent and was leaving in a week for the front. They had a good lunch together. He talked about spies and British intrigue and pan-Slavism and the assassination of Jaurès and the Socialist revolution and laughed all the time and said everything was well on its way to ballyhack. She thought he was wonderful and wanted to say something about their being engaged and felt very tender towards him and scared he'd be killed, but suddenly it was time for her to go back to the office and neither of them had brought the matter up. He walked back to the Riggs Building with her and said goodbye and gave her a big kiss right there in front of everybody and ran off promising he'd write from New York. At that moment Alice came up on her way to Mrs. Robinson's and Janey found herself telling her that she was engaged to be married to Jerry Burnham and that he was going to Europe to the war as a war correspondent.

When her father died in early September, it was a great relief to all concerned. Only, coming back from Oak Hill Cemetery all the things she'd wanted as a girl came back to her, and the thought of Alec, and everything seemed so unhappy that she couldn't stand it. Her mother was very quiet and her eyes were very red and she kept saying that she was so glad that there'd be room on the lot for her to be buried in Oak Hill too. She'd have hated for him to be buried in any other cemetery than Oak Hill. It was so beautiful and all the nicest people in Georgetown were buried there.

With the insurance money Mrs. Williams did over the house and fixed up the two top floors to rent out as apartments. That was the chance Janey had been waiting for for so long to get a place of her own and she and Alice got a room in a house on Massachusetts Avenue near the Carnegie

179

Library, with cooking privileges. So one Saturday afternoon she phoned from the drugstore for a taxicab and set out with her suitcase and trunk and a pile of framed pictures from her room on the seat beside her. The pictures were two color prints of Indians by Remington, a Gibson girl, a photograph of the battleship *Connecticut* in the harbor of Villefranche that Joe had sent her and an enlarged photograph of her father in uniform standing at the wheel of an imaginary ship against a stormy sky furnished by a photographer in Norfolk, Virginia. Then there were two unframed colorprints by Maxfield Parrish that she'd bought recently and a framed snapshot of Joe in baseball clothes. The little picture of Alec she'd wrapped among her things in her suitcase. The cab smelt musky and rumbled along the streets. It was a crisp autumn day, the gutters were full of dry leaves. Janey felt scared and excited as if she were starting out all alone on a journey.

That fall she read a great many newspapers and magazines and *The Beloved Vagabond*, by W. J. Locke. She began to hate the Germans that were destroying art and culture, civilization, Louvain. She waited for a letter from Jerry, but a letter never came.

One afternoon she was coming out of the office a little late, who should be standing in the hall by the elevator but Joe. "Hello, Janey," he said. "Gee, you look like a million dollars." She was so glad to see him she could hardly speak, could only squeeze his arm tight. "I just got paid off . . . I thought I better come up here and see the folks before I spent all my jack . . . I'll take you out and set you up to a big feed an' a show if you want . . ." He was sunburned and his shoulders were broader than when he left. His big hands and knotty wrists stuck out of a new-looking blue suit that was too tight for him at the waist. The sleeves were too short too.

"Did you go to Georgetown?" she asked him.

"Yare."

"Did you go up to the cemetery?"

"Mommer wanted me to go, but what's the use?"

"Poor mother, she's so sentimental about it . . ."

They walked along. Joe didn't say anything. It was a hot day. Dust blew down the street.

Janey said: "Joe, dear, you must tell me all about your adventures . . . You must have been to some wonderful places. It's thrilling having a brother in the navy."

"Janey, pipe down about the navy, will you? . . . I don't want to hear about it. I deserted in B.A., see, and shipped out East on a limey, on an English boat . . . That's a dog's life too, but anything's better than the U.S.N."

180

"But, Joe . . ."

"Ain't nothin' to worry about . . ."

"But, Joe, what happened?"

"You won't say a word to a livin' soul, will you, Janey?
You see I got in a scrap with a petty officer tried to ride me
too damn hard. I socked him in the jaw an' kinda mauled
him, see, an' tnings looked pretty bad for me, so I made
tracks for the tall timber. . . . That's all."

"Oh, Joe, and I was hoping you'd get to be an officer."

"A gob get to be an officer . . . ? A fat chance."

She took him to the Mabillion, where Jerry had taken her.
At the door Joe peered in critically. "Is this the swellest joint
you know, Janey? I got a hundred iron men in my pocket."

"Oh, this is dreadfully expensive . . . It's a French restaurant. And you oughtn't to spend all your money on me."

"Who the hell else do you want me to spend it on?"

Joe sat down at a table and Janey went back to 'phone
Alice that she wouldn't be home till late. When she got back
to the table, Joe was pulling some little packages wrapped in
red and greenstriped tissuepaper out of his pockets.

"Oh, what's that?"

"You open 'em, Janey . . . It's yours."

She opened the packages. They were some lace collars and an embroidered tablecloth.

"The lace is Irish and that other's from Madeira . . . I had a Chinese vase for you too, but some sonofabit . . . sonofagun snitched it on me."

"That was awful sweet of you to think of me . . . I appreciate it."

Joe fidgeted with his knife and fork. "We gotta git a move on, Janey, or we'll be late for the show . . . I got tickets for *The Garden of Allah*."

When they came out of the Belasco onto Lafayette Square that was cool and quiet with a rustle of wind in the trees, Joe said, "Ain't so much; I seen a real sandstorm onct," and Janey felt bad about her brother being so rough and uneducated. The play made her feel like when she was little, full of uneasy yearn for foreign countries and a smell of incense and dark eyes and dukes in tailcoats tossing money away on the gaming tables of Monte Carlo, monks and the mysterious East. If Joe was only a little better educated he'd be able to really appreciate all the interesting ports he visited. He left her on the stoop of the house on Massachusetts Avenue.

"Where are you going to stay, Joe?" she asked.

"I guess I'll shove along back to New York an' pick up a berth. . . . Sailoring's a pretty good graft with this war on."

"You mean tonight?" He nodded.

"I wish I had a bed for you, but I couldn't very well on account of Alice."

"Naw, I doan want to hang round this dump . . . I jus' came up to say hello."

"Well, goodnight, Joe, be sure and write."

"Goodnight, Janey, I sure will."

She watched him walk off down the street until he went out of sight in the shadows of the trees. It made her unhappy to see him go all alone down the shadowed street. It wasn't quite the shambling walk of a sailor, but he looked like a workingman all right. She sighed and went into the house. Alice was waiting up for her. She showed Alice the lace and they tried on the collars and agreed that it was very pretty and quite valuable.

Janey and Alice had a good time that winter. They took to smoking cigarettes and serving tea to their friends Sunday afternoons. They read novels by Arnold Bennett and thought of themselves as bachelor girls. They learned to play bridge and shortened their skirts. At Christmas Janey got a hundred-dollar bonus and a raise to twenty a week from Dreyfus and Carroll. She began telling Alice that she was an old stickinthemud to stay on at Mrs. Robinson's. For herself she began to have ambitions of a business career. She wasn't afraid of men any more and kidded back and forth with young clerks in the elevator about things that would have made her blush the year before. When Johnny Edwards or Morris Byer took her out to the movies in the evening, she didn't mind having them put their arms around her, or having them kiss her once or twice while she was fumbling in her bag for her latchkey. She knew just how to catch a boy's hand by the wrist and push it away without making any scene when he tried to get too intimate. When Alice used to talk warningly about men having just one idea, she'd laugh and say, "Oh, they're not so smart." She discovered that just a little peroxide in the water when she washed her hair made it blonder and took away that mousey look. Sometimes when she was getting ready to go out in the evening, she'd put a speck of rouge on her little finger and rub it very carefully on her lips.

The Camera Eye (15)

in the mouth of the Schuylkill Mr. Pierce came on board ninetysix years old and sound as a dollar He'd been officeboy in Mr. Pierce's office about the time He'd enlisted and missed the battle of Antietam on account of having dysentery so bad and Mr. Pierce's daughter Mrs. Black called Him Jack and smoked little brown cigarettes and we played *Fra Diavolo* on the phonograph and everybody was very jolly when Mr. Pierce tugged at his dundrearies and took a toddy and Mrs. Black lit cigarettes one after another and they talked about old days and about how His father had wanted Him to be a priest and His poor mother had had such trouble getting together enough to eat for that family of greedy boys and His father was a silent man and spoke mostly Portugee and when he didn't like the way a dish was cooked that came on the table he'd pick it up and sling it out of the window and He wanted to go to sea and studied law at the University and in Mr. Pierce's office and He sang

Oh who can tell the joy he feels
As o'er the foam his vessel reels

and He mixed up a toddy and Mr. Pierce pulled at his dundrearies and everybody was very jolly and they talked about the schooner *Mary Wentworth* and how Colonel Hodgeson and Father Murphy looked so hard on the cheery glass and He mixed up a toddy and Mr. Pierce pulled at his dundrearies and Mrs. Black smoked the little brown cigarettes one after another and everybody was very jolly with *Fra Diavolo* playing on the phonograph and the harbor smell and the ferryboats and the Delaware all silveryripply used to be all marshes over there where we used to go duckshooting and He sang *Vittoria* with the phonograph

and Father Murphy got a terrible attack of gout and had to be carried off on a shutter and Mr. Pierce ninety-six years old and sound as a dollar took a sip of toddy and tugged at his dundrearies silveryripply and the harbor-smell came on the fresh wind and smoke from the ship-yards in Camden and lemon rye sugary smell of toddy-glasses and everybody was very jolly

Newsreel XII

Flow, river, flow
Down to the sea
Bright stream bring my loved one
Home to me

FIGHTING AT TORREON

at the end of the last campaign, writes Champ Clark Missouri's brilliant Congressman, I had about collapsed from overwork, nervous tension, loss of sleep and appetite and constant speaking, but three bottles of Electric Bitters made me allright

ROOSEVELT IS MADE LEADER OF NEW PARTY

BRYAN'S THROAT CUT BY CLARK; AIDS PARKER

True, dear one, true
I'm trying hard to be
But hear me say
It's a very very long long way
From the banks of the Seine

the crime for which Richardson was sentenced to die in the electric chair was the confessed murder of his for-

185

mer sweetheart nineteen-year-old Avis Linnell of Hyannis a pupil in the New England Conservatory of Music at Boston.

The girl stood in the way of the minister's marriage to a society girl and heiress of Brookline both through an engagement that still existed between the two and because of a condition in which Miss Linnell found herself.

The girl was deceived into taking a poison given her by Richardson which she believed would remedy that condition and died in her room at the Young Women's Christian Association.

ROOSEVELT TELLS FIRST TIME HOW US GOT PANAMA

HUNDRED THOUSAND PEOPLE UNABLE TO ENTER BIG HALL ECHO CHEERING

at dinnertime the Governor said he hadn't heard directly from Mr. Bryan during the day. "At the present rate of gain," Mr. Wilson said, "after reading the results of the fifteenth ballot, I figure it'll take about 175 more ballots to land me"

Redhaired Youth Says Stories of Easy Money Led Him to Crime

interest in the case was intensified on December 20 when it became known that the ex-clergyman had mutilated himself in his cell at the Charles Street Jail.

FIVE MEN DIE AFTER GETTING TO SOUTH POLE

DIAZ TRAINS HEAVY GUNS ON BUSINESS SECTION

> *It's a very very long long way*
> *From the banks of the Seine*
> *For a girl to go and stay*
> *On the banks of the Saskatchewan*

The Boy Orator of the Platte

It was in the Chicago Convention in '96 that the prizewinning boy orator, the minister's son whose lips had never touched liquor, let out his silver voice so that it filled the gigantic hall, filled the ears of the plain people:

> *Mr. Chairman and gentlemen of the convention:*
> *I would be presumptuous indeed*
> *to present myself against*
> *the distinguished gentleman to whom you have listened,*
> *if this were a mere measuring of abilities;*
> *but this is not a contest between persons.*
> *The humblest citizen in all the land,*
> *when clad in the armor of a righteous cause,*
> *is stronger than all the hosts of error.*
> *I come to speak to you in defence of a cause as holy as the*
> *cause of Liberty . . .*

a youngish bigmouthed man in a white tie
barnstormer, exhorter, evangelist,

his voice charmed the mortgageridden farmers of the great plains, rang through weatherboarded schoolhouses in the Missouri Valley, was sweet in the ears of small storekeepers hungry for easy credit, melted men's innards like the song of a thrush or a mockin' in the gray quiet before sunup, or a sudden roar in winter wheat or a bugler playing taps and the flag flying;

silver tongue of the plain people:

> *. . . the man who is employed for wages is as much a*
> *businessman as his employer;*
> *the attorney in a country town is as much a businessman*
> *as the corporation counsel in a giant metropolis;*
> *the merchant in a crossroads store is as much a business-*
> *man as the merchant of New York;*
> *the farmer who goes forth in the morning and toils all day,*
> *who begins in the spring and toils all summer, and who by*
> *the application of brain and muscle to the natural resources*
> *of the country creates wealth, is as much a businessman as*
> *the man who goes upon the board of trade and bets upon the*
> *price of grain;*
> *the miners who go down a thousand feet in the earth*
> *or climb two thousand feet upon the cliffs*

and bring forth from their hiding places
         the precious metals
                  to be poured in the channels of trade,
are as much businessmen
         as the few financial magnates
                  who
                           in a back room
                           corner the money of the world.

The hired man and the country attorney sat up and listened,
   this was big talk for the farmer who'd mortgaged his crop
to buy fertilizer, big talk for the smalltown hardware man,
groceryman, feed and corn merchant, undertaker, truckgar-
dener . . .

Having behind us
         the producing masses
                  of this nation and the world,
supported by the commercial interests, the laboring interests,
         and the toilers everywhere,
we will answer
                  their demand
                           for a gold standard
                                    by saying to them:
You shall not press down upon the brow of labor this crown
         of thorns,
                  you shall not crucify mankind upon a cross of gold.

They roared their lungs out (*crown of thorns and cross of
gold*)
   carried him round the hall on their shoulders, hugged him,
loved him, named their children after him, nominated him
for President,
   boy orator of the Platte,
                           silver tongue of the plain people.
But MacArthur and Forrest, two Scotchmen in the Rand,
had invented the cyanide process for extracting gold from
ore, South Africa flooded the gold market; there was no need
for a prophet of silver.

The silver tongue chanted on out of the big mouth, chanting Pacifism, Prohibition, Fundamentalism,
   nibbling radishes on the lecture platform,
   drinking grapejuice and water,
   gorging big cornbelt meals;
            Bryan grew gray in the hot air of Chautauqua tents,
in the applause, the handshakes, the backpattings, the cigar-

smoky air of committeerooms at Democratic conventions, a
silver tongue in a big mouth.

   In Dayton he dreamed of turning the trick again, of
setting back the clocks for the plain people, branding, flaying,
making a big joke

   of Darwinism and the unbelieving outlook of city
folks, scientists, foreigners with beards and monkey morals.

   In Florida he'd spoken every day at noon on a float
under an awning selling lots for Coral Gables . . . he had to
speak, to feel the drawling voices hush, feel the tense approv-
ing ears, the gust of handclaps.

   Why not campaign again through the length and
breadth to set up again the tottering word for the plain
people who wanted the plain word of God?

   (crown of thorns and cross of gold)
the plain prosperous comfortable word of God
for plain prosperous comfortable midamerican folks?

He was a big eater. It was hot. A stroke killed him.

Three days later down in Florida the company delivered
the electric horse he'd ordered to exercise on
when he'd seen the electric horse the President
exercised on in the White House.

The Camera Eye (16)

   it was hot as a bakeoven going through the canal from
Delaware City and turtles sunning themselves tumbled off
into the thick ocher ripple we made in passing and He
was very gay and She was feeling well for once and He
made us punch of tea and mint and a little Saint Croix
rum but it was hot as the hinges of Delaware and we saw
scarlet tanagers and redwing blackbirds and kingfishers
cackled wrathfully as the yellow wave from the white bow
rustled the reeds and the cattails and the sweetflag and
He talked about law reform and what politicians were
like and where were the Good Men in this country and
said Why thinking the way I think I couldn't get elected
to be notary public in any county in the state not with all
the money in the world no not even dogcatcher

J. Ward Moorehouse

He was born in Wilmington, Delaware, on the Fourth of July. Poor Mrs. Moorehouse could hear the firecrackers popping and crackling outside the hospital all through her laborpains. And when she came to a little and they brought the baby to her, she asked the nurse in a trembling husky whisper if she thought it could have a bad effect on the baby all that noise, prenatal influence you know. The nurse said the little boy ought to grow up to be very patriotic and probably President, being born on the Glorious Fourth, and went on to tell a long story about a woman who'd been frightened by having a beggar stick his hand out suddenly right under her nose just before the child was born and the child had been born with six fingers, but Mrs. Moorehouse was too weak to listen and went off to sleep. Later Mr. Moorehouse came by on his way home from the depot where he worked as stationagent and they decided to call the kid John Ward after Mrs. Moorehouse's father who was a farmer in Iowa and pretty well off. Then Mr. Moorehouse went round to Healy's to get tanked up because he was a father and because it was the Glorious Fourth and Mrs. Moorehouse went off to sleep again.

Johnny grew up in Wilmington. He had two brothers, Ben and Ed, and three sisters, Myrtle, Edith, and Hazel, but everybody said he was the bright boy of the family as well as the eldest. Ben and Ed were stronger and bigger than he was, but he was the marbles champion of the public school, getting considerable fame one term by a corner in agates he maneuvered with the help of a little Jewish boy named Ike Goldberg; they managed to rent out agates to other boys for a cent a week for ten.

When the Spanish War came on, everybody in Wilmington was filled with martial enthusiasm, all the boys bothered their parents to buy them Rough Rider suits and played filibuster and Pawnee Indian wars and Colonel Roosevelt and Remember the *Maine* and the White Fleet and the *Oregon* steaming through the Straits of Magellan. Johnny was down on the wharf one summer evening when Admiral Cervera's squadron was sighted in battle formation passing through the Delaware Capes by a detachment of the state militia who immediately opened fire on an old colored man crabbing out in the river. Johnny ran home like Paul Revere and Mrs. Moorehouse gathered up her six children and, pushing two of them in a babycarriage and dragging the other four after her, made for the railway station to find her husband. By the time they'd decided to hop on the next train to Philadelphia, news went round that the Spanish squadron was just some boats fishing for menhaden and that the militiamen were being confined in barracks for drunkenness. When the old colored man had hauled in his last crabline, he sculled back to shore and exhibited to his cronies several splintery bulletholes in the side of his skiff.

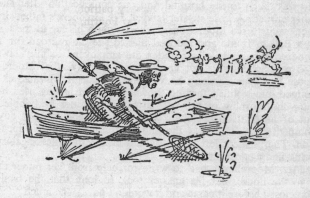

When Johnny graduated from highschool as head of the debating team, class orator, and winner of the prize essay contest with an essay entitled "Roosevelt, the Man of the Hour," everybody felt he ought to go to college. But the financial situation of the family was none too good, his father said, shaking his head. Poor Mrs. Moorehouse, who had been sickly since the birth of her last child, had been taken to the hospital to have an operation and would stay there for some time to come. The younger children had had measles, whooping cough, scarlet fever, and mumps all year. The amortization on the house was due and Mr. Moorehouse had not gotten the expected raise that New Year's. So instead of getting a job as assistant freight agent or picking peaches down near Dover, the way he had other summers, Johnny went round Delaware, Maryland, and Pennsylvania as agent for a bookdistributing firm. In September he received a congratulatory note from them saying that he was the first agent they had ever had who sold a hundred consecutive sets of Bryant's *History of the United States*. On the strength of it he went out to West Philadelphia and applied for a scholarship at the U. of P. He got the scholarship, passed the exams, and enrolled himself as a freshman, indicating B.S. as the degree he was working for. The first term he commuted from Wilmington to save the expense of a room. Saturdays and Sundays he picked up a little money taking subscriptions for Stoddard's *Lectures*. Everything would have gone right if his father hadn't slipped on the ice on the station steps one January morning in Johnny's sophomore year and broken his hip. He was taken to the hospital and one complication after another ensued. A little shyster lawyer, Ike Goldberg's father, in fact, went to see Moorehouse, who lay with his leg in the air in a Balkan frame and induced him to sue the railroad for a hundred thousand dollars under the employers' liability law. The railroad lawyers got up witnesses to prove that Moorehouse had been drinking heavily and the doctor who had examined him testified that he showed traces of having used liquor the morning of the fall, so by midsummer he hobbled out of hospital on crutches, without a job and without any compensation. That was the end of Johnny's college education. The incident left in his mind a lasting bitterness against drink and against his father.

Mrs. Moorehouse had to write for help from her father to save the house, but his answer took so long that the bank foreclosed before it came and it wouldn't have done much good anyway because it was only a hundred dollars in ten-dollar bills in a registered envelope and just about paid the cost of moving to a floor in a fourfamily frame house down by the Pennsylvania freightyards. Ben left highschool and got a job as assistant freightagent and Johnny went into the office of Hillyard and Miller, Real Estate. Myrtle and her mother baked pies evenings and made angelcake to send to the Woman's Exchange and Mr. Moorehouse sat in an invalid chair in the front parlor cursing shyster lawyers and the lawcourts and the Pennsylvania Railroad.

This was a bad year for Johnny Moorehouse. He was twenty and didn't drink or smoke and was keeping himself clean for the lovely girl he was going to marry, a girl in pink organdy with golden curls and a sunshade. He'd sit in the musty little office of Hillyard and Miller, listing tenements for rent, furnished rooms, apartments, desirable lots for sale, and think of the Boer War and the Strenuous Life and prospecting for gold. From his desk he could see a section of a

street of frame houses and a couple of elmtrees through a grimy windowpane. In front of the window was in summer a conical wiremesh flytrap where caught flies buzzed and sizzled, and in winter a little openface gas-stove that had a peculiar feeble whistle all its own. Behind him, back of a groundglass screen that went partway to the ceiling, Mr. Hillyard and Mr. Miller sat facing each other at a big double desk, smoking cigars and fiddling with papers. Mr. Hillyard was a sallowfaced man with black hair a little too long who had been on the way to making a reputation for himself as a criminal lawyer when, through some scandal that nobody ever mentioned, as it was generally agreed in Wilmington that he had lived it down, he had been disbarred. Mr. Miller was a little roundfaced man who lived with his elderly mother. He had been forced into the real-estate business by the fact that his father had died leaving him building lots scattered over Wilmington and the outskirts of Philadelphia and nothing else to make a living from. Johnny's job was to sit in the outer office and be polite to prospective buyers, to list the properties, attend to advertising, type the firm's letters, empty the wastebaskets and the dead flies out of the flytrap, take customers to visit apartments, houses, and building lots, and generally make himself useful and agreeable. It was on this job that he found out that he had a pair of bright blue eyes and that he could put on an engaging boyish look that people liked. Old ladies looking for houses used to ask specially to have that nice young man show them round, and business men who dropped in for a chat with Mr. Hillyard or Mr. Miller would nod their heads and look wise and say, "Bright boy, that." He made eight dollars a week.

Outside of the Strenuous Life and a lovely girl to fall in love with him, there was one thing Johnny Moorehouse's mind dwelt on as he sat at his desk listing desirable five and sevenroom dwelling-houses, drawingroom, diningroom, kitchen and butler's pantry, three master's bedrooms and bath, maid's room, water, electricity, gas, healthy location on gravelly soil in restricted residential area: He wanted to be a songwriter. He had a fair tenor voice and could carry *Larboard Watch Ahoy* or *I Dreamt I Dwelt in Marble Halls* or *Through Pleasures and Palaces Sadly I Roam* very adequately. Sunday afternoons he took music lessons with Miss O'Higgins, a shriveled little Irishwoman, unmarried, of about thirtyfive, who taught him the elements of the piano and listened with rapture to his original compositions that she took down for him on musicpaper that she had all ready ruled when he came. One song that began

> *Oh, show me the state where the peaches bloom*
> *Where maids are fair . . . It's Delaware*

she thought good enough to send to a music publisher in Philadelphia, but it came back, as did his next composition that Miss O'Higgins—he called her Marie by this time and she declared she couldn't take any money from him for her lessons, at least not until he was rich and had made a name for himself—that Marie cried over and said was as beautiful as MacDowell. It began

> *The silver bay of Delaware*
> *Rolls through peachblossoms to the sea*
> *And when my heart is bowed with care*
> *Its memory sweet comes back to me.*

Miss O'Higgins had a little parlor with gilt chairs in it where she gave her music lessons. It was very heavily hung with lace curtains and with salmoncolored brocaded portieres she had bought at an auction. In the center was a black walnut table piled high with worn black leather albums. Sunday afternoons after the lesson was over she'd bring out tea and cookies and cinnamon toast and Johnny would sit there

194

sprawled in the horsehair armchair that had to have a flow-ered cover over it winter and summer on account of its being so worn and his eyes would be so blue and he'd talk about things he wanted to do and poke fun at Mr. Hillyard and Mr. Miller and she'd tell him stories of great composers, and her cheeks would flush and she'd feel almost pretty and feel that after all there wasn't such a terrible disparity in their ages. She supported by her music lessons an invalid mother and a father who had been a well-known baritone and patriot in Dublin his younger days but who had taken to drink, and she was madly in love with Johnny Moorehouse.

Johnny Moorehouse worked on at Hillyard and Miller's sitting in the stuffy office, chafing when he had nothing to do until he thought he'd go mad and run amok and kill some-body, sending songs to the music publishers that they always sent back, reading the *Success Magazine,* full of sick longing for the future: to be away from Wilmington and his father's grumbling and pipesmoking and the racket his little brothers and sisters made and the smell of corned beef and cabbage and his mother's wrinkled crushed figure and her overworked hands.

But one day he was sent down to Ocean City, Maryland, to report on some lots the firm had listed there. Mr. Hillyard would have gone himself only he had a carbuncle on his neck. He gave Johnny the return ticket and ten dollars for the trip.

It was a hot July afternoon. Johnny ran home to get a bag and to change his clothes and got down to the station just in time to make the train. The ride was hot and sticky down through peachorchards and pinebarrens under a blazing slaty sky that flashed back off sandy patches in scraggly cornfields and whitewashed shacks and strips of marshwater. Johnny had taken off the jacket of his gray flannel suit and folded it on the seat beside him to keep it from getting mussed and

laid his collar and tie on top of it so that they'd be fresh when he got in, when he noticed a darkeyed girl in a ruffled pink dress and a wide white leghorn hat sitting across the aisle. She was considerably older than he was and looked like the sort of fashionably dressed woman who'd be in a parlorcar rather than in a daycoach. But Johnny reflected that there wasn't any parlorcar on this train. Whenever he wasn't looking at her, he felt that she was looking at him.

The afternoon grew overcast and it came on to rain, big drops spattered against the car windows. The girl in pink ruffles was struggling to put her window down. He jumped over and put it down for her. "Allow me," he said. "Thanks." She looked up and smiled into his eyes. "Oh, it's so filthy on this horrid train." She showed him her white gloves all smudged from the windowfastenings. He sat down again on the inside edge of his seat. She turned her full face to him. It was an irregular brown face with ugly lines from the nose to the ends of the mouth, but her eyes set him tingling. "You won't think it's too unconventional of me if we talk, will you?" she said. "I'm bored to death on this horrid train, and there isn't any parlorcar though the man in New York swore that there was."

"I bet you been traveling all day," said Johnny, looking shy and boyish.

"Worse than that. I came down from Newport on the boat last night."

The casual way she said Newport quite startled him. "I'm going to Ocean City," he said.

"So am I. Isn't it a horrid place? I wouldn't go there for a minute if it weren't for Dad. He pretends to like it."

"They say that Ocean City has a great future . . . I mean in a kind of a realestate way," said Johnny.

There was a pause.

"I got on in Wilmington," said Johnny with a smile.

"A horrid place, Wilmington . . . I can't stand it."

"I was born and raised there . . . I suppose that's why I like it," said Johnny.

"Oh, I didn't mean there weren't awfully nice people in Wilmington . . . lovely old families . . . Do you know the Rawlinses?"

"Oh, that's all right . . . I don't want to spend all my life in Wilmington, anyway . . . Gosh, look at it rain."

It rained so hard that a culvert was washed out and the train was four hours late into Ocean City. By the time they got in they were good friends; it had thundered and lightened and she'd been so nervous and he'd acted very strong and protecting and the car had filled up with mosquitoes and they

197

had both been eaten up and they'd gotten very hungry together. The station was pitchblack and there was no porter and it took him two trips to get her bags out and even then they almost forgot her alligatorskin handbag and he had to go back into the car a third time to get it and his own suit-

case. By that time an old darkey with a surrey had appeared who said he was from the Ocean House. "I hope you're going there too," she said. He said he was and they got in, though they had no place to put their feet because she had so many bags. There were no lights in Ocean City on account of the storm. The surreywheels ground through a deep sandbed; now and then that sound and the clucking of the driver at his horse were drowned by the roar of the surf from the beach. The only light was from the moon continually hidden by driving clouds. The rain had stopped, but the tense air felt as if another downpour would come any minute. "I certainly would have perished in the storm if it hadn't been for you," she said; then suddenly she offered him her hand like a man: "My name's Strang . . . Annabelle Marie Strang . . . Isn't that a funny name?" He took her hand. "John Moorehouse is mine . . . Glad to meet you, Miss Strang." The palm of her hand was hot and dry. It seemed to press into his. When he let go he felt that she had expected him to hold her hand longer. She laughed a husky low laugh. "Now we're introduced, Mr. Moorehouse, and everything's quite all right . . . I certainly shall give Dad a piece of my mind. The idea of his not meeting his only daughter at the station."

In the dark hotel lobby lit by a couple of smoked oillamps he saw her, out of the corner of his eye, throw her arms round a tall whitehaired man, but by the time he had scrawled John W. Moorehouse in his most forceful handwriting in the register and gotten his roomkey from the clerk, they had gone. Up in the little pine bedroom it was very hot. When he pulled up the window, the roar of the surf came in through the rusty screen mingling with the rattle of rain on the roof. He changed his collar and washed in tepid water he poured from the cracked pitcher on the washstand and went down to the diningroom to try to get something to eat. A goat-toothed waitress was just bringing him soup when Miss Strang came in followed by the tall man. As the only lamp was on the table he was sitting at, they came towards it and he got up and smiled. "Here he is, Dad," she said. "And you owe him for the driver that brought us from the station . . . Mr. Morris, you must meet my father, Doctor Strang . . . The name was Morris, wasn't it?" Johnny blushed. "Moorehouse, but it's quite all right. . . . I'm glad to meet you, sir."

Next morning Johnny got up early and went round to the office of the Ocean City Improvement and Realty Company that was in a new greenstained shingled bungalow on the freshly laidout street back of the beach. There was no one there yet, so he walked round the town. It was a muggy gray day and the cottages and the frame stores and the unpainted shacks along the railroad track looked pretty desolate. Now and then he slapped a mosquito on his neck. He had on his last clean collar and he was worried for fear it would get wilted. Whenever he stepped off the board sidewalks he got sand in his shoes, and sharp beachburrs stuck to his ankles. At last he found a stout man in a white linen suit sitting on the steps of the realestate office. "Good morning, sir," he said. "Are you Colonel Wedgewood?" The stout man was too out of breath to answer and only nodded. He had one big silk handkerchief stuck into his collar behind and with another was mopping his face. Johnny gave him the letter he had from his firm and stood waiting for him to say something. The fat man read the letter with puckered brows and led the way into the office. "It's this asthma," he gasped between great wheezing breaths. "Cuts ma wind when Ah trah to hurry. Glad to meet you, son."

Johnny hung round old Colonel Wedgewood the rest of the morning, looking blue-eyed and boyish, listening politely to stories of the Civil War and General Lee and his white horse Traveller and junketings befoa de woa on the Easten Shoa, ran down to the store to get a cake of ice for the cooler, made a little speech about the future of Ocean City as a summer resort—"Why, what have they got at Atlantic City or Cape May that we haven't got here?" roared the Colonel—went home with him to his bungalow for lunch, thereby missing the train he ought to have taken back to Wilmington, refused a mint julep—he neither drank nor smoked—but stood admiringly by while the Colonel concocted and drank two good stiff ones, for his asthma, used his smile and his blue eyes and his boyish shamble on the Colonel's colored cook Mamie and by four o'clock he was laughing about the Governor of North Carolina and the Governor of South Carolina and had accepted a job with the Queen City Improvement and Realty Company at fifteen dollars a week, with a small furnished cottage thrown in. He went back to the hotel and wrote Mr. Hillyard, inclosing the deeds for the lots and his

REAL
ESTATE

expense account, apologized for leaving the firm at such short notice, but explained that he owed it to his family who were in great need to better himself as much as he could; then he wrote to his mother that he was staying on in Ocean City and please to send him his clothes by express; he wondered whether to write Miss O'Higgins, but decided not to. After all, bygones were bygones.

When he had eaten supper he went to the desk to ask for his bill, feeling pretty nervous for fear he wouldn't have enough money to pay it, and was just coming out with two quarters in his pocket and his bag in his hand when he met Miss Strang. She was with a short dark man in white flannels whom she introduced as Monsieur de la Rochevillaine. He was a Frenchman but spoke good English. "I hope you're not leaving us," she said. "No, ma'am, I'm just moving down the beach to one of Colonel Wedgewood's cottages." The Frenchman made Johnny uneasy; he stood smiling suave as a barber beside Miss Strang. "Oh, you know our fat friend, do you? He's a great crony of Dad's. I think he's just too boring with his white horse Traveller." Miss Strang and the Frenchman

smiled both at once as if they had some secret in common. The Frenchman stood beside her swinging easily on the balls of his feet as if he were standing beside some piece of furniture he owned and was showing off to a friend. Johnny had a notion to paste him one right where the white flannel bulged into a pot belly. "Well, I must go," he said. "Won't you come back later? There's going to be dancing. We'd love to have you." "Yes, come back by all means," said the Frenchman. "I will if I can," said Johnny, and walked off with his suitcase in his hand, feeling sticky under the collar and sore. "Drat that

Frenchman," he said aloud. Still, there was something about the way Miss Strang looked at him. He guessed he must be falling in love.

It was a hot August, the mornings still, the afternoons piling up sultry into thundershowers. Except when there were clients to show about the scorched sandlots and pinebarrens laid out into streets, Johnny sat in the office alone under the twoflanged electric fan. He was dressed in white flannels and a pink tennis shirt rolled up to the elbows, drafting the lyrical description of Ocean City (Maryland) that was to preface the advertising booklet that was the Colonel's pet idea: "The lifegiving surges of the broad Atlantic beat on the crystalline beaches of Ocean City (Maryland) . . . the tonic breath of the pines brings relief to the asthmatic and the consumptive . . . nearby the sportsman's paradise of Indian River spreads out its broad estuary teeming with . . ." In the afternoon the Colonel would come in sweating and wheezing and Johnny would read him what he had written and he'd say, "Bully, ma boy, bully," and suggest that it be all done over. And Johnny would look up a new batch of words in a dogeared *Century Dictionary* and start off again.

It would have been a fine life except that he was in love. Evenings he couldn't keep away from the Ocean House. Each time he walked up the creaking porch steps past the old ladies rocking and fanning with palmleaf fans, and went through the screen doors into the lobby, he felt sure that this time he'd find Annabelle Marie alone, but each time the Frenchman was with her as smiling and cool and potbellied as ever. They both made a fuss over Johnny and petted him like a little dog or a precocious child; she taught him to dance the "Boston," and the Frenchman, who it turned out was a duke or a baron or something, kept offering him drinks and cigars and scented cigarettes. Johnny was shocked to death when he found out that she smoked, but somehow it went with dukes and Newport and foreign travel and that sort of thing. She used some kind of musky perfume and the smell of it and the slight rankness of cigarette smoke in her hair made him dizzy and feverish when he danced with her. Some nights he tried to tire out the Frenchman playing pool, but then she'd disappear to bed and he'd have to go off home cursing under his breath. While he undressed he could still feel a little tingle of musk in his nostrils. He was trying to make up a song:

> By the moonlight sea
> I pine for thee
> Anabelle Marie . . .

202

Then it 'ud suddenly sound too damn silly and he'd stride up and down his little porch in his pajamas, with the mosquitoes shrilling about his head and the pound of the sea and the jeer of the dryflies and katydids in his ears, cursing being young and poor and uneducated and planning how he'd make a big enough pile to buy out every damn Frenchman; then he'd be the one she'd love and look up to and he wouldn't care if she did have a few damn Frenchmen for mascots if she wanted them. He'd clench his fists and stride around the porch muttering, "By gum, I can do it."

Then one evening he found Annabelle Marie alone. The Frenchman had gone on the noon train. She seemed glad to see Johnny, but there was obviously something on her mind. She had too much powder on her face and her eyes looked red; perhaps she'd been crying. It was moonlight. She put her hand on his arm, "Moorehouse, walk down the beach with me," she said. "I hate the sight of all these old hens in rocking chairs." On the walk that led across a scraggly lawn down to the beach they met Doctor Strang.

"What's the matter with Rochevillaine, Annie?" he said. He was a tall man with a high forehead. His lips were compressed and he looked worried.

"He got a letter from his mother . . . She won't let him."

"He's of age, isn't he?"

"Dad, you don't understand the French nobility . . . The family council won't let him . . . They could tie up his income."

"You'll have enough for two . . . I told him that."

"Oh, shut up about it, can't you? . . ." She suddenly started to blubber like a child. She ran past Johnny and back to the hotel, leaving Johnny and Doctor Strang facing each other on the narrow boardwalk. Doctor Strang saw Johnny for the first time. "H'm . . . excuse us," he said as he brushed past and walked with long strides up the walk, leaving Johnny to go down to the beach and look at the moon all by himself.

But the nights that followed, Annabelle Marie did walk out along the beach with him and he began to feel that perhaps she hadn't loved the Frenchman so much after all. They would go far beyond the straggling cottages and build a fire and sit side by side looking into the flame. Their hands sometimes brushed against each other as they walked; when she'd want to get to her feet he'd take hold of her two hands and pull her up towards him and he always planned to pull her to him and kiss her, but he hadn't the nerve.

One night was very warm and she suddenly suggested they go in bathing.

203

"But we haven't our suits."

"Haven't you ever been in without? It's much better . . . Why, you funny boy, I can see you blushing even in the moonlight."

"Do you dare me?"

"I doubledare you."

He ran up the beach a way and pulled off his clothes and went very fast into the water. He didn't dare look and only got a glimpse out of the corner of an eye of white legs and breasts and a wave spuming white at her feet. While he was putting his clothes on again, he was wondering if he wanted to get married to a girl who'd go in swimming with a fellow all naked like that, anyway. He wondered if she'd done it with that damn Frenchman. "You were like a marble faun," she said when he got back beside the fire where she was coiling her black hair round her head. She had hairpins in her

204

mouth and spoke through them. "Like a very nervous marble faun . . . I got my hair wet."

He hadn't intended to, but he suddenly pulled her to him and kissed her. She didn't seem at all put out, but made herself little in his arms and put her face up to be kissed again. "Would you marry a feller like me without any money?"

"I hadn't thought of it, darling, but I might."

"You're pretty wealthy, I guess, and I haven't a cent, and I have to send home money to my folks . . . but I have prospects."

"What kind of prospects?" She pulled her face down and ruffled his hair and kissed him.

"I'll make good in this realestate game. I swear I will."

"Will it make good, poor baby?"

"You're not so much older'n me . . . How old are you, Annabelle?"

"Well, I admit to twentyfour, but you mustn't tell anybody, or about tonight or anything."

"Who would I be telling about it, Annabelle Marie?"

Walking home, something seemed to be on her mind because she paid no attention to anything he said. She kept humming under her breath.

Another evening they were sitting on the porch of his cottage smoking cigarettes—he would occasionally smoke a cigarette now to keep her company—he asked her what it was worrying her. She put her hands on his shoulders and shook him: "Oh, Moorehouse, you're such a fool . . . but I like it."

"But there must be something worrying you, Annabelle . . . You didn't look worried the day we came down on the train together."

"If I told you . . . Gracious, I can imagine your face." She laughed her hard gruff laugh that always made him feel uncomfortable.

"Well, I wish I had the right to make you tell me . . . You ought to forget that damn Frenchman."

"Oh, you're such a little innocent," she said. Then she got up and walked up and down the porch.

"Won't you sit down, Annabelle? Don't you like me even a little bit?"

She rubbed her hand through his hair and down across his face. "Of course I do, you little blue-eyed ninny . . . But can't you see it's everything driving me wild, all those old cats round the hotel talk about me as if I was a scarlet woman because I occasionally smoke a cigarette in my own room . . . Why, in England some of the most aristocratic women smoke right in public without anybody saying 'boo' to

205

them . . . And then I'm worried about Dad; he's sinking too much money in realestate. I think he's losing his mind."

"But there's every indication of a big boom coming down here. It'll be another Atlantic City in time."

"Now look here, 'fess up, how many lots have been sold this month?"

"Well, not so many . . . But there are some important sales pending . . . There's that corporation that's going to build the new hotel."

"Dad'll be lucky if he gets fifty cents out on the dollar . . . and he keeps telling me how rattlebrained I am. He's a physician and not a financial wizard and he ought to realize it. It's all right for somebody like you who has nothing to lose and a way to make in the world to be messing around in realestate . . . As for that fat Colonel I don't know whether he's a fool or a crook."

"What kind of a doctor is your father?"

"Do you mean to say you never heard of Doctor Strang? He's the bestknown nose and throat specialist in Philadelphia . . . Oh, it's so cute . . ." She kissed him on the cheek ". . . and ignorant . . ." she kissed him again . . . "and pure."

"I'm not so pure," he said quickly and looked at her hard in the eyes. Their faces began to blush looking at each other. She let her head sink slowly on his shoulder.

His heart was pounding. He was dizzy with the smell of her hair and the perfume she wore. He pulled her to her feet, with his arm round her shoulders. Tottering a little, her leg against his leg, the stiffness of her corset against his ribs, her hair against his face, he pulled her through the little living-room into the bedroom and locked the door behind them. Then he kissed her as hard as he could on the lips. She sat down on the bed and began to take off her dress, a little coolly he thought, but he'd gone too far to pull back. When she took off her corset, she flung it in the corner of the room. "There," she said. "I hate the beastly things." She got up and walked towards him in her chemise and felt for his face in the dark.

"What's the matter, darling?" she whispered fiercely. "Are you afraid of me?"

Everything was much simpler than Johnny expected. They giggled together while they were dressing. Walking back along the beach to the Ocean House, he kept thinking: "Now she'll have to marry me."

In September a couple of cold northeasters right after Labor Day emptied the Ocean House and the cottages. The Colonel talked bigger about the coming boom and his advertising campaign, and drank more. Johnny took his meals with him now instead of at Mrs. Ames's boardinghouse. The booklet was finished and approved and Johnny had made a couple of trips to Philadelphia with the text and the photographs to get estimates from printers. Running through Wilmington on the train without getting off there gave him a pleasant feeling of independence. Doctor Strang looked more and more wor-

ried and talked about protecting his investments. They had not talked of Johnny's engagement to his daughter, but it seemed to be understood. Annabelle's moods were unaccountable. She kept saying she was dying of boredom. She teased and nagged at Johnny continually. One night he woke suddenly to find her standing beside the bed. "Did I scare you?" she said. "I couldn't sleep . . . Listen to the surf." The wind was shrilling round the cottage and a tremendous surf roared on the beach. It was almost daylight before he could get her to get out of bed and go back to the hotel. "Let 'em see me . . . I don't care," she said. Another time when they were walking along the beach she was taken with nausea and he had to stand waiting while she was sick behind a sand-dune, then he supported her, white and trembling, back to the Ocean House. He was worried and restless. On one of his trips to Philadelphia he went round to the *Public Ledger* to see if he could get a job as a reporter.

One Saturday afternoon he sat reading the paper in the lobby of the Ocean House. There was no one else there, most of the guests had left. The hotel would close the fifteenth. Suddenly he found himself listening to a conversation. The two bellhops had come in and were talking in low voices on the bench against the wall.

"Well, I got mahn awright this summer, damned if I didn't, Joe."

"I would of too if I hadn't gotten sick."

"Didn't I tell you not to monkey round with that Lizzie? Man, I b'lieve every sonofabitch in town slep' with that jane, not excludin' niggers."

"Say, did you . . . You know the blackeyed one? You said you would."

Johnny froze. He held the paper rigid in front of him.

The bellhop gave out a low whistle. "Hotstuff," he said. "Jeez, what these society dames gits away with 's got me beat."

"Didye, honest?"

"Well, not exactly . . . 'Fraid I might ketch somethin'. But

208

that Frenchman did . . . Jeez, he was in her room all the time."

"I know he was. I caught him onct." They laughed. "They'd forgot to lock the door."

"Was she all neked?"

"I guess she was . . . under her kimono . . . He's cool as a cucumber and orders icewater."

"Whah didn't ye send up Mr. Greeley?"

"Hell, why should I? Frenchman wasn't a bad scout. He gave me five bucks."

"I guess she can do what she goddam pleases. Her dad about owns this dump, they tell me, him and ole Colonel Wedgewood."

"I guess that young guy in the realestate office is gettin' it now . . . looks like he'd marry her."

"Hell, I'd marry her maself if a girl had that much kale."

Johnny was in a cold sweat. He wanted to get out of the lobby without their seeing him. A bell rang and one of the boys ran off. He heard the other one settling himself on the bench. Maybe he was reading a magazine or something. Johnny folded up the paper quietly and walked out onto the porch. He walked down the street without seeing anything. For a while he thought he'd go down to the station and take the first train out and throw the whole business to ballyhack, but there was the booklet to get out, and there was a chance that if the boom did come he might get in on the ground floor, and this connection with money and the Strangs; opportunity knocks but once at a young man's door. He went back to his cottage and locked himself in his bedroom. He stood a minute looking at himself in the glass of the bureau. The neatly parted light hair, the cleancut nose and chin; the image blurred. He found he was crying. He threw himself face down on the bed and sobbed.

When he went up to Philadelphia the next time to read proof on the booklet:

OCEAN CITY (Maryland)

VACATIONLAND SUPREME

He also took up a draft of the wedding invitations to be engraved:

Doctor Alonso B. Strang
announces the marriage of his daughter
Annabelle Marie
to Mr. J. Ward Moorehouse

at Saint Stephen's Protestant Episcopal Church,
Germantown, Pennsylvania, on November fifteenth
nineteen hundred and nine at twelve noon

Then there was an invitation to the reception to be sent to a special list. It was to be a big wedding because Doctor Strang had so many social obligations. Annabelle decided on J. Ward Moorehouse as more distinguished than John W. and began to call him Ward. When they asked him about inviting his family, he said his mother and father were both invalids and his brothers and sisters too little to enjoy it. He wrote his mother that he was sure she'd understand, but that as things were and with Dad the way he was . . . he was sure she'd understand. Then one evening Annabelle told him she was going to have a baby.

"I thought maybe that was it."

Her eyes were suddenly scaringly cold black in his. He hated her at that minute, then he smiled blue-eyed and boyish. "I mean you being so nervous and everything." He laughed and took her hand. "Well, I'm goin' to make you an honest woman, ain't I?" He had the drop on her now. He kissed her.

She burst out crying.

"Oh, Ward, I wish you wouldn't say 'ain't.' "

"I was just teasing, dear . . . But isn't there some way?"

"I've tried everything . . . Dad would know, but I don't dare tell him. He knows I'm pretty independent . . . but . . ."

"We'll have to stay away for a year after we're married . . . It's rotten for me. I was just offered a job on the *Public Ledger*."

"We'll go to Europe . . . Dad'll fix us up for our honeymoon . . . He's glad to get me off his hands and I've got money in my own right, mother's money."

"Maybe it's all a mistake."

"How can it be?"

"How long is it since you . . . noticed . . . ?"

Her eyes were suddenly black and searching in his again. They stared at each other and hated each other. "Quite long enough," she said and pulled his ear as if he were a child, and went swishing upstairs to dress. The Colonel was tickled to death about the engagement and had invited them all to dinner to celebrate it.

The wedding came off in fine style and J. Ward Moorehouse found himself the center of all eyes in a wellfitting frock coat and a silk hat. People thought he was very handsome. His mother back in Wilmington let flatiron after flat-

iron cool while she pored over the account in the papers; finally she took off her spectacles and folded the papers carefully and laid them on the ironing board. She was very happy.

The young couple sailed the next day from New York on the *Teutonic*. The crossing was so rough that only the last two days was it possible to go out on deck. Ward was sick and was taken care of by a sympathetic cockney steward who spoke of Annabelle as the "Madam" and thought she was his mother. Annabelle was a good sailor, but the baby made her feel miserable and whenever she looked at herself in her handmirror she was so haggard that she wouldn't get out of her bunk. The stewardess suggested gin with a dash of bitters in it and it helped her over the last few days of the crossing. The night of the captain's dinner she finally appeared in the diningroom in an evening gown of black valenciennes and everybody thought her the bestlooking woman on the boat. Ward was in a fever for fear she'd drink too much champagne as he had seen her put away four ponies of gin and bitters and a Martini cocktail while dressing. He had made friends with an elderly banker, Mr. Jarvis Oppenheimer, and his wife, and he was afraid that Annabelle would seem a little fast to them. The captain's dinner went off without a hitch, however, and Annabelle and Ward found that they made a good team. The captain, who had known Doctor Strang, came and sat with them in the smoking room afterwards and had a glass of champagne with them and with Mr. and Mrs. Oppenheimer and they heard people asking each other who could that charming scintillating brilliant young couple be, somebody interesting surely, and when they went to bed after having seen the lighthouses in the Irish Sea, they felt that all the seasick days had been thoroughly worth while.

Annabelle didn't like it in London where the dark streets were dismal in a continual drizzle of sleet, so they only stayed a week at the Cecil before crossing to Paris. Ward was sick again on the boat from Folkstone to Boulogne and couldn't keep track of Annabelle whom he found in the diningsaloon drinking brandy and soda with an English army of-

ficer when the boat reached the calm water between the long jetties of Boulogne harbor. It wasn't so bad as he expected being in a country where he didn't know the language and Annabelle spoke French very adequately and they had a first-class compartment and a basket with a cold chicken and sandwiches in it and some sweet wine that Ward drank for the first time—when in Rome do as the Romans do—and they were quite the honeymoon couple on the train going down to Paris. They drove in a cab from the station to the Hotel Wagram, with only their handbaggage because the hotel porter took care of the rest, through streets shimmering with green gaslight on wet pavements. The horse's hoofs rang sharp on the asphalt and the rubbertired wheels of the cab spun smoothly and the streets were crowded in spite of the fact that it was a rainy winter night and there were people sitting out at little marbletop tables round little stoves in front of cafés and there were smells in the air of coffee and wine and browning butter and baking bread. Annabelle's eyes caught all the lights; she looked very pretty, kept nudging him to show him things and patting his thigh with one hand. Annabelle had written to the hotel, where she had stayed before with her father, and they found a white bedroom and parlor waiting for them and a roundfaced manager who was very elegant and very affable to bow them into it and a fire in the grate. They had a bottle of champagne and some pâté de foie gras before going to bed and Ward felt like a king. She took off her traveling clothes and put on a negligee and he put on a smoking jacket that she had given him and that he hadn't worn and all his bitter feelings of the last month melted away.

213

They sat a long time looking into the fire smoking Muratti cigarettes out of a tin box. She kept fondling his hair and rubbing her hand round his shoulders and neck. "Why aren't you more affectionate, Ward?" she said in low gruff tones. "I'm the sort of woman likes to be carried off her feet . . . Take care . . . You may lose me . . . Over here the men know how to make love to a woman."

"Gimme a chance, won't you? . . . First thing I'm going to get a job with some American firm or other. I think Mr. Oppenheimer'll help me do that. I'll start in taking French lessons right away. This'll be a great opportunity for me."

"You funny boy."

"You don't think I'm going to run after you like a poodle-dog, do you, without making any money of my own? . . . Nosiree, bobby." He got up and pulled her to her feet. "Let's go to bed."

Ward went regularly to the Berlitz School for his French lessons and went round to see Notre Dame and Napoleon's tomb and the Louvre with old Mr. Oppenheimer and his wife. Annabelle, who said that museums gave her a head-ache, spent her days shopping and having fittings with dress-makers. There were not many American firms in Paris, so the only job Ward could get, even with the help of Mr. Oppenheimer who knew everyone, was on Gordon Bennett's news-paper, the Paris edition of the *New York Herald*. The job consisted of keeping track of arriving American business men, interviewing them on the beauties of Paris and on international relations. This was his meat and enabled him to make many valuable contacts. Annabelle thought it was all too boring and refused to be told anything about it. She made him put on a dress suit every evening and take her to the opera and theaters. This he was quite willing to do as it was good for his French.

She went to a very famous specialist for women's diseases who agreed that on no account should she have a baby at this time. An immediate operation was necessary and would be a little dangerous, as the baby was so far along. She didn't tell Ward and only sent word from the hospital when it was over. It was Christmas Day. He went immediately to see her. He heard the details in chilly horror. He'd gotten used to the idea of having a baby and thought it would have a steadying effect on Annabelle. She lay looking very pale in the bed in the private sanatorium and he stood beside the bed with his fists clenched without saying anything. At length the nurse said to him that he was tiring madame and he went away. When Annabelle came back from the hospital after four or five days announcing gaily that she was fit as a fiddle and was

going to the south of France, he said nothing. She got ready to go, taking it for granted that he was coming, but the day she left on the train to Nice he told her he was going to stay on in Paris. She looked at him sharply and then said with a laugh, "You're turning me loose, are you?"

"I have my business and you have your pleasure," he said.

"All right, young man, it's a go."

He took her to the station and put her on the train, gave the conductor five francs to take care of her and came away from the station on foot. He'd had enough of the smell of musk and perfume for a while.

Paris was better than Wilmington, but Ward didn't like it. So much leisure and the sight of so many people sitting round eating and drinking got on his nerves. He felt very homesick the day the Ocean City booklet arrived inclosed with an enthusiastic letter from Colonel Wedgewood. Things were moving at last, the Colonel said; as for himself he was putting every cent he could scrape up, beg or borrow, into options. He even suggested that Ward send him a little money to invest for him, now that he was in a position to risk a stake on the surety of a big turnover; risk wasn't the word because the whole situation was sewed up in a bag; nothing to do but shake the tree and let the fruit fall into their mouths. Ward went down the steps from the office of Morgan Harjes where he got his mail and out onto Boulevard Haussmann. The heavy coated paper felt good to his fingers. He put the letter in his pocket and walked down the boulevard with the honk of horns and the ring of horses' hoofs and the shuffle of steps in his ears, now and then reading a phrase. Why, it almost made him want to go back to Ocean City (Maryland) himself. A little ruddy sunlight was warming the winter gray of the streets. A smell of roasting coffee came from somewhere; Ward thought of the white crackling sunlight of windswept days at home; days that lashed you full of energy and hope; the Strenuous Life. He had a date to lunch with Mr. Oppenheimer at a very select little restaurant down in the slums somewhere called the Tour d'Argent. When he got into a redwheeled taximeter cab it made him feel good again that the driver understood his directions. After all it was educational, made up for those years of college he missed. He had read through the booklet for the third time when he reached the restaurant.

He got out at the restaurant and was just paying the taxi when he saw Mr. Oppenheimer and another man arriving down the quai on foot. Mr. Oppenheimer wore a gray overcoat and a gray derby of the same pearly color as his moustaches; the other man was a steelgray individual with a thin nose and chin. When he saw them Ward decided that he must be more careful about his clothes in the future.

They ate lunch for a long time and a great many courses, although the steelgray man, whose name was McGill—he was manager of one of Jones and Laughlin's steel plants in Pittsburgh—said his stomach wouldn't stand anything but a

chop and a baked potato and drank whiskey and soda instead of wine. Mr. Oppenheimer enjoyed his food enormously and kept having long consultations about it with the head waiter. "Gentlemen, you must indulge me a little . . . this for me is a debauch," he said. "Then, not being under the watchful eye of my wife, I can take certain liberties with my digestion . . . My wife has entered the sacred precincts of a fitting at her corsetière's and is not to be disturbed . . . You, Ward, are not old enough to realize the possibilities of food." Ward looked embarrassed and boyish and said he was enjoying the duck very much. "Food," went on Mr. Oppenheimer, "is the last pleasure of an old man."

When they were sitting over Napoleon brandy in big bowl-shaped glasses and cigars, Ward got up his nerve to bring out the Ocean City (Maryland) booklet that had been burning a hole in his pocket all through lunch. He laid it on the table modestly. "I thought maybe you might like to glance at it, Mr. Oppenheimer, as . . . as something a bit novel in the advertising line."

Mr. Oppenheimer took out his glasses and adjusted them on his nose, took a sip of brandy and looked through the book with a bland smile. He closed it, let a little curling blue cigarsmoke out through his nostrils and said, "Why, Ocean City must be an earthly paradise indeed . . . Don't you lay it on . . . er . . . a bit thick?"

"But you see, sir, we've got to make the man in the street just crazy to go there . . . there's got to be a word to catch your eye the minute you pick it up."

Mr. McGill, who up to that time hadn't looked at Ward, turned a pair of hawkgray eyes on him in a hard stare. With a heavy red hand he reached for the booklet. He read it intently right through while Mr. Oppenheimer went on to talk about the bouquet of the brandy and how you should warm the glass a little in your hand and take it in tiny sips, rather inhaling it than drinking it. Suddenly Mr. McGill brought his fist down on the table and laughed a dry quick laugh that didn't move a muscle of his face. "By gorry, that'll get 'em, too," he said. "I reckon it was Mark Twain said there was a sucker born every minute . . ." He turned to Ward and said, "I'm sorry I didn't ketch your name, young feller; do you mind repeating it?"

"With pleasure . . . It's Moorehouse, J. Ward Moorehouse."

"Where do you work?"

"I'm on the *Paris Herald* for the time being," said Ward, blushing.

"Where do you live when you're in the States?"

217

"My home's in Wilmington, Delaware, but I don't guess I'll go back there when we go home. I've been offered some editorial work on the *Public Ledger* in Philly."

Mr. McGill took out a visiting card and wrote an address on it.

"Well, if you ever think of coming to Pittsburgh, look me up."

"I'd be delighted to see you."

"His wife," put in Mr. Oppenheimer, "is the daughter of Doctor Strang, the Philadelphia nose and throat specialist . . . By the way, Ward, how is the dear girl? I hope Nice has cured her of her tonsillitis."

"Yes, sir," said Ward, "she writes that she's much better."

"She's a lovely creature . . . charming . . ." said Mr. Oppenheimer, draining the last sip out of his brandyglass with upcast eyes.

Next day Ward got a wire from Annabelle that she was coming up to Paris. He met her at the train. She introduced a tall Frenchman with a black Vandyke beard, who was helping her off with her bags when Ward came up, as "Monsieur Forelle, my traveling companion." They didn't get a chance to talk until they got into the cab together. The cab smelt musty, as they had to keep the windows closed on account of the driving rain.

"Well, my dear," Annabelle said, "have you got over the pet you were in when I left? . . . I hope you have because I have bad news for you."

"What's the trouble?"

"Dad's gotten himself in a mess financially . . . I knew it'd happen. He has no more idea of business than a cat . . . Well, that fine Ocean City boom of yours collapsed before it had started and Dad got scared and tried to unload his sandlots and naturally nobody'd buy them . . . Then the Improvement and Realty Company went bankrupt and that precious Colonel of yours has disappeared and Dad has got himself somehow personally liable for a lot of the concern's debts. . . . And there you are. I wired him we were coming home as soon as we could get a sailing. I'll have to see what I can do . . . He's helpless as a child about business."

"That won't make me mad. I wouldn't have come over here anyway if it wasn't for you."

"Just all selfsacrifice, aren't you?"

"Let's not squabble, Annabelle."

The last days in Paris Ward began to like it. They heard *La Bohème* at the opera and were both very much excited about it. Afterwards they went to a café and had some cold partridge and wine and Ward told Annabelle about how he'd

218

wanted to be a songwriter and about Marie O'Higgins and how he'd started to compose a song about her and they felt very fond of each other. He kissed her again and again in the cab going home and the elevator going up to their room seemed terribly slow.

They still had a thousand dollars on the letter of credit Doctor Strang had given them as a wedding present, so that Annabelle bought all sorts of clothes and hats and perfumes and Ward went to an English tailor near the Church of the Madeleine and had four suits made. The last day Ward bought her a brooch in the shape of a rooster, made of Limoges enamel and set with garnets, out of his salary from the *Paris Herald*. Eating lunch after their baggage had gone to the boat train they felt very tender about Paris and each other and the brooch. They sailed from Havre on the *Touraine* and had a completely calm passage, a gray glassy swell all the way, although the month was February. Ward wasn't seasick. He walked round and round the firstclass every morning before Annabelle got up. He wore a Scotch tweed cap and a Scotch tweed overcoat to match, with a pair of fieldglasses slung over his shoulder, and tried to puzzle out some plan for the future. Wilmington anyway was far behind like a ship hull down on the horizon.

The steamer with tugboats chugging at its sides nosed its way through the barges and tugs and carferries and red whistling ferryboats of New York harbor against a howling icy-bright northwest wind.

Annabelle was grouchy and said it looked horrid, but Ward felt himself full of enthusiasm when a Jewish gentleman in a checked cap pointed out the Battery, the Custom House, the Aquarium, and Trinity Church.

They drove right from the dock to the ferry and ate in the redcarpeted diningroom at the Pennsylvania Station in Jersey City. Ward had fried oysters. The friendly darkey waiter in a white coat was like home. "Home to God's country," Ward said, and decided he'd have to go down to Wilmington and say hello to the folks. Annabelle laughed at him and they sat stiffly in the parlorcar of the Philadelphia train without speaking.

Doctor Strang's affairs were in very bad shape and, as he was busy all day with his practice, Annabelle took them over completely. Her skill in handling finance surprised both Ward and her father. They lived in Doctor Strang's big old house on Spruce Street. Ward, through a friend of Doctor Strang's, got a job on the *Public Ledger* and was rarely home. When he had any spare time he listened to lectures on economics and business at the Drexel Institute. Evenings Annabelle took

220

to going out with a young architect named Joachim Beale who was very rich and owned an automobile. Beale was a thin young man with a taste for majolica and Bourbon whiskey and he called Annabelle "my Cleopatra."

Ward came in one night and found them both drunk sitting with very few clothes on in Annabelle's den in the top of the house. Doctor Strang had gone to a medical conference in Kansas City. Ward stood in the doorway with his arms folded and announced that he was through and would sue for divorce and left the house, slamming the door behind him and

went to the Y.M.C.A. for the night. Next afternoon when he got to the office he found a special delivery letter from Annabelle begging him to be careful what he did, as any publicity would be disastrous to her father's practice, and offering to do anything he suggested. He immediately answered it:

DEAR ANNABELLE:
   I now realize that you have intended all along to use me only as a screen for your disgraceful and unwomanly conduct. I now understand why you prefer the company of foreigners, bohemians, and such to that of ambitious young Americans.

I have no desire to cause you or your father any pain or publicity, but in the first place you must refrain from degrading the name of Moorehouse while you still legally bear it and also I shall feel that when the divorce is satisfactorily arranged, I shall be entitled to some compensation for the loss of time, etc., and the injury to my career that has come through your fault. I am leaving tomorrow for Pittsburgh where I have a position awaiting me and work that I hope will cause me to forget you and the great pain your faithlessness has caused me.

He wondered for a while how to end the letter, and finally wrote

                                                        sincerely JWM

and mailed it.

He lay awake all night in the upper berth in the sleeper for Pittsburgh. Here he was twenty-three years old and he hadn't a college degree and he didn't know any trade and he'd given up the hope of being a songwriter. God damn it, he'd never be valet to any society dame again. The sleeper was stuffy, the pillow kept getting in a knot under his ear, snatches of the sales talk for Bancroft's or Bryant's histories, . . . "Through peach-orchards to the sea . . ." Mr. Hillyard's voice addressing the jury from the depths of the realestate office in Wilmington: "Realestate, sir, is the one safe sure steady conservative investment, impervious to loss by flood and fire; the owner of realestate links himself by indissoluble bonds to the growth of his city or nation . . . improve or not at his leisure and convenience and sit at home in quiet and assurance letting the riches drop into his lap that are produced by the unavoidable and inalienable growth in wealth of a mighty nation . . ." "For a young man with proper connections and if I may say so pleasing manners and a sound classical education," Mr. Oppenheimer had said, "banking should offer a valuable field for the cultivation of the virtues of energy, diplomacy, and perhaps industry. . ." A hand was tugging at his bedclothes.

"Pittsburgh, sah, in forty-five minutes," came the colored porter's voice. Ward pulled on his trousers, noticed with dismay that they were losing their crease, dropped from the berth, stuck his feet in his shoes that were sticky from being hastily polished with inferior polish, and stumbled along the aisle past dishevelled people emerging from their bunks, to the men's washroom. His eyes were glued together and he wanted a bath. The car was unbearably stuffy and the washroom smelt of underwear and of other men's shaving soap.

Through the window he could see black hills powdered with
snow, an occasional coaltipple, rows of gray shacks all alike,
a riverbed scarred with minedumps and slagheaps, purple lacing of trees along the hill's edge cut sharp against a red sun;
then against the hill, bright and red as the sun, a blob of
flame from a smelter. Ward shaved, cleaned his teeth, washed
his face and neck as best he could, parted his hair. His jaw
and cheekbones were getting a square look that he admired.
"Cleancut young executive," he said to himself as he fastened
his collar and tied his necktie. It was Annabelle had taught
him the trick of wearing a necktie the same color as his eyes.
As he thought of her name a faint tactile memory of her lips
troubled him, of the musky perfume she used. He brushed
the thought aside, started to whistle, stopped for fear the
other men dressing might think it peculiar and went and
stood on the platform. The sun was well up now, the hills
were pink and black and the hollows blue where the smoke
of breakfast fires collected. Everything was shacks in rows,
ironworks, coaltipples. Now and then a hill threw a row of
shacks or a group of furnaces up against the sky. Stragglings

of darkfaced men in dark clothes stood in the slush at the crossings. Coalgrimed walls shut out the sky. The train passed through tunnels under crisscrossed bridges, through deep cuttings. "Pittsburgh Union Station," yelled the porter. Ward put a quarter into the colored man's hand, picked out his bag from a lot of other bags, and walked with a brisk firm step down the platform, breathing deep the cold coalsmoky air of the trainshed.

The Camera Eye (17)

the spring you could see Halley's Comet over the elms from the back topfloor windows of the Upper House Mr. Greenleaf said you would have to go to confirmation class and be confirmed when the bishop came and next time you went canoeing you told Skinny that you wouldn't be confirmed because you believed in camping and canoeing and Halley's Comet and the Universe and the sound the rain made on the tent the night you'd both read *The Hound of the Baskervilles* and you'd hung out the steak on a tree and a hound must have smelt it because he kept circling round you and howling something terrible and you were so scared (but you didn't say that, you don't know what you said)

and not in church and Skinny said if you'd never been baptized you couldn't be confirmed and you went and told Mr. Greenleaf and he looked very chilly and said you'd better not go to confirmation class any more and after that you had to go to church Sundays but you could go to either one you liked so sometimes you went to the Congregational and sometimes to the Episcopalian and the Sunday the Bishop came you couldn't see Halley's Comet any more and you saw the others being confirmed and it lasted for hours because there were a lot of little girls being confirmed too and all you could hear was mumble mumble this thy child mumble mumble this thy child and you wondered if you'd be alive next time Halley's Comet came round

Newsreel XIII

I was in front of the national palace when the firing began. I ran across the Plaza with other thousands of scurrying men women and children scores of whom fell in their flight to cover

NEW HIGH MOUNTAINS FOUND

Oh Jim O'Shea was cast away upon an Indian Isle
The natives there they liked his hair
They liked his Irish smile

BEDLAM IN ART

BANDITS AT HOME IN WILDS

Washington considers unfortunate illogical and unnatural the selection of General Huerta as provisional president of Mexico in succession to the overthrown president

THREE FLEE CITY FEAR WEB

He'd put sand in the hotel sugar writer says he came to America an exile and found only sordidness.

LUNG YU FORMER EMPRESS OF CHINA DIES IN THE FORBIDDEN CITY

La cucaracha la cucaracha
Ya no quiere caminar
Porque no tiene

IGNORING OF LOWER CLASSES IN ORGANIZING OF
REPUBLIC MAY CAUSE ANOTHER UPRISING

SIX HUNDRED AMERICANS FLEE CAPITAL

You shall have rings on your fingers
And bells on your toes
Elephants to ride upon
My little Irish rose
So come to your nabob and on next Saint Patrick's day
Be Mrs. Mumbo Jumbo Jijibhoy Jay O'Shea

Eleanor Stoddard

When she was small she hated everything. She hated her father, a stout redhaired man smelling of whiskers and stale pipetobacco. He worked in an office in the stockyards and came home with the stockyards stench on his clothes and told bloody jokes about butchering sheep and steers and hogs and men. Eleanor hated smells and the sight of blood. Nights she used to dream she lived alone with her mother in a big clean white house in Oak Park in winter when there was snow on the ground and she'd been setting a white linen tablecloth with bright white silver and she'd set white flowers and the white meat of chicken before her mother who was a society lady in a dress of white samite, but there'd suddenly be a tiny red speck on the table and it would grow and grow and her mother would make helpless fluttering motions with her hands and she'd try to brush it off but it would grow a spot of blood welling into a bloody blot spreading over the tablecloth and she'd wake up out of the nightmare smelling the stockyards and screaming.

When she was sixteen in highschool she and a girl named Isabelle swore together that if a boy ever touched them they'd kill themselves. But that fall the girl got pneumonia after scarlet fever and died.

The only other person Eleanor liked was Miss Oliphant, her English teacher. Miss Oliphant had been born in England. Her parents had come to Chicago when she was a girl in her teens. She was a great enthusiast for the English language, tried to get her pupils to use the broad "a" and felt that she had a right to some authority in matters pertaining to English literature due to being distantly related to a certain Mrs. Oliphant who'd been an English literary lady in the middle nineteenth century and had written so beautifully about Florence. So she'd occasionally have her more promising pupils, those who seemed the children of nicer parents, to tea in her little flat where she lived all alone with a sleepy blue Persian cat and a bullfinch, and talk to them about Goldsmith and Doctor Johnson's pithy sayings and Keats and *cor cordium* and how terrible it was he died so young and Tennyson and how rude he'd been to women and about how they changed the guard at Whitehall and the grapevine Henry the Eighth planted at Hampton Court and the ill-fated Mary Queen of Scots. Miss Oliphant's parents had been Catholics and had considered the Stuarts the rightful heirs to the British throne, and used to pass their wineglasses over the water

227

pitcher when they drank to the king. All this thrilled the boys and girls very much and particularly Eleanor and Isabelle, and Miss Oliphant used to give them high grades for their compositions and encourage them to read. Eleanor was very fond of her and very attentive in class. Just to hear Miss Oliphant pronounce a phrase like "The Great Monuments of English Prose," or "the Little Princes in the Tower" or "Saint George and Merrie England" made small chills go up and down her spine. When Isabelle died, Miss Oliphant was so lovely about it, had her to tea with her all alone and read her "Lycidas" in a clear crisp voice and told her to read "Adonais" when she got home, but that she couldn't read it to her because she knew she'd break down if she did. Then she talked about her best friend when she'd been a girl who'd been an Irish girl with red hair and a clear warm white skin like Crown Darby, my dear, and how she'd gone to India and died of the fever, and how Miss Oliphant had never thought to survive her grief and how Crown Darby had been invented and the inventor had spent his last penny working on the formula for this wonderful china and had needed some gold as the last ingredient, and they had been starving to death and there had been nothing left but his wife's wedding ring and how they kept the fire in the furnace going with their chairs and tables and at last he had produced his wonderful china that the royal family used exclusively.

It was Miss Oliphant who induced Eleanor to take courses at the Art Institute. She had reproductions on her walls of pictures by Rossetti and Burne-Jones and talked to Eleanor about the pre-Raphaelite Brotherhood. She made her feel that Art was something ivory white and very pure and noble and distant and sad.

When her mother died of pernicious anaemia Eleanor was a thin girl of eighteen, working days in a laceshop in the Loop and studying commercial art evenings at the Art Institute. After the funeral she went home and packed her belongings and moved to Moody House. She hardly ever went to see her father. He sometimes called her up on the phone, but whenever she could she avoided answering. She wanted to forget all about him.

In the laceshop they liked her because she was so refined and gave the place what old Mrs. Lang who owned the store called "an indefinable air of chic," but they only paid her ten dollars a week and five of that went for rent and board. She didn't eat much, but the food was so bad in the dininghall and she hated sitting with the other girls so that sometimes she had to get an extra bottle of milk to drink in her room and some weeks she'd find herself without money to buy pencils and drawingpaper with and would have to go by to see her father and get a couple of dollars from him. He gave it to her gladly enough, but somehow that made her hate him more than ever.

Evenings she used to sit in her little sordid cubbyhole of a room with its ugly bedspread and ugly iron bed, while a sound of hymnsinging came up from the common hall, reading Ruskin and Pater out of the public library. Sometimes she would let the book drop on her knees and sit all evening staring at the dim reddish electriclight bulb that was all the management allowed.

Whenever she asked for a raise Mrs. Lang said, "Why, you'll be marrying soon and leaving me, dear; a girl with your style, indefinable chic can't stay single long, and then you won't need it."

Sundays she usually took the train out to Pullman where her mother's sister had a little house. Aunt Betty was a quiet housewifely little woman who laid all Eleanor's peculiarities to girlish fancies and kept a bright lookout for a suitable young man she could corral as a beau for her. Her husband, Uncle Joe, was foreman in a rolling mill. Many years in the rolling mill had made him completely deaf, but he claimed that actually in the mill he could hear what was said perfectly. If it was summer he spent Sunday hoeing his gardenpatch where he specialized in lettuce and asters. In winter or in bad weather he'd be sitting in the front room reading the *Railroad Man's Magazine*. Aunt Betty would cook an elaborate dinner from recipes out of the *Ladies' Home Journal* and they'd ask Eleanor to arrange the flowers for them on the dinnertable. After dinner Aunt Betty would wash the dishes and Eleanor would wipe them, and while the old people took their nap she would sit in the front room reading the society section of the *Chicago Tribune*. After supper if it was fine the old people would walk down to the station with her and put her on the train, and Aunt Betty would say that it was a shocking shame for a lovely girl like her to be living all alone in the big city. Eleanor would smile a bright bitter smile and say that she wasn't afraid.

The cars going home would be crowded Sunday nights with young men and girls sticky and mussed up and sunburned from an outing in the country or on the dunes. Eleanor hated them and the Italian families with squalling brats that filled the air with a reek of wine and garlic and the Germans redfaced from a long afternoon's beer drinking and the drunk Finn and Swedish workmen who stared at her with a blue alcoholic gleam out of wooden faces. Sometimes a

229

man would try to start something and she'd have to move into another car.

Once, when the car was very crowded, a curlyhaired man rubbed himself up against her suggestively. The crowd was so thick she couldn't pull herself away from him. She could hardly keep from screaming out for help; it was only that she felt it was so vulgar to make a fuss. Uncontrollable dizziness came over her when she finally forced her way out at her station, and she had to stop at a drugstore on the way home for a little aromatic spirits of ammonia. She rushed through the hall of Moody House and up to her room still trembling. She was nauseated and one of the other girls found her being sick in the bathroom and looked at her so queerly. She was very unhappy at times like that and thought of suicide. She had painful cramps during her monthly periods and used to have to stay in bed at least one day every month. Often she felt miserable for a whole week.

One fall day she had phoned Mrs. Lang that she was sick and would have to stay in bed. She went back up to her room and lay down on the bed and read *Romola*. She was reading through the complete works of George Eliot that were in the Moody House library. When the old scrubwoman opened the door to make the bed she said, "Sick . . . I'll clean up, Mrs. Koontz." In the afternoon she got hungry and the sheets were all rumply under her back and although she felt rather ashamed of herself for feeling able to go out when she'd told Mrs. Lang she was too sick to move, she suddenly felt she would suffocate if she stayed in her room another minute. She dressed carefully and went downstairs feeling a little furtive. "So you're not so sick after all," said Mrs. Biggs, the matron, when she passed her in the hall. "I just felt I needed a breath of air." "Too bad about you," she heard Mrs. Biggs say under her breath as she went out the door. Mrs. Biggs was very suspicious of Eleanor because she was an art student.

Feeling a little faint she stopped at a drugstore and had some aromatic spirits of ammonia in water. Then she took a car down to Grant Park. A tremendous northwest wind was blowing grit and papers in whirls along the lakefront.

She went into the Art Institute and up into the Stickney Room to see the Whistlers. She liked the Art Institue better than anything else in Chicago, better than anything else in the world, the quiet, the absence of annoying men, the smooth smell of varnish from the paintings. Except on Sundays when the crowd came and it was horrid. Today there was no one in the Stickney Room but another girl well-dressed in a gray fox neckpiece and a little gray hat with a

feather in it. The other girl was looking fixedly at the portrait of Manet. Eleanor was interested; she rather pretended to look at the Whistlers than look at them. Whenever she could she looked at the other girl. She found herself standing beside the other girl also looking at the portrait of Manet. Suddenly their eyes met. The other girl had palebrown almondshaped eyes rather far apart.

"I think he's the best painter in the world," she said combatively as if she wanted somebody to deny it.

"I think he's a lovely painter," said Eleanor, trying to keep her voice from trembling. "I love that picture."

"You know that's not by Manet himself, that's by Fantin-Latour," said the other girl.

"Oh, yes, of course," said Eleanor.

There was a pause. Eleanor was afraid that would be all but the other girl said, "What other pictures do you like?"

Eleanor looked carefully at the Whistler; then she said slowly, "I like Whistler and Corot."

"I do, too, but I like Millet best. He's so round and warm . . . Have you ever been to Barbizon?"

"No, but I'd love to." There was a pause. "But I think Millet's a little coarse, don't you?" Eleanor ventured.

"You mean that chromo of the Angelus? Yes, I simply loathe and despise religious feeling in a picture, don't you?"

Eleanor didn't quite know what to say to that, so she shook her head and said, "I love Whistler so; when I've been looking at them I can look out of the window and everything looks, you know, pastelly like that."

"I have an idea," said the other girl who had been looking at a little watch she had in her handbag. "I don't have to be home till six. Why don't you come and have tea with me? I know a little place where you can get very good tea, a German pastry shop. I don't have to be home till six and we can have a nice long chat. You won't think it's unconventional of me asking you, will you? I like unconventionality, don't you? Don't you hate Chicago?"

Yes, Eleanor did hate Chicago and conventional people and all that. They went to the pastryshop and drank tea and the girl in gray, whose name was Eveline Hutchins, took hers with lemon in it. Eleanor talked a great deal and made the other girl laugh. Her father, Eleanor found herself explaining, was a painter who lived in Florence and whom she hadn't seen since she was a little girl. There had been a divorce and her mother had married again, a business man connected with Armour and Company, and now her mother was dead and she had only some relatives at Lake Forest; she studied at the Art Institute, but was thinking of giving it up because the teachers didn't suit her. She thought living in Chicago was just too horrible and wanted to go East.

"Why don't you go to Florence and live with your father?" asked Eveline Hutchins.

"Well, I might some day, when my ship comes in," said Eleanor.

"Oh, well, I'll never be rich," said Eveline. "My father's a clergyman . . . Let's go to Florence together, Eleanor, and call on your father. If we arrived there he couldn't very well throw us out."

"I'd love to take a trip some day."

"It's time I was home. By the way, where do you live? Let's meet tomorrow afternoon and look at all the pictures together."

"I'm afraid I'll be busy tomorrow."

"Well, maybe you can come to supper some night. I'll ask mother when I can have you. It's so rare to meet a girl you can talk to. We live on Drexel Boulevard. Here's my card. I'll send you a postcard and you'll promise to come, won't you?"

"I'd love to, if it's not earlier than seven . . . You see I have an occupation that keeps me busy every afternoon except Sunday, and Sundays I usually go out to see my relatives in . . ."

"In Lake Forest?"

"Yes . . . When I'm in town I live at a sort of Y.W.C.A. place, Moody House; it's plebeian but convenient . . . I'll write down the address on this card." The card was of Mrs. Lang's, "Imported Laces and Hand-Embroidered Fabrics." She wrote her address on it, scratched out the other side and handed it to Eveline.

"That's lovely," she said, "I'll drop you a card this very night and you'll promise to come, won't you?"

Eleanor saw her onto the streetcar and started to walk slowly along the street. She had forgotten all about feeling sick, but now that the other girl had gone she felt let down and shabbily dressed and lonely picking her way through the windy evening bustle of the streets.

Eleanor made several friends through Eveline Hutchins. The first time she went to the Hutchinses she was too awed to notice much, but later she felt freer with them, particularly, as she discovered that they all thought her an interesting girl and very refined. There were Doctor and Mrs. Hutchins and two daughters and a son away at college. Doctor Hutchins was a Unitarian minister and very broadminded and Mrs. Hutchins did watercolors of flowers that were declared to show great talent. The elder daughter, Grace, had been at school in the East, at Vassar, and was thought to have shown ability in a literary way, the son was taking postgraduate Greek at Harvard and Eveline was taking the most interesting courses right there at Northwestern. Doctor Hutchins was a softvoiced man with a large smooth pinkish face and large smooth white deadlooking hands. The Hutchinses were all planning to go abroad next year which would be Doctor Hutchins's sabbatical. Eleanor had never heard talk like that before and it thrilled her.

Then one evening Eveline took her to Mrs. Shuster's. "You mustn't say anything about Mrs. Shuster at home, will you?" said Eveline as they were coming down from the Elevated. "Mr. Shuster is an art dealer and my father thinks they're a little too Bohemian . . . It's just because Annie Shuster came to our house one night and smoked all through dinner. . . . I said we'd go to the concert at the Auditorium."

Eleanor had made herself a new dress, a very simple white dress, with a little green on it, not exactly an evening dress, but one she could wear any time, for the occasion, and when

Annie Shuster, a dumpy little red-haired woman with a bouncy manner of walking and talking, helped them off with their wraps in the hall she exclaimed how pretty it was.

"Why, yes, it's lovely," said Eveline. "In fact, you're looking pretty as a peach tonight, Eleanor."

"I bet that dress wasn't made in this town . . . Looks like Paris to me," said Mrs. Shuster.

Eleanor smiled deprecatingly and blushed a little and looked handsomer than ever.

There were a great many people packed into two small

rooms and cigarette smoke and coffeecups and smell of some kind of punch. Mr. Shuster was a whitehaired grayfaced man with a head too large for his body and a tired manner. He talked like an Englishman. There were several young men standing around him; one of them Eleanor had known casually when she had studied at the Art Institute. His name was Eric Egstrom and she had always liked him; he was towhaired and blue-eyed and had a little blond mustache. She could see that Mr. Shuster thought a lot of him. Eveline took her around and introduced her to everybody and asked everybody questions that seemed sometimes disconcerting. Men and women both smoked and talked about books and pictures and about people Eleanor had never heard of. She looked around and didn't say much and noticed the Greek silhouettes on the orange lampshades and the pictures on the walls which looked very odd indeed and the two rows of yellowbacked French books on the shelves and felt that she might learn a great deal there.

They went away early because Eveline had to go by the Auditorium to see what the program at the concert was for fear she might be asked about it, and Eric and another young man took them home. After they'd left Eveline at her house, they asked Eleanor where she lived and she hated to say Moody House because it was in such a horridlooking street, so she made them walk with her to an Elevated station and ran up the steps quickly and wouldn't let them come with her, although it scared her to go home alone as late as it was.

Many of Mrs. Lang's customers thought Eleanor was French, on account of her dark hair, her thin oval face and her transparent skin. In fact, one day when a Mrs. McCormick that Mrs. Lang suspected might be one of "the" McCormicks asked after that lovely French girl who waited on her before, Mrs. Lang got an idea. Eleanor would have to be French from now on; so she bought her twenty tickets at the Berlitz School and said she could have the hour off in the morning between nine and ten if she would go and take French lessons there. So all through December and January Eleanor studied French three times a week, with an old man in a smelly alpaca jacket and began to slip a phrase in now and then as unconcernedly as she could when she was talking to the customers, and when there was anybody in the shop Mrs. Lang always called her "Mademoiselle."

She worked hard and borrowed yellowbacked books from the Shusters to read in the evenings with a dictionary and soon she knew more French than Eveline did who had had a French governess when she was little. One day at the Berlitz School she found she had a new teacher. The old man had pneumonia and she had a young Frenchman instead. He was a thin young man with a sharp blue-shaved chin and large brown eyes with long lashes. Eleanor liked him at once, his thin aristocratic hands and his aloof manner. After half an hour they had forgotten all about the lesson and were talking English. He spoke English with a funny accent but fluently. She particularly liked the throaty way he pronounced "r."

Next time she was all tingling going up the stairs to see if it would be the same young man. It was. He told her that the old man had died. She felt she ought to be sorry but she wasn't. The young man noticed how she felt and screwed his face up into a funny half-laughing, half-crying expression and said, "Vae victis." Then he told her about his home in France and how he hated the conventional bourgeois life there and

235

how he'd come to America because it was the land of youth and the future and skyscrapers and the Twentieth Century Limited and how beautiful he thought Chicago was. Eleanor had never heard anyone talk like that and told him he must have gone through Ireland and kissed the blarney stone. Then he looked very aggrieved and said, "Mademoiselle, c'est la pure vérité," and she said she believed him absolutely and how interesting it was to meet him and how she must introduce him to her friend Eveline Hutchins. Then he went on to tell her how he'd lived in New Orleans and how he'd come as a steward on a French Line boat and how he'd worked as dishwasher and busboy and played the piano in cabarets and worse places than that and how much he loved Negroes and how he was a painter and wanted so much to get a studio and paint but that he hadn't the money yet. Eleanor was a little chilled by the part about dishwashing and cabarets and colored people, but when he said he was interested in art she felt she really would have to introduce him to Eveline and she felt very bold and unconventional when she asked him to meet them at the Art Institute Sunday afternoon. After all if they decided against it they wouldn't have to go.

Eveline was thrilled to death, but they got Eric Egstrom to come along too, on account of Frenchmen having such a bad reputation. The Frenchman was very late and they began to be afraid he wasn't coming or that they'd missed him in the crowd, but at last Eleanor saw him coming up the big staircase. His name was Maurice Millet—no, no relation of the painter's—and he shocked them all very much by refusing to look at any paintings in the Art Institute by saying that he thought it ought to be burned down and used a lot of words like cubism and futurism that Eleanor had never heard before. But she could see at once that he had made a great hit with Eveline and Eric; in fact, they hung on his every word and all through tea neither of them paid any attention to Eleanor. Eveline invited Maurice to the house and they all went to supper to Drexel Boulevard, where Maurice was very polite to Doctor and Mrs. Hutchins, and on to the Shusters' afterwards. They left the Shusters' together and Maurice said that the Shusters were impossible and had very bad paintings on their walls, "Tout ça c'est affreusement pompier," he said. Eleanor was puzzled, but Eveline and Eric said that they understood perfectly that he meant they knew as little about art as a firemen's convention, and they laughed a great deal.

The next time she saw Eveline, Eveline confessed that she was madly in love with Maurice and they both cried a good deal and decided that after all their beautiful friendship could stand even that. It was up in Eveline's room at Drexel Boulevard. On the mantel was a portrait Eveline was trying to do of him in pastels from memory. They sat side by side on the bed, very close, with their arms round each other and talked solemnly about each other and Eleanor told about how she felt about men; Eveline didn't feel quite that way, but nothing could ever break up their beautiful friendship and they'd always tell each other everything.

About that time Eric Egstrom got a job in the interior decorating department at Marshall Field's that paid him fifty a week. He got a fine studio with a northlight in an alley off North Clark Street and Maurice went to live with him there. The girls were there a great deal and they had many friends in and tea in glasses Russian style and sometimes a little Virginia Dare wine, so they didn't have to go to the Shusters' any more. Eleanor was always trying to get in a word alone with Eveline; and the fact that Maurice didn't like Eveline

the way Eveline liked him made Eveline very unhappy, but Maurice and Eric seemed to be thoroughly happy. They slept in the same bed and were always together. Eleanor used to wonder about them sometimes, but it was so nice to know boys who weren't horrid about women. They all went to the opera together and to concerts and art exhibitions—it was Eveline or Eric who usually bought the tickets and paid when they ate in restaurants—and Eleanor had a better time those few months than she'd ever had in her life before. She never went out to Pullman any more and she and Eveline talked about getting a studio together when the Hutchinses came back from their trip abroad. The thought that every day brought June nearer and that then she would lose Eveline and have to face the horrid gritty dusty sweaty Chicago summer alone made Eleanor a little miserable sometimes, but Eric was trying to get her a job in his department at Marshall Field's, and she and Eveline were following a course of lectures on interior decorating at the University evenings, and that gave her something to look forward to.

Maurice painted the loveliest pictures in pale buffs and violets of longfaced boys with big luminous eyes and long lashes, and longfaced girls that looked like boys, and Russian wolfhounds with big luminous eyes, and always in the back there were a few girders or a white skyscraper and a big puff of white clouds and Eveline and Eleanor thought it was such a shame that he had to go on teaching at the Berlitz School.

The day before Eveline sailed for Europe they had a little party at Egstrom's place. Maurice's pictures were around the walls and they were all glad and sorry and excited and tittered a great deal. Then Egstrom came in with the news that he had told his boss about Eleanor and how she knew French and had studied art and was so goodlooking and everything and Mr. Spotmann had said to bring her around at noon tomorrow, and that the job, if she could hold it down, would pay at least twenty-five a week. There had been an old lady in to see Maurice's paintings and she was thinking of buying one; they all felt very gay and drank quite a lot of wine, so that in the end when it was time for goodbyes it was Eveline who felt lonesome at going away from them all, instead of Eleanor feeling lonesome at being left behind as she had expected.

When Eleanor walked back along the platform from seeing the Hutchinses all off for New York the next evening, and their bags all labeled for the steamship *Baltic* and their eyes all bright with the excitement of going East and going abroad and the smell of coalsmoke and the clang of engine bells and scurry of feet, she walked with her fists clenched and her sharppointed nails dug into the palms of her hands, saying to herself over and over again: "I'll be going, too; it's only a question of time; I'll be going, too."

239

The Camera Eye (18)

she was a very fashionable lady and adored bullterriers and had a gentleman friend who was famous for his resemblance to King Edward

she was a very fashionable lady and there were white lilies in the hall No my dear I can't bear the scent of them in the room and the bullterriers bit the trades people and the little newsy No my dear they never bite nice people and they're quite topping with Billy and his friends

we all went coaching in a fourinhand and the man in the back blew a long horn and that's where Dick Whittington stood with his cat and the bells   there were hampers full of luncheon and she had gray eyes and was very kind to her friend's little boy though she loathed simply loathed most children and her gentleman friend who was famous for his resemblance to King Edward couldn't bear them or the bullterriers and she kept asking Why do you call him that?

and you thought of Dick Whittington and the big bells of Bow, three times Lord Mayor of London, and looked into her gray eyes and said Maybe because I called him that the first time I saw him and I didn't like her and I didn't like the bullterriers and I didn't like the fourinhand but I wished Dick Whittington three times Lord Mayor of London boomed the big bells of Bow and I wished Dick Whittington I wished I was home but I hadn't any home and the man in the back blew a long horn

Eleanor Stoddard

Working at Marshall Field's was very different from working at Mrs. Lang's. At Mrs. Lang's she had only one boss, but in the big store she seemed to have everybody in the department over her. Still she was so refined and cold and had such a bright definite little way of talking that, although people didn't like her much, she got along well. Even Mrs. Potter

and Mr. Spotmann, the department heads, were a little afraid of her. News got around that she was a society girl and didn't really have to earn a living at all. She was very sympathetic with the customers about their problems of homemaking and had a little humble-condescending way with Mrs. Potter and admired her clothes, so that at the end of a month Mrs. Potter said to Mr. Spotmann, "I think we have quite a find in the Stoddard girl," and Mr. Spotmann, without opening his white trap of an old woman's mouth, said, "I've thought so all along."

When Eleanor stepped out on Randolph one sunny afternoon with her first week's pay envelope in her hand she felt pretty happy. She had such a sharp little smile on her thin lips that a couple of people turned to look at her as she walked along ducking her head into the gusty wind to keep her hat from being blown off. She turned down Michigan Avenue towards the Auditorium looking at the bright shop windows and the very-pale blue sky and the piles of dovegray fluffy clouds over the lake and the white blobs of steam from the locomotives. She went into the deep amberlit lobby of the Auditorium Annex, sat down all by herself at a wicker table in the corner of the lounge and sat there a long while all by herself drinking a cup of tea and eating buttered toast, ordering the waiter about with a crisp little refined monied voice.

Then she went to Moody House, packed her things and moved to the Eleanor Club, where she got a room for seven-fifty with board. But the room wasn't much better and everything still had the gray smell of a charitable institution, so the next week she moved again to a small residential hotel on the Northside where she got room and board for fifteen a week. As that only left her a balance of three-fifty—it had turned out that the job only paid twenty, which actually only meant eighteen-fifty when insurance was taken off—she had to go to see her father again. She so impressed him with her rise in the world and the chances of a raise that he promised her five a week, although he was only making twenty himself and was planning to marry again, to a Mrs. O'Toole, a widow with five children who kept a boardinghouse out Elsdon Way.

Eleanor refused to go to see her future stepmother, and made her father promise to send her the money in a money-order each week, as he couldn't expect her to go all the way out to Elsdon to get it. When she left him she kissed him on the forehead and made him feel quite happy. All the time she was telling herself that this was the very last time.

Then she went back to the Hotel Ivanhoe and went up to her room and lay on her back on the comfortable brass bed looking round at her little room with its white woodwork and its pale yellow wallpaper with darker satiny stripes and the lace curtains in the window and the heavy hangings. There was a crack in the plaster of the ceiling and the carpet was worn, but the hotel was very refined, she could see that, full of old couples living on small incomes and the help were very elderly and polite and she felt at home for the first time in her life.

When Eveline Hutchins came back from Europe the next spring wearing a broad hat with a plume on it, full of talk of the Salon des Tuileries and the Rue de la Paix and museums and art exhibitions and the opera, she found Eleanor a changed girl. She looked older than she was, dressed quietly and fashionably, had a new bitter sharp way of talking. She was thoroughly established in the interior decorating department at Marshall Field's and expected a raise any day, but she wouldn't talk about it. She had given up going to classes or haunting the Art Institute and spent a great deal of time with an old maiden lady who also lived at the Ivanhoe who was reputed to be very rich and very stingy, a Miss Eliza Perkins.

The first Sunday she was back, Eleanor had Eveline to tea at the hotel and they sat in the stuffy lounge talking in refined whispers with the old lady. Eveline asked about Eric and Maurice, and Eleanor supposed that they were all right, but hadn't seen them much since Eric had lost his job at Marshall Field's. He wasn't turning out so well as she had hoped, she said. He and Maurice had taken to drinking a great deal and going round with questionable companions, and Eleanor rarely got a chance to see them. She had dinner every evening with Miss Perkins and Miss Perkins thought a great deal of her and bought her clothes and took her with her driving in the park and sometimes to the theater when there was something really worth while on, Minnie Maddern Fiske or Guy Bates Post in an interesting play. Miss Perkins was the daughter of a wealthy saloonkeeper and had been played false in her youth by a young lawyer whom she had trusted to invest some money for her and whom she had fallen in love with. He had run away with another girl and a number of cash certificates. Just how much she had left Eleanor hadn't been able to find out, but as she always took the best seats at the theater and liked going to dinner at expensive hotels and restaurants and hired a carriage by the half-day whenever she wanted one, she gathered that she must still be well off.

After they had left Miss Perkins to go to the Hutchinses for supper, Eveline said: "Well, I declare—I don't see what you see in that . . . that little old maid . . . And here I was just bursting to tell you a million things and to ask you a million questions . . . I think it was mean of you."

"I'm very devoted to her, Eveline. I thought you'd be interested in meeting any dear friend of mine."

"Oh, of course I am, dear, but, gracious, I can't make you out."

"Well, you won't have to see her again, though I could tell by her manner that she thought you were lovely."

Walking from the Elevated station to the Hutchinses it was more like old times again. Eleanor told about the hard feelings that were growing between Mr. Spotmann and Mrs. Potter and how they both wanted her to be on their side, and made Eveline laugh, and Eveline confessed that on the *Kroonlan* coming back she had fallen very much in love with a man from Salt Lake City, such a relief after all those foreigners, and Eleanor teased her about it and said he was probably a Mormon and Eveline laughed and said, No, he was a judge, and admitted that he was married already. "You see," said Eleanor, "of course he's a Mormon." But Eveline said that she knew he wasn't and that if he'd divorce his wife she'd marry him in a minute. Then Eleanor said she didn't believe in divorce and if they hadn't gotten to the door they would have started quarrelling.

That winter she didn't see much of Eveline. Eveline had many beaux and went out a great deal to parties and Eleanor used to read about her on the society page Sunday mornings.

244

She was very busy and often too tired at night even to go to the theater with Miss Perkins. The row between Mrs. Potter and Mr. Spotmann had come to a head and the management had moved Mrs. Potter to another department and she had let herself plunk into an old Spanish chair and had broken down and cried right in front of the customers and Eleanor had had to take her to the dressingroom and borrow smelling salts for her and help her do up her peroxide hair into the big pompadour again and consoled her by saying that she would probably like it much better over in the other building anyway. After that Mr. Spotmann was very goodnatured for several months. He occasionally took Eleanor out to lunch with him and they had a little joke that they laughed about together about Mrs. Potter's pompadour wobbling when she'd cried in front of the customers. He sent Eleanor out on many little errands to wealthy homes, and the customers liked her because she was so refined and sympathetic and the other employees in the department hated her and nicknamed her "teacher's pet." Mr. Spotmann even said that he'd try to get her a percentage on commissions and talked often about giving her that raise to twentyfive a week.

Then one day Eleanor got home late to supper and the old clerk at the hotel told her that Miss Perkins had been stricken with heartfailure while eating steak and kidney pie for lunch and had died right in the hotel diningroom and that the body had been removed to the Irving Funeral Chapel and asked her if she knew any of her relatives that should be notified. Eleanor knew nothing except that her financial business was handled by the Corn Exchange Bank and that she thought that she had nieces in Mound City, but didn't know their names. The clerk was very worried about who would pay for the removal of the body and the doctor and a week's unpaid hotel bill and said that all her things would be held under seal until some qualified person appeared to claim them. He seemed to think Miss Perkins had died especially to spite the hotel management.

Eleanor went up to her room and locked the door and threw herself on the bed and cried a little, because she'd been fond of Miss Perkins.

Then a thought crept into her mind that made her heart beat fast. Suppose Miss Perkins had left her a fortune in her will. Things like that happened. Young men who opened church pews, coachmen who picked up a handbag; old ladies were always leaving their fortunes to people like that. She could see it in headlines—

MARSHALL FIELD EMPLOYEE INHERITS MILLION

She couldn't sleep all night and in the morning she found the manager of the hotel and offered to do anything she could. She called up Mr. Spotmann and coaxed him to give her the day off, explaining that she was virtually prostrated by Miss Perkins's death. Then she called up the Corn Exchange Bank and talked to a Mr. Smith who had been in charge of the Perkins estate. He assured her that the bank would do everything in its power to protect the heirs and the residuary legatees and said that the will was in Miss Perkins's safe-deposit box and that he was sure everything was in proper legal form.

Eleanor had nothing to do all day, so she got hold of Eveline for lunch and afterwards they went to Keith's together. She felt it wasn't just proper to go to the theater with her old friend still lying at the undertaker's, but she was so nervous and hysterical she had to do something to take her mind off this horrible shock. Eveline was very sympathetic and they felt closer than they had since the Hutchinses had gone abroad. Eleanor didn't say anything about her hopes.

At the funeral there were only Eleanor and the Irish chambermaid at the hotel, an old woman who sniffled and crossed herself a great deal, and Mr. Smith and a Mr. Sullivan who was representing the Mound City relatives. Eleanor wore black and the undertaker came up to her and said, "Excuse me, miss, but I can't refrain from remarking how lovely you look, just like a Bermuda lily." It wasn't as bad as she had expected and afterwards Eleanor and Mr. Smith and Mr. Sullivan, the representative of the law firm who had charge of the interests of the relatives, were quite jolly together coming out of the crematorium.

It was a sparkling October day and everybody agreed that October was the best month in the year and that the minister had read the funeral service very beautifully. Mr. Smith asked Eleanor wouldn't she eat lunch with them as she was mentioned in the will, and Eleanor's heart almost stopped beating and she cast down her eyes and said she'd be very pleased.

They all got into a taxi. Mr. Sullivan said it was pleasant to roll away from the funeral chapel and such gloomy thoughts. They went to lunch at de Yonghe's and Eleanor made them laugh telling them about how they'd acted at the hotel and what a scurry everybody had been in, but when they handed her the menu said that she couldn't eat a thing. Still when she saw the planked whitefish she said that she'd take just a little to pick to pieces on her plate. It turned out that the windy October air had made them all hungry and the long ride in the taxi. Eleanor enjoyed her lunch very much and after the whitefish she ate a little Waldorf salad and then a peach melba.

The gentlemen asked her whether she would mind if they smoked cigars and Mr. Smith put on a rakish look and said would she have a cigarette and she blushed and said no, she never smoked and Mr. Sullivan said he'd never respect a woman who smoked and Mr. Smith said some of the girls of the best families in Chicago smoked and as for himself he didn't see the harm in it if they didn't make chimneys of themselves. After lunch they walked across the street and went up in the elevator to Mr. Sullivan's office and there they sat down in big leather chairs and Mr. Sullivan and Mr. Smith put on solemn faces and Mr. Smith cleared his throat and began to read the will. Eleanor couldn't make it out at first and Mr. Smith had to explain to her that the bulk of the fortune of three million dollars was left to the Florence Crittenton home for wayward girls, but that the sum of one thousand dollars each was to the three nieces in Mound City and that a handsome diamond brooch in the form of a locomotive was left to Eleanor Stoddard and, "If you call at the Corn Exchange Bank some time tomorrow, Miss Stoddard," said Mr. Smith, "I shall be very glad to deliver it to you."

Eleanor burst out crying.

They both were very sympathetic and so touched that Miss Stoddard should be so touched by the remembrance of her old friend. As she left the office, promising to call for the brooch tomorrow, Mr. Sullivan was just saying in the friendliest voice, "Mr. Smith, you understand that I shall have to endeavor to break that will in the interests of the Mound City Perkinses," and Mr. Smith said in the friendliest voice, "I suppose so, Mr. Sullivan, but I don't see that you can get very far with it. It's an ironclad, copper-riveted document if I do say so as shouldn't, because I drew it up myself."

So the next day at eight Eleanor was on her way down to Marshall Field's again and there she stayed for several years. She got the raise and the percentages on commissions and she and Mr. Spotmann got to be quite thick, but he never tried to make love to her and their relations were always formal; that was a relief to Eleanor because she kept hearing stories about floorwalkers and department heads forcing their attentions on the young girl employees and Mr. Elwood of the furniture department had been discharged for that very reason, when it came out that little Lizzie Dukes was going to have a baby, but perhaps that hadn't been all Mr. Elwood's fault as Lizzie Dukes didn't look as if she was any better than she should be; anyway, it seemed to Eleanor as if she'd spend the rest of her life furnishing other people's new drawingrooms and diningrooms, matching curtains and samples of upholstery and wallpaper, smoothing down indignant women customers who'd been sent an Oriental china dog instead of an inlaid teak teatable or who even after they'd chosen it themselves weren't satisfied with the pattern on that cretonne.

She found Eveline Hutchins waiting for her one evening when the store closed. Eveline wasn't crying but was deathly pale. She said she hadn't had anything to eat for two days and wouldn't Eleanor have some tea with her over at the Sherman House or anywhere.

They went to the Auditorium Annex and sat in the lounge and ordered tea and cinnamon toast and then Eveline told her that she'd broken off her engagement with Dirk McArthur and that she'd decided not to kill herself but to go to work. "I'll never fall in love with anybody again, that's all, but I've got to do something and you're just wasting yourself in that stuffy department store, Eleanor; you know you never get a chance to show what you can do; you're just wasting your ability."

Eleanor said that she hated it like poison, but what was she to do? "Why not do what we've been talking about all these years . . . Oh, people make me so mad, they never will have any nerve or do anything that's fun or interesting . . . I bet you if we started a decorating business we'd have lots of orders. Sally Emerson'll give us her new house to decorate and then everybody else'll just have to have us to be in the swim . . . I don't think people really want to live in the horrible stuffy places they live in; it's just that they don't know any better."

Eleanor lifted her teacup and drank several little sips. She looked at her little white carefully manicured hand with pointed nails holding the teacup. Then she said, "But where'd we get the capital? We'd have to have a little capital to start on."

"Dad'll let us have something, I think, and maybe Sally Emerson might; she's an awfully good sport and then our first commission'll launch us . . . Oh, do come on, Eleanor, it'll be such fun."

" 'Hutchins and Stoddard, Interior Decorating,' " said Eleanor, putting down her teacup, "or maybe 'Miss Hutchins and Miss Stoddard'; why, my dear, I think it's a grand idea!"

"Don't you think just 'Eleanor Stoddard and Eveline Hutchins' would be better?"

"Oh, well, we can decide on the name when we hire a studio and have it put in the telephone book. Why don't we put it this way, Eveline dear . . . if you can get your friend Mrs. Emerson to give us the decorating of her new house, we'll go in for it, if not we'll wait until we have a genuine order to start off on."

"All right; I know she will. I'll run right out and see her now." Eveline had a high color now. She got to her feet and leaned over Eleanor and kissed her. "Oh, Eleanor, you're a darling."

"Wait a minute, we haven't paid for our tea," said Eleanor.

The next month the office was unbearable, and the customers' complaints and leaving the Ivanhoe in a hurry every morning and being polite to Mr. Spotmann and thinking up little jokes to make him laugh. Her room at the Ivanhoe seemed small and sordid and the smell of cooking that came up through the window and the greasesmell of the old elevator. Several days she called up that she was sick and then found that she couldn't stay in her room and roamed about the city going to shops and movingpicture shows and then getting suddenly dead tired and having to come home in a taxi that she couldn't afford. She even went back to the Art Institute once in a while, but she knew all the pictures by heart and hadn't the patience to look at them any more. Then at last Eveline got Mrs. Philip Paine Emerson to feeling that her new house couldn't do without a novel note in the diningroom and they got her up an estimate much less than any of the established decorators was asking, and Eleanor had the pleasure of watching Mr. Spotmann's astonished face when she refused to stay even with a raise to forty a week and said that she had a commission with a friend to decorate the new Paine Emerson mansion in Lake Forest.

"Well, my dear," said Mr. Spotmann, snapping his square white mouth, "if you want to commit suicide of your career I won't be the one to stop you. You can leave right this minute if you want to. Of course you forfeit the Christmas bonus."

Eleanor's heart beat fast. She looked at the gray light that came through the office, and the yellow cardcatalogue case and the letters on a file and the little samples dangling from them. In the outer office Ella Bowen the stenographer had stopped typing; she was probably listening. Eleanor sniffed the lifeless air that smelt of chintz and furniturevarnish and steamheat and people's breath and then she said, "All right, Mr. Spotmann, I will."

It took her all day to get her pay and to collect the insurance money due her and she had a long wrangle with a cashier about the amount, so that it was late afternoon before she stepped out into the driving snow of the streets and went into a drugstore to call up Eveline.

Eveline had already rented two floors of an old Victorian house off Chicago Avenue, and they were busy all winter decorating the office and showrooms downstairs and the apartment upstairs where they were going to live, and doing Sally Emerson's diningroom. They got a colored maid named Amelia who was a very good cook although she drank a little, and they had cigarettes and cocktails at the end of the afternoon and little dinners with wine, and found a downattheheels French dressmaker to make them evening gowns to wear when they went out with Sally Emerson and her set, and rode in taxis and got to know a lot of really interesting people. By spring when they finally got a check for five hundred dollars out of Philip Paine Emerson they were a thousand dollars in the hole but they were living the way they liked. The diningroom was considered a little extreme, but some people liked it, and a few more orders came. They made many friends and started going round with artists again and with special writers on the *Daily News* and the *American*, who took them out to dinner in foreign restaurants that were very smoky and where they talked a great deal about modern French painting and the Middle West and going to New York. They went to the Armory Show and had a photograph of Brancusi's Golden Bird over the desk in the office and copies of the *Little Review* and *Poetry* among the files of letters from clients and unpaid bills from wholesalers.

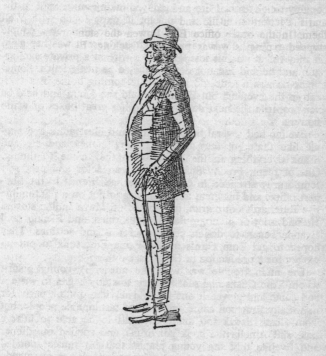

Eleanor went out a great deal with Tom Custis, who was an elderly redfaced man, fond of music, and chorusgirls and drinking, who belonged to all the clubs and for years had been a great admirer of Mary Garden. He had a box at the opera and a Stevens-Duryea and nothing to do except go to tailors and visit specialists and occasionally blackball a Jew or a newcomer applying for membership in some club he belonged to. The Armours had bought out his father's meatpacking concern when he was still a college athlete and he hadn't done a stroke of work since. He claimed to be thoroughly sick of social life and enjoyed taking an interest in the girls' decorating business. He kept in close touch with Wall Street and would occasionally turn over to Eleanor a couple of shares that he was trading in. If they rose it was her gain, if they fell it was his loss. He had a wife in a private sanitarium and he and Eleanor decided they'd be just friends. Sometimes he was a little too affectionate coming home in a taxicab in the evening, but Eleanor would scold him and he'd be very contrite the next day, and send her great boxes of white flowers.

Eveline had several beaux, writers and illustrators and people like that, but they never had any money and ate and drank everything in the house when they came to dinner. One of them, Freddy Seargeant, was an actor and producer temporarily stranded in Chicago. He had friends in the Shubert office, and his great ambition was to put on a pantomime like Reinhardt's *Sumurun*, only based on Maya Indian stories. He had a lot of photographs of Maya ruins, and Eleanor and Eveline began to design costumes for it and settings. They hoped to get Tom Custis or the Paine Emersons to put up money for a production in Chicago.

The main trouble was with the music. A young pianist whom Tom Custis had sent to Paris to study began to write it and came and played it one night. They had quite a party for him. Sally Emerson came and a lot of fashionable people, but Tom Custis drank too many cocktails to be able to hear a note and Amelia the cook got drunk and spoiled the dinner and Eveline told the young pianist that his music sounded like movie music and he went off in a huff. When everybody had gone, Freddy Seargeant and Eveline and Eleanor roamed around the ravaged apartment feeling very bad indeed. Freddy Seargeant twisted his black hair, slightly splotched with gray, in his long hands and said he was going to kill himself, and Eleanor and Eveline quarrelled violently.

"But it did sound like movingpicture music and, after all, why shouldn't it?" Eveline kept saying. Then Freddy Seargeant got his hat and went out saying, "You women are mak-

ing life a hell for me," and Eveline burst out crying and got
hysterical and Eleanor had to send for a doctor.

The next day they scraped up fifty dollars to send Freddy
back to New York, and Eveline went back to live at the
house on Drexel Boulevard, leaving Eleanor to carry on the
decorating business all alone.

Next spring Eleanor and Eveline sold for five hundred

some chandeliers that they had picked up in a junk shop on
the west side for twenty-five dollars and were just writing out
checks for their more pressing debts when a telegram arrived.

SIGNED CONTRACT WITH SHUBERTS PRODUCTION RETURN
OF THE NATIVE   WILL YOU DO SCENERY COSTUMES HUN-
DRED FIFTY A WEEK EACH   MUST COME ON NEW YORK
IMMEDIATELY   MUST HAVE YOU   WIRE IMMEDIATELY
HOTEL DES ARTISTES CENTRAL PARK SOUTH   FREDDY

"Eleanor, we've got to do it," said Eveline, taking a ciga-

253

rette out of her handbag and walking round the room puffing at it furiously. "It'll be a rush, but let's make the Twentieth Century this afternoon." "It's about noon now," said Eleanor in a trembly voice. Without answering Eveline went to the phone and called up the Pullman office. That evening they sat in their section looking out of the window at the steelworks of Indiana Harbor, the big cement works belching puttycolored smoke, the flaring furnaces of Gary disappearing in smokeswirling winter dusk. Neither of them could say anything.

The Camera Eye (19)

the methodist minister's wife was a tall thin woman who sang little songs at the piano in a spindly lost voice who'd heard you liked books and grew flowers and vegetables and was so interested because she'd once been an episcopalian and loved beautiful things and had had stories she had written published in a magazine and she was younger than her husband who was a silent blackhaired man with a mouth like a mousetrap and tobaccojuice on his chin and she wore thin white dresses and used perfume and talked in a bell-like voice about how things were lovely as a lily and the moon was bright as a bubble full to bursting behind the big pine when we walked back along the shore and you felt you ought to put your arm round her and kiss her only you didn't want to and anyway you wouldn't have had the nerve walking slow through the sand and the pine needles under the big moon swelled to bursting like an enormous drop of quicksilver and she talked awful sad about the things she had hoped for and you thought it was too bad

you liked books and Gibbon's *Decline and Fall of the Roman Empire* and Captain Marryat's novels and wanted to go away and to sea and to foreign cities Carcassonne Marakesh Isfahan and liked things to be beautiful and wished you had the nerve to hug and kiss Martha the colored girl they said was half Indian old Emma's daughter and little redheaded Mary I taught how to swim if I only had the nerve breathless nights when the moon was full but Oh God not lilies

Newsreel XIV

BOMBARDIER STOPS AUSTRALIAN

colonel says Democrats have brought distress to nation
I'll resign when I die Huerta snarls in grim defi and half
Mexico will die with me   no flames were seen but the
vast plume of blackened steam from the crater waved a
mile high in the sky and volcanic ash fell on Macomber
Flats thirteen miles distant
    Eggs noisy? No Pokerchips.

> *Way down on the levee*
> *In old Alabamy*
> *There's daddy and mammy*
> *And Ephram and Sammy*

MOONFAIRIES DANCE ON RAVINIA GREENS

WILSON WILL TAKE ADVICE OF BUSINESS

admits he threw bomb   policewoman buys drinks
after one loses on wheat   slain as burglar

> *On a moonlight night*
> *You can find them all*
> *While they are waiting*
> *Banjoes are syncopating*
> *What's that they're all saying*
> *What's that they're all singing*

recognizing James scrawl the president seized the

cracker and pulled out the fuse. A stream of golden gum-drops fell over the desk; then glancing at the paper the Chief Executive read, "Don't eat too many of them because Mamma says they'll make you sick if you do."

RIDING SEAWOLF IN MEXICAN WATERS

They all keep aswaying
  Ahumming and swinging
It's the good ship Robert E. Lee
  That's come to carry the cotton away

ISADORA DUNCAN'S NEW HAPPINESS

I.W.W. troublemakers overran a Garibaldi birthday celebration at Rosebank Staten Island this afternoon, insulted the Italian flag, pummeled and clubbed members of the Italian Rifle Society and would have thrown the American flag to the dirt if

SIX UNCLAD BATHING GIRLS BLACK
EYES OF HORRID MAN

Indian divers search for drowned boy's body. Some of the witnesses say they saw a woman in the crowd. She was hit with a brick. The man in gray took refuge behind her skirts to fire. The upper decks and secluded parts of the boat are the spooners' paradise where liberties are often taken with intoxicated young girls whose mothers should not have permitted them to go on a public boat unescorted.

MIDWEST MAY MAKE OR BREAK WILSON

TELL CAUSES OF UNREST IN LABOR WORLD

"I'm a Swiss admiral proceeding to America," and the copper called a taxi

See them shuffling along
  Hear their music and song
It's simply great, mate,
  Waiting on the levee

Waiting
for
  the
    Robert
      E.
        Lee.

Emperor of the Caribbean

When Minor C. Keith died all the newspapers carried his picture, a brighteyed man with a hawknose and a respectable bay window, and an uneasy look under the eyes.

Minor C. Keith was a rich man's son, born in a family that liked the smell of money, they could smell money halfway round the globe in that family.

His Uncle was Henry Meiggs, the Don Enrique of the West Coast. His father had a big lumber business and handled realestate in Brooklyn;

young Keith was a chip of the old block.

(Back in fortynine Don Enrique had been drawn to San Francisco by the gold rush. He didn't go prospecting in the hills, he didn't die of thirst sifting alkalidust in Death Valley. He sold outfits to the other guys. He stayed in San Francisco and played politics and high finance until he got in too deep and had to get aboard ship in a hurry.

The vessel took him to Chile. He could smell money in Chile.

He was the capitalista yanqui. He'd build the railroad from Santiago to Valparaiso. There were guano deposits on the Chincha Islands. Meiggs could smell money in guano. He dug himself a fortune out of guano, became a power on the West Coast, juggled figures, railroads, armies, the politics of the local caciques and politicos: they were all chips in a huge pokergame. Behind a big hand he heaped up the dollars.

He financed the unbelievable Andean railroads.

When Thomas Guardia got to be dictator of Costa Rica he wrote to Don Enrique to build him a railroad;

Meiggs was busy in the Andes, a $75,000 dollar contract was hardly worth his while,

so he sent for his nephew Minor Keith.

They didn't let grass grow under their feet in that family.

257

at sixteen Minor Keith had been on his own, selling collars and ties in a clothingstore.

After that he was a lumber surveyor and ran a lumber business.

When his father bought Padre Island off Corpus Christi, Texas, he sent Minor down to make money out of it.

Minor Keith started raising cattle on Padre Island and seining for fish,

but cattle and fish didn't turn over money fast enough

so he bought hogs and chopped up the steers and boiled the meat and fed it to the hogs and chopped up the fish and fed it to the hogs,

but hogs didn't turn over money fast enough

so he was glad to be off to Limon.

Limon was one of the worst pestholes on the Caribbean, even the Indians died there of malaria, yellowjack, dysentery.

Keith went back up to New Orleans on the steamer *John G. Meiggs* to hire workers to build the railroad. He offered a dollar a day and grub and hired seven hundred men. Some of them had been down before in the filibustering days of William Walker.

Of that bunch about twentyfive came out alive.

The rest left their whiskey-scalded carcasses to rot in the swamps.

On another load he shipped down fifteen hundred; they all died to prove that only Jamaica Negroes could live in Limon.

Minor Keith didn't die.

In 1882 there were twenty miles of railroad built and Keith was a million dollars in the hole;

the railroad had nothing to haul.

Keith made them plant bananas so that the railroad might have something to haul, to market the bananas he had to go into the shipping business;

this was the beginning of the Caribbean fruittrade.

All the while the workers died of whiskey, malaria, yellowjack, dysentery.

Minor Keith's three brothers died.

Minor Keith didn't die.

He built railroads, opened retail stores up and down the coast in Bluefields, Belize, Limon, bought and sold rubber, vanilla, tortoiseshell, sarsaparilla, anything he could buy cheap he bought, anything he could sell dear he sold.

In 1918 in co-operation with the Boston Fruit Company he

formed the United Fruit Company that has since become one of the most powerful industrial units in the world.

In 1912 he incorporated the International Railroads of Central America;

all of it built out of bananas;

in Europe and the United States people had started to eat bananas,

so they cut down the jungles through Central America to plant bananas,

and built railroads to haul the bananas,

and every year more steamboats of the Great White Fleet steamed north loaded with bananas,

and that is the history of the American empire in the Caribbean,

and the Panama Canal and the future Nicaragua Canal and the marines and the battleships and the bayonets.

Why that uneasy look under the eyes, in the picture of Minor C. Keith the pioneer of the fruit trade, the railroad-builder, in all the pictures the newspapers carried of him when he died?

The Camera Eye (20)

when the streetcarmen went out on strike in Lawrence in sympathy with what the hell they were a lot of wops anyway bohunks hunkies that didn't wash their necks ate garlic with squalling brats and fat oily wives the damn dagoes they put up a notice for volunteers good clean young

to man the streetcars and show the foreign agitators this was still a white man's

well this fellow lived in Matthews and he'd always wanted to be a streetcar conductor they said Mr. Grover had been a streetcar conductor in Albany and drank and was seen on the street with floosies

well this fellow lived in Matthews and he went over to Lawrence with his roommate and they reported in Lawrence and people yelled at them Blacklegs Scabs but those that weren't wops were muckers a low element they liked each other a lot this fellow did and his roommate and he got up on the platform and twirled the bright brass handle and clanged the bell

it was in the carbarn his roommate was fiddling with something between the bumpers and this fellow twirled the shiny brass handle and the car started and he ran down his roommate and his head was mashed just like that between the bumpers killed him dead just like that right there in the carbarn and now the fellow's got to face his roommate's folks

J. Ward Moorehouse

In Pittsburgh Ward Moorehouse got a job as a reporter on the *Times Dispatch* and spent six months writing up Italian weddings, local conventions of Elks, obscure deaths, murders and suicides among Lithuanians, Albanians, Croats, Poles, the difficulties over naturalization papers of Greek restaurant keepers, dinners of the Sons of Italy. He lived in a big red frame house, at the lower end of Highland Avenue, kept by a Mrs. Cook, a crotchety old woman from Belfast who had been forced to take lodgers since her husband, who had been a foreman in one of the Homestead mills, had been crushed by a crane dropping a load of pigiron over him. She made Ward his breakfasts and his Sunday dinners and stood over him while he was eating them alone in the stuffy furniture-crowded diningroom telling him about her youth in the north of Ireland and the treachery of papists and the virtues of the defunct Mr. Cook.

It was a bad time for Ward. He had no friends in Pittsburgh and he had colds and sore throats all through the cold grimy sleety winter. He hated the newspaper office and the inclines and the overcast skies and the breakneck wooden stairs he was always scrambling up and down, and the smell of poverty and cabbage and children and washing in the rattletrap tenements where he was always seeking out Mrs. Piretti whose husband had been killed in a rumpus in a saloon on Locust Street or Sam Burkovich who'd been elected president of the Ukrainian singing society, or some woman with sudsy hands whose child had been slashed by a degenerate. He never got home to the house before three or four in the morning and by the time he had breakfast round noon there never seemed to be any time to do anything before he had to call up the office for assignments again. When he had first gotten to Pittsburgh he had called to see Mr. McGill, whom he'd met with Jarvis Oppenheimer in Paris. Mr. McGill remembered him and took down his address and told him to keep in touch because he hoped to find an opening for him in the new information bureau that was being organized by the Chamber of Commerce, but the weeks went by and he got no word from Mr. McGill. He got an occasional dry note from Annabelle Marie about legal technicalities; she would divorce him charging nonsupport, desertion and cruelty. All he had to do was to refuse to go to Philadelphia when the papers were served on him. The perfume on the blue notepaper raised a faint rancor of desire for women in him. But he must keep himself clean and think of his career.

The worst time was his weekly day off. Often he'd stay all day sprawled on the bed, too depressed to go out into the black slush of the streets. He sent to correspondence schools for courses in journalism and advertising and even for a

course in the care of fruit trees on the impulse to throw up everything and go West and get a job on a ranch or something; but he felt too listless to follow them and the little booklets accumulated week by week on the table in his room. Nothing seemed to be leading anywhere. He'd go over and over again his whole course of action since he'd left Wilmington that day on the train to go down to Ocean City. He must have made a mistake somewhere but he couldn't see where. He took to playing solitaire, but he couldn't even keep his mind on that. He'd forget the cards and sit at the table with a gingerbreadcolored velveteen cloth on it, looking past the spot of dusty artificial ferns ornamented with a crepe paper cover and a dusty pink bow off a candybox, down into the broad street where trolleycars went by continually scraping round the curve and where the arclights coming on in the midafternoon murk shimmered a little in the black ice of the gutters. He thought a lot about the old days at Wilmington and Marie O'Higgins and his piano lessons and fishing in an old skiff along the Delaware when he'd been a kid; he'd get so nervous that he'd have to go out and would go and drink a hot chocolate at the sodafountain on the next corner and then go downtown to a cheap movie or vaudeville show. He took to smoking three stogies a day, one after each meal. It gave him something he could vaguely look forward to.

He called once or twice to see Mr. McGill at his office in the Frick Building. Each time he was away on a business trip. He'd have a little chat with the girl at the desk while waiting and then go away reluctantly, saying, "Oh, yes, he said he was going on a trip," or, "He must have forgotten the appointment," to cover his embarrassment when he had to go away. He was loath to leave the brightly lit office anteroom, with its great shiny mahogany chairs with lions' heads on the arms and the tables with lions' claws for feet and the chirrup of typewriters from behind partitions, and telephone bells ringing and welldressed clerks and executives bustling in and out. Down at the newspaper office it was noisy with clanging presses and smelt sour of printer's ink and moist rolls of paper and sweating copyboys running round in green eyeshades. And not to know any really nice people, never to get an assignment that wasn't connected with working people or foreigners or criminals; he hated it.

One day in the spring he went to the Schenley to interview a visiting travel lecturer. He felt good about it as he hoped to wheedle a by-line out of the city editor. He was picking his way through the lobby crowded by the arrival of a state convention of Kiwanians when he ran into Mr. McGill.

"Why, hello, Moorehouse," said Mr. McGill, in a casual tone as if he'd been seeing him all along. "I'm glad I ran into you. Those fools at the office mislaid your address. Have you a minute to spare?"

"Yes, indeed, Mr. McGill," said Ward. "I have an appointment to see a man, but he can wait."

"Never make a man wait if you have an appointment with him," said Mr. McGill.

"Well, this isn't a business appointment," said Ward, looking up into Mr. McGill's face with his boyish blue-eyed smile. "He won't mind waiting a minute."

They went into the writing room and sat down on a tapestried sofa. Mr. McGill explained that he had just been appointed temporary general manager to reorganize the Bessemer Metallic Furnishings and Products Company that handled a big line of byproducts of the Homestead Mills. He was looking for an ambitious and energetic man to handle the advertising and promotion.

"I remember that booklet you showed me in Paris, Moorehouse, and I think you're the man."

Ward looked at the floor. "Of course that would mean giving up my present work."

"What's that?"

"Newspaper work."

"Oh, drop that; there's no future in that . . . We'd have to make someone else nominal advertising manager for reasons we won't go into now . . . but you'll be the actual executive. What kind of a salary would you expect?"

Ward looked Mr. McGill in the eyes, the blood stopped in his ears while he heard his own voice saying casually: "How about a hundred a week?"

Mr. McGill stroked his mustache and smiled. "Well, we'll thrash that out later," he said, getting to his feet. "I think I can advise you strongly to give up your present work . . . I'll call up Mr. Bateman about it . . . so that he'll understand why we're taking you away from him . . . No hard feelings, you understand, on account of your resigning suddenly . . . never want hard feelings . . . Come down and see me tomorrow at ten. You know the office in the Frick Building."

"I think I've got some valuable ideas about advertising, Mr. McGill. It's the work I'm most interested in doing," said Ward.

Mr. McGill wasn't looking at him any more. He nodded and went off. Ward went on up to interview his lecturer, afraid to let himself feel too jubilant yet.

The next day was his last in a newspaper office. He accepted a salary of seventyfive with a promise of a raise as soon as returns warranted it, took a room and bath at the Schenley, had an office of his own in the Frick Building where he sat at a desk with a young man named Oliver Taylor who was a nephew of one of the directors who was being worked up through the organization. Oliver Taylor was a firstrate tennis player and belonged to all the clubs and was only too glad to let Moorehouse do the work. When he found that Moorehouse had been abroad and had had his clothes made in England, he put him up at the Sewickley Country Club and took him out with him for drinks after officehours. Little by little Moorehouse got to know people and to be invited out as

an eligible bachelor. He started to play golf with an instructor on a small course over in Allegheny where he hoped nobody he knew would go. When he could play a fair game he went over to Sewickley to try it out.

One Sunday afternoon Oliver Taylor went with him and pointed out all the big executives of the steel mills and the mining properties and the oil industry out on the links on a Sunday afternoon, making ribald remarks about each one that Ward tittered at a little bit, but that seemed to him in very bad taste. It was a sunny May afternoon and he could smell locustblossoms on the breeze off the fat lands along the Ohio, and there were the sharp whang of the golfballs and the flutter of bright dresses on the lawn round the clubhouse, and frazzles of laughter and baritone snatches of the safe talk of business men coming on the sunny breeze that still had a little scorch of furnace smoke in it. It was hard to keep the men he was introduced to from seeing how good he felt.

The rest of the time he did nothing but work. He got his stenographer, Miss Rodgers, a plainfaced spinster who knew the metal products business inside out from having worked fifteen years in Pittsburgh offices, to get him books on the industry that he read at his hotel in the evenings, so that at executive conferences he astonished them by his knowledge of the processes and products of industry. His mind was full of augerbits, canthooks, mauls, sashweights, axes, hatchets, monkeywrenches; sometimes in the lunch hour he'd stop in to a hardware store on the pretext of buying a few brads or tacks and talk to the storekeeper. He read *Crowds Junior* and various books on psychology, tried to imagine himself a hardware merchant or the executive of Hammacher Schlemmer or some other big hardware house, and puzzled over what kind of literature from a factory would be appealing to him. Shaving while his bath was running in the morning, he would see long processions of andirons, grates, furnace fittings, pumps, sausagegrinders, drills, calipers, vises, casters, drawerpulls pass between his face and the mirror and wonder how they could be made attractive to the retail trade. He was shaving himself with a Gillette; why was he shaving with a Gillette instead of some other kind of razor? "Bessemer" was a good name, smelt of money and mighty rolling mills and great executives stepping out of limousines. The thing to do was to interest the hardware buyer, to make him feel a part of something mighty and strong, he would think as he picked out a necktie. "Bessemer," he'd say to himself as he ate breakfast. Why should our cotterpins appeal more than any other cotterpins, he'd ask himself as he stepped on the streetcar. Jolting in the straphanging crowd on the way downtown, staring at the headlines in the paper without seeing them, chainlinks and anchors and ironcouplings and malleable elbows and unions and bushings and nipples and pipecaps would jostle in his head. "Bessemer."

When he asked for a raise he got it, to a hundred and twentyfive dollars.

At a country club dance he met a blond girl who danced very well. Her name was Gertrude Staple and she was the only daughter of old Horace Staple who was director of several corporations, and was reputed to own a big slice of Standard Oil stock. Gertrude was engaged to Oliver Taylor, though they did nothing but quarrel when they were together, so she confided to Ward while they were sitting out a dance. Ward's dress-suit fitted well and he looked much younger than most of the men at the dance. Gertrude said that the men in Pittsburgh had no allure. Ward talked about Paris and she said that she was bored to tears and would rather live in Nome, Alaska, than in Pittsburgh. She was awfully pleased that he knew Paris and he talked about the Tour d'Argent and the Hotel Wagram and the Ritz Bar and he felt very sore that he hadn't a car, because he noticed that she was making it easy for him to ask her to let him take her home. But next day he sent her some flowers with a little note in French that he thought would make her laugh. The next Saturday afternoon he went to an automobile school to take lessons in driving a car, and strolled past the Stutz sales agency to see what kind of terms he could get to buy a roadster on.

One day Oliver Taylor came into the office with a funny smile on his face and said, "Ward, Gertrude's got a crush on you. She can't talk about anything else . . . Go ahead; I don't give a damn. She's too goddam much trouble for me to handle. She tires me out in a half an hour."

"It's probably just because she doesn't know me," said Ward, blushing a little.

"Too bad her old man won't let her marry anything but a millionaire. You might get some lovin' out of it, though."

"I haven't got the time for that stuff," said Ward.

"It don't leave me time for anything else," said Taylor. "Well, so long . . . You hold down the fort; I've got a luncheon date with a swell girl . . . she's a warm baby an' she's dancing in the *Red Mill*, first row, third from the left." He winked, and slapped Ward on the back and went off.

The next time that Ward went to call at the big house of the Staples that lay back from the trees, he went in a red

Stutz roadster that he'd taken out on trial. He handled it well
enough, although he turned in too quickly at the drive and
slaughtered some tulips in a flowerbed. Gertrude saw him
from the library window and kidded him about it. He said he
was a rotten driver, always had been and always would be.
She gave him tea and a cocktail at a little table under an apple-
tree back of the house and he wondered all the time he was
talking to her whether he ought to tell her about his divorce.
He told her about his unhappy life with Annabelle Strang.
She was very sympathetic. She knew of Doctor Strang. "And
I was hoping you were just an adventurer . . . from plowboy
to president, you know . . . that sort of thing."

"But I am," he said, and they both laughed and he could
see that she was really crazy about him.

That night they met at a dance and walked down to the
end of the conservatory where it was very steamy among the
orchids, and he kissed her and told her that she looked like a
pale yellow orchid. After that they always sneaked off whenever they got a chance. She had a way of going limp suddenly in his arms under his kisses that made him sure that

she loved him. But when he got home after those evenings, he'd be too nervous and excited to sleep, and would pace up and down the room wanting a woman to sleep with, and cursing himself out. Often he'd take a cold bath and tell himself he must attend to business and not worry about those things or let a girl get under his skin that way. The streets in the lower part of town were full of prostitutes, but he was afraid of catching a disease or being blackmailed. Then one night after a party Taylor took him to a house that he said was thoroughly reliable where he met a pretty dark Polish girl who couldn't have been more than eighteen, but he didn't go there very often, as it cost fifty dollars, and he was always nervous when he was in the place for fear there'd be a police raid and he'd have blackmail to pay.

One Sunday afternoon Gertrude told him that her mother had scolded her for being seen about with him so much on account of his having a wife in Philadelphia. The notice of the decree had come the morning before. Ward was in high spirits and told her about it and asked her to marry him. They were at the free organ recital in Carnegie Institute, a good place to meet because nobody who was anybody ever went there. "Come over to the Schenley and I'll show you the decree." The music had started. She shook her head, but patted his hand that lay on the plush seat beside her knee. They went out in the middle of the number. The music got on their nerves. They stood talking a long while in the vestibule. Gertrude looked miserable and haggard. She said she was in wretched health and that her father and mother would never consent to her marrying a man who didn't have as much income as she did and she wished she was a poor stenographer or telephone girl that could do as she liked and that she loved him very much and would always love him and thought she'd take to drink or dope or something because life was just too terrible.

Ward was very cold and kept his jaw set square and said that she couldn't really care for him and that as far as he was concerned that was the end and that if they met they'd be good friends. He drove her out Highland Avenue in the Stutz that wasn't paid for yet and showed her the house he'd lived in when he first came to Pittsburgh and talked of going out West and starting an advertising business of his own and finally left her at a friend's house in Highland Park where she'd told her chauffeur to pick her up at six.

He went back to the Schenley and had a cup of black coffee sent up to his room and felt very bitter and settled down to work on some copy he was getting out, saying, "To hell with the bitch," all the time under his breath.

He didn't worry much about Gertrude in the months that followed because a strike came on at Homestead and there were strikers killed by the mine guards and certain writers from New York and Chicago who were sentimentalists began to take a good deal of space in the press with articles flaying the steel industry and the feudal conditions in Pittsburgh as they called them, and the Progressives in Congress were making a howl, and it was rumored that people wanting to make politics out of it were calling for a congressional investigation. Mr. McGill and Ward had dinner together all alone at the Schenley to talk about the situation, and Ward said that what was necessary was an entirely new line in the publicity of the industry. It was the business of the industry to educate the public by carefully planned publicity extending over a term of years. Mr. McGill was very much impressed and said he'd talk around at directors' meetings about the feasibility of founding a joint information bureau for the entire industry. Ward said he felt he ought to be at the head of it, because he was just wasting his time at the Bessemer Products; that had all simmered down to a routine job that anybody could take care of. He talked of going to Chicago and starting an advertising agency of his own. Mr. McGill smiled and stroked his steelgray mustache and said, "Not so fast, young man; you stay around here a while yet and on my honor you won't regret it," and Ward said that he was willing, but here he'd been in Pittsburgh five years and where was he getting?

The information bureau was founded, and Ward was put in charge of the actual work at ten thousand dollars a year and began to play stocks a little with his surplus money, but there were several men over him earning higher salaries who didn't do anything but get in his way, and he was very restless. He felt he ought to be married and have an establishment of his own. He had many contacts in different branches of the casting and steel and oil industries, and felt he ought to entertain. Giving dinners at the Fort Pitt or the Schenley was expensive and somehow didn't seem solid.

Then one morning he opened his newspaper to find that Horace Staple had died of angina pectoris the day before while going up in the elevator of the Carnegie Building, and that Gertrude and her mother were prostrated at their palatial residence in Sewickley. He immediately sat down in the writingroom, although it would make him late at the office, and wrote Gertrude a note:

> DEAREST GERTRUDE:
> In this terrible moment of grief, allow me to remind you that I think of you constantly. Let me know at once if I can be of any use to you in any way. In the valley of the shadow of death we must realize that the Great Giver to whom we owe all love and wealth and all affection around the jocund fireside is also the Grim Reaper . . .

After staring at the words, chewing the end of the pen a minute, he decided that it was a bit thick about the Grim Reaper and copied the note out again leaving out the last sentence, signed it "Your Devoted Ward," and sent it out to Sewickley by special messenger.

At noon he was just leaving for lunch when the office boy told him there was a lady on his phone. It was Gertrude. Her voice was trembly, but she didn't seem too terribly upset. She begged him to take her out to dinner that night somewhere where they wouldn't be seen because the house and everything gave her the creeps and that she'd go mad if she heard any more condolences. He told her to meet him in the lobby of the Fort Pitt and he'd run her out to some little place where they could be quiet and talk.

That evening there was an icy driving wind. The sky had been leaden all day with inky clouds driving out of the northwest. She was so muffled up in furs that he didn't recognize her when she came into the lobby. She held out her hand to him and said, "Let's get out of here," as soon as she came up to him. He said he knew a little roadhouse on the way to McKeesport, but thought the drive would be too cold for her in his open roadster. She said, "Let's go; do let's . . . I love a blizzard." When she got into the car she said in a trembling voice, "Glad to see your old flame, Ward?" and he said, "God, Gertrude, I am; but are you glad to see me?" And then she said, "Don't I look glad?" Then he started to mumble something about her father, but she said, "Please let's not talk about that."

The wind was howling behind them all the way up the Monongahela Valley, with occasional lashing flurries of snow. Tipples and bessemer furnaces and tall ranks of chimneys stood out inky black against a low woolly sky that caught all the glare of flaming metal and red slag and the white of arcs and of locomotive headlights. At one crossing they almost ran into a train of coalcars. Her hand tightened on his arm when the car skidded as he put on the brakes.

"That was a narrow squeak," he said through clenched teeth.

"I don't care. I don't care about anything tonight," she said.

He had to get out to crank the car as he had stalled the motor. "It'll be all right if we don't freeze to death," he said. When he'd clambered back into the car, she leaned over and kissed him on the cheek. "Do you still want to marry me? I love you, Ward." The motor raced as he turned and kissed her hard on the mouth the way he'd kissed Annabelle that day in the cottage at Ocean City. "Of course I do, dear," he said.

The roadhouse was kept by a French couple, and Ward talked French to them and ordered a chicken dinner and red wine and hot whiskey toddies to warm them up while they were waiting. There was no one else in the roadhouse and he had a table placed right in front of the gaslogs at the end of a pink and yellow diningroom, dimly lit, a long ghostly series of empty tables and long windows blocked with snow. Through dinner he told Gertrude about his plans to form an agency of his own and said he was only waiting to find a suitable partner and he was sure that he could make it the biggest in the country, especially with this new unexploited angle of the relations between capital and labor. "Why, I'll be able to help you a lot with capital and advice and all sorts of things, once we're married," she said, looking at him with flushed cheeks and sparkling eyes. "Of course you can, Gertrude."

She drank a great deal during dinner and wanted more hot

whiskies afterwards, and he kissed her a great deal and ran
his hand up her leg. She didn't seem to care what she did and
kissed him right in front of the roadhouse keeper. When they
went out to get in the car to go home, the wind was blowing
sixty miles an hour and the snow had blotted out the road

and Ward said it would be suicide to try to drive to Pittsburgh a night like that and the roadhouse keeper said that he
had a room all ready for them and that monsieur et madame
would be mad to start out, particularly as they'd have the
wind in their faces all the way. At that Gertrude had a moment of panic and said she'd rather kill herself than stay.
Then she suddenly crumpled up in Ward's arms sobbing hys-
terically, "I want to stay, I want to stay, I love you so."

They called up the Staple house and talked to the night-
nurse who said that Mrs. Staple was resting more easily, that
she'd been given an opiate and was sleeping quietly as a

child, and Gertrude told her that when her mother woke to tell her she was spending the night with her friend Jane English and that she'd be home as soon as the blizzard let them get a car on the road. Then she called up Jane English and told her that she was distracted with grief and had taken a room at the Fort Pitt to be alone. And if her mother called to tell her she was asleep. Then they called up the Fort Pitt and reserved a room in her name. Then they went up to bed. Ward was very happy and decided he loved her very much and she seemed to have done this sort of thing before because the first thing she said was: "We don't want to make this a shotgun wedding, do we, darling?"

Six months later they were married, and Ward resigned his position with the information bureau. He'd had a streak of luck on the Street and decided to take a year off for a honeymoon in Europe. It turned out that the Staple fortune was all left to Mrs. Staple in trust and that Gertrude would only have an annuity of fifteen thousand dollars until her mother died, but they were planning to meet the old lady at Carlsbad and hoped to coax some capital out of her for the new adver-

tising agency. They sailed in the bridal suite on the *Deutschland* to Plymouth and had a fine passage and Ward was only seasick one day.

The Camera Eye (21)

that August it never rained a drop and it had hardly rained in July   the truck garden was in a terrible state and all through the Northern Neck of Virginia it was no use pulling cornfodder because the lower leaves were all withered and curled up at the edges   only the tomatoes gave a crop.

when they weren't using Rattler on the farm you'd ride him (he was a gelding sorrel threeyearold and stumbled) through the tall woods of white pine and the sandbed roads on fire with trumpetvine and through swamps dry and cracked crisscross like alligator hide

past the Morris's house where all the Morris children looked dry and dusty and brown.

and round along the rivershore past Harmony Hall where Sydnor a big sixfoot-six barefoot man with a long face and a long nose with a big wart on his nose 'ud be ashamblin' around and not knowin' what to do on account of the drought and his wife sick and ready to have another baby and the children with hoopin' cough and his stomach trouble

and past Sandy Pint agin past the big pine

and Miss Emily 'ud be alookin' over the fence astandin' beside the crapemyrtle (Miss Emily wore poke bonnets and always had a few flowers and a couple of broilers for sale and the best blood in the South flowed in her veins Tancheford that's how we spell it but we pronounce it Tofford if only the boys warnt so noaccount always drinkin' an' carryin' on down by the rivershoa an' runnin' whiskey over from Mar'land instead o' fishin' an' agoin' out blind drunk and gettin' the trapnets cut up or lost   Miss Emily took a drop herself now and then but she always put a good face on things lookin' over the picket fence astandin' by the crapemyrtle bush visitin' with the people passin' along the road)

then down to Lynch's Pint where old Bowie Franklin was (he warn't much account neither looked like a bantam rooster Bowie Franklin did with his long scrawny neck an' his ruptured walk couldn't do much work and he didn't have money to spend on liquor so he just fed his gray fowls that warn't much account and looked just like Bowie did and hung round the wharf and sometimes when the boat was in or there were some fisherman in the crick on account of it blowin' so hard down the bay somebody'd slip him a drink o' whiskey an' he'd be a whole day asleepin' it off)

Rattler sweat somethin' awful on account o' bein' fed corn in this hot weather and the old saddle stank and the horsedoctors buzzed round his flanks and it was time for supper and you'd ride slowly home hating the goddamn exhausted land and the drought that wouldn't let the garden grow and the katydids and the dryflies jeering out of the sapling gums and persimmons ghostly with dust along the road and the sickleshaped beach where the seanettles stung you when you tried to swim out and the chiggers and the little scraps of talk about what was going on up to the Hague or Warsaw or Pekatone and the phone down at the cottage that kept ringing whenever any farmer's wife along the line took up the receiver to talk to any other farmer's wife and all down the line you could hear the receivers click as they all ran to the receiver to listen to what was said

and the land between the rivers was flat drained of all strength by tobacco in the early Walter Raleigh Captain John Smith Pocahontas days but what was it before the war that drained out the men and women?

and I rode Rattler the threeyearold sorrel gelding who stumbled so much and I hated the suncaked hardpans and the clay subsoil and the soughing pines and the noaccount gums and persimmonbushes and the brambles.

there was only the bay you could like sparkling to the horizon and the southeast wind that freshened every afternoon and the white sails of bugeyes

Newsreel XV

lights go out as "Home Sweet Home" is played to patrons low wages cause unrest, woman says

There's a girl in the heart of Maryland
With a heart that belongs to me

WANT BIG WAR OR NONE

the mannequin who is such a feature of the Paris racecourse surpasses herself in the launching of novelties. She will put on the most amazing costume and carry it with perfect sangfroid. Inconsistency is her watchword.

Three German staff officers who passed nearby were nearly mobbed by enthusiastic people who insisted on shaking their hands

GIRL STEPS ON MATCH; DRESS IGNITED; DIES

And Mary-land
Was fairy-land
When she said that mine she'd be

DANUBE SHOTS SIGNAL FOR EARLY STRIFE

I'm against capital punishment as are all levelminded women. I hate to think any woman would attend a hanging. It is a terrible thing for the state to commit murder

CZAR LOSES PATIENCE WITH AUSTRIA

panic in exodus from Carlsbad   disappearance of Major reveals long series of assassinations   décolleté in broad daylight lingerie frocks that by no possible means could be associated with the tub What shall be worn next? Paris cries choirboys go camping professor to tour woods Belgrade Falls

GENERAL WAR NEAR

ASSASSIN SLAYS DEPUTY JAURES

LIVES TWO HOURS AFTER HE'S DEAD

I lost a friend and a pal when Garros gave up his life but I expect to lose more friends in the profession before this war is over

LOST TRUNKS SHOW UP IN LONDON

conventions of one sort or another are inevitably side-stepped or trod upon during the languid or restful days of summer, and because of the relaxation just now there are several members of the younger set whose debutante days lie in the distance of two or even three seasons hence enjoying the glory of

BLACK POPE ALSO DEAD

large quantities of Virginia tobacco to be imported to England especially for the use of British troops on the continent

> *There's a girl in the heart of Maryland*
> *With a heart that belongs to me*

Prince of Peace

Andrew Carnegie
was born in Dunfermline in Scotland,
came over to the States in an immigrant
ship worked as bobbinboy in a textile factory
fired boilers
clerked in a bobbin factory at $2.50 a week

ran round Philadelphia with telegrams as a Western Union messenger
learned the Morse code was telegraph operator on the Pennsy lines
was a military telegraph operator in the Civil War and

always saved his pay;
whenever he had a dollar he invested it.
Andrew Carnegie started out buying Adams Express and Pullman stock when they were in a slump;
he had confidence in railroads,
he had confidence in communications,
he had confidence in transportation,
he believed in iron.
Andrew Carnegie believed in iron, built bridges Bessemer plants blast furnaces rolling mills;
Andrew Carnegie believed in oil;
Andrew Carnegie believed in steel;
always saved his money
whenever he had a million dollars he invested it.
Andrew Carnegie became the richest man in the world
and died.
Bessemer Duquesne Rankin Pittsburgh Bethlehem Gary
Andrew Carnegie gave millions for peace
and libraries and scientific institutes and endowments and thrift
whenever he made a billion dollars he endowed an institution to promote universal peace
always
except in time of war.

The Camera Eye (22)

all week the fog clung to the sea and the cliffs at noon there was just enough warmth of the sun through the fog to keep the salt cod drying on the flakes   gray flakes green sea gray houses white fog   at noon there was just enough sun to ripen bakeapple and wildpear on the moorlands to warm the bayberry and sweetfern mealtimes in the boardinghouse everybody waited for the radio operators   the radio operators could hardly eat   yes it was war

Will we go in? will Britain go in?

*Obligations according to the treaty of . . . handed the
ambassador his passports*   every morning they put out
the cod on the flakes spreading them even in the faint glow
of the sun through the fog

a steamer blowing in the distance the lap of the waves
against piles along the seaweedy rocks scream of gulls
clatter of boardinghouse dishes

*War declared expedit . . . Big battle in the North Sea
German Fleet Destroyed* BRITISH FLEET DESTROYED
GERMAN SQUADRON OFF CAPE RACE *loyal Newfoundland-
ers to the colors Port closed at St. Johns Port aux
Basques*

and every evening they brought in the cod off the
flakes clatter of boardinghouse dishes and everybody
waiting for the radio operators

lap of the waves against the piles of the wharf, scream
of gulls circling and swooping white in the white fog a
steamer blowing in the distance and every morning they
spread out the cod on the flakes

J. Ward Moorehouse

When Ward came back from his second honeymoon
abroad he was thirtytwo, but he looked older. He had the
capital and the connections and felt that the big moment had
come. The war talk in July had decided him to cut short his
trip. In London he'd picked up a young man named Edgar
Robbins who was in Europe for International News. Edgar
Robbins drank too much and was a fool about the women,
but Ward and Gertrude took him around with them everywhere and confided in each other that they wanted to
straighten him out. Then one day Robbins took Ward aside
and said that he had syphilis and would have to follow the
straight and narrow. Ward thought the matter over a little
and offered him a job in the New York office that he was
going to open as soon as he got home. They told Gertrude it
was liver trouble and she scolded him like a child when he
took a drink and on the boat back to America they felt he
was completely devoted to both of them. Ward didn't have to
write any copy after that and could put in all his time organizing the business. Old Mrs. Staple had been induced to put
fifty thousand dollars into the firm. Ward rented an office at

100 Fifth Avenue, fitted it up with Chinese porcelain vases and cloisonné ashtrays from Vantine's and had a tigerskin rug in his private office. He served tea in the English style every afternoon and put himself in the telephone book as J. Ward Moorehouse, Public Relations Counsel. While Robbins was drafting the literature to be sent out, Ward went to Pittsburgh and Chicago and Bethelehem and Philadelphia to reestablish contacts.

In Philadelphia he was walking into the lobby of the Bellevue Stratford when he met Annabelle Marie. She greeted him amiably and said she'd heard of him and his publicity business and they had dinner together, talking about old times.

"You certainly have improved," Annabelle Marie kept saying. Ward could see that she regretted the divorce a little, but he felt he couldn't say the same for her. The lines on her face had deepened and she didn't finish her sentences, and had a parrot screech to her voice. She was tremendously made up and he wondered if she took drugs. She was busy divorcing Beale who she said had turned homosexual on her. Ward said dryly that he had married again and was very happy. "Who wouldn't be with the Staple fortune back of them?" she said. Her little air of ownership irritated Ward and he excused himself right after dinner, saying he had work to do. Annabelle looked at him through halfclosed eyes with her head to one side, said "I wish you luck," and went up in the hotel elevator in a shrill cackle of laughter.

Next day he took the Pennsylvania to Chicago, traveling in a drawing room. Miss Rosenthal, his secretary, and Morton, his English valet, went with him. He had his dinner in the drawingroom with Miss Rosenthal, a sallowfaced girl, shrewd and plain, who he felt was devoted to his interests. She had been with him in Pittsburgh with Bessemer Products. When the coffee had been cleared away and Morton had poured them each out a swallow of brandy that Miss Rosenthal giggled over a great deal declaring it would go to her head, he started to dictate. The train rumbled and lurched and now and then he could smell coalsmoke and the hot steamygreasy

body of the engine up ahead, hot shiny steel charging through the dark Appalachians. He had to talk loudly to be heard. The rumble of the train made the cords of his voice vibrate. He forgot everything in his own words . . . American industry like a steamengine, like a highpower locomotive on a great express train charging through the night of old individualistic methods. . . . What does a steamengine require? Co-operation, co-ordination of the inventor's brain, the promoter's brain that made the development of these highpower products possible . . . Co-ordination of capital, the storedup energy of the race in the form of credit intelligently directed . . . labor, the prosperous contented American working man to whom the unprecedented possibilities of capital collected in great corporations had given the full dinnerpail, cheap motor transport, insurance, short working hours . . . a measure of comfort and prosperity unequaled before or since in the tragic procession of recorded history or in the known regions of the habitable globe.

But he had to stop dictating because he found he'd lost his voice. He sent Miss Rosenthal to bed and went to bed himself, but he couldn't sleep; words, ideas, plans, stock quotations kept unrolling in endless tickertape in his head.

Next afternoon at the LaSalle he had a call from Judge Bowie C. Planet. Ward sat waiting for him to come up, looking out at the very pale blue Lake Michigan sky. In his hand he had a little filing card on which was written:

Planet, Bowie C . . . Tennessee Judge, married Elsie Wilson Denver; small copper lead interests. . . . Anaconda? unlucky oil speculator . . . member one-horse lawfirm Planet and Wilson, Springfield, Illinois.

"All right, Miss Rosenthal," he said when there was a knock at the door. She went off into the other room with the filing card.

Morton opened the door to let in a roundfaced man with a black felt hat and a cigar.

"Hello, Judge," Ward said, getting to his feet and holding out his hand. "How's everything? Won't you sit down?"

Judge Planet advanced slowly into the room. He had a curious rolling gait as if his feet hurt him. They shook hands, and Judge Planet found himself sitting facing the steelbright light that came through the big windows back of Moorehouse's desk.

"Won't you have a cup of tea, sir?" asked Morton, who advanced slowly with a tray glittering with silver teathings. The judge was so surprised that he let the long ash that he'd been carrying on his cigar to prove to himself he was sober drop off on his bulging vest. The judge's face remained round

282

and bland. It was the face of a mucker from which all the lines of muckerdom had been carefully massaged away. The judge found himself sipping a cup of lukewarm tea with milk in it.

"Clears the head, clears the head," said Ward, whose cup was cooling untasted before him.

Judge Planet puffed silently on his cigar.

"Well, sir," he said, "I'm very glad to see you."

At that moment Morton announced Mr. Barrow, a skinny man with popeyes and a big adamsapple above a stringy necktie. He had a nervous manner of speaking and smoked too many cigarettes. He had the look of being stained with nicotine all over, face, fingers, teeth yellow.

On Ward's desk there was another little filing card that read:

Barrow, G. H., labor connections, reformer type. Once sec. Bro. locomotive engineers; unreliable.

As he got to his feet, he turned the card over. After he'd shaken hands with Mr. Barrow, placed him facing the light and encumbered him with a cup of tea, he began to talk.

"Capital and labor," he began in a slow careful voice as if dictating, "as you must have noticed, gentlemen, in the course of your varied and useful careers, capital and labor, those two great forces of our national life neither of which can exist without the other are growing further and further apart; any cursory glance at the newspapers will tell you that. Well, it has occurred to me that one reason for this unfortunate state of affairs has been the lack of any private agency that might fairly present the situation to the public. The lack of properly distributed information is the cause of most of the misunderstandings in this world . . . The great leaders of American capital, as you probably realize, Mr. Barrow, are firm believers in fairplay and democracy and are only too anxious to give the worker his share of the proceeds of industry if they can only see their way to do so in fairness to the public and the investor. After all, the public is the investor whom we all aim to serve."

"Sometimes," said Mr. Barrow, "but hardly . . ."

"Perhaps you gentlemen would have a whiskey and soda." Morton stood sleekhaired between them with a tray on which were decanters, tall glasses full of ice and some open splits of Apollinaris.

"I don't mind if I do," said Judge Planet.

Morton padded out, leaving them each with a clinking glass. Outside the sky was beginning to glow with evening a little. The air was wine-colored in the room. The glasses made things chattier. The judge chewed on the end of a fresh cigar.

"Now, let's see if I'm getting you right, Mr. Moorehouse. You feel that with your connections with advertising and big business you want to open up a new field in the shape of an agency to peaceably and in a friendly fashion settle labor disputes. Just how would you go about it?"

"I am sure that organized labor would co-operate in such a movement," said G. H. Barrow, leaning forward on the edge of his chair. "If only they could be sure that . . . well, that . . ."

"That they weren't getting the wool pulled over their eyes," said the judge, laughing.

"Exactly."

"Well, gentlemen, I'm going to put my cards right down on

the table. The great motto upon which I have built up my business has always been co-operation."

"I certainly agree with you there," said the judge, laughing again and slapping his knee. "The difficult question is how to bring about that happy state."

"Well, the first step is to establish contact . . . Right at this moment under our very eyes we see friendly contact being established."

"I must admit," said G. H. Barrow with an uneasy laugh, "I never expected to be drinking a highball with a member of the firm of Planet and Wilson."

The judge slapped his fat thigh. "You mean on account of the Colorado trouble . . . ? You needn't be afraid. I won't eat you, Mr. Barrow . . . But frankly, Mr. Moorehouse, this doesn't seem to me to be just the time to launch your little project."

"This war in Europe . . ." began G. H. Barrow.

"Is America's great opportunity . . . You know the proverb about when thieves fall out . . . Just at present I admit we find ourselves in a moment of doubt and despair, but as soon as American business recovers from the first shock and begins to pull itself together . . . Why, gentlemen, I just came back from Europe; my wife and I sailed the day Great Britain declared war . . . I can tell you it was a narrow squeak . . . Of one thing I can assure you with comparative certainty, whoever wins, Europe will be economically ruined. This war is America's great opportunity. The very fact of our neutrality . . ."

"I don't see who will be benefited outside of the munitions-makers," said G. H. Barrow.

Ward talked a long time, and then looked at his watch, that lay on the desk before him, and got to his feet. "Gentlemen, I'm afraid you'll have to excuse me. I have just time to dress for dinner." Morton was already standing beside the desk with their hats. It had gotten dark in the room. "Lights, please, Morton," snapped Ward.

As they went out Judge Planet said, "Well, it's been a very pleasant chat, Mr. Moorehouse, but I'm afraid your schemes are a little idealistic."

"I've rarely heard a businessman speak with such sympathy and understanding of the labor situation," said G. H. Barrow.

"I only voice the sentiments of my clients," said Ward as he bowed them out.

Next day he spoke at a Rotary Club luncheon on "Labor Troubles: A Way Out." He sat at a long table in the big hotel banquet hall full of smells of food and cigarettes, and scurrying waiters. He spread the food a little round his plate with a fork, answering when he was spoken to, joking a little with Judge Planet, who sat opposite him, trying to formulate sentences out of the haze of phrases in his mind. At last it was time for him to get to his feet. He stood at the end of the long table with a cigar in his hand, looking at the two rows of heavyjowled faces turned towards him.

"When I was a boy down along the Delaware . . ." He stopped. A tremendous clatter of dishes was coming from behind the swinging doors through which waiters were still scuttling with trays. The man who had gone to the door to make them keep quiet came stealthily back. You could hear his shoes creak across the parquet floor. Men leaned forward along the table. Ward started off again. He was going on now; he hardly knew what he was saying, but he had raised a laugh out of them. The tension relaxed. "American business has been slow to take advantage of the possibilities of modern publicity . . . education of the public and employers and employees, all equally servants of the public . . . Co-operation . . . stockownership giving the employee an interest in the industry . . . avoiding the grave dangers of socialism and demagoguery and worse . . . It is in such a situation that the public relations counsel can step in in a quiet manly way and say, Look here, men, let's talk this over eye to eye . . . But his main importance is in times of industrial peace . . . when two men are sore and just about to hit one another is no time to preach public service to them . . . The time for an educational campaign and an oral crusade that will drive home to the rank and file of the mighty Colossus of American uptodate industry is right now, today."

There was a great deal of clapping. He sat down and sought out Judge Planet's face with his blue-eyed smile. Judge Planet looked impressed.

Newsreel XVI

The Philadelphian had completed the thirteenth lap and was two miles away on the fourteenth. His speed it is thought must have been between a hundred and a hundred and ten miles an hour. His car wavered for a flash and then careered to the left. It struck a slight elevation and jumped. When the car alighted it was on four wheels atop of a high embankment. Its rush apparently was unimpeded. Wishart turned the car off the embankment and attempted to regain the road. The speed would not permit the slight turn necessary, however, and the car plowed through the frontyard of a farmer residing on the course. He escaped one tree but was brought up sideways against another. The legs being impeded by the steering gear they were torn from the trunk as he was thrown through

> *I want to go*
> *To Mexico*
> *Under the Stars and Stripes to fight the foe*

SNAPS CAMERA; ENDS LIFE

gay little chairs and tables stand forlornly on the sidewalk for there are few people feeling rich enough to take even a small drink.

PLUMBER HAS HUNDRED LOVES

BRINGS MONKEYS HOME

missing rector located losses in U.S. crop report let baby go naked if you want it to be healthy if this mystery is ever solved you will find a woman at the bottom of the mystery said Patrolman E. B. Garfinkle events leading up to the present war run continuously back to the French Revolution

they seemed to stagger like drunken men suddenly hit between the eyes after which they made a run for us shouting some outlandish cry we could not make out

> *And the ladies of the harem*
> *Knew exactly how to wear 'em*
> *In Oriental Baghdad long ago.*

The Camera Eye (23)

this friend of mother's was a very lovely woman with lovely blond hair and she had two lovely daughters   the blond one married an oil man who was bald as the palm of your hand and went to live in Sumatra   the dark one married a man from Bogota and it was a long trip in a dugout canoe up the Magdalena River and the natives were Indians and slept in hammocks and had such horrible diseases and when the woman had a baby it was the husband who went to bed and used poisoned arrows and if you got a wound in that country it never healed but festered white and maturated and the dugout tipped over so easily into the warm steamy water full of ravenous fish that if you had a scratch on you or an unhealed wound it was the smell of blood attracted them sometimes they tore people to pieces

it was eight weeks up the Magdalena River in dugout canoes and then you got to Bogota

poor Jonas Fenimore came home from Bogota a very sick man and they said it was elephantiasis   he was a good fellow and told stories about the steamy jungle and the thunderstorms and the crocodiles and the horrible diseases and the ravenous fish and he drank up all the whiskey in the sideboard and when he went in swimming you could see that there were thick blotches on his legs like the scale of an apple and he liked to drink whiskey and he talked about Colombia becoming one of the richest countries in the world and oil and rare woods for veneering and tropical butterflies

but the trip up the Magdalena River was too long and too hot and too dangerous and he died

they said it was whiskey and elephantiasis

and the Magdalena River

Eleanor Stoddard

When they first arrived in New York, Eleanor, who'd never been East before, had to rely on Eveline for everything. Freddy met them at the train and took them to get rooms at the Brevoort. He said it was a little far from the theater, but much more interesting than an uptown hotel, all the artists and radicals and really interesting people stayed there and it was very French. Going down in the taxi he chattered about the lovely magnificent play and his grand part, and what a fool the director Ben Freelby was, and how one of the backers had only put up half the money he'd promised; but that Josephine Gilchrist, the business manager, had the sum virtually lined up now and the Shuberts were interested and they would open out of town at Greenwich exactly a month from today. Eleanor looked out at Fifth Avenue and the chilly spring wind blowing women's skirts, a man chasing a derby hat, the green buses, taxicabs, the shine on shopwindows; after all, this wasn't so very different from Chicago. But at lunch at the Brevoort it was very different, Freddy seemed to know so many people and introduced them to everybody as if he was very proud of them. They were all names she had heard or read of in the book column of the *Daily News.* Everybody seemed very friendly. Freddy talked French to the waiter and the hollandaise sauce was the most delicious she had ever eaten.

That afternoon on the way to rehearsal, Eleanor had her first glimpse of Times Square out of the taxicab window. In the dark theater they found the company sitting waiting for Mr. Freelby. It was very mysterious, with just a single big electric light bulb hanging over the stage and the set for some other play looking all flat and dusty.

A grayhaired man with a broad sad face and big circles

under his eyes came in. That was the famous Benjamin Freelby; he had a tired fatherly manner and asked Eveline and Eleanor up to his apartment to dinner with Freddy that night so that they could talk at their ease about the settings and the costumes. Eleanor was relieved that he was so kind and tired and thought that after all she and Eveline were much better dressed than any of those New York actresses. Mr. Freelby made a great fuss about there being no lights; did they expect him to rehearse in the dark? The stagemanager with the manuscript in his hand ran round looking for the electrician and somebody was sent to call up the office. Mr. Freelby walked about the stage and fretted and fumed and said, "This is monstrous." When the electrician arrived wiping his mouth with the back of his hand, and finally switched on the houselights and some spots, Mr. Freelby had to have a table and chair and a reading light on the table. Nobody seemed to be able to find a chair the right height for him. He kept fuming up and down, tugging at his coarse gray hair and saying, "This is monstrous." At last he got settled and he said to Mr. Stein, the stagemanager, a lanky man who sat in another chair near him, "We'll start with act one, Mr. Stein. Has everybody their parts?" Several actors got on the stage and stood round and the rest talked in low voices. Mr. Freelby "shushed" them and said, "Please, children, we've got to be quiet," and the rehearsal was in progress.

From that time on everything was a terrible rush. Eleanor never seemed to get to bed. The scenepainter, Mr. Bridgeman, at whose studios the scenery was painted, found objections to everything; it turned out that someone else, a pale young man with glasses who worked for Mr. Bridgeman, would have to design the scenery from their sketches and that they couldn't have their names in the program at all except for the costumes on account of not belonging to the scene designer's union. When they weren't wrangling at the Bridgeman Studios they were dashing about the streets in taxicabs with samples of materials. They never seemed to get to bed before four or five in the morning. Everybody was so temperamental and Eleanor had quite a siege each week to get a check out of Miss Gilchrist.

When the costumes were ready, all in early Victorian style, and Eleanor and Freddy and Mr. Freelby went to see them at the costumers' they really looked lovely, but the costumers wouldn't deliver them without a check and nobody could find Miss Gilchrist, and everybody was running round in taxis, and at last late that night Mr. Freelby said he'd give his personal check. The transfer company had its truck at the door with the scenery, but wouldn't let the flats be carried into the theater until they had a check. Mr. Bridgeman was there, too, saying his check had come back marked *no funds* and he and Mr. Freelby had words in the box office. At last Josephine Gilchrist appeared in a taxi with five hundred dollars in bills on account for Mr. Bridgeman and for the transfer company. Everybody smiled when they saw the crisp orangebacked bills. It was a great relief.

When they had made sure that the scenery was going into the theater, Eleanor and Eveline and Freddy Seargeant and Josephine Gilchrist and Mr. Freelby all went to Bustanoby's to get a bite to eat and Mr. Freelby set them up to a couple of bottles of Pol Roger and Josephine Gilchrist said that she felt it in her bones that the play would be a hit and that didn't often happen with her, and Freddy said the stagehands liked it and that was always a good sign and Mr. Freelby said Ike Gold, the Shuberts' officeboy, had sat through the run-through with the tears running down his cheeks, but nobody knew what theater they'd open in after a week in Greenwich and a week in Hartford and Mr. Freelby said he'd go and talk to J.J. about it personally first thing in the morning.

Friends from Chicago called up who wanted to get into the dress rehearsal. It made Eleanor feel quite important, especially when Sally Emerson called up. The dress rehearsal dragged terribly, half the scenery hadn't come and the Wessex villagers didn't have any costumes, but everybody said that it was a good sign to have a bad dress rehearsal.

Opening night Eleanor didn't get any supper and had only a half an hour to dress in. She was icy all over with excitement. She hoped the new chartreuse tulle evening dress she'd charged at Tappé's looked well, but she didn't have time to worry. She drank a cup of black coffee and it seemed as if the taxi never would get uptown. When she got to the theater the lobby was all lit up and full of silk hats and bare powdered backs and diamonds and eveningwraps and all the first-nighters looked at each other and waved to their friends and talked about who was there and kept trooping up the aisle halfway through the first act. Eleanor and Eveline stood stiffly side by side in the back of the theater and nudged each other when a costume looked good and agreed that the actors were too dreadful and that Freddy Seargeant was the worst. At the party that Sally Emerson gave for them afterwards at the duplex apartment of her friends the Careys everybody said that the scenery and costumes were lovely and that they were sure the play would be a great success. Eleanor and Eveline were the center of everything and Eleanor was annoyed because Eveline drank a little too much and was noisy.

Eleanor met a great many interesting people and decided that she'd stay on in New York whatever happened.

The play failed after two weeks and Eleanor and Eveline never did get seven hundred and fifty dollars that the management owed them. Eveline went back to Chicago, and Eleanor rented an apartment on Eighth Street. Sally Emerson had decided that Eleanor had great talent and got her husband to put up a thousand dollars to start her New York decorating business on. Eveline Hutchins's father was sick, but she wrote from Chicago that she'd be on whenever she could.

While Sally Emerson was in New York that summer, Eleanor went out with her all the time and got to know many rich people. It was through Alexander Parsons that she got the job to decorate the house the J. Ward Moorehouses were building near Great Neck. Mrs. Moorehouse walked round the unfinished house with her. She was a washedout blonde who kept explaining that she'd do the decorating herself only she hadn't the strength since her operation. She'd been in bed most of the time since her second child was born and told Eleanor all about her operation. Eleanor hated to hear about women's complaints and nodded coldly from time to time, making businesslike comments about furniture and draperies and now and then jotting notes on the decoration down on a piece of paper. Mrs. Moorehouse asked her to stay to lunch in the little cottage where they were living until they got the house finished. The little cottage was a large house in Dutch

Colonial style full of pekinese dogs and maids in flounced aprons and a butler. As they went into the diningroom, Eleanor heard a man's voice in an adjoining room and smelt cigarsmoke. At lunch she was introduced to Mr. Moorehouse

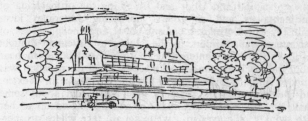

and a Mr. Perry. They had been playing golf and were talking about Tampico and oilwells. Mr. Moorehouse offered to drive her back to town after lunch and she was relieved to get away from Mrs. Moorehouse. She hadn't had a chance to talk about her ideas for decorating the new house yet, but, going in, Mr. Moorehouse asked her many questions about it and they laughed together about how ugly most people's houses were, and Eleanor thought that it was very interesting to find a business man who cared about those things. Mr. Moorehouse suggested that she prepare the estimates and bring them to his office. "How will Thursday do?" Thursday would be fine and he had no date that day and they'd have a bite of lunch together if she cared to. "Mealtime's the only time I get to devote to the things of the spirit," he said with a blue twinkle in his eye, so they both said "Thursday" again when he let Eleanor out at the corner of Eighth Street and Fifth Avenue and Eleanor thought he looked as if he had a sense of humor and thought she liked him much better than Tom Custis.

Eleanor found that she had to have many interviews with Ward Moorehouse as the work went on. She had him to dinner at her place on Eighth Street and she had her Martinique maid Augustine cook sauté chicken with red peppers and tomatoes. They had cocktails with absinthe in them and a bottle of very good burgundy and Ward Moorehouse enjoyed sitting back on the sofa and talking and she enjoyed listening and began to call him J. W. After that they were friends quite apart from the work on the house at Great Neck.

He told Eleanor about how he'd been a boy in Wilmington, Delaware, and the day the militia fired on the old darkey and thought it was the Spanish fleet and about his unhappy first marriage and about how his second wife was an invalid and about his work as a newspaperman and in advertising offices, and Eleanor, in a gray dress with just a touch of sparkly something on one shoulder and acting the discreet little homebody, led him on to explain about the work he was doing keeping the public informed about the state of relations between capital and labor and stemming the propaganda of sentimentalists and reformers, upholding American ideas against crazy German socialistic ideas and the panaceas of discontented dirtfarmers in the Northwest. Eleanor thought his ideas were very interesting, but she liked better to hear about the stock exchange and how the Steel Corporation was founded and the difficulties of the oil companies in Mexico, and Hearst and great fortunes. She asked him about some small investment she was making, and he looked up at her with twinkly blue eyes in a white square face where prosperity was just beginning to curve over the squareness of the jowl and said, "Miss Stoddard, may I have the honor of being your financial adviser?"

Eleanor thought his slight Southern accent and oldschool gentlemanly manners very attractive. She wished she had a more distinctivelooking apartment and that she'd kept some of the crystal chandeliers instead of selling them. It was twelve o'clock before he left, saying he'd had a very pleasant evening, but that he must go to answer some longdistance calls. Eleanor sat before the mirror at her dressingtable rubbing cold cream on her face by the light of two candles. She wished her neck wasn't so scrawny and wondered how it would be to start getting a henna rinse now and then when she got her hair washed.

The Camera Eye (24)

raining in historic Quebec   it was raining on the Château in historic Quebec where gallant Wolfe in a threecornered hat sat in a boat in a lithograph and read Gray's "Elegy" to his men gallant Wolfe climbing up the cliffs to meet gallant Montcalm in a threecornered hat on the plains of Abraham with elaborate bows and lace ruffles on the uniforms in the hollow squares and the gallantry and the command to fire and the lace ruffles ruined in the mud on the plains of Abraham

but the Château was the Château Frontenac worldfamous hostelry historic in the gray rain in historic gray

Quebec and we were climbing up from the Saguenay River Scenic Steamer Greatest Scenic Route in the World the Chautauqua Lecturer and his wife and the baritone from Athens Kentucky where they have a hill called the Acropolis exactly the way it is in Athens Greece and culture and a reproduction of the Parthenon exactly the way it is in Athens Greece

stony rain on stony streets and out onto the platform and the St. Lawrence people with umbrellas up walking back and forth on the broad wooden rainy platform looking over the slatepointed roofs of Quebec and the coal wharves and the grain elevators and the ferries and the *Empress of Ireland* with creamcolored funnels steaming in from the Other Side and Levis and green hills across the river and the Isle of Orléans green against green and the stony rain on the shining gray slatepointed roofs of Quebec

but the Chautauqua Lecturer wants his dinner and quarrels with his wife and makes a scene in the historic diningroom of the historic Château Frontenac and the headwaiter comes and the Chautauqua Lecturer's a big thick curlyhaired angry man with a voice used to bawling in tents about the Acropolis just like it is in Athens Greece and the Parthenon just like it is in Athens Greece and the Winged Victory and the baritone is too attentive to the small boy who wants to get away and wishes he hadn't said he'd come and wants to shake the whole bunch

but it's raining in historic Quebec and walking down the street alone with the baritone he kept saying about how there were bad girls in a town like this and boys shouldn't go with bad girls and the Acropolis and the bel canto and the Parthenon and voice culture and the beautiful statues of Greek boys and the Winged Victory and the beautiful statues

but I finally shook him and went out on the cars to see the Falls of Montmorency famous in song and story and a church full of crutches left by the sick in Sainte Anne de Beaupré

and the gray rainy streets full of girls

Janey

In the second year of the European War Mr. Carroll sold out his interest in the firm of Dreyfus and Carroll to Mr. Dreyfus and went home to Baltimore. There was a chance that the state Democratic convention would nominate him for Governor. Janey missed him in the office and followed all the reports of Maryland politics with great interest. When Mr. Carroll didn't get the nomination Janey felt quite sorry about it. Round the office there got to be more and more foreigners and talk there took on a distinctly pro-German trend that she didn't at all like. Mr. Dreyfus was very polite and generous with his employees, but Janey kept thinking of the ruthless invasion of Belgium and the horrible atrocities and didn't like to be working for a Hun, so she began looking round for another job. Business was slack in Washington and she knew it was foolish to leave Mr. Dreyfus, but she couldn't help it, so she went to work for Smedley Richards, a realestate operator on Connecticut Avenue, at a dollar less a week. Mr. Richards was a stout man who talked a great deal about the gentleman's code and made love to her. For a couple of weeks she kept him off, but the third week he took to drinking and kept putting his big beefy hands on her and borrowed a dollar one day and at the end of the week said he wouldn't be able to pay her for a day or two, so she just didn't go back and there she was out of a job.

It was scary being out of a job; she dreaded having to go back to live at her mother's with the boarders and her sisters' noisy ways. She read the ads in *The Star* and *The Post* every day and answered any she saw, but someone had always been there ahead of her, although she got to the address the first thing in the morning. She even put her name down at an employment agency. The woman at the desk was a stout woman with bad teeth and a mean smile, she made Janey pay two dollars as a registration fee and showed her the waiting list of expert stenographers she had and said that girls ought to marry and that trying to earn their own living was stuff and nonsense because it couldn't be done. The bad air and the pinched faces of the girls waiting on benches made her feel

quite sick so she went and sat a little while in the sun in Lafayette Square getting her courage up to tell Alice, who was
still at Mrs. Robinson's, that she hadn't found a job yet. A
young man with a red face sat down beside her and tried to
start talking to her, so she had to walk on. She went into a
drugstore and had a chocolate milk, but the sodajerker tried
to kid her a little, and she burst out crying. The sodajerker
looked scared to death and said, "Beg pardon, miss, I didn't
mean no offence." Her eyes were still red when she met Alice
coming out of the Riggs Building; Alice insisted on paying
for a thirtyfivecent lunch for her at The Brown Teapot, although Janey couldn't eat a thing. Alice had an Itoldyouso
manner that made Janey mad, and she said that it was too
late now for her to try to go back to Mrs. Robinson's because
Mrs. Robinson didn't have work for the girls she had there as
it was. That afternoon Janey felt too discouraged to look for
work and roamed round the Smithsonian Institution trying to
interest herself in the specimens of Indian beadwork and war

JACKSON

canoes and totempoles, but everything gave her the creeps and she went up to the room and had a good cry. She thought of Joe and Jerry Burnham and wondered why she never got letters from them, and thought of the poor soldiers in the trenches and felt very lonely. By the time Alice came home she'd washed her face and put on powder and rouge and was bustling briskly about their room; she joked Alice about the business depression and said that if she couldn't get a job in Washington she'd go to Baltimore or New York or Chicago to get a job. Alice said that sort of talk made her miserable. They went out and ate a ham sandwich and a glass of milk for supper to save money.

All that fall Janey went round trying to get work. She got so that the first thing she was conscious of in the morning when she woke up was the black depression of having nothing to do. She ate Christmas dinner with her mother and sisters and told them that she'd been promised twentyfive a week after the first of the year to keep them from sympathizing with her. She wouldn't give them the satisfaction.

At Christmas she got a torn paper package from Joe through the mail with an embroidered kimono in it. She went through the package again and again hoping to find a letter, but there was nothing but a little piece of paper with Merry Xmas scrawled on it. The package was postmarked St. Nazaire in France and was stamped OUVERT PAR LA CENSURE. It made the war seem very near to her and she hoped Joe wasn't in any danger over there.

One icy afternoon in January when Janey was lying on the bed reading *The Old Wives' Tale,* she heard the voice of Mrs. Baghot, the landlady, calling her. She was afraid it was about the rent that they hadn't paid that month yet, but it was Alice on the phone. Alice said for her to come right over because there was a man calling up who wanted a stenographer for a few days and none of the girls were in and she thought Janey might just as well go over and see if she wanted the job. "What's the address? I'll go right over." Alice told her the address. Her voice was stuttering excitedly at the other end of the line. "I'm so scared . . . if Mrs. Robinson finds out she'll be furious." "Don't worry, and I'll explain it to the man," said Janey.

The man was at the Hotel Continental on Pennsylvania Avenue. He had a bedroom and a parlor littered with typewritten sheets and paper-covered pamphlets. He wore shell-rimmed spectacles that he kept pulling off and putting on as if he wasn't sure whether he saw better with them or without them. He started to dictate without looking at Janey, as soon as she'd taken off her hat and gotten pad and pencil out of her handbag. He talked in jerks as if delivering a speech, striding back and forth on long thin legs all the while. It was some sort of article to be marked "For immediate release," all about capital and labor and the eighthour day and the Brotherhood of Locomotive Engineers. It was with a little feeling of worry that she worked out that he must be a laborleader. When he'd finished dictating he went out of the room abruptly and told her please to type it out as soon as she could that he'd be back in a minute. There was a Remington on the table, but she had to change the ribbon, and typed in a great hurry for fear he would come back and find her not

finished. Then she sat there waiting, with the article and the carbon copies all piled on the table looking neat and crisp. An hour passed and he didn't come. Janey got restless, roamed about the room, looked into the pamphlets. They were all about labor and economics and didn't interest her. Then she looked out of the window and tried to crane her neck out to see what time it said by the clock on the postoffice tower. But she couldn't see it, so she went over to the phone to ask the office if Mr. Barrow was in the hotel please to tell him his manuscript was ready. The desk said it was five o'clock and that Mr. Barrow hadn't come in yet, although he'd left word that he'd be back immediately. As she set down the receiver she knocked a letter on lavender paper off the stand. When she picked it up, as she had nothing to do and was tired of playing naughts and crosses with herself, she read it. She was ashamed of herself but once she'd started she couldn't stop.

DEAR G.H.

I hate to do this but honestly, kid, I'm in a hell of a fix for jack. You've got to come across with two thousand iron men ($2000) or else I swear I'll stop behaving like a lady and raise the roof. I hate to do this, but I know you've got it or else I wouldn't plague you like I do. I mean business this time

—the little girl you used to love
QUEENIE

Janey blushed and put the letter back exactly the way it had been. Weren't men awful, always some skeleton in the closet. It was dark outside and Janey was getting hungry and uneasy when the telephone rang. It was Mr. Barrow, who said that he was sorry he'd kept her waiting and that he was at the Shoreham in Mr. Moorehouse's suite and would she mind coming right over—no, not to bring the manuscript—but he had some more dictation for her right there, J. Ward Moorehouse it was, she must know the name. Janey didn't know the name, but the idea of going to take dictation at the Shoreham quite thrilled her and this letter and everything. This was some excitement like when she used to go round with Jerry Burnham. She put on her hat and coat, freshened up her face a little in the mirror over the mantel and walked through the stinging January evening to the corner of F and Fourteenth, where she stood waiting for the car. She wished she had a muff; the lashing wind bit into her hands in her thin gloves and into her legs just above the shoe-tops. She wished she was a wealthy married woman living in Chevy Chase and waiting for her limousine to come by and take her home to her husband and children and a roaring open fire. She remembered Jerry Burnham and wondered if she could have married him if she'd handled it right. Or Johnny Edwards; he'd gone to New York when she'd refused him, and was making big money in a broker's office. Or Morris Byer. But he was a Jew. This year she hadn't had any beaux. She was on the shelf; that was about the size of it.

At the corner before the Shoreham she got out of the car. The lobby was warm. Welldressed people stood around talking in welldressed voices. It smelt of hothouse flowers. At the desk they told her to go right up to apartment number eight on the first floor. A man with a wrinkled white face under a flat head of sleek black hair opened the door. He wore a sleek black suit and had a discreet skating walk. She said she was the stenographer for Mr. Barrow and he beckoned her into the next room. She stood at the door waiting for someone to notice her. At the end of the room there was a big fireplace where two logs blazed. In front of it was a broad table piled with magazines, newspapers, and typewritten manuscripts. On one end stood a silver teaservice, on the other a tray with decanters, a cocktail shaker and glasses. Everything had a wellpolished silvery gleam, chairs, tables, teaset, and the watchchain and the teeth and sleek prematurely gray hair of the man who stood with his back to the fire.

Immediately she saw him Janey thought he must be a fine man. Mr. Barrow and a little baldheaded man sat in deep chairs on either side of the fireplace listening to what he said with great attention.

"It's a very important thing for the future of this country," he was saying in a low earnest voice. "I can assure you that the great executives and the powerful interests in manufacturing and financial circles are watching these developments with the deepest interest. Don't quote me in this; I can assure you confidentially that the President himself . . ." His eye caught Janey's. "I guess this is the stenographer. Come right in, Miss . . ."

"Williams is the name," said Janey.

His eyes were the blue of alcoholflame, with a boyish flicker in them; this must be J. Ward Moorehouse whose name she ought to know.

"Have you a pencil and paper? That's fine; sit right down at the table. Morton, you'd better carry away those teathings." Morton made the teathings disappear noiselessly. Janey sat down at the end of the table and brought out her pad and pencil. "Hadn't you better take off your hat and coat, or you won't feel them when you go out?" There was something homey in his voice, different when he talked to her than when he talked to the men. She wished she could work for him. Anyway she was glad she had come.

"Now, Mr. Barrow, what we want is a statement that will allay unrest. We must make both sides in this controversy understand the value of co-operation. That's a great word, co-operation . . . First we'll get it down in rough . . . You'll please make suggestions from the angle of organized labor, and you, Mr. Jonas, from the juridical angle. Ready, Miss Williams . . . Released by J. Ward Moorehouse, Public Relations Counsel, Hotel Shoreham, Washington, D.C., January 15, 1916 . . ." Then Janey was too busy taking down the dictation to catch the sense of what was being said.

That evening when she got home she found Alice already in bed. Alice wanted to go to sleep, but Janey chattered like a magpie about Mr. Barrow and labor troubles and J. Ward Moorehouse and what a fine man he was, and so kind and friendly and had such interesting ideas for collaboration between capital and labor, and spoke so familiarly about what the President thought and what Andrew Carnegie thought and what the Rockefeller interests or Mr. Schick or Senator La Follette intended, and had such handsome boyish blue eyes, and was so nice, and the silver teaservice, and how young he looked in spite of his prematurely gray hair, and the open fire and the silver cocktail shaker and the crystal glasses.

"Why, Janey," broke in Alice, yawning, "I declare you must have a crush on him. I never heard you talk about a man that way in my life."

Janey blushed and felt very sore at Alice. "Oh, Alice, you're so silly . . . It's no use talking to you about anything."

She got undressed and turned out the light. It was only when she got to bed that she remembered that she hadn't had any supper. She didn't say anything about it because she was sure Alice would say something silly.

Next day she finished the job for Mr. Barrow. All morning she wanted to ask him about Mr. Moorehouse, where he lived, whether he was married or not, where he came from, but she reflected it wouldn't be much use. That afternoon, after she had been paid, she found herself walking along H Street past the Shoreham. She pretended to herself that she wanted to look in the storewindows. She didn't see him, but she saw a big shiny black limousine with a monogram that she couldn't make out without stooping and it would look funny if she stooped; she decided that was his car.

She walked down the street to the corner opposite the big gap in the houses where they were tearing down the Arlington. It was a clear sunny afternoon. She walked round Lafayette Square looking at the statue of Andrew Jackson on a rearing horse among the bare trees.

There were children and nursemaids grouped on the benches. A man with a grizzled vandyke with a black portfolio under his arm sat down on one of the benches and immediately got up again and strode off; foreign diplomat, thought Janey, and how fine it was to live in the Capital City where there were foreign diplomats and men like J. Ward Moorehouse. She walked once more round the statue of Andrew Jackson rearing green and noble on a green noble horse in the russet winter afternoon sunlight and then back towards the Shoreham, walking fast as if she were late to an appointment. She asked a bellboy where the public stenographer was. He sent her up to a room on the second floor where she asked an acideyed woman with a long jaw, who was typing away with her eyes on the little sector of greencarpeted hall she could see through the halfopen door, whether she knew of anyone who wanted a stenographer.

The acideyed woman stared at her. "Well, this isn't an agency, you know."

"I know; I just thought on the chance . . ." said Janey, feeling everything go suddenly out of her. "Do you mind if I sit down a moment?"

The acideyed woman continued staring at her.

"Now, where have I seen you before . . . ? No, don't remind me . . . You . . . you were working at Mrs. Robinson's the day I came in to take out her extra work. There, you see, I remember you perfectly." The woman smiled a yellow smile.

"I'd have remembered you," said Janey, "only I'm so tired of going round looking for a job."

"Don't I know?" sighed the woman.

"Don't you know anything I could get?"

"I'll tell you what you do . . . They were phoning for a girl to take dictation in number eight. They're using 'em up like . . . like sixty in there, incorporating some concern or something. Now, my dear, you listen to me, you go in there and take off your hat like you'd come from somewhere and start taking dictation and they won't throw you out, my dear, even if the other girl just came, they use 'em up too fast."

Before Janey knew what she was doing, she'd kissed the acideyed woman on the edge of the jaw and had walked fast along the corridor to number eight and was being let in by the sleekhaired man who recognized her and asked "Stenographer?"

"Yes," said Janey, and in another minute she had taken out her pad and paper and taken off her hat and coat and was sitting at the end of the shinydark mahogany table in front of the crackling fire, and the firelight glinted on silver decanters and hotwater pitchers and teapots and on the black perfectly shined shoes and in the flameblue eyes of J. Ward Moorehouse.

There she was sitting taking dictation from J. Ward Moorehouse.

At the end of the afternoon the sleekhaired man came in

and said, "Time to dress for dinner, sir," and J. Ward Moorehouse grunted and said, "Hell." The sleekhaired man skated a little nearer across the thick carpet. "Beg pardon, sir, Miss Rosenthal's fallen down and broken 'er 'ip. Fell on the hice in front of the Treasury Buildin', sir."

"The hell she has . . . Excuse me, Miss Williams," he said and smiled. Janey looked up at him indulgent-understandingly and smiled too. "Has she been fixed up all right?"

"Mr. Mulligan took her to the orspital, sir."

"That's right . . . You go downstairs, Morton, and send her some flowers. Pick out nice ones."

"Yessir . . . About five dollars' worth, sir?"

"Two-fifty's the limit, Morton, and put my card in."

Morton disappeared. J. Ward Moorehouse walked up and down in front of the fireplace for a while as if he were going to dictate. Janey's poised pencil hovered above the pad.

J. Ward Moorehouse stopped walking up and down and looked at Janey. "Do you know anyone, Miss Williams . . . I want a nice smart girl as stenographer and secretary, someone I can repose confidence in . . . Damn that woman for breaking her hip."

Janey's head swam. "Well, I'm looking for a position of that sort myself."

J. Ward Moorehouse was still looking at her with a quizzical blue stare. "Do you mind telling me, Miss Williams, why you lost your last job?"

"Not at all. I left Dreyfus and Carroll, perhaps you know them . . . I didn't like what was going on round there. It would have been different if old Mr. Carroll had stayed, though Mr. Dreyfus was very kind, I'm sure."

"He's an agent of the German government."

"That's what I mean. I didn't like to stay after the President's proclamation."

"Well, round here we're all for the Allies, so it'll be quite all right. I think you're just the person I like . . . Of course, can't be sure, but all my best decisions are made in a hurry. How about twentyfive a week to begin on?"

"All right, Mr. Moorehouse; it's going to be very interesting work, I'm sure."

"Tomorrow at nine please, and send these telegrams from me as you go out:

MRS. J. WARD MOOREHOUSE
GREAT NECK LONG ISLAND NEW YORK
MAY HAVE TO GO MEXICO CITY EXPLAIN SALT-
WORTHS UNABLE ATTEND DINNER HOPE EVERY-
THING ALLRIGHT LOVE TO ALL

WARD

"Do you mind traveling, Miss Williams?"

"I've never traveled, but I'm sure I'd like it."

"I may have to take a small office force down with me
. . . oil business. Let you know in a day or two . . ."

"Thank you; that'll be all today. When you've typed those
out and sent the wires, you may go."

J. Ward Moorehouse went through a door in the back, taking his coat off as he went. When Janey had typed the articles
and was slipping out of the hotel lobby to send the wires at

the Western Union, she caught a glimpse of him in a dress-suit with a gray felt hat on and a buffcolored overcoat over his arm. He was hurrying into a taxi and didn't see her. It was very late when she went home. Her cheeks were flushed, but she didn't feel tired. Alice was sitting up reading on the edge of the bed. "Oh, I was so worried . . ." she began, but Janey threw her arms round her and told her she had a job as private secretary to J. Ward Moorehouse and that she was going to Mexico. Alice burst out crying, but Janey was feeling so happy she couldn't stop to notice it, but went on to tell her everything about the afternoon at the Shoreham.

The Electrical Wizard

Edison was born in Milan, Ohio, in eighteen-fortyseven;

Milan was a little town on the Huron River that for a while was the wheatshipping port for the whole Western Reserve; the railroads took away the carrying trade, the Edison family went up to Port Huron in Michigan to grow up with the country;

his father was a shinglemaker who puttered round with various small speculations; he dealt in grain and feed and lumber and built a wooden tower a hundred feet high; tourists and excursionists paid a quarter each to go up the tower and look at the view over Lake Huron and the St. Clair River and Sam Edison became a solid and respected citizen of Port Huron.

Thomas Edison went to school for only three months because the teacher thought he wasn't right bright. His mother taught him what she knew at home and read eighteenth-century writers with him, Gibbon and Hume and Newton, and let him rig up a laboratory in the cellar.

Whenever he read about anything he went down cellar and tried it out.

When he was twelve he needed money to buy books and chemicals; he got a concession as newsbutcher on the daily train from Detroit to Port Huron. In Detroit there was a public library and he read it.

He rigged up a laboratory on the train and whenever he read about anything he tried it out. He rigged up a printing press and printed a paper called *The Herald*, when the Civil War broke out he organized a newsservice and cashed in on

308

the big battles. Then he dropped a stick of phosphorus and set the car on fire and was thrown off the train.

By that time he had considerable fame in the country as the boy editor of the first newspaper to be published on a moving train. The London *Times* wrote him up.

He learned telegraphy and got a job as night operator at Stratford Junction in Canada, but one day he let a freight-train get past a switch and had to move on.

(During the Civil War a man that knew telegraphy could get a job anywhere.)

Edison traveled round the country taking jobs and dropping them and moving on, reading all the books he could lay his hands on; whenever he read about a scientific experiment he tried it out, whenever he could get near an engine he'd tinker with it, whenever they left him alone in a telegraph office he'd do tricks with the wires. That often lost him the job and he had to move on.

He was tramp operator through the whole Middle West: Detroit, Cincinnati, Indianapolis, Louisville, New Orleans, always broke, his clothes stained with chemicals, always trying tricks with the telegraph.

He worked for the Western Union in Boston.

In Boston he doped out the model of his first patent, an automatic voterecorder for use in Congress, but they didn't want an automatic voterecorder in Congress, so Edison had the trip to Washington and made some debts and that was all he got out of that; he worked out a stockticker and burglar alarms and burned all the skin off his face with nitric acid.

But New York was already the big market for stocks and ideas and gold and greenbacks.

(This part is written by Horatio Alger:)

When Edison got to New York he was stony broke and had debts in Boston and Rochester. This was when gold was at a premium and Jay Gould was trying to corner the gold market. Wall Street was crazy. A man named Law had rigged up an electric indicator (Callahan's invention) that indicated the price of gold in brokers' offices. Edison, looking for a job, broke and with no place to go, had been hanging round the central office passing the time of day with the operators when the general transmitter stopped with a crash in the middle of a rush day of nervous trading; everybody in the office lost his head. Edison stepped up and fixed the machine and landed a job at three hundred dollars a month.

In sixtynine, the year of Black Friday, he started an electrical engineering firm with a man named Pope.

From then on he was on his own; he invented a stock ticker and it sold. He had a machineshop and a laboratory; whenever he thought of a device he tried it out. He made forty thousand dollars out of the Universal Stock Ticker.

He rented a shop in Newark and worked on an automatic telegraph and on devices for sending two and four messages at the same time over the same wire.

In Newark he tinkered with Sholes on the first typewriter, and invented the mimeograph, the carbon rheostat, the microtasimeter, and first made paraffin paper.

Something he called etheric force worried him; he puzzled a lot about etheric force but it was Marconi who cashed in on the Hertzian waves. Radio was to smash the ancient universe. Radio was to kill the old Euclidian God, but Edison was never a man to worry about philosophical concepts;

he worked all day and all night tinkering with cogwheels and bits of copperwire and chemicals in bottles; whenever he thought of a device he tried it out. He made things work. He wasn't a mathematician. I can hire mathematicians but mathematicians can't hire me, he said.

In eighteen-seventysix he moved to Menlo Park where he invented the carbon transmitter that made the telephone a commercial proposition, that made the microphone possible

he worked all day and all night and produced

    the phonograph

        the incandescent electric lamp

and systems of generation, distribution, regulation and measurement of electric current, sockets, switches, insulators, manholes. Edison worked out the first system of electric light using the direct current and small unit lamps and the multiple arc that were installed in London Paris New York and Sunbury Pennsylvania,

            the threewire system,

               the magnetic ore separator,

                  an electric railway.

He kept them busy at the Patent Office filing patents and caveats.

To find a filament for his electric lamp that would work, that would be a sound commercial proposition, he tried all kinds of paper and cloth, thread, fishline, fibre, celluloid, boxwood, coconutshells, spruce, hickory, bay, mapleshavings, rosewood, punk, cork, flax, bamboo, and the hair out of a redheaded Scotchman's beard;

whenever he got a hunch he tried it out.

In eighteen-eightyseven he moved to the huge laboratories at West Orange.

He invented rockcrushers and the fluoroscope and the reeled film for movie cameras and the alkaline storage battery and the long kiln for burning out portland cement and the kinetophone that was the first talking movie and the poured cement house that is to furnish cheap artistic identical sanitary homes for workers in the electrical age.

Thomas A. Edison at eightytwo worked sixteen hours a day;

he never worried about mathematics or the social system or generalized philosophical concepts;

in collaboration with Henry Ford and Harvey Firestone who never worried about mathematics or the social system or generalized philosophical concepts;

he worked sixteen hours a day trying to find a substitute for rubber; whenever he read about anything he tried it out; whenever he got a hunch he went to the laboratory and tried it out.

The Camera Eye (25)

those spring nights the streetcar wheels screech grinding in a rattle of loose trucks round the curved tracks of Harvard Square dust hangs in the powdery arclight glare allnight till dawn can't sleep

haven't got the nerve to break out of the bellglass

four years under the ethercone breathe deep gently now that's the way be a good boy one two three four five six get A's in some courses but don't be a grind be interested in literature but remain a gentleman don't be seen with Jews or Socialists

and all the pleasant contacts will be useful in Later Life say hello pleasantly to everybody crossing the yard

sit looking out into the twilight of the pleasantest four years of your life

grow cold with culture like a cup of tea forgotten between an incenseburner and a volume of Oscar Wilde cold and not strong like a claret lemonade drunk at a Pop Concert in Symphony Hall

311

    four years I didn't know you could do what you Mi-
chelangelo wanted say
    Marx
        to all
the professors with a small Swift break all the Gree-
noughs in the shooting gallery
    but tossed with eyes smarting all the spring night read-
ing *The Tragical History of Doctor Faustus* and went
mad listening to the streetcar wheels screech grinding in a
rattle of loose trucks round Harvard Square and the
trains crying across the saltmarshes and the rumbling
siren of a steamboat leaving dock and the blue peter
flying and millworkers marching with a red brass band
through the streets of Lawrence Massachusetts
    it was like the Magdeburg spheres the pressure outside
sustained the vacuum within
    and I hadn't the nerve
                to jump up and walk outofdoors and tell

them all to go take a flying
            Rimbaud
                at the moon

Newsreel XVII

an attack by a number of hostile airships developed before midnight. Bombs were dropped somewhat indiscriminately over localities possessing no military importance

RAILROADS WON'T YIELD AN INCH

We shall have to make the passage under conditions not entirely advantageous to us, said Captain Koenig of the *Deutschland* ninety miles on his way passing Solomon's Island at 2:30. Every steamer passed blew his whistle in salute.

> *You made me what I am today*
> *I hope you're satisfied*
> *You dragged me down and down and down*
> *Until the soul within me died*

Sir Roger Casement was hanged in Pentonville Gaol at nine o'clock this morning.

U-BOAT PASSES CAPES UNHINDERED

clad only in kimono girl bathers shock dairy lunch instead of firstclass café on amusement dock heavy losses shown in U.S. crop report Italians cheered as Austrians leave hot rolls in haste to get away giant wall of water rushes down valley professor says Beethoven gives the impression of a juicy steak

PRISON'S MAGIC TURNS CITY JUNK INTO GOLD MINE

Mac

The rebels took Juarez and Huerta fled and the steamboats
to Europe were packed with cientificos making for Paris and
Venustiano Carranza was president in Mexico City. Somebody got Mac a pass on the Mexican Central down to the
capital. Encarnacion cried when he left and all the anarchists
came down to the station to see him off. Mac wanted to join
Zapata. He'd picked up a little Spanish from Encarnacion
and a vague idea of the politics of the revolution. The train
took five days. Five times it was held up while the section
hands repaired the track ahead. Occasionally at night bullets
came through the windows. Near Caballos a bunch of men
on horses rode the whole length of the train waving their big
hats and firing as they went. The soldiers in the caboose woke
up and returned the fire and the men rode off in a driving
dustcloud. The passengers had to duck under the seats when
the firing began or lie flat in the aisle. After the attack had
been driven off, an old woman started to shriek and it was
found that a child had been hit through the head. The
mother was a stout dark woman in a flowered dress. She
went up and down the train with the tiny bloody body
wrapped in a shawl asking for a doctor, but anybody could
see that the child was dead.

Mac thought the trip would never end. He bought peppery food and lukewarm beer from old Indian women at stations, tried to drink pulque and to carry on conversations with his fellowpassengers. At last they passed Queretaro and the train began going fast down long grades in the cold bright air. Then the peaks of the great volcanos began to take shape in the blue beyond endless crisscrosspatterned fields of centuryplants and suddenly the train was rattling between garden walls, through feathery trees. It came to a stop with a clang of couplings: Mexico City.

Mac felt lost wandering round the bright streets among the lowvoiced crowds, the men all dressed in white and the women all in black or dark blue. The streets were dusty and sunny and quiet. There were stores open and cabs and trolleycars and polished limousines. Mac was worried. He had only two dollars. He'd been on the train so long he'd forgotten what he intended to do when he reached his destination. He wanted clean clothes and a bath. When he'd wandered round a good deal he saw a place marked "American Bar." His legs were tired. He sat down at a table. A waiter came over and asked him in English what he wanted. He couldn't think of anything else so he ordered a whiskey. He drank the whiskey and sat there with his head in his hands. At the bar were a lot of Americans and a couple of Mexicans in tengallon hats rolling dice for drinks. Mac ordered another whiskey.

A beefy redeyed man in a rumpled khaki shirt was roaming uneasily about the bar. His eye lit on Mac and he sat down at his table. "Mind if I set here awhile, pardner?" he asked. "Those sonsobitches too damn noisy. Here, sombrero . . . wheresat damn waiter? Gimme a glass-beer. Well, I got the old woman an' the kids off today . . . When are you pullin' out?"

"Why, I just pulled in," said Mac.

"The hell you say . . . This ain't no place for a white man . . . These bandits'll be on the town any day . . . It'll be horrible, I tell you. There won't be a white man left alive . . . I'll get some of 'em before they croak me, though . . . By God, I can account for twentyfive of 'em, no, twentyfour." He pulled a Colt out of his pocket, emptied the chamber into his hand and started counting the cartridges, "Eight," then he started going through his pockets and ranged the cartridges in a row on the deal table. There were only twenty. "Some sonvabitch robbed me."

A tall lanky man came over from the bar and put his hand on the redeyed man's shoulder. "Eustace, you'd better put that away till we need it . . . You know what to do, don't you?" He turned to Mac; "As soon as the shooting begins, all

315

American citizens concentrate at the Embassy. There we'll sell our lives to the last man."

Somebody yelled from the bar, "Hey, big boy, have another round," and the tall man went back to the bar.

"You fellers seem to expect trouble," said Mac.

"Trouble—my God! You don't know this country. Did you just come in?"

"Blew in from Juarez just now."

"You can't have. Railroad's all tore up at Queretaro."

"Well, they musta got it fixed," said Mac. "Say, what do they say round here about Zapata?"

"My God, he's the bloodthirstiest villain of the lot . . . They roasted a feller was foreman of a sugar mill down in Morelos on a slow fire and raped his wife and daughters right before his eyes . . . My God, pardner, you don't know what kind of country this is! Do you know what we ought to do . . . d'you know what we'd do if we had a man in the White House instead of a yellowbellied potatomouthed reformer? We'd get up an army of a hundred thousand men and clean this place up . . . It's a hell of a fine country, but there's not one of them damn greasers worth the powder and shot to shoot 'em . . . smoke 'em out like vermin, that's what I say . . . Every mother's sonvabitch of 'em 's a Zapata under the skin."

"What business are you in?"

"I'm an oil prospector, and I've been in this lousy hole fifteen years and I'm through. I'd have gotten out on the train to Vera Cruz today only I have some claims to settle up an' my furniture to sell . . . You can't tell when they'll cut the railroad and then we won't be able to get out and President Wilson'll let us be shot down right here like rats in a trap . . . If the American public realized conditions down here . . . My God, we're the laughingstock of all the other nations . . . What's your line o' work, pardner?"

"Printer . . . linotype operator."

"Looking for a job?"

Mac had brought out a dollar to pay for his drinks. "I guess I'll have to," he said. "That's my last dollar but one."

"Why don't you go round to the *Mexican Herald?* They're always needin' English language printers . . . They can't keep anybody down here . . . Ain't fit for a white man down here no more . . . Look here, pardner, that drink's on me."

"Well, we'll have another then, on me."

"The fat's in the fire in this country now, pardner . . . everything's gone to hell . . . might as well have a drink while we can."

That evening, after he'd eaten some supper in a little American lunchroom, Mac walked round the Alameda to get the whiskey out of his head before going up to the *Mexican Herald* to see if he could get a job. It would only be for a couple of weeks, he told himself, till he could get wise to the lay of the land. The tall trees on the Alameda and the white statues and the fountains and the welldressed couples strolling round in the gloaming and the cabs clattering over the cobbles looked quiet enough, and the row of stonyeyed Indian women selling fruit and nuts and pink and yellow and green candies in booths along the curb. Mac decided that the man he'd talked to in the bar had been stringing him along because he was a tenderfoot.

He got a job all right at the *Mexican Herald* at thirty mex dollars a week, but round the printing plant everybody talked just like the men in the bar. That night an old Polish American who was a proofreader there took him round to a small hotel to get him a flop and lent him a couple of cartwheels till payday.

"You get your wages in advance as much as you can," said the old Pole; "one of these days there will be a revolution and then goodbye *Mexican Herald* . . . unless Wilson makes intervention mighty quick."

"Sounds all right to me; I want to see the social revolution," said Mac.

The old Pole laid his finger along his nose and shook his head in a peculiar way and left him.

When Mac woke up in the morning, he was in a small

317

room calsomined bright yellow. The furniture was painted blue and there were red curtains in the window. Between the curtains the long shutters were barred with vivid violet sunlight that cut a warm path across the bedclothes. A canary was singing somewhere and he could hear the flap pat flap of a woman making tortillas. He got up and threw open the shutters. The sky was cloudless above the redtile roofs. The street was empty and full of sunlight. He filled his lungs with cool thin air and felt the sun burning his face and arms and neck as he stood there. It must be early. He went back to bed and fell asleep again.

When Wilson ordered the Americans out of Mexico several months later, Mac was settled in a little apartment in the Plaza del Carmen with a girl named Concha and two white Persian cats. Concha had been a stenographer and interpreter with an American firm and had been the mistress of an oilman for three years, so she spoke pretty good English. The oilman had jumped on the train for Vera Cruz in the panic at the time of the flight of Huerta, leaving Concha high and dry. She had taken a fancy to Mac from the moment she had first seen him going into the postoffice. She made him very comfortable, and when he talked to her about going out to join Zapata, she only laughed and said peons were ignorant savages and fit only to be ruled with the whip. Her mother, an old woman with a black shawl perpetually over her head, came to cook for them and Mac began to like Mexican food, turkey with thick chocolate brown sauce, and enchiladas with cheese. The cats were named Porfirio and Venustiano and always slept on the foot of their bed. Concha was very thrifty and made Mac's pay go much further than he could and never complained when he went out batting round town and came home late with a headache from drinking tequila. Instead of trying to get on the crowded trains to Vera Cruz, Mac took a little money he had saved up and bought up the office furniture that wildeyed American businessmen were selling out for anything they could get for it. He had it piled in the courtyard back of the house where they lived. Buying it had been Concha's idea in the first place and he used to tease her about how they'd never get rid of it again, but she'd nod her head and say, "Wait a minute."

Concha liked it very much when he'd have friends in to eat with him Sundays. She would wait on them very pleasantly and send her little brother Antonio round for beer and cognac and always have cakes in the house to bring out if anybody dropped in. Mac would sometimes think how much pleasanter this was than when he'd lived with Maisie in San

Diego, and began to think less often about going out to join Zapata.

The Polish proofreader, whose name was Korski, turned out to be a political exile, a Socialist, and a wellinformed man. He would sit all afternoon over a half a glass of cognac talking about European politics; since the collapse of the European Socialist parties at the beginning of the war he had taken no part in anything; from now on he'd be an onlooker. He had a theory that civilization and a mixed diet were causing the collapse of the human race.

Then there was Ben Stowell, an independent oil promoter who was trying to put through a deal with Carranza's government to operate some oilwells according to the law. He was broke most of the time and Mac used to lend him money, but he always talked in millions. He called himself a progressive in politics and thought that Zapata and Villa were honest men. Ben Stowell would always take the opposite side of any argument from Korski and would infuriate the old man by his antisocial attitude. Mac wanted to make some money to send up to Maisie for the kids' schooling. It made him feel good to send Rose up a box of toys now and then. He and Ben would have long talks about the chances of making money in Mexico. Ben Stowell brought round a couple of young radical politicians who enjoyed sitting through the afternoon talking about socialism and drinking and learning English. Mac usually didn't say much, but sometimes he got sore and gave them a broadside of straight I.W.W. doctrine. Concha would finish all arguments by bringing on supper and saying with a shake of her head, "Every poor man socialista . . . a como no? But when you get rich, quick you all very much capitalista."

One Sunday Mac and Concha and some Mexican newspapermen and Ben Stowell and his girl, Angustias, who was a chorusgirl at the Lirico, went out on the trolley to Xochimilco. They hired a boat with a table in it and an awning and an Indian to pole them round through the poplarboarded canals among the rich flower patches and vegetable gardens. They drank pulque and they had a bottle of whiskey with them, and they bought the girls calla lilies. One of the Mexicans played a guitar and sang.

In the afternoon the Indian brought the boat back to a landing and they strolled off in couples into the woods. Mac suddenly felt very homesick and told Concha about his children in the U.S. and about Rose particularly, and she burst into tears and told him how much she loved children, but that when she was seventeen she had been very sick and they'd thought she was going to die and now she couldn't have any children, only Porfirio and Venustiano. Mac kissed her and told her that he'd always look after her.

When they got back to the trolley station, loaded down with flowers, Mac and Ben let the girls go home alone and went to a cantina to have a drink. Ben said he was pretty tired of this sort of thing and wished he could make his pile and go back to the States to marry and have a home and a family. "You see, Mac," he said, "I'm forty years old. Christ, a man can't bat around all his life." "Well, I'm not far from it," said Mac. They didn't say much, but Ben walked up with Mac as far as the office of the *Mexican Herald* and then went downtown to the Iturbide to see some oilmen who were staying there. "Well, it's a great life if you don't weaken," he said as he waved his hand at Mac and started down the street. He was a stocky bullnecked man with a bowlegged walk.

Several days later Ben came around to the Plaza del Carmen before Mac was out of bed. "Mac, you come and eat with me this noon," he said. "There's a guy named G. H. Barrow here I want to kinda show the town a little bit. He might be useful to us . . . I want to know what he's after anyway." The man was writing articles on the Mexican situation and was said to have some connection with the A.F. of L. At lunch he asked anxiously if the water was safe and whether it wasn't dangerous to walk round the streets after nightfall. Ben Stowell kidded him along a little and told him stories of generals and their friends breaking into a bar and shooting into the floor to make the customers dance and then using the place for a shooting gallery. "The shooting gallery, that's what they call congress here," said Mac. Barrow said he was going to a meeting of the Union Nacional de Trabajadores that afternoon and would they mind going with him to interpret for him. It was Mac's day off, so they said, "All right." He said he'd been instructed to try to make contacts with the Pan-American Federation of Labor. Gompers would come down himself if something could be lined up. He said he'd been a shipping clerk and a Pullman conductor and had been in the office of the Railroad Brotherhood, but now he was working for the A.F. of L. He wished American workers had more ideas about the art of life. He'd been at the Second International meetings at Amsterdam and felt the European workers understood the art of life. When Mac asked him why the hell the Second International hadn't done something to stop the World War, he said the time wasn't ripe yet and spoke about German atrocities.

"The German atrocities are a Sunday school picnic to what goes on every day in Mexico," said Ben.

Then Barrow went on to ask whether Mexicans were as immoral as it was made out. The beer they were drinking with their lunch was pretty strong and they all loosened up a little. Barrow wanted to know whether it wasn't pretty risky going out with girls here on account of the high percentage of syphilis. Mac said yes, but that he and Ben could show him some places that were all right if he wanted to look 'em over. Barrow tittered and looked embarrassed and said he'd just as

321

soon look 'em over. "A man ought to see every side of things when he's investigating conditions."

Ben Stowell slapped his hand on the edge of the table and said that Mac was just the man to show him the backside of Mexico.

They went to the meeting that was crowded with slender dark men in blue denim. At first they couldn't get in on account of the crowd packed in the aisles and in the back of the hall, but Mac found an official he knew who gave them seats in a box. The hall was very stuffy and the band played and there was singing and speeches were very long. Barrow said listening to a foreign language made him sleepy, and suggested that they walk around town; he'd heard that the red light district was . . . he was interested in conditions.

Outside the hall they ran across Enrique Salvador, a newspaperman that Ben knew. He had a car and a chauffeur. He shook hands and laughed and said the car belonged to the chief of police who was a friend of his and wouldn't they like to ride out to San Angel? They went out the long avenue past Chapultepec, the Champs Elysées of Mexico, Salvador called it. Near Tacubaya Salvador pointed out the spot where Carranza's troops had had a skirmish with the Zapatistas the week before and a corner where a rich clothing merchant had been murdered by bandits, and G. H. Barrow kept asking was it quite safe to go so far out in the country, and Salvador said, "I am a newspaperman. I am everybody's friend."

Out at San Angel they had some drinks and when they got back to the city they drove round the Pajaritos district. G. H. Barrow got very quiet and his eyes got a watery look when he saw the little lighted cribhouses, each one with a bed and some paperflowers and a crucifix that you could see through the open door, past a red or blue curtain, and the dark quiet Indian girls in short chemises standing outside their doors or sitting on the sill.

"You see," said Ben Stowell, "it's easy as rolling off a log . . . But I don't advise you to get too careless round here . . . Salvador'll show us a good joint after supper. He ought to know because he's a friend of the chief of police and he runs most of them."

But Barrow wanted to go into one of the cribs, so they got out and talked to one of the girls and Salvador sent the chauffeur to get a couple of bottles of beer. The girl received them very politely and Barrow tried to get Mac to ask her questions, but Mac didn't like asking her questions, so he let Salvador do it. When G. H. Barrow put his hand on her bare shoulder and tried to pull her chemise off and asked how much did she want to let him see her all naked, the girl didn't

322

understand and tore herself away from him and yelled and cursed at him and Salvador wouldn't translate what she said. "Let's get this bastard outa here," said Ben in a low voice to Mac, "before we have to get in a fight or somethin'."

They had a tequila each before dinner at a little bar where nothing was sold but tequila out of varnished kegs. Salvador showed G. H. Barrow how to drink it, first putting salt on the hollow between his thumb and forefinger and then gulping the glass of tequila, licking up the salt and swallowing some chile sauce to finish up with, but he got it down the wrong way and choked.

At supper they were pretty drunk and G. H. Barrow kept saying that Mexicans understood the art of life and that was meat for Salvador who talked about the Indian genius and the Latin genius and said that Mac and Ben were the only gringos he ever met he could get along with, and insisted on their not paying for their meal. He'd charge it to his friend the chief of police. Next they went to a cantina beside a theater where there were said to be French girls, but the French girls weren't there. There were three old men in the cantina playing a cello, a violin, and a piccolo. Salvador made them play *La Adelita* and everybody sang it and then *La Cucaracha*. There was an old man in a broadbrimmed hat with a huge shiny pistolholster on his back, who drank up his drink quickly when they came in and left the bar. Salvador whispered to Mac that he was General Gonzales and had left in order not to be seen drinking with gringos.

Ben and Barrow sat with their heads together at a table in the corner talking about the oil business. Barrow was saying that there was an investigator for certain oil interests coming down; he'd be at the Regis almost any day now and Ben was saying he wanted to meet him and Barrow put his arm around his shoulder and said he was sure Ben was just the man this investigator would want to meet to get an actual working knowledge of conditions. Meanwhile Mac and Salvador were dancing the Cuban danzon with the girls. Then Barrow got to his feet a little unsteadily and said he didn't want to wait for the French girls, but why not go to that place where they'd been and try some of the dark meat, but Salvador insisted on taking them to the house of Remedios near the American embassy. "Quelque cosa de chic," he'd say in bad French. It was a big house with a marble stairway and crystal chandeliers and salmon-brocaded draperies and lace curtains and mirrors everywhere. "Personne que les henerales vieng aqui," he said when he'd introduced them to the madam, who was a darkeyed grayhaired woman in black with a black shawl who looked rather like a nun. There was only one girl left unoccupied, so they fixed up Barrow with her and arranged about the price and left him. "Whew, that's a relief," said Ben when they came out. The air was cold and the sky was all stars.

Salvador had made the three old men with their instruments get back into the back of the car and said he felt romantic and wanted to serenade his novia and they went out towards Guadalupe speeding like mad along the broad causeway. Mac and the chauffeur and Ben and Salvador and the three old men singing *La Adelita* and the instruments chirping, all off key. In Guadalupe they stopped under some buttonball trees against the wall of a house with big grated windows and sang *Cielito lindo* and *La Adelita* and *Cuatro milpas*, and Ben and Mac sang *Just to keep her from the foggy dew* and were just starting *Oh, bury me not on the lone prairie* when a girl came to the window and talked a long time in low Spanish to Salvador.

Salvador said, "Elle dit que nous make escandalo and must go away. Très chic."

By that time a patrol of soldiers had come up and were about to arrest them all when the officer arrived and recognized the car and Salvador and took them to have a drink with him at his billet. When they all got home to Mac's place

324

they were very drunk. Concha, whose face was drawn from waiting up, made up a mattress for Ben in the diningroom, and as they were all going to turn in Ben said, "By heavens, Concha, you're a swell girl. When I make my pile I'll buy you the handsomest pair of diamond earrings in the Federal District." The last they saw of Salvador he was standing up in the front seat of the car as it went round the corner on two wheels conducting the three old men in *La Adelita* with big gestures like an orchestra leader.

Before Christmas Ben Stowell came back from a trip to Tamaulipas feeling fine. Things were looking up for him. He'd made an arrangement with a local general near Tampico to run an oilwell on a fifty-fifty basis. Through Salvador he'd made friends with some members of Carranza's cabinet and was hoping to be able to turn over a deal with some of the big claimholders up in the States. He had plenty of cash and took a room at the Regis. One day he went round to the printing plant and asked Mac to step out in the alley with him for a minute.

"Look here, Mac," he said, "I've got an offer for you . . . You know old Worthington's bookstore? Well, I got drunk last night and bought him out for two thousand pesos . . . He's pulling up stakes and going home to blighty, he says."

"The hell you did!"

"Well, I'm just as glad to have him out of the way."

"Why, you old whoremaster, you're after Lisa."

"Well, maybe she's just as glad to have him out of the way, too."

"She's certainly a goodlooker."

"I got a lot a news I'll tell you later . . . Ain't goin' to be healthy round the *Mexican Herald* maybe . . . I've got a proposition for you, Mac . . . Christ knows I owe you a hellova lot . . . You know that load of office furniture you have out back Concha made you buy that time?" Mac nodded. "Well, I'll take it off your hands and give you a half interest in that bookstore. I'm opening an office. You know the book business . . . you told me yourself you did . . . the profits of the first year are yours and after that we split two ways, see? You certainly ought to make it pay. That old fool Worthington did, and kept Lisa into the bargain . . . Are you on?"

"Jeez, lemme think it over, Ben . . . but I got to go back to the daily bunksheet."

So Mac found himself running a bookstore on the Calle Independencia with a line of stationery and a few typewriters. It felt good to be his own boss for the first time in his life. Concha, who was a storekeeper's daughter, was delighted. She kept the books and talked to the customers so that Mac didn't have much to do but sit in the back and read and talk to his friends. That Christmas Ben and Lisa, who was a tall Spanish girl said to have been a dancer in Malaga, with a white skin like a camellia and ebony hair, gave all sorts of parties in an apartment with American-style bath and kitchen that Ben rented out in the new quarter towards Chapultepec. The day the Asociacion de Publicistas had its annual banquet Ben stopped into the bookstore feeling fine and told Mac he wanted him and Concha to come up after supper and wouldn't Concha bring a couple of friends, nice wellbehaved girls not too choosy, like she knew. He was giving a party for G. H. Barrow who was back from Vera Cruz and a big contact man from New York who was wangling something. Ben didn't know just what. He'd seen Carranza yesterday and at the banquet everybody'd kowtowed to him.

"Jeez, Mac, you oughta been at that banquet; they took one of the streetcars and had a table the whole length of it and an orchestra and rode us out to San Angel and back and then all round town."

"I saw 'em starting out," said Mac, "looked too much like a funeral to me."

"Jeez, it was swell, though. Salvador an' everybody was there and this guy Moorehouse, the big hombre from New York, jeez, he looked like he didn't know if he was comin' or goin'. Looked like he expected a bomb to go off under the seat any minute . . . hellova good thing for Mexico if one had, when you come to think of it. All the worst crooks in town was there."

The party at Ben's didn't come off so well. J. Ward Moorehouse didn't make up to the girls as Ben had hoped. He brought his secretary, a tired blond girl, and they both looked scared to death. They had a dinner Mexican style and champagne and a great deal of cognac and a victrola played records by Victor Herbert and Irving Berlin and a little itinerant band attracted by the crowd played Mexican airs on the street outside. After dinner things were getting a little noisy inside, so Ben and Moorehouse took chairs out on the balcony and had a long talk about the oil situation over their cigars. J. Ward Moorehouse explained that he had come down in a purely unofficial capacity you understand to make contacts, to find out what the situation was and just what there was behind Carranza's stubborn opposition to American investors and that the big businessmen he was in touch with in the States desired only fair play and that he felt that if their point of view could be thoroughly understood through some information bureau or the friendly co-operation of Mexican newspapermen . . .

Ben went back into the diningroom and brought out Enrique Salvador and Mac. They all talked over the situation and J. Ward Moorehouse said that speaking as an old newspaperman himself he thoroughly understood the situation of the press, probably not so different in Mexico City from that in Chicago or Pittsburgh, and that all the newspapermen wanted was to give each fresh angle of the situation its proper significance in a spirit of fair play and friendly co-operation, but that he felt that the Mexican business in Mexico just as the American press was misinformed about the aims of Mexican politics. If Mr. Enrique would call by the Regis he'd be delighted to talk to him more fully, or to any one of you gentlemen, and if he wasn't in, due to the great press of appointments and the very few days he had to spend in the Mexican capital, his secretary, Miss Williams, would be only too willing to give them any information they wanted and a few specially prepared strictly confidential notes on the attitude of the big American corporations with which he was purely informally in touch.

After that he said he was sorry, but he had telegrams waiting for him at the Regis, and Salvador took him and Miss Williams, his secretary, home in the chief of police's automobile.

"Jeez, Ben, that's a smooth bastard," said Mac to Ben after J. Ward Moorehouse had gone.

"Mac," said Ben, "that baby's got a slick cream of millions all over him. By gum, I'd like to make some of these contacts he talks about . . . By gorry, I may do it yet . . . You just watch your Uncle Dudley, Mac. I'm goin' to associate with the big hombres after this."

After that the party was not so refined. Ben brought out a lot more cognac and the men started taking the girls into the bedrooms and hallways and even into the pantry and kitchen. Barrow cottoned onto a blonde named Nadia who was half English and talked to her all evening about the art of life. After everybody had gone Ben found them locked up in his bedroom.

Mac got to like the life of a storekeeper. He got up when he wanted to and walked up the sunny streets past the cathedral and the façade of the National Palace and up Independencia where the sidewalks had been freshly sprinkled with water and a morning wind was blowing through, sweet with the smell of flowers and roasting coffee. Concha's little brother Antonio would have the shutters down and be sweeping out the store by the time he got there. Mac would sit in the back reading or would roam about the store chatting with people in English and Spanish. He didn't sell many books,

328

but he kept all the American and European papers and magazines and they sold well, especially the *Police Gazette* and *La Vie Parisienne*. He started a bank account and was planning to take on some typewriter agencies. Salvador kept telling him he'd get a contract to supply stationery to some government department and make him a rich man.

One morning he noticed a big crowd in the square in front of the National Palace. He went into one of the cantinas under the arcade and ordered a glass of beer. The waiter told him that Carranza's troops had lost Torreón and that Villa and Zapata were closing in on the Federal District. When he got to the bookstore, news was going down the street that Carranza's government had fled and that the revolutionists would be in the city before night. The storekeepers began to put up their shutters. Concha and her mother came crying, saying that it would be worse than the terrible week when Madero fell and that the revolutionists had sworn to burn and loot the city. Antonio ran in saying that the Zapatistas were bombarding Tacuba. Mac got a cab and went over to the Chamber of Deputies to see if he could find anybody he knew. All the doors were open to the street and there were papers littered along the corridors. There was nobody in the theater but an old Indian and his wife who were walking round hand in hand looking reverently at the gilded ceiling and the paintings and the tables covered with green plush. The old man carried his hat in his hand as if he were in church.

Mac told the cabman to drive to the paper where Salvador worked, but the janitor there told him with a wink that Salvador had gone to Vera Cruz with the chief of police. Then he went to the Embassy where he couldn't get a word with anybody. All the anterooms were full of Americans who had come in from ranches and concessions and who were cursing out President Wilson and giving each other the horrors with stories of the revolutionists. At the consulate Mac met a Syrian who offered to buy his stock of books. "No, you don't," said Mac and went back down Independencia.

When he got back to the store, newsboys were already running through the street crying, "Viva la revolucion revindicadora." Concha and her mother were in a panic and said they must get on the train to Vera Cruz or they'd all be murdered. The revolutionists were sacking convents and murdering priests and nuns. The old woman dropped on her knees in the corner of the room and began chanting Ave Marias.

"Aw, hell!" said Mac, "let's sell out and go back to the States. Want to go to the States, Concha?" Concha nodded vigorously and began to smile through her tears. "But what the devil can we do with your mother and Antonio?" Concha said she had a married sister in Vera Cruz. They could leave them there if they could ever get to Vera Cruz.

Mac, the sweat pouring off him, hurried back to the consulate to find the Syrian. They couldn't decide on the price. Mac was desperate because the banks were all closed and there was no way of getting any money. The Syrian said that he was from the Lebanon and an American citizen and a Christian and that he'd lend Mac a hundred dollars if Mac would give him a sixtyday note hypothecating his share in the bookstore for two hundred dollars. He said that he was an American citizen and a Christian and was risking his life to save Mac's wife and children. Mac was so flustered he noticed just in time that the Syrian was giving him a hundred dollars mex and that the note was made out in American dollars. The Syrian called upon God to protect them both and said it was an error and Mac went off with two hundred pesos in gold.

He found Concha all packed. She had closed up the store and was standing on the pavement outside with some bundles, the two cats in a basket, and Antonio and her mother, each wrapped in a blanket.

They found the station so packed full of people and baggage they couldn't get in the door. Mac went round to the yards and found a man named McGrath he knew who worked for the railroad. McGrath said he could fix them up, but that they must hurry. He put them into a secondclass coach out in the yards and said he'd buy their tickets, but would probably have to pay double for them. Sweat was pouring from under Mac's hatband when he finally got the two women seated and the basket of cats and bundles and Antonio stowed away. The train was already full, although it hadn't backed into the station yet. After several hours the train pulled out, a line of dusty soldiers fighting back the people on the platform who tried to rush the train as it left. Every seat was taken, the aisles were full of priests and nuns, there were welldressed people hanging onto the platforms.

Mac didn't have much to say sitting next to Concha in the dense heat of the slowmoving train. Concha sighed a great deal and her mother sighed, "Ay, de mi dios," and they gnawed on chickenwings and ate almond paste. The train was often stopped by groups of soldiers patrolling the line. On sidings were many boxcars loaded with troops, but nobody seemed to know what side they were on. Mac looked out at the endless crisscross ranks of centuryplants and the crumbling churches and watched the two huge snowy volcanos, Popocatepetl and Ixtacihuatl, change places on the horizon;

330

then there was another goldenbrown cone of an extinct volcano slowly turning before the train; then it was the blue-white peak of Orizaba in the distance growing up taller and taller into the cloudless sky.

After Huamantla they ran down through clouds. The rails rang under the merry clatter of the wheels curving down steep grades in the misty winding valley through moist forestgrowth. They began to feel easier. With every loop of the train the air became warmer and damper. They began to see orange and lemontrees. The windows were all open. At stations women came through selling beer and pulque and chicken and tortillas.

At Orizaba it was sunny again. The train stopped a long time. Mac sat drinking beer by himself in the station restaurant. The other passengers were laughing and talking, but Mac felt sore.

When the bell rang he didn't want to go back to Concha and her mother and their sighs and their greasy fingers and their chickenwings.

He got on another car. Night was coming on full of the smells of flowers and warm earth.

It was late the next day when they got into Vera Cruz. The town was full of flags and big red banners stretched from wall to wall of the orange and lemon and banana-colored streets with their green shutters and the palms waving in the seawind. The banners read: "Viva Obregon," "Viva La Revolucion Revindicadora," "Viva El Partido Laborista."

In the main square a band was playing and people were dancing. Sacred daws flew cawing among the dark umbrella-shaped trees.

Mac left Concha and her bundles and the old woman and Antonio on a bench and went to the Ward Line office to see about passage to the States. There everybody was talking about submarine warfare and America entering the Great War and German atrocities and Mac found that there was no boat for a week and that he didn't have enough cash even for two steerage passages. He bought himself a single steerage passage. He'd begun to suspect that he was making a damn fool of himself and decided to go without Concha.

When he got back to where she was sitting, she'd bought custardapples and mangos. The old woman and Antonio had gone off with the bundles to find her sister's house. The white cats were out of their basket and were curled up on the bench beside her. She looked up at Mac with a quick confident blackeyed smile and said that Porfirio and Venustiano were happy because they smelt fish. He gave her both hands to help her to her feet. At that moment he couldn't tell her he'd decided to go back to the States without her. Antonio came running up and said that they'd found his aunt and that she'd put them up and that everybody in Vera Cruz was for the revolution.

Going through the main square again, Concha said she was thirsty and wanted a drink. They were looking around for an empty table outside of one of the cafés when they caught sight of Salvador. He jumped to his feet and embraced Mac and cried, "Viva Obregon," and they had a mint julep American style. Salvador said that Carranza had been murdered in the mountains by his own staff officers and that onearmed Obregon had ridden into Mexico City dressed in white cotton like a peon wearing a big peon hat at the head of his Yaqui Indians and that there'd been no disorder and that the principles of Madero and Juarez were to be re-established and that a new era was to dawn.

They drank several mint juleps and Mac didn't say anything about going back to America.

He asked Salvador where his friend, the chief of police, was, but Salvador didn't hear him. Then Mac said to Concha suppose he went back to America without her, but she said he was only joking. She said she liked Vera Cruz and would like to live there. Salvador said that great days for Mexico were coming, that he was going back up the next day. That night they all ate supper at Concha's sister's house. Mac furnished the cognac. They all drank to the workers, to the trade-unions, to the partido laborista, to the social revolution and the agraristas.

Next morning Mac woke up early with a slight headache. He slipped out of the house alone and walked out along the breakwater. He was beginning to think it was silly to give up his bookstore like that. He went to the Ward Line office and took his ticket back. The clerk refunded him the money and he got back to Concha's sister's house in time to have chocolate and pastry with them for breakfast.

Proteus

Steinmetz was a hunchback,
son of a hunchback lithographer.

He was born in Breslau in eighteen-sixtyfive, graduated with highest honors at seventeen from the Breslau Gymnasium, went to the University of Breslau to study mathematics; mathematics to Steinmetz was muscular strength and long walks over the hills and the kiss of a girl in love and big evenings spent swilling beer with your friends;

on his broken back he felt the topheavy weight of society the way workingmen felt it on their straight backs, the way poor students felt it, was a member of a Socialist club, editor of a paper called *The People's Voice*.

Bismarck was sitting in Berlin like a big paperweight to keep the new Germany feudal, to hold down the empire for his bosses the Hohenzollerns.

Steinmetz had to run off to Zurich for fear of going to jail; at Zurich his mathematics woke up all the professors at the Polytechnic;

but Europe in the eighties was no place for a penniless German student with a broken back and a big head filled with symbolic calculus and wonder about electricity that is mathematics made power
and a Socialist at that.

With a Danish friend he sailed for America steerage on an old French line boat *La Champagne*,

lived in Brooklyn at first and commuted to Yonkers where he had a twelvedollar a week job with Rudolph Eichemeyer, who was a German exile from fortyeight, an inventor and electrician and owner of a factory where he made hatmaking machinery and electrical generators.

In Yonkers he worked out the theory of the Third Harmonics and

the law of hysteresis which states in a formula the hundredfold relations between the metallic heat, density, frequency, when the poles change places in the core of a magnet under an alternating current.

It is Steinmetz's law of hysteresis that makes possible all the transformers that crouch in little boxes and gableroofed houses in all the hightension lines all over everywhere. The mathematical symbols of Steinmetz's law are the patterns of all transformers everywhere.

In eighteen-ninetytwo, when Eichemeyer sold out to the corporation that was to form General Electric, Steinmetz was entered in the contract along with other valuable apparatus. All his life Steinmetz was a piece of apparatus belonging to General Electric.

First his laboratory was at Lynn, then it was moved and the little hunchback with it to Schenectady, the electric city.

General Electric humored him, let him be a Socialist, let him keep a greenhouseful of cactuses lit up by mercury lights, let him have alligators, talking crows, and a gila monster for pets, and the publicity department talked up the wizard, the medicine man who knew the symbols that opened up the doors of Ali Baba's cave.

Steinmetz jotted a formula on his cuff and next morning a thousand new powerplants had sprung up and the dynamos sang dollars and the silence of the transformers was all dollars,

and the publicity department poured oily stories into the ears of the American public every Sunday and Steinmetz became the little parlor magician,

who made a toy thunderstorm in his laboratory and made all the toy trains run on time and the meat stay cold in the icebox and the lamp in the parlor and the great lighthouses and the searchlights and the revolving beams of light that guide airplanes at night towards Chicago, New York, St. Louis, Los Angeles,

and they let him be a Socialist and believe that human society could be improved the way you can improve a dynamo, and they let him be pro-German and write a letter offering his services to Lenin because mathematicians are so impractical who make up formulas by which you can build powerplants, factories, subway systems, light, heat, air, sunshine, but not human relations that affect the stockholders' money and the directors' salaries.

Steinmetz was a famous magician and he talked to Edison tapping with the Morse code on Edison's knee

334

because Edison was so very deaf
and he went out West
to make speeches that nobody understood
and he talked to Bryan about God on a railroad train
and all the reporters stood round while he and Einstein
met face to face,
but they couldn't catch what they said
and Steinmetz was the most valuable piece of apparatus
General Electric had
until he wore out and died.

Janey

The trip to Mexico and the private car the Mexican government put at the disposal of J. Ward Moorehouse to go back north in was lovely but a little tiresome, and it was so dusty going across the desert. Janey bought some very pretty things so cheap, some turquoise jewelry and pink onyx to take home to Alice and her mother and sisters as presents. Going up in the private car J. Ward kept her busy dictating and there was a big bunch of men always drinking and smoking cigars and laughing at smutty stories in the smokingroom or on the observation platform. One of them was that man Barrow she'd done some work for in Washington. He always stopped to talk to her now and she didn't like the way his eyes were when he stood over her table talking to her, still he was an interesting man and quite different from what she'd imagined a laborleader would be like, and it amused her to think that she knew about Queenie and how startled he'd be if he knew she knew. She kidded him a good deal and she thought maybe he was getting a crush on her, but he was the sort of man who'd be like that with any woman.

They didn't have a private car after Laredo and the trip wasn't so nice. They went straight through to New York. She had a lower in a different car from J. Ward and his friends, and in the upper berth there was a young fellow she took quite a fancy to. His name was Buck Saunders and he was from the Panhandle of Texas and talked with the funniest drawl. He'd punched cows and worked in the Oklahoma oilfields and saved up some money and was going to see Washington City. He was tickled to death when she said she was from Washington and she told him all about what he ought

335

to see, the Capitol and the White House and the Lincoln Memorial and the Washington Monument and the Old Soldiers' Home and Mount Vernon. She said to be sure to go out to Great Falls and told him about canoeing on the canal and how she'd been caught in a terrible thunderstorm once near Cabin John's Bridge. They ate several meals together in the diningcar and he told her she was a dandy girl and awful easy to talk to and how he had a girl in Tulsa, Oklahoma, and how he was going to get a job in Venezuela, down at Maracaibo in the oilfields, because she'd thrown him over to marry a rich dirtfarmer who struck oil in his cowpasture. G. H. Barrow kidded Janey about her fine handsome pickup and she said what about him and the redheadedlady who got off in St. Louis, and they laughed and she felt quite devilish and that G. H. Barrow wasn't so bad after all. When Buck got off the train in Washington, he gave her a snapshot of himself taken beside an oilderrick and said he'd write every day and would come to New York to see her if she'd let him, but she never heard from him.

She liked Morton, the cockney valet, too, because he always spoke to her so respectfully. Every morning he'd come and report on how J. Ward was feeling. " 'E looks pretty black this mornin', Miss Williams," or, " 'E was whistlin' while 'e was shavin. Is 'e feelin' good? Rath-er."

When they got to the Pennsylvania Station, New York, she had to stay with Morton to see that the box of files was sent to the office at 100 Fifth Avenue and not out to Long Island where J. Ward's home was. She saw Morton off in a Pierce Arrow that had come all the way in from Great Neck to get the baggage, and went alone to the office in a taxicab with her typewriter and the papers and files. She felt scared and excited looking out of the taxicab window at the tall white buildings and the round watertanks against the sky and the puffs of steam way up and the sidewalks crowded with people and all the taxicabs and trucks and the shine and jostle and clatter. She wondered where she'd get a room to live, and how she'd find friends and where she'd eat. It seemed terribly scary being all alone in the big city like that and she wondered that she'd had the nerve to come. She decided she'd try to find Alice a job and that they'd take an apartment together, but where would she go tonight?

When she got to the office, everything seemed natural and reassuring and so handsomely furnished and polished so bright and typewriters going so fast and much more stir and bustle than there'd been in the offices of Dreyfus and Carroll; but everybody looked Jewish and she was afraid they wouldn't like her and afraid she wouldn't be able to hold down the job.

A girl named Gladys Compton showed her her desk, that she said had been Miss Rosenthal's desk. It was in a little passage just outside J. Ward's private office opposite the door to Mr. Robbins's office. Gladys Compton was Jewish and was Mr. Robbins's stenographer and said what a lovely girl Miss Rosenthal had been and how sorry they all were in the office about her accident and Janey felt that she was stepping into a dead man's shoes and would have a stiff row to hoe. Gladys Compton stared at her with resentful brown eyes that had a slight squint in them when she looked hard at anything and said she hoped she'd be able to get through the work, that sometimes the work was simply killing, and left her.

When things were closing up at five, J. Ward came out of his private office. Janey was so pleased to see him standing by her desk. He said he'd talked to Miss Compton and asked her to look out for Janey a little at first and that he knew it was hard for a young girl finding her way around a new city, finding a suitable place to live and that sort of thing, but that Miss Compton was a very nice girl and would help her out and he was sure everything would work out fine. He gave her a blue-eyed smile and handed her a closely written packet of notes and said would she mind coming in the office a little early in the morning and having them all copied and on his desk by nine o'clock. He wouldn't usually ask her to do work like that, but all the typists were so stupid and everything was in confusion owing to his absence. Janey felt only too happy to do it and warm all over from his smile.

She and Gladys Compton left the office together. Gladys Compton suggested that seeing as she didn't know the city hadn't she better come home with her. She lived in Flatbush with her father and mother and of course it wouldn't be what Miss Williams was accustomed to, but they had a spare room that they could let her have until she could find her way around, and that it was clean at least and that was more than you could say about many places. They went by the station to get her bag. Janey felt relieved not to have to find her way alone in all that crowd. Then they went down into the subway and got on an expresstrain that was packed to the doors and Janey didn't think she could stand it being packed in close with so many people. She thought she'd never get there and the trains made so much noise in the tunnel she couldn't hear what the other girl was saying.

At last they got out into a wide street with an elevated running down it where the buildings were all one or two stories and the stores were groceries and vegetable and fruit stores. Gladys Compton said, "We eat kosher, Miss Williams, on account of the old people. I hope you don't mind; of course Benny—Benny's my brudder—and I haven't any prejudices." Janey didn't know what kosher was, but she said of course she didn't mind, and told the other girl about how funny the food was down in Mexico, so peppery you couldn't hardly eat it.

When they got to the house Gladys Compton began to pronounce her words less precisely and was very kind and thoughtful. Her father was a little old man with glasses on the end of his nose and her mother was a fat pearshaped woman in a wig. They talked Yiddish among themselves. They did everything they could to make Janey comfortable and gave her a nice room and said they'd give her board and lodging for ten dollars a week as long as she wanted to stay and when she wanted to move she could go away and no hard feelings. The house was a yellow two family frame house on a long block of houses all exactly alike, but it was well heated and the bed was comfortable. The old man was a watchmaker and worked at a Fifth Avenue jeweler's. In the old country their name had been Kompshchski, but they said that in New York nobody could pronounce it. The old man had wanted to take the name of Freedman, but his wife thought Compton sounded more refined. They had a good supper with tea in glasses and soup with dumplings and red caviar and gefültefisch, and Janey thought it was very nice knowing people like that. The boy Benny was still in highschool, a gangling youth with heavy glasses who ate with his head hung over his plate and had a rude way of contradicting anything anybody said. Gladys said not to mind him, that he was very good in his studies and was going to study law. When the strangeness had worn off a little, Janey got to like the Comptons, particularly old Mr. Compton, who was very kind and treated everything that happened with gentle heartbroken humor.

The work at the office was so interesting. J. Ward was beginning to rely on her for things. Janey felt it was going to be a good year for her.

The worst thing was the threequarters of an hour ride in the subway to Union Square mornings. Janey would try to read the paper and to keep herself in a corner away from the press of bodies. She liked to get to the office feeling bright and crisp, with her dress feeling neat and her hair in nice order, but the long jolting ride fagged her out, made her feel as if she wanted to get dressed and take a bath all over again. She liked walking along Fourteenth Street, all garish and shimmering in the sunny early morning dust, and up Fifth Avenue to the office. She and Gladys were always among the first to get in. Janey kept flowers on her desk and would sometimes slip in and put a couple of roses in a silver vase on J. Ward's broad mahogany desk. Then she'd sort the mail, lay

his personal letters in a neat pile on the corner of the blotter-pad that was in a sort of frame of red illuminated Italian leather, read the other letters, look over his engagement book and make up a small typewritten list of engagements, interviews, copy to be got out, statements to the press. She laid the list in the middle of the blotter under a rawcopper paperweight from the Upper Peninsula of Michigan, checking off with a neat W. the items she could attend to without consulting him.

By the time she was back at her desk correcting the spelling in the copy that had emanated from Mr. Robbins's office the day before, she began to feel a funny tingle inside her; soon J. Ward would be coming in. She told herself it was all nonsense, but every time the outer office door opened she looked up expectantly. She began to worry a little; he might have had an accident driving in from Great Neck. Then, when she'd given up expecting him, he'd walk hurriedly through with a quick smile all around and the groundglass

340

door of his private office would close behind him. Janey would notice whether he had a fresh haircut or not. One day he had a splatter of mud on the trouserleg of his blue serge suit and she couldn't keep her mind off it all morning trying to think of a pretext to go in and tell him about it. Rarely he'd look at her directly with a flash of blue eyes as he passed, or stop and ask her a question. Then she'd feel fine.

The work at the office was so interesting. It put her right in the midst of headlines like when she used to talk to Jerry Burnham back at Dreyfus and Carroll's. There was the Onondaga Salt Products account and literature about bathsalts and chemicals and the employees' baseball team and cafeteria and old-age pensions, and Marigold Copper and combating subversive tendencies among the miners who were mostly foreigners who had to be educated in the principles of Americanism, and the Citrus Center Chamber of Commerce's campaign to educate the small investors in the North in the stable building qualities of the Florida fruit industry, and the slogan to be launched, "Put an Alligator Pear on Every Breakfast Table" for the Avocado Producers Co-operative. That concern occasionally sent up a case so that everybody in the office had an alligator pear to take home, except Mr. Robbins, who wouldn't take his, but said they tasted like soap. Now the biggest account of all was the Southwestern Oil campaign to counter the insidious anti-American propaganda of the British oilcompanies in Mexico and to oppose the intervention lobby of the Hearst interests in Washington.

In June Janey went to her sister Ellen's wedding. It was funny being in Washington again. Going on the train Janey looked forward a whole lot to seeing Alice, but when she saw her they couldn't seem to find much to talk about. She felt out of place at her mother's. Ellen was marrying a law student at Georgetown University who had been a lodger and the house was full of college boys and young girls after the wedding. They all laughed and giggled around and Mrs. Williams and Francie seemed to enjoy it all right, but Janey was glad when it was time for her to go down to the station and take the train to New York again. When she said goodbye to Alice she didn't say anything about her coming down to New York to get an apartment.

She felt pretty miserable on the train sitting in the stuffy parlorcar looking out at towns and fields and signboards. Getting back to the office the next morning was like getting home.

It was exciting in New York. The sinking of the *Lusitania* had made everybody feel that America's going into the war was only a question of months. There were many flags up on

Fifth Avenue. Janey thought a great deal about the war. She had a letter from Joe from Scotland that he'd been torpedoed on the steamer *Marchioness* and that they'd been ten hours in an open boat in a snowstorm off Pentland Firth with the current carrying them out to sea, but that they'd landed and he was feeling fine and that the crew had gotten bonuses and that he was making big money anyway. When she'd read the letter she went in to see J. Ward with a telegram that had just come from Colorado and told him about her brother being torpedoed and he was very much interested. He talked about being patriotic and saving civilization and the historic beauties of Rheims Cathedral. He said he was ready to do his duty when the time came, and that he thought America's entering the war was only a question of months.

A very welldressed woman came often to see J. Ward. Janey looked enviously at her lovely complexion and her neat dresses, not ostentatious but very chic, and her manicured nails and her tiny feet. One day the door swung open so that she could hear her and J. Ward talking familiarly together. "But, J.W., my darling," she was saying, "this office is a fright. It's the way they used to have their offices in Chicago in the early eighties." He was laughing. "Well, Eleanor, why don't you redecorate it for me? Only the work would have to be done without interfering with business. I can't move, not with the press of important business just now."

Janey felt quite indignant about it. The office was lovely the way it was, quite distinctive, everybody said so. She wondered who this woman was who was putting ideas into J. Ward's head. Next day when she had to make out a check for two hundred and fifty dollars on account to Stoddard and Hutchins, Interior Decorators, she almost spoke her mind, but after all it was hardly her business. After that Miss Stoddard seemed to be around the office all the time. The work was done at night so that every morning when Janey came in, she found something changed. It was all being done over in black and white with curtains and upholstery of a funny claret-color. Janey didn't like it at all, but Gladys said it was in the modern style and very interesting. Mr. Robbins refused to have his private cubbyhole touched and he and J. Ward almost had words about it, but in the end he had his own way and the rumor went round that J. Ward had had to increase his salary to keep him from going to another agency.

Labor Day Janey moved. She was sorry to leave the Comptons, but she'd met a middleaged woman named Eliza Tingley who worked for a lawyer on the same floor as J. Ward's office. Eliza Tingley was a Baltimorean, had passed a bar examination herself, and Janey said to herself that she

342

was a woman of the world. She and her twin brother, who was a certified accountant, had taken a floor of a house on West Twentythird Street in the Chelsea district and they asked Janey to come in with them. It meant being free from the subway and Janey felt that the little walk over to Fifth Avenue every morning would do her good. The minute she'd seen Eliza Tingley in the lunchcounter downstairs she'd taken a fancy to her. Things at the Tingleys were free and easy and Janey felt at home there. Sometimes they had a drink in the evening. Eliza was a good cook and they'd take a long time over dinner and play a couple of rubbers of threehanded bridge before going to bed. Saturday night they'd almost always go to the theater. Eddy Tingley would get the seats at a cutrate agency he knew. They subscribed to the *Literary Digest* and to the *Century* and the *Ladies' Home Journal* and Sundays they had roast chicken or duck and read the magazine section of the *New York Times*.

The Tingleys had a good many friends and they liked Janey and included her in everything and she felt that she was living the way she'd like to live. It was exciting too that winter with rumors of war all the time. They had a big map of Europe hung up on the livingroom wall and marked the positions of the Allied armies with little flags. They were heart and soul for the Allies, and names like Verdun or Chemin des Dames started little shivers running down their spines. Eliza wanted to travel and made Janey tell her over and over again every detail of her trip to Mexico; they began to plan a trip abroad together when the war was over and Janey began to save money for it. When Alice wrote from Washington that maybe she would pull up stakes in Washington and go down to New York, Janey wrote saying that it was so hard for a girl to get a job in New York just at present and that maybe it wasn't such a good idea.

All that fall J. Ward's face looked white and drawn. He got in the habit of coming into the office Sunday afternoons and Janey was only too glad to run around there after dinner to help him out. They'd talk over the events of the week in the office and J. Ward would dictate a lot of private letters to her and tell her she was a treasure and leave her there typing away happily. Janey was worried too. Although new accounts came in all the time the firm wasn't in a very good financial condition. J. Ward had made some unfortunate plunges in the Street and was having a hard time holding things together. He was anxious to buy out the large interest still held by old Mrs. Staple and talked of notes his wife had gotten hold of and that he was afraid his wife would use unwisely. Janey could see that his wife was a disagreeable peevish woman trying to use her mother's money as a means of keeping a hold on J. Ward. She never said anything to the Tingleys about J. Ward personally, but she talked a great deal about the business and they agreed with her that the work was so interesting. She was looking forward to this Christmas because J. Ward had hinted that he would give her a raise.

A rainy Sunday afternoon she was typing off a confidential letter to Judge Planet inclosing a pamphlet from a detective agency describing the activities of labor agitators among the Colorado miners, and J. Ward was walking up and down in front of the desk staring with bent brows at the polished toes of his shoes when there was a knock on the outer office door. "I wonder who that could be?" said J. Ward. There was something puzzled and nervous about the way he spoke. "It may be Mr. Robbins forgotten his key," said Janey. She went to see. When she opened the door Mrs. Moorehouse brushed past her. She wore a wet slicker and carried an umbrella, her face was pale and her nostrils were twitching. Janey closed the door gently and went to her own desk and sat down. She was worried. She took up a pencil and started drawing scrolls round the edge of a piece of typewriter paper. She couldn't help hearing what was going on in J. Ward's private office. Mrs. Moorehouse had shot in slamming the groundglass door behind her. "Ward, I can't stand it . . . I won't stand it another minute," she was screaming at the top of her voice. Janey's heart started beating very fast. She heard J. Ward's voice low and conciliatory, then Mrs. Moorehouse's. "I won't be treated like that, I tell you. I'm not a child to be treated like that . . . You're taking advantage of my condition. My health won't stand being treated like that."

"Now look here, Gertrude, on my honor as a gentleman," J. Ward was saying. "There's nothing in it, Gertrude. You lie there in bed imagining things and you shouldn't break in like this. I'm a very busy man. I have important transactions that demand my complete attention."

Of course it's outrageous, Janey was saying to herself.

"You'd still be in Pittsburgh working for Bessemer Products, Ward, if it wasn't for me and you know it . . . You may despise me, but you don't despise Dad's money . . . but I'm through, I tell you. I'm going to start divorce . . ."

"But, Gertrude, you know very well there's no other woman in my life."

"How about this woman you're seen round with all the time . . . what's her name . . . Stoddard? You see, I know more than you think . . . I'm not the kind of woman you think I am, Ward. You can't make a fool of me, do you hear?"

Mrs. Moorehouse's voice rose into a rasping shriek. Then she seemed to break down and Janey could hear her sobbing. "Now, Gertrude," came Ward's voice soothingly, "you've gotten yourself all wrought up over nothing . . . Eleanor Stoddard and I have had a few business dealings . . . She's a bright woman and I find her stimulating . . . intellectually, you understand . . . We've occasionally eaten dinner together, usually with mutual friends, and that's absolutely . . ." Then his voice sunk so low that Janey couldn't hear what he was saying. She began to think she ought to slip out. She didn't know what to do.

She'd half gotten to her feet when Mrs. Moorehouse's voice soared to a hysterical shriek again. "Oh, you're cold as a fish . . . You're just a fish. I'd like you better if it was true, if you were having an affair with her . . . But I don't care; I won't be used as a tool to use Dad's money."

The door of the private office opened and Mrs. Moorehouse came out, gave Janey a bitter glare as if she suspected her relations with J. Ward too, and went out. Janey sat down at her desk again trying to look unconcerned. Inside the private office she could hear J. Ward striding up and down with a heavy step. When he called her his voice sounded weak:

"Miss Williams."

She got up and went into the private office with her pencil and pad in one hand. J. Ward started to dictate as if nothing had happened, but halfway through a letter to the president of the Ansonia Carbide Corporation he suddenly said, "Oh hell," and gave the wastebasket a kick that sent it spinning against the wall.

"Excuse me, Miss Williams; I'm very much worried . . . Miss Williams, I'm sure I can trust you not to mention it to a soul . . . You understand, my wife is not quite herself; she'd been ill . . . the last baby . . . you know those things sometimes happen to women."

Janey looked up at him. Tears had started into her eyes, "Oh, Mr. Moorehouse, how can you think I'd not understand? . . . Oh, it must be dreadful for you, and this is a great work and so interesting." She couldn't say any more. Her lips couldn't form any words. "Miss Williams," J. Ward was saying, "I . . . er . . . appreciate . . . er." Then he picked up the wastepaper basket. Janey jumped up and helped him pick up the crumpled papers and trash that had scattered over the floor. His face was flushed from stooping. "Grave responsibilities . . . Irresponsible woman may do a hell of a lot of damage, you understand." Janey nodded and nodded. "Well, where were we? Let's finish up and get out of here."

They set the wastebasket under the desk and started in on the letters again.

All the way home to Chelsea, picking her way through the slush and pools of water on the streets, Janey was thinking of what she'd like to have said to J. Ward to make him understand that everybody in the office would stand by him whatever happened.

When she got in the apartment, Eliza Tingley said a man had called her up. "Sounded like a rather rough type; wouldn't give his name; just said to say Joe had called up and that he'd call up again." Janey felt Eliza's eyes on her inquisitively.

"That's my brother Joe, I guess . . . He's a . . . he's in the merchant marine."

Some friends of the Tingleys came in, they had two tables of bridge and were having a very jolly evening when the telephone rang again, and it was Joe. Janey felt herself blushing as she talked to him. She couldn't ask him up and still she wanted to see him. The others were calling to her to play her hand. He said he had just got in and that he had some presents for her and he'd been clear out to Flatbush and that the yids there had told him she lived in Chelsea now and he was

in the cigarstore at the corner of Eighth Avenue. The others
were calling to her to play her hand. She found herself saying
that she was very busy doing some work and wouldn't he
meet her at five tomorrow at the office building where she
worked. She asked him again how he was and he said, "Fine,"
but he sounded disappointed. When she went back to her
table they all kidded her about the boyfriend and she laughed
and blushed, but inside she felt mean because she hadn't
asked him to come up.

Next evening it snowed. When she stepped out of the elevator crowded to the doors at five o'clock, she looked eagerly
round the vestibule. Joe wasn't there. As she was saying
goodnight to Gladys she saw him through the door. He was

standing outside with his hands deep in the pockets of a blue
peajacket. Big blobs of snowflakes spun round his face that
looked lined and red and weatherbeaten.

"Hello, Joe," she said.

"Hello, Janey."

"When did you get in?"

"A couple a days ago."

"Are you in good shape, Joe? How do you feel?"

347

"I gotta rotten head today . . . Got stinkin' last night."

"Joe, I was so sorry about last night, but there were a lot of people there and I wanted to see you alone so we could talk."

Joe grunted.

"That's awright, Janey . . . Gee, you're lookin' swell. If any of the guys saw me with you they'd think I'd picked up somethin' pretty swell awright."

Janey felt uncomfortable. Joe had on heavy workshoes and there were splatters of gray paint on his trouserlegs. He had a package wrapped in newspaper under his arm.

"Let's go eat somewheres . . . Jeez, I'm sorry I'm not rigged up better. We lost all our duffle, see, when we was torpedoed."

"Were you torpedoed again?"

Joe laughed, "Sure, right off Cape Race. It's a great life . . . Well, that's strike two . . . I brought along your shawl, though, by God if I didn't . . . I know where we'll eat; we'll eat at Lüchow's."

"Isn't Fourteenth Street a little . . ."

"Naw, they got a room for ladies . . . Janey, you don't think I'd take you to a dump wasn't all on the up an' up?"

Crossing Union Square a seedylooking young man in a red sweater said, "Hi, Joe." Joe dropped back of Janey for a minute and he and the young man talked with their heads together. Then Joe slipped a bill in his hand, said, "So long, Tex," and ran after Janey, who was walking along feeling a little uncomfortable.

She didn't like Fourteenth Street after dark.

"Who was that, Joe?"

"Some damn AB or other. I knew him down New Orleans . . . I call him Tex. I don't know what his name is . . . He's down on his uppers."

"Were you down in New Orleans?"

Joe nodded. "Took a load a molasses out on the *Henry B. Higginbotham* . . . Piginbottom we called her. Well, she's layin' easy now on the bottom awright . . . on the bottom of the Grand Banks."

When they went in the restaurant the headwaiter looked at them sharply and put them at a table in the corner of a little inside room. Joe ordered a big meal and some beer, but Janey didn't like beer, so he had to drink hers too. After Janey had told him all the news about the family and how she liked her job and expected a raise Christmas and was so happy living with the Tingleys who were so lovely to her, there didn't seem to be much to say. Joe had bought tickets to the Hippodrome, but they had plenty of time before that

started. They sat silent over their coffee and Joe puffed at a cigar. Janey finally said it was a shame the weather was so mean and that it must be terrible for the poor soldiers in the trenches and she thought the Huns were just too barbarous and the *Lusitania* and how silly the Ford peace ship idea was. Joe laughed in the funny abrupt way he had of laughing now, and said, "Pity the poor sailors out at sea on a night like this." He got up to get another cigar.

Janey thought what a shame it was he'd had his neck shaved when he had a haircut; his neck was red and had little wrinkles in it and she thought of the rough life he must be leading, and when he came back she asked him why he didn't get a different job.

"You mean in a shipyard? They're making big money in shipyards, but hell, Janey, I'd rather knock around . . . It's all for the experience, as the feller said when they blew his block off."

"No, but there are boys not half so bright as you are with nice clean jobs right in my office . . . and a future to look forward to."

"All my future's behind me," said Joe with a laugh. "Might go down to Perth Amboy get a job in a munitions factory, but I rather be blowed up in the open, see?"

Janey went on to talk about the war and how she wished we were in it to save civilization and poor little helpless Belgium.

"Can that stuff, Janey," said Joe. He made a cutting gesture with his big red hand above the tablecloth. "You people don't understand it, see . . . The whole damn war's crooked from start to finish. Why don't they torpedo any French Line boats? Because the Frogs have it all set with the Jerries, see, that if the Jerries leave their boats alone they won't shell the German factories back of the front. What we wanta do 's sit back and sell 'em munitions and let 'em blow 'emselves to hell. An' those babies are makin' big money in Bordeaux and Toulouse or Marseilles while their own kin are shootin' daylight into each other at the front, and it's the same thing with the limeys . . . I'm tellin' ye, Janey, this war's crooked, like every other goddam thing."

Janey started to cry. "Well, you needn't curse and swear all the time."

"I'm sorry, sister," said Joe humbly, "but I'm just a bum an' that's about the size of it an' not fit to associate with a nicedressed girl like you."

"No, I didn't mean that," said Janey, wiping her eyes.

"Gee, but I forgot to show you the shawl." He unwrapped the paper package. Two Spanish shawls spilled out on the table, one of black lace and the other green silk embroidered with big flowers.

"Oh, Joe, you oughtn't to give me both of them . . . You ought to give one to your best girl."

"The kinda girls I go with ain't fit to have things like that . . . I bought those for you, Janey."

Janey thought the shawls were lovely and decided she'd give one of them to Eliza Tingley.

They went to the Hippodrome, but they didn't have a very good time. Janey didn't like shows like that much and Joe kept falling asleep. When they came out of the theater it was bitterly cold. Gritty snow was driving hard down Sixth Avenue almost wiping the "L" out of sight. Joe took her home in a taxi and left her at her door with an abrupt "Solong, Janey." She stood a moment on the step with her key in her hand and watched him walking west towards Tenth Avenue and the wharves, with his head sunk in his peajacket.

That winter the flags flew every day on Fifth Avenue. Janey read the paper eagerly at breakfast; at the office there was talk of German spies and submarines and atrocities and propaganda. One morning a French military mission came to

call on J. Ward, handsome pale officers with blue uniforms and red trousers and decorations. The youngest of them was on crutches. They'd all of them been severely wounded at the front. When they'd left, Janey and Gladys almost had words because Gladys said officers were a lot of lazy loafers and she'd rather see a mission of private soldiers. Janey wondered if she oughtn't to tell J. Ward about Gladys's pro-Germanism, whether it mightn't be her patriotic duty. The Comptons might be spies; weren't they going under an assumed name? Benny was a scientist or worse, she knew that. She decided she'd keep her eyes right open.

The same day G. H. Barrow came in. Janey was in the private office with them all the time. They talked about President Wilson and neutrality and the stockmarket and the delay in transmission in the *Lusitania* note. G. H. Barrow had had an interview with the President. He was a member of a committee endeavoring to mediate between the railroads and the Brotherhoods that were threatening a strike. Janey liked him better than she had on the private car coming up from Mexico, so that when he met her in the hall just as he was leaving the office she was quite glad to talk to him and when he asked her to come out to dinner with him, she accepted and felt very devilish.

All the time G. H. Barrow was in New York, he took Janey out to dinner and the theater. Janey had a good time and she could always kid him about Queenie if he tried to get too friendly going home in a taxi. He couldn't make out where she'd found out about Queenie and he told her the whole story and how the woman kept hounding him for money, but he said that now he was divorced from his wife and there was nothing she could do. After making Janey swear she'd never tell a soul, he explained that through a legal technicality he'd been married to two women at the same time and that Queenie was one of them and that now he'd divorced them both, and there was nothing on earth Queenie could do, but the newspapers were always looking for dirt and particularly liked to get something on a liberal like himself devoted to the cause of labor. Then he talked about the art of life and said American women didn't understand the art of life; at least women like Queenie didn't. Janey felt very sorry for him, but when he asked her to marry him she laughed and said she really would have to consult counsel before replying. He told her all about his life and how poor he'd been as a boy and then about jobs as stationagent and freightagent and conductor and the enthusiasm with which he'd gone into work for the Brotherhood and how his muckraking articles on conditions in the rail-

352

roads had made him a name and money so that all his old associates felt he'd sold out, but that, so help me, it wasn't true. Janey went home and told the Tingleys all about the proposal, only she was careful not to say anything about Queenie or bigamy, and they all laughed and joked about it, and it made Janey feel good to have been proposed to by such an important man and she wondered why it was such interesting men always fell for her and regretted they always had that dissipated look, but she didn't know whether she wanted to marry G. H. Barrow or not.

At the office next morning, she looked him up in *Who's Who* and there he was, *Barrow, George Henry, publicist* . . . but she didn't think she could ever love him. At the office that day J. Ward looked very worried and sick and Janey felt so sorry for him and quite forgot about G. H. Barrow. She was called into a private conference J. Ward was having with Mr. Robbins and an Irish lawyer named O'Grady, and they said did she mind if they rented a safe-deposit box in her name to keep certain securities in and started a private account for her at the Bankers Trust. They were forming a new corporation. There were business reasons why something of the sort might become imperative. Mr. Robbins and J. Ward would own more than half the stock of a new concern and would work for it on a salary basis. Mr. Robbins looked very worried and a little drunk and kept lighting cigarettes and forgetting them on the edge of the desk and kept saying, "You know very well, J. W., that anything you do is O.K. by me." J. Ward explained to Janey that she'd be an officer of the new corporation, but of course would in no way be personally liable. It came out that old Mrs. Staple was suing J. Ward to recover a large sum of money, and that his wife had started divorce proceedings in Pennsylvania and that she was refusing to let him go home to see the children and that he was living at the McAlpin.

"Gertrude's lost her mind," said Mr. Robbins genially. Then he slapped J. Ward on the back. "Looks like the fat was in the fire now," he roared. "Well, I'm goin' out to lunch; a man must eat . . . and drink . . . even if he's a putative bankrupt."

J. Ward scowled and said nothing and Janey thought it was in very bad taste to talk like that and so loud too.

When she went home that evening she told the Tingleys that she was going to be a director of the new corporation and they thought it was wonderful that she was getting ahead so fast and that she really ought to ask for a raise even if business was in a depressed state. Janey smiled, and said, "All in good time." On the way home she had stopped in the tele-

graph office on Twentythird Street and wired G. H. Barrow,
who had gone up to Washington: LET'S JUST BE FRIENDS.

Eddy Tingley brought out a bottle of sherry and at dinner
he and Eliza drank a toast. "To the new executive," and
Janey blushed crimson and was very pleased. Afterwards they
played a rubber of dummy bridge.

The Camera Eye (26)

the garden was crowded and outside Madison Square
was full of cops that made everybody move on and the
bombsquad all turned out

we couldn't get a seat so we ran up the stairs to the top
gallery and looked down through the blue air at the faces
thick as gravel and above them on the speakers' stand
tiny black figures and a man was speaking and whenever
he said war there were hisses and whenever he said Russia there was clapping on account of the revolution I
didn't know who was speaking somebody said Max East-
man and somebody said another guy but we clapped and
yelled for the revolution and hissed for Morgan and the
capitalist war and there was a dick looking into our faces
as if he was trying to remember them

then we went to hear Emma Goldman at the Bronx
Casino but the meeting was forbidden and the streets
around were very crowded and there were moving vans
moving through the crowd and they said the moving vans
were full of cops with machineguns and there were little
policedepartment Fords with searchlights and they
charged the crowd with the Fords and the searchlights   everybody talked machineguns revolution civil
liberty freedom of speech but occasionally somebody got
into the way of a cop and was beaten up and shoved into a
patrol wagon and the cops were scared and they said they
were calling out the fire department to disperse the crowd
and everybody said it was an outrage and what about Washington and Jefferson and Patrick Henry?

Afterwards we went to the Brevoort it was much nicer
everybody who was anybody was there and there was

Emma Goldman eating frankfurters and sauerkraut and everybody looked at Emma Goldman and at everybody else that was anybody and everybody was for peace and the co-operative commonwealth and the Russian revolution and we talked about red flags and barricades and suitable posts for machineguns

   and we had several drinks and welsh rabbits and paid our bill and went home, and opened the door with a latchkey and put on pajamas and went to bed and it was comfortable in bed

Newsreel XVIII

Goodbye, Piccadilly, farewell, Leicester Square
It's a long long way to Tipperary

WOMAN TRAPS HUSBAND WITH GIRL IN HOTEL

to such a task we can dedicate our lives
and our fortunes, everything that we are,
and everything that we have, with the pride of those who know
that the day has come when America is privileged to spend her
blood and her might for the principles that gave her birth
and happiness and the peace that she has treasured. God helping her she can do no other

> *It's a long way to Tipperary*
> *It's a long way to go*
> *It's a long way to Tipperary*
> *And the sweetest girl I know*

TRAITORS BEWARE

FOUR MEN IN EVANSTON FINED FOR KILLING BIRDS

WILSON WILL FORCE DRAFT

food gamblers raise price of canned foods   move for dry U S in war   files charges when men ignore national air

356

MOONEY CASE INCENTIVE

Goodbye, Piccadilly, farewell, Leicester Square
It's a long long way to Tipperary
But my heart's right there.

HOUSE REFUSES TO ALLOW T. R. TO RAISE TROOPS

the American Embassy was threatened today with an
attack by a mob of radical Socialists led by Nicolai Lenin
an exile who recently returned from Switzerland via Germany.

ALLIES TWINE FLAGS ON TOMB OF WASHINGTON

Eleanor Stoddard

Eleanor thought that things were very exciting that winter.
She and J. W. went out a great deal together, to all the
French operas and to first nights. There was a little French
restaurant where they ate hors d'oeuvres way east of Fiftysix
Street. They went to see French paintings in the galleries up
Madison Avenue. J. W. began to get interested in art, and
Eleanor loved going round with him because he had such a
romantic manner about everything and he used to tell her she
was his inspiration and that he always got good ideas when
he'd been talking to her. They often talked about how silly
people were who said that a man and a woman couldn't have
a platonic friendship. They wrote each other little notes in
French every day. Eleanor often thought it was a shame J.
W. had such a stupid wife who was an invalid too, but she
thought that the children were lovely and it was nice that
they both had lovely blue eyes like their father.

She had an office now all by herself and had two girls
working with her to learn the business and had quite a lot of
work to do. The office was in the first block above Madison
Square on Madison Avenue and she had just had her own

name on it. Eveline Hutchins didn't have anything to do with it any more as Doctor Hutchins had retired and the Hutchinses had all moved out to Santa Fe. Eveline sent her an occasional box of Indian curios or pottery and the watercolors the Indian children did in the schools, and Eleanor found they sold very well. In the afternoon she'd ride downtown in a taxi and look up at the Metropolitan Life tower and the Flatiron Building and the lights against the steely Manhattan

sky and think of crystals and artificial flowers and gilt patterns on indigo and claretcolored brocade.

The maid would have tea ready for her and often there would be friends waiting for her, young architects or painters. There'd always be flowers, calla lilies with the texture of icecream or a bowl of freesias. She'd talk a while before slipping off to dress for dinner. When J. W. phoned that he couldn't come she'd feel very bad. If there was still anybody there who'd come to tea she'd ask him to stay and have pot-luck with her.

The sight of the French flag excited her always or when a band played *Tipperary;* and one evening when they were going to see *The Yellow Jacket* for the third time, she had on a new furcoat that she was wondering how she was going to pay for, and she thought of all the bills at her office and the house on Sutton Place she was remodeling on a speculation and wanted to ask J. W. about a thousand he'd said he'd invested for her and wondered if there'd been any turnover yet. They'd been talking about the air raids and poison gas and the effect of the war news downtown and the Bowmen of Mons and the Maid of Orleans and she said she believed in the supernatural, and J. W. was hinting something about reverses on the Street and his face looked drawn and worried; but they were crossing Times Square through the eighto'clock crowds and the skysigns flashing on and off. The fine little triangular men were doing exercises on the Wrigley sign and suddenly a grindorgan began to play *The Marseillaise* and it was too beautiful; she burst into tears and they talked about Sacrifice and Dedication and J. W. held her arm tight through the fur coat and gave the organgrinder man a dollar. When they got to the theater Eleanor hurried down to the ladies' room to see if her eyes had got red. But when she looked in the mirror they weren't red at all and there was a flash of heartfelt feeling in her eyes, so she just freshened up her face and went back up to the lobby, where J. W. was waiting for her with the tickets in his hand; her gray eyes were flashing and had tears in them.

Then one evening J. W. looked very worried indeed and said when he was taking her home from the opera where they'd seen *Manon* that his wife didn't understand their relations and was making scenes and threatening to divorce him. Eleanor was indignant and said she must have a very coarse nature not to understand that their relations were pure as driven snow. J. W. said she had and that he was very worried and he explained that most of the capital invested in his agency was his mother-in-law's and that she could bankrupt him if she wanted to, which was much worse than a divorce. At that Eleanor felt very cold and crisp and said that she would rather go out of his life entirely than break up his home and that he owed something to his lovely children. J. W. said she was his inspiration and he had to have her in his life and when they got back to Eighth Street they walked back and forth in Eleanor's white glittering drawingroom in the heavy smell of lilies wondering what could be done. They smoked many cigarettes, but they couldn't seem to come to any decision. When J. W. left he said with a sigh. "She may have detectives shadowing me this very minute," and he went away very despondent.

After he'd gone, Eleanor walked back and forth in front of the long Venetian mirror between the windows. She didn't know what to do. The decorating business was barely breaking even. She had the amortization to pay off on the house on Sutton Place. The rent of her apartment was two months overdue and there was her fur coat to pay for. She'd counted on the thousand dollars' worth of shares J. W. had said would be hers if he made the killing he expected in that Venezuela Oil stock. Something must have gone wrong or else he would have spoken of it. When Eleanor went to bed she didn't sleep. She felt very miserable and lonely. She'd have to go back to the drudgery of a department store. She was losing her looks and her friends and now if she had to give up J. W. it would be terrible. She thought of her colored maid Augustine with her unfortunate loves that she always told Eleanor about and she wished she'd been like that. Maybe she'd been wrong from the start to want everything so justright and beautiful. She didn't cry, but she lay all night with her eyes wide and smarting staring at the flowered molding round the ceiling that she could see in the light that filtered in from the street through her lavender tulle curtains.

A couple of days later at the office she was looking at some antique Spanish chairs an old furniture dealer was trying to sell her when a telegram came:

DISAGREEABLE DEVELOPMENTS MUST SEE YOU INADVISABLE USE TELEPHONE MEET ME TEA AT FIVE OCLOCK PRINCE GEORGE HOTEL

It wasn't signed. She told the man to leave the chairs and when he'd gone stood a long time looking down at a pot of lavender crocuses with yellow pistils she had on her desk. She was wondering if it would do any good if she went out to Great Neck and talked to Gertrude Moorehouse. She called Miss Lee who was making up some curtains in the other room and asked her to take charge of the office and that she'd phone during the afternoon.

She got into a taxi and went up to the Pennsylvania Station. It was a premature spring day. People were walking along the street with their overcoats unbuttoned. The sky was a soft mauve with frail clouds like milkweed floss. In the smell of furs and overcoats and exhausts and bundledup bodies came an unexpected scent of birchbark. Eleanor sat bolt upright in the back of the taxi driving her sharp nails into the palms of her graygloved hands. She hated these treacherous days when winter felt like spring. They made the lines come out on her face, made everything seem to crumble about her, there seemed to be no firm footing any more. She'd go out and talk to Gertrude Moorehouse as one woman to another. A scandal would ruin everything. If she talked to her awhile she'd make her realize that there had never been anything between her and J. W. A divorce scandal would ruin everything. She'd lose her clients and have to go into bankruptcy and the only thing to do would be to go back to Pullman to live with her uncle and aunt.

She paid the taximan and went down the stairs to the Long Island Railroad. Her knees were shaky and she felt desperately tired as she pushed her way through the crowd to the information desk. No, she couldn't get a train to Great Neck till 2:13. She stood in line a long time for a ticket. A man stepped on her foot. The line of people moved maddeningly slow past the ticketwindow. When she got to the window it was several seconds before she could remember the name of the place she wanted a ticket for. The man looked at her through the window, with peevish shoebutton eyes. He wore a green eyeshade and his lips were too red for his pale face. The people behind were getting impatient. A man with a tweed coat and a heavy suitcase was already trying to brush past her. "Great Neck and return." As soon as she'd bought the ticket the thought came to her that she wouldn't have time to get out there and back by five o'clock. She put the ticket in her gray silk purse that had a little design in jet on it. She thought of killing herself. She would take the subway downtown and go up in the elevator to the top of the Woolworth Building and throw herself off.

Instead she went out to the taxistation. Russet sunlight was pouring through the gray colonnade, the blue smoke of exhausts rose into it crinkled like watered silk. She got into a taxi and told the driver to take her round Central Park. Some of the twigs were red and there was a glint on the long buds of beeches, but the grass was still brown and there were piles of dirty snow in the gutters. A shivery raw wind blew across the ponds. The taximan kept talking to her. She couldn't catch what he said and got tired of making random answers and told him to leave her at the Metropolitan Art Museum. While she was paying him a newsboy ran by crying "Extra!" Eleanor bought a paper for a nickel and the taximan bought a paper. "I'll be a sonova . . ." she heard the taximan exclaim, but she ran up the steps fast for fear she'd have to talk to him. When she got in the quiet silvery light of the museum she opened up the paper. A rancid smell of printer's ink

came from it; the ink was still sticky and came off on her gloves.

DECLARATION OF WAR

A matter of hours now Washington observers declare.
German's note thoroughly unsatisfactory.

She left the newspaper on a bench and went to look at the Rodins. After she'd looked at the Rodins she went to the Chinese wing. By the time she was ready to go down Fifth Avenue in the bus—she felt she'd been spending too much on taxis—she felt elated. All the way downtown she kept remembering the Age of Bronze. When she made out J. W. in the stuffy pinkish light of the hotel lobby she went towards him with a springy step. His jaw was set and his blue eyes were on fire. He looked younger than last time she'd seen him. "Well, it's come at last," he said. "I just wired Washington offering my services to the government. I'd like to see 'em try and pull a railroad strike now." "It's wonderful and terrible," said Eleanor. "I'm trembling like a leaf."

362

They went to a little table in the corner behind some heavy draperies to have tea. They had hardly sat down before the orchestra started playing *The Star-Spangled Banner*, and they had to get to their feet. There was great bustle in the hotel. People kept running about with fresh editions of the papers, laughing and talking loud. Perfect strangers borrowed each other's newspapers, chatted about the war, lit cigarettes for each other.

"I have an idea, J. W.," Eleanor was saying, holding a piece of cinnamontoast poised in her pointed fingers, "that if I went out and talked to your wife as one woman to another, she'd understand the situation better. When I was decorating the house she was so kind and we got along famously."

"I have offered my services to Washington," said Ward. "There may be a telegram at the office now. I'm sure that Gertrude will see that it is her simple duty."

"I want to go, J. W.," said Eleanor. "I feel I must go."

"Where?"

"To France."

"Don't do anything hasty, Eleanor."

"No, I feel I must . . . I could be a very good nurse . . . I'm not afraid of anything; you ought to know that, J. W."

The orchestra played *The Star-Spangled Banner* again; Eleanor sang some of the chorus in a shrill little treble voice. They were too excited to sit still long and went over to J. W.'s office in a taxi. The office was in great excitement. Miss Williams had had a flagpole put up in the center window and was just raising the flag on it. Eleanor went over to her and they shook hands warmly. The cold wind was rustling the papers on the desk and typewritten pages were sailing across the room, but nobody paid any attention. Down Fifth Avenue a band was coming near playing *Hail, Hail, the Gang's All Here*. All along office windows were brightly lit, flags were slapping against their poles in the cold wind, clerks and stenographers were leaning out and cheering, dropping out papers that sailed and whirled in the bitter eddying wind.

"It's the Seventh Regiment," somebody said and they all clapped and yelled. The band was clanging loud under the window. They could hear the tramp of the militiamen's feet. All the automobiles in the stalled traffic tooted their horns. People on the tops of the busses were waving small flags. Miss Williams leaned over and kissed Eleanor on the cheek. J. W. stood by looking out over their heads with a proud smile on his face.

After the band had gone and traffic was running again they put the window down and Miss Williams went around picking up and arranging loose papers. J. W. had a telegram from

Washington accepting his services on the Public Information Committee that Mr. Wilson was gathering about him and said he'd leave in the morning. He called up Great Neck and asked Gertrude if he could come out to dinner and bring a friend. Gertrude said he might and that she hoped she'd be able to stay up to see them. She was excited by the warnews, but she said the thought of all that misery and slaughter gave her horrible pains in the back of the head.

"I have a hunch that if I take you out to dinner at Gertrude's, everything will be all right," he said to Eleanor. "I'm rarely wrong in my hunches."

"Oh, I know she'll understand," said Eleanor.

As they were leaving the office they met Mr. Robbins in the hall. He didn't take his hat off or the cigar out of his mouth. He looked drunk. "What the hell is this, Ward?" he said. "Are we at war or not?"

"If we're not we will be before morning," said J. W.

"It's the goddamnedest treason in history," said Mr. Robbins. "What did we elect Wilson for instead of Old Fuzzywhiskers except to keep us out of the goddam mess?"

"Robbins, I don't agree with you for a minute," said J. W. "I think it's our duty to save . . ." But Mr. Robbins had disappeared through the office door leaving a strong reek of whiskey behind him.

"I'd have given him a piece of my mind," said Eleanor, "if I hadn't seen that he was in no condition."

Driving out to Greak Neck in the Pierce Arrow was thrilling. A long red afterglow lingered in the sky. Crossing the Queensboro Bridge with the cold wind back of them was like flying above lights and blocks of houses and the purple bulk of Blackwell's Island and the steamboats and the tall chimneys and the blue light of powerplants. They talked of Edith Cavell and airraids and flags and searchlights and the rumble of armies advancing and Joan of Arc. Eleanor drew the fur robe up to her chin and thought about what she'd say to Gertrude Moorehouse.

When they got to the house she felt a little afraid of a scene. She stopped in the hall to do up her face with a pocketmirror she had in her bag.

Gertrude Moorehouse was sitting in a long chair beside a crackling fire. Eleanor glanced around the room and was pleased at how lovely it looked. Gertrude Moorehouse went very pale when she saw her. "I wanted to talk to you," said Eleanor.

Gertrude Moorehouse held out her hand without getting up. "Excuse me for not getting up, Miss Stoddard," she said, "but I'm absolutely prostrated by the terrible news."

"Civilization demands a sacrifice . . . from all of us," said Eleanor.

"Of course it is terrible what the Huns have done, cutting the hands off Belgian children and all that," said Gertrude Moorehouse.

"Mrs. Moorehouse," said Eleanor. "I want to speak to you about this unfortunate misunderstanding of my relations with your husband . . . Do you think I am the sort of woman who could come out here and face you if there was anything in these horrible rumors? Our relations are pure as driven snow."

"Please don't speak of it, Miss Stoddard. I believe you."

When J. W. came in they were sitting on either side of the fire talking about Gertrude's operation.

Eleanor got to her feet. "Oh, I think it's wonderful of you, J. W."

J. W. cleared his throat and looked from one to the other. "It's little less than my duty," he said.

"What is it?" asked Gertrude.

"I have offered my services to the government to serve in whatever capacity they see fit for the duration of the war."

"Not at the front," said Gertrude with a startled look.

"I'm leaving for Washington tomorrow . . . Of course I shall serve without pay."

"Ward, that's noble of you," said Gertrude. He walked over slowly until he stood beside her chair, then he leaned over and kissed her on the forehead. "We must all make our sacrifices . . . My dear, I shall trust you and your mother . . ."

"Of course, Ward, of course . . . It's all been a silly mis-understanding." Gertrude flushed red. She got to her feet. "I've been a damn suspicious fool . . . but you mustn't go to the front, Ward. I'll talk mother around" . . . She went up to him and put her hands on his shoulders. Eleanor stood back against the wall looking at them. He wore a smoothfitting tuxedo. Gertrude's salmoncolored teagown stood out against the black. His light hair was ashgray in the light from the crystal chandelier against the tall ivorygray walls of the room. His face was in shadow and looked very sad. Eleanor thought how little people understood a man like that, how beautiful the room was, like a play, like a Whistler, like Sarah Bernhardt. Emotion misted her eyes.

"I'll join the Red Cross," she said. "I can't wait to get to France."

Newsreel XIX

U.S. AT WAR

UPHOLD NATION CITY'S CRY

Over there
Over there

at the annual meeting of the stockholders of the Colt Patent Firearms Manufacturing Company a $2,500,000 melon was cut. The present capital stock was increased. The profits for the year were 259 per cent

JOYFUL SURPRISE OF BRITISH

The Yanks are coming
We're coming o-o-o-ver

PLAN LEGISLATION TO KEEP COLORED PEOPLE
FROM WHITE AREAS

many millions paid for golf about Chicago Hindu agitators in nationwide scare Armour urges U.S. save earth from famine

ABUSING FLAG TO BE PUNISHED

Labor deputies peril to Russia acts have earmarks of dishonorable peace London hears

*And we won't come home
Till it's over over there.*

The Camera Eye (27)

there were priests and nuns on the *Espagne* the Atlantic was glassgreen and stormy covers were clamped on the portholes and all the decklights were screened and you couldn't light a match on deck

but the stewards were very brave and said the Boche wouldn't sink a boat of the Compagnie Générale anyway, because of the priests and nuns and the Jesuits and the Comité des Forges promising not to bombard the Bassin de la Briey where the big smelters were and stock in the company being owned by the Prince de Bourbon and the Jesuits and the priests and nuns

anyhow everybody was very brave except for Colonel and Mrs. Knowlton of the American Red Cross who had waterproof coldproof submarineproof suits like eskimosuits and they wore them and they sat up on deck with the suits all blown up and only their faces showing and there were firstaid kits in the pockets and in the belt there was a waterproof container with milkchocolate and crackers and maltedmilk tablets.

and in the morning you'd walk round the deck and there would be Mr. Knowlton blowing up Mrs. Knowlton

or Mrs. Knowlton blowing up Mr. Knowlton

the Roosevelt boys were very brave in stiff visored new American army caps and sharpshooter medals on the khaki whipcord and they talked all day about We must come in We must come in

as if the war were a swimming pool

and the barman was brave and the stewards were brave

they'd all been wounded and they were very glad that they were stewards and not in the trenches

and the pastry was magnificent

at last it was the zone and a zigzag course we sat quiet in the bar and then it was the mouth of the Gironde and a French torpedoboat circling round the ship in the early pearl soft morning and the steamers following the little patrolboat on account of the minefields the sun was rising red over the ruddy winegrowing land and the Gironde was full of freighters and airplanes in the sun and battleships

the Garonne was red   it was autumn there were barrels of new wine and shellcases along the quays in front of the grayfaced houses and the masts of stocky sailboats packed against the great red iron bridge

at the Hotel of the Seven Sisters everybody was in mourning but business was brisk on account of the war and every minute they expected the government to come down from Paris

up north they were dying in the mud and the trenches but business was good in Bordeaux and the winegrowers and the shipping agents and the munitionsmakers crowded into the Chapon Fin and ate ortolans and mushrooms and truffles and there was a big sign

MEFIEZ-VOUS

les oreilles ennemis vous écoutent

red wine twilight and yellowgravelled squares edged with winebarrels and a smell of chocolate in the park gray statues and the names of streets

Street of Lost Hopes, Street of the Spirit of the Laws, Street of Forgotten Footsteps

and the smell of burning leaves and the grayfaced Bourbon houses crumbling into red wine twilight

at the Hotel of the Seven Sisters after you were in bed late at night you suddenly woke up and there was a secretserviceagent going through your bag

and he frowned over your passport and peeped in your books and said Monsieur c'est la petite visite

Fighting Bob

La Follette was born in the town limits of Primrose; he worked on a farm in Dane County, Wisconsin, until he was nineteen.

At the University of Wisconsin he worked his way through. He wanted to be an actor, studied elocution and Robert Ingersoll and Shakespeare and Burke;

(who will ever explain the influence of Shakespeare in the last century, Marc Antony over Caesar's bier, Othello to the Venetian Senate, and Polonius, everywhere Polonius?)

riding home in a buggy after commencement he was Booth and Wilkes writing the Junius papers and Daniel Webster and Ingersoll defying God and the togaed great grave and incorruptible as statues magnificently spouting through the capitoline centuries;

he was the star debater in his class,

and won an interstate debate with an oration on the character of Iago.

He went to work in a law office and ran for district attorney. His schoolfriends canvassed the county riding round evenings. He bucked the machine and won the election.

It was the revolt of the young man against the state republican machine

and Boss Keyes the postmaster in Madison who ran the county was so surprised he about fell out of his chair.

That gave La Follette a salary to marry on. He was twentyfive years old.

Four years later he ran for Congress; the university was with him again; he was the youngsters' candidate. When he was elected he was the youngest representative in the house.

He was introduced round Washington by Philetus Sawyer the Wisconsin lumber king who was used to stacking and selling politicians the way he stacked and sold cordwood.

He was a Republican and he'd bucked the machine. Now they thought they had him. No man could stay honest in Washington.

Booth played Shakespeare in Baltimore that winter. Booth never would go to Washington on account of the bitter memory of his brother. Bob La Follette and his wife went to every performance.

In the parlor of the Plankinton Hotel in Milwaukee during the state fair, Boss Sawyer the lumber king tried to bribe him to influence his brother-in-law who was presiding judge over the prosecution of the Republican state treasurer;

Bob La Follette walked out of the hotel in a white rage. From that time it was war without quarter with the Republican machine in Wisconsin until he was elected governor and wrecked the Republican machine;

this was the tenyears war that left Wisconsin the model state where the voters, orderloving Germans and Finns, Scandinavians fond of their own opinion, learned to use the new leverage, direct primaries, referendum and recall.

La Follette taxed the railroads

John C. Payne said to a group of politicians in the lobby of the Ebbitt House in Washington "La Follette's a damn fool if he thinks he can buck a railroad with five thousand miles of continuous track, he'll find he's mistaken . . . We'll take care of him when the time comes."

But when the time came the farmers of Wisconsin and the young lawyers and doctors and businessmen just out of school

> took care of him
> and elected him governor three times
> and then to the United States Senate,

where he worked all his life making long speeches full of statistics, struggling to save democratic government, to make a farmers' and small businessmen's commonwealth, lonely with his back to the wall, fighting corruption and big business and high finance and trusts and combinations of combinations and the miasmic lethargy of Washington.

He was one of "the little group of willful men expressing no opinion but their own"

who stood out against Woodrow Wilson's armed ship bill that made war with Germany certain; they called it a filibuster, but it was six men with nerve straining to hold back a crazy steamroller with their bare hands;

the press pumped hatred into its readers against La Follette,

the traitor;

they burned him in effigy in Illinois;

in Wheeling they refused to let him speak.

In nineteen-twentyfour La Follette ran for President and without money or political machine rolled up four and a half million votes

but he was a sick man, incessant work and the breathed out air of committee rooms and legislative chambers choked him

and the dirty smell of politicians,
and he died,
an orator haranguing from the capitol of a lost republic;
but we will remember

how he sat firm in March nineteen-seventeen while Woodrow Wilson was being inaugurated for the second time, and for three days held the vast machine at deadlock. They wouldn't let him speak; the galleries glared hatred at him; the Senate was a lynching party,

a stumpy man with a lined face, one leg stuck out in the aisle and his arms folded and a chewed cigar in the corner of his mouth

and an undelivered speech on his desk,
a willful man expressing no opinion but his own.

Charley Anderson

Charley Anderson's mother kept a railroad boardinghouse near the Northern Pacific station at Fargo, North Dakota. It was a gabled frame house with porches all round, painted mustard yellow with chocolate-brown trim, and out back there was always washing hanging out on sagging lines that ran from a pole near the kitchen door to a row of broken-down chickenhouses. Mrs. Anderson was a quietspoken grayhaired woman with glasses; the boarders were afraid of her and did their complaining about the beds, or the food, or the eggs weren't fresh to waddling bigarmed Lizzie Green from the north of Ireland who was the help and cooked and did all the housework. When any of the boys came home drunk, it was Lizzie with a threadbare man's overcoat pulled over her nightgown who came out to make them shut up. One of the brakemen tried to get fresh with Lizzie one night and got such a sock in the jaw that he fell clear off the front porch. It was Lizzie who washed and scrubbed Charley when he was little, who made him get to school on time and put arnica on his knees when he skinned them and soft soap on his chilblains and mended

the rents in his clothes. Mrs. Anderson had already raised three
children who had grown up and left home before Charley
came, so that she couldn't seem to keep her mind on Charley.
Mr. Anderson had also left home about the time Charley was
born; he'd had to go West on account of his weak lungs,
couldn't stand the hard winters, was how Mrs. Anderson put
it. Mrs. Anderson kept the accounts, preserved or canned
strawberries, peas, peaches, beans, tomatoes, pears, plums, applesauce as each season came round, made Charley read a
chapter of the Bible every day and did a lot of churchwork.

Charley was a chunky little boy with untidy towhair and
gray eyes. He was a pet with the boarders and liked things allright except Sundays when he'd have to go to church twice
and to Sundayschool and then right after dinner his mother
would read him her favorite sections of Matthew or Esther or
Ruth and ask him questions about the chapters he'd been as-
signed for the week. This lesson took place at a table with a
red tablecloth next to a window that Mrs. Anderson kept
banked with pots of patienceplant, wandering jew, begonias
and ferns summer and winter. Charley would have pins and
needles in his legs and the big dinner he'd eaten would have
made him drowsy and he was terribly afraid of committing

373

the sin against the Holy Ghost, which his mother hinted was inattention in church or in Sundayschool or when she was reading him the Bible. Winters the kitchen was absolutely quiet except for the faint roaring of the stove or Lizzie's heavy step or puffing breath as she stacked the dinnerdishes she'd just washed back in the cupboard. Summers it was much worse. The other kids would have told him about going swimming down in the Red River or fishing or playing follow my leader in the lumberyard or on the coalbunkers back of the roundhouse, and the caught flies would buzz thinly in the festooned tapes of flypaper and he'd hear the yardengine shunting freightcars or the through train for Winnipeg whistling for the station and the bell clanging, and he'd feel sticky and itchy in his stiff collar and he'd keep looking up at the loudticking porcelain clock on the wall. It made the time go too slowly to look up at the clock often, so he wouldn't let himself look until he thought fifteen minutes had gone by, but when he looked again it'd only be five minutes and he'd feel desperate. Maybe it'd be better to commit the sin against the Holy Ghost right there and be damned good and proper once and for all and run away with a tramp the way Dolphy Olsen did, but he didn't have the nerve.

By the time he was ready for highschool he began to find funny things in the Bible, like the kids talked about when they got tired playing toad in the hole in the deep weeds back of the lumberyard fence, the part about Onan and the Levite and his concubine and the Song of Solomon, it made him feel funny and made his heart pound when he read it, like listening to scraps of talk among the railroadmen in the boardinghouse, and he knew what hookers were and what was happening when women got so fat in front and it worried him and he was careful when he talked to his mother not to let her know he knew about things like that.

Charley's brother Jim had married the daughter of a liverystable owner in Minneapolis. The spring Charley was getting ready to graduate from the eighth grade they came to visit Mrs. Anderson. Jim smoked cigars right in the house and jollied his mother and while he was there there was no talk of Biblereading. Jim took Charley fishing one Sunday up the Cheyenne and told him that if he came down to the Twin Cities when school was over he'd give him a job helping round the garage he was starting up in part of his fatherinlaw's liverystable. It sounded good when he told the other guys in school that he had a job in the city for the summer. He was glad to get out, as his sister Esther had just come back from taking a course in nursing and nagged him all the time about talking

374

slang and not keeping his clothes neat and eating too much pie.

He felt fine the morning he went over to Moorhead all alone, carrying a suitcase Esther had lent him, to take the train for the Twin Cities. At the station he tried to buy a package of cigarettes, but the man at the newsstand kidded him and said he was too young. When he started it was a fine spring day and a little too hot. There was sweat on the flanks of the big horses pulling the long line of flourwagons that was crossing the bridge. While he was waiting in the station the air became stifling and a steamy mist came up. The sunlight shone red on the broad backs of the grain elevators along the track. He heard one man say to another, "Looks to me like it might be a tornado," and when he got on the train he half leaned out of the open window watching purple thunderheads building up in the northwest beyond the brightgreen wheat that stretched clear to the clouds. He kinda hoped it would be a tornado because he'd never seen one, but when the light-

ning began cracking like a whip out of the clouds he felt a little scared, though being on the train with the conductor and the other passengers made it seem safer. It wasn't a tornado, but it was a heavy thundershower and the wheatfields turned to zinc as great trampling hissing sheets of rain advanced slowly across them. Afterwards the sun came out and Charley opened the window and everything smelt like spring and there were birds singing in all the birchwoods and in the dark firs round all the little shining lakes.

Jim was there to meet him at the Union Depot in a Ford truck. They stopped at the freight station and Charley had to help load a lot of heavy packages of spare parts shipped from Detroit and marked "Vogel's Garage." Charley tried to look as if he'd lived in a big city all his life, but the clanging trolleycars and the roughshod hoofs of truckhorses striking sparks out of the cobbles and the goodlooking blond girls and the stores and the big German beersaloons and the hum that came from mills and machineshops went to his head. Jim looked tall and thin in his overalls and had a new curt way of talking. "Kid, you see you mind yourself a little up to the house; the old man's an old German, Hedwig's old man, an' a little pernickety, like all old Germans are," said Jim when they'd filled the truck and were moving slowly through the heavy traffic. "Sure, Jim," said Charley, and he began to feel a little uneasy about what it 'ud be like living in Minneapolis. He wished Jim 'ud smile a little more.

Old man Vogel was a stocky redfaced man with untidy gray hair and a potbelly, fond of dumpling and stews with plenty of rich sauce on them and beer, and Jim's wife Hedwig was

his only daughter. His wife was dead, but he had a middleaged German woman everybody addressed as Aunt Hart-

mann to keep house for him. She followed the men around all
the time with a mop and between her and Hedwig, whose blue
eyes had a peevish look because she was going to have a baby
in the fall, the house was so spotless that you could have eaten
a fried egg off the linoleum anywhere. They never let the windows be opened for fear of the dust coming in. The house was
right on the street and the liverystable was in the yard behind,
entered through an alley beyond which was the old saddler's
shop that had just been done over as a garage. When Jim and
Charley drove up the signpainters were on a stepladder out
front putting up the new shiny red and white sign that read
"VOGEL'S GARAGE." "The old bastard," muttered Jim. "He
said he'd call it Vogel and Anderson's, but what the hell!" Everything smelt of stables, and a colored man was leading a
skinny horse around with a blanket over him.

All that summer Charley washed cars and drained transmis-
sions and relined brakes. He was always dirty and greasy in
greasy overalls, in the garage by seven every morning and not
through till late in the evening when he was too tired to do

anything but drop into the cot that had been fixed for him in the attic over the garage. Jim gave him a dollar a week for pocket money and explained that he was mighty generous to do it, as it was to Charley's advantage to learn the business. Saturday nights he was the last one to get a bath and there usually wasn't anything but lukewarm water left, so that he'd have a hard time getting cleaned up. Old man Vogel was a socialist and no churchgoer and spent all day Sunday drinking beer with his cronies. At Sunday dinner everybody talked German, and Jim and Charley sat at the table glumly without saying anything, but old Vogel plied them with beer and made jokes at which Hedwig and Aunt Hartmann always laughed uproariously, and after dinner Charley's head would be swimming from the beer that tasted awful bitter to him, but he felt he had to drink it, and old man Vogel would tease him to smoke a cigar and then tell him to go out and see the town. He'd walk out feeling overfed and a little dizzy and take the streetcar to St. Paul to see the new state capitol or to Lake Harriet or go out to Big Island Park and ride on the rollercoaster or walk around the Parkway until his feet felt like they'd drop off. He didn't know any kids his own age at first, so he took to reading for company. He'd buy every number of *Popular Mechanics* and the *Scientific American* and *Adventure* and the *Wide World Magazine*. He had it all planned to start building a yawlboat from the plans in the *Scientific American* and to take a trip down the Mississippi River to the Gulf. He'd live by shooting ducks and fishing for catfish. He started saving up his dollars to buy himself a shotgun.

He liked it all right at old man Vogel's, though, on account of not having to read the Bible or go to church, and he liked tinkering with motors and learned to drive the Ford truck. After a while he got to know Buck and Slim Jones, two brothers about his age who lived down the block. He was a pretty big guy to them on account of working in a garage. Buck sold newspapers and had a system of getting into movingpicture shows by the exit doors and knew all the best fences to see ballgames from. Once Charley got to know the Jones boys he'd run round to their place as soon as he was through dinner Sundays and they'd have a whale of a time getting hitches all over the place on graintrucks, riding on the back bumpers of streetcars and getting chased by cops and going out on the lumber booms and going swimming and climbing round above the falls and he'd get back all sweaty and with his good suit dirty and be bawled out by Hedwig for being late for supper. Whenever old Vogel found the Jones boys hanging round the garage he'd chase them out, but when he and Jim were away, Gus the colored stableman would come over smelling of

378

horses and tell them stories about horseraces and fast women and whiskeydrinking down at Louisville and the proper way to take a girl the first time and how he and his steady girl just did it all night without stopping not even for a minute.

Labor Day old man Vogel took Jim and his daughter and Aunt Hartmann out driving in the surrey behind a fine pair of bays that had been left with him to sell and Charley was left to take care of the garage in case somebody came along who wanted gas or oil. Buck and Slim came round and they all talked about how it was Labor Day and wasn't it hell to pay that they weren't going out anywhere. There was a doubleheader out at the Fair Grounds and lots of other ballgames around. The trouble started by Charley showing Buck how to drive the truck, then to show him better he had to crank her up, then before he knew it he was telling them he'd take them for a ride round the block. After they'd ridden round the block he went back and closed up the garage and they went joyriding out towards Minnehaha. Charley said to himself he'd drive very carefully and be home hours before the folks got back, but somehow he found himself speeding down an asphalt boulevard and almost ran into a ponycart full of little girls that turned in suddenly from a side road. Then on the way home they were drinking sarsaparilla out of the bottles and having a fine time when Buck suddenly said there was a cop on a motorcycle following them. Charley speeded up to get away from the cop, made a turn too sharp and stopped

with a crash against a telegraph pole. Buck and Slim beat it as fast as they could run and there was Charley left to face the cop.

The cop was a Swede and cursed and swore and bawled him out and said he'd take him to the hoosegow for driving without a license, but Charley found his brother Jim's license under the seat and said his brother had told him to take the car back to the garage after they'd delivered a load of apples out at Minnehaha and the cop let him off and said to drive more carefully another time. The car ran all right except one fender was crumpled up and the steering wheel was a little funny. Charley drove home so slow that the radiator was boiling over when he got back and there was the surrey standing in front of the house and Gus holding the bays by the head and all the family just getting out.

There was nothing he could say. The first thing they saw was the crumpled fender. They all lit into him and Aunt Hartmann yelled the loudest and old Vogel was purple in the face and they all talked German at him and Hedwig yanked at his coat and slapped his face and they all said Jim 'd have to give him a licking. Charley got sore and said nobody was going to give him a licking and then Jim said he reckoned he'd better go back to Fargo anyway, and Charley went up and packed his suitcase and went off without saying goodbye to any of them that evening with his suitcase in one hand and five back numbers of the *Argosy* under his arm. He had just enough jack saved up to get a ticket to Barnesville. After that he had to play hide and seek with the conductor until he dropped off the train at Moorhead. His mother was glad to see him and said he was a good boy to get back in time to visit with her a little before highschool opened and talked about his being confirmed. Charley didn't say anything about the Ford truck and decided in his mind he wouldn't be confirmed in any damned church. He ate a big breakfast that Lizzie fixed for him and went into his room and lay down on the bed. He wondered if not wanting to be confirmed was the sin against the Holy Ghost, but the thought didn't scare him as much as it used to. He was sleepy from sitting up on the train all night and fell asleep right away.

Charley dragged through a couple of years of highschool, making a little money helping around the Moorhead Garage evenings, but he didn't like it home any more after he got back from his trip to the Twin Cities. His mother wouldn't let him work Sundays and nagged him about being confirmed and his sister Esther nagged him about everything and Lizzie treated him as if he was still a little kid, called him "Pet" before the boarders, and he was sick of schooling, so the spring when he was seventeen, after commencement, he went down to Minneapolis again looking for a job on his own this time. As he had money to keep him for a few days, the first thing he did was to go down to Big Island Park. He wanted to ride on the rollercoasters and shoot in the shootinggalleries and go swimming and pick up girls. He was through with hick towns like Fargo and Moorhead where nothing ever happened.

It was almost dark when he got to the lake. As the little steamboat drew up to the wharf, he could hear the jazzband through the trees, and the rasp and rattle of the rollercoaster and yells as a car took a dip. There were a dancing pavilion and colored lights among the trees and a smell of girls' perfumery and popcorn and molasses candy and powder from the shootinggallery and the barkers were at it in front of their booths. As it was Monday evening there weren't very many people. Charley went round the rollercoaster a couple of times and got to talking with the young guy who ran it about what the chances were of getting a job round there.

The guy said to stick around, Svenson the manager would be there when they closed up at eleven, and he thought he might be looking for a guy. The guy's name was Ed Walters; he said it wasn't much of a graft, but that Svenson was pretty straight; he let Charley take a couple of free rides to see how the rollercoaster worked and handed him out a bottle of cream soda and told him to keep his shirt on. This was his second year in the amusement game and he had a sharp foxface and a wise manner.

Charley's heart was thumping when a big hollowfaced man with coarse sandy hair came round to collect the receipts at the ticket booth. That was Svenson. He looked Charley up and down and said he'd try him out for a week and to remember that this was a quiet family amusement park and that he wouldn't stand for any rough stuff and told him to come round at ten the next morning. Charley said "So long" to Ed Walters and caught the last boat and car back to town. When he got out of the car it was too late to take his bag out of the station parcelroom; he didn't want to spend money on a room or to go out to Jim's place, so he slept on a bench in front of the City Hall. It was a warm night and it made him feel good to be sleeping on a bench like a regular hobo. The arclights kept getting in his eyes, though, and he was nervous about the cop; it'd be a hell of a note to get pinched for a vag and lose the job out at the park. His teeth were chattering when he woke up in the gray early morning. The arclights spluttered pink against a pale lemonyellow sky; the big business blocks with all their empty windows looked funny and gray and de-

serted. He had to walk fast pounding the pavement with his heels to get the blood going through his veins again.

He found a stand where he could get a cup of coffee and a doughnut for five cents and went out to Lake Minnetonka on the first car. It was a bright summer day with a little north in the wind. The lake was very blue and the birchtrunks looked very white and the little leaves danced in the wind green-yellow against the dark evergreens and the dark blue of the sky. Charley thought it was the most beautiful place he'd ever seen. He waited a long time drowsing in the sun on the end of the wharf for the boat to start over to the island. When he got there the park was all locked up, there were shutters on all the booths and the motionless red and blue cars of the rollercoaster looked forlorn in the morning light. Charley roamed round for a while, but his eyes smarted and his legs ached and his suitcase was too heavy, so he found a place sheltered by the wall of a shack from the wind and lay down in the warm sun on the pineneedles and went to sleep with his suitcase beside him.

He woke up with a start. His Ingersoll said eleven. He had a cold sinking feeling. It'd be lousy to lose the job by being late. Svenson was there sitting in the ticket booth at the roller-coaster with a straw hat on the back of his head. He didn't say anything about the time. He just told Charley to take his coat off and help MacDonald the engineer oil up the motor.

Charley worked on that rollercoaster all summer until the park closed in September. He lived in a little camp over at Excelsior with Ed Walters and a wop named Spagnolo who had a candy concession.

In the next camp Svenson lived with his six daughters. His wife was dead. Anna the eldest was about thirty and was cashier at the amusement park, two of them were waitresses at the Tonka Bay Hotel and the others were in highschool and didn't work. They were all tall and blond and had nice complexions. Charley fell for the youngest, Emiscah, who was just about his age. They had a float and a springboard and they all went in swimming together. Charley wore a bathingsuit upper and a pair of khaki pants all summer and got very sunburned. Ed's girl was Zona and all four of them used to go out canoeing after the amusement park closed, particularly warm nights when there was a moon. They didn't drink, but they smoked cigarettes and played the phonograph and kissed and cuddled up together in the bottom of the canoe. When they'd got back to the boys' camp, Spagnolo would be in bed and they'd haze him a little and put junebugs under his blankets and he'd curse and swear and toss around. Emiscah was a great hand for making fudge, and Charley was crazy about her and she seemed to like him. She taught him how to frenchkiss and would stroke his hair and rub herself up against him like a cat, but she never let him go too far, and he wouldn't have thought it was right anyway. One night all four of them went out and built a fire under a pine in a patch of big woods up the hill back of the camps. They toasted marshmallows and sat round the fire telling ghoststories. They had blankets and Ed knew how to make a bed with hemlock twigs stuck in the ground and they all four of them slept in the same blankets and tickled each other and roughhoused around and it took them a long time to get to sleep. Part of the time Charley lay between the two girls and they cuddled up close to him, but he got a hardon and couldn't sleep and was worried for fear the girls would notice.

He learned to dance and to play poker and when Labor Day came he hadn't saved any money, but he felt he'd had a wonderful summer.

He and Ed got a room together in St. Paul. He got a job as machinist's assistant in the Northern Pacific shops and made fair money. He learned to run an electric lathe and started a course in nightschool to prepare for civil engineering at the Mechanical Arts High. Ed didn't seem to have much luck about jobs, all he seemed to be able to do was pick up a few

dollars now and then as attendant at a bowling alley. Sundays they often ate dinner with the Svensons. Mr. Svenson was running a small movie house called the Leif Ericsson on Fourth Street, but things weren't going so well. He took it for granted that the boys were engaged to two of his daughters and was only too glad to see them come around. Charley took Emiscah out every Saturday night and spent a lot on candy and taking her to vaudeville shows and to a Chink restaurant where you could dance afterwards. At Christmas he gave her his seal ring and after that she admitted that she was engaged to him. They'd go back to the Svensons' and sit on the sofa in the parlor hugging and kissing.

She seemed to enjoy getting him all wrought up, then she'd run off and go and fix her hair or put some rouge on her face and be gone a long time and he'd hear her upstairs giggling with her sisters. He'd walk up and down in the parlor, where there was only one light in a flowered shade, feeling nervous and jumpy. He didn't know what to do. He didn't want to get married because that 'ud keep him from traveling round the country and getting ahead in studying engineering. The other guys at the shop who weren't married went down the line or picked up streetwalkers, but Charley was afraid of getting a disease, and he never seemed to have any time what with nightschool and all, and besides it was Emiscah he wanted.

After he'd given her a last rough kiss, feeling her tongue in his mouth and his nostrils full of her hair and the taste of her mouth in his mouth, he'd walk home with his ears ringing,

384

feeling sick and weak; when he got to bed he couldn't sleep, but would toss around all night thinking he was going mad and Ed'd grunt at him from the other side of the bed for crissake to keep still.

In February Charley got a bad sore and the doctor he went to said it was diphtheria and sent him to the hospital. He was terribly sick for several days after they gave him the antitoxin. When he was getting better Ed and Emiscah came to see him and sat on the edge of his bed and made him feel good. Ed was all dressed up and said he had a new job and was making big money, but he wouldn't tell what it was. Charley got the idea that Ed and Emiscah were going round together a little since he'd been sick, but he didn't think anything of it.

The man in the next cot, who was also recovering from diphtheria, was a lean grayhaired man named Michaelson. He'd been working in a hardware store that winter and was having a hard time. Up to a couple of years before he'd had a farm in Iowa in the cornbelt, but a series of bad crops had ruined him, the bank had foreclosed and taken the farm and

385

offered to let him work it as a tenant, but he'd said he'd be damned if he'd work as a tenant for any man and had pulled up his stakes and come to the city, and here he was fifty years old with a wife and three small children to support trying to start from the ground up again. He was a great admirer of Bob La Follette and had a theory that the Wall Street bankers were conspiring to seize the government and run the country by pauperizing the farmer. He talked all day in a thin wheezy voice until the nurse made him shut up, about the Non-Partisan League and the Farmer-Labor Party and the destiny of the great Northwest and the need for workingmen and farmers to stick together to elect honest men like Bob La Follette. Charley had joined a local of an A. F. of L. union that fall and Michaelson's talk, broken by spells of wheezing and coughing, made him feel excited and curious about politics. He decided he'd read the papers more and keep up with what was going on in the world. What with this war and everything you couldn't tell what might happen.

When Michaelson's wife and children came to see him he introduced them to Charley and said that being laid up next to a bright young fellow like that made being sick a pleasure. It made Charley feel bad to see how miserably pale and illfed they looked and what poor clothes they had on in this zero weather. He left the hospital before Michaelson did and the last thing Michaelson said when Charley leaned over him to shake his dry bony hand was "Boy, you read Henry George, do you hear . . . ? He knows what's the trouble with this country; damme if he don't."

Charley was so glad to be walking on his pins down the snowy street in the dry icecold wind and to get the smell of iodoform and sick people out of his head that he forgot all about it.

First thing he did was to go to Svensons'. Emiscah asked him where Ed Walters was. He said he hadn't been home and didn't know. She looked worried when he said that and he wondered about it. "Don't Zona know?" asked Charley. "No, Zona's got a new feller; that's all she thinks about." Then she smiled and patted his hand and babied him a little bit and they sat on the sofa and she brought out some fudge she'd made and they held hands and gave each other sticky kisses and Charley felt happy. When Anna came in she said how thin he looked and that they'd have to feed him up, and he stayed to supper. Mr. Svenson said to come and eat supper with them every night for a while until he was on his feet again. After supper they all played hearts in the front parlor and had a fine time.

When Charley got back to his lodginghouse, he met the

landlady in the hall. She said his friend had left without paying the rent and that he'd pay up right here and now or else she wouldn't let him go up to his room. He argued with her and said he'd just come out of the hospital and she finally said she'd let him stay another week. She was a big softlooking woman with puckered cheeks and a yellow chintz apron full of little pockets. When Charley got up to the hall bedroom where he'd slept all winter with Ed, it was miserably cold and lonely. He got into the bed between the icy sheets and lay shivering, feeling weak and kiddish and almost ready to cry, wondering why the hell Ed had gone off without leaving him word and why Emiscah had looked so funny when he said he didn't know where Ed was.

Next day he went to the shop and got his old job back, though he was so weak he wasn't much good. The foreman was pretty decent about it and told him to go easy for a few days, but he wouldn't pay him for the time he was sick because he wasn't an old employee and hadn't gotten a certificate from the company doctor. That evening he went to the bowlingalley where Ed used to work. The barkeep upstairs said Ed had beaten it to Chi on account of some flimflam about raffling off a watch. "Good riddance, if you ask me," he said. "That bozo has all the makin's of a bad egg."

He had a letter from Jim saying that ma had written from Fargo that she was worried about him and that Charley had better let Jim take a look at him, so he went over to the Vogels' next Sunday. First thing he did when he saw Jim was to say that busting up the Ford had been a damn fool kid's trick and they shook hands on it and Jim said nobody would say anything about it and that he'd better stay and eat with them. The meal was fine and the beer was fine. Jim's kid was darn cute; it was funny to think that he was an uncle. Even Hedwig didn't seem so peevish as before. The garage was making good money and old man Vogel was going to give up the liverystable and retire. When Charley said he was studying at nightschool, old Vogel began to pay more attention to him. Somebody said something about La Follette and Charley said he was a big man.

"Vat is the use being a big man if you are wrong?" said old Vogel with beersuds in his mustache. He took another draft out of his stein and looked at Charley with sparkling blue eyes. "But dot's only a beginning . . . ve vill make a Sozialist out of you yet." Charley blushed and said, "Well, I don't know about that," and Aunt Hartmann piled another helping of hasenpfeffer and noodles and mashed potatoes on his plate.

One raw March evening he took Emiscah to see *The Birth*

of a Nation. The battles and the music and the bugles made them all jelly inside. They both had tears in their eyes when the two boys met on the battlefield and died in each other's arms on the battlefield. When the Ku Klux Klan charged across the screen Charley had his leg against Emiscah's leg and she dug her fingers into his knee so hard it hurt. When they came out Charley said by heck he thought he wanted to go up to Canada and enlist and go over and see the Great War. Emiscah said not to be silly and then looked at him kinda funny and asked him if he was pro-British. He said he didn't care and that the only fellows that would gain would be the bankers, whoever won. She said "Isn't it terrible? Let's not talk about it any more."

When they got back to the Svensons', Mr. Svenson was sitting in the parlor in his shirtsleeves reading the paper. He got up and went to meet Charley with a worried frown on his face and was just about to say something when Emiscah shook her head. He shrugged his shoulders and went out. Charley asked Emiscah what was eating the old man. She grabbed hold of him and put her head on his shoulder and burst out crying. "What's the matter, kitten; what's the matter, kitten?" he kept asking. She just cried and cried until he could feel her tears on his cheek and neck and said, "For crissake, snap out of it, kitten; you're wilting my collar."

She let herself drop on the sofa and he could see that she was working hard to pull herself together. He sat down beside her and kept patting her hand. Suddenly she got up and stood in the middle of the floor. He tried to put his arms around her to pet her, but she pushed him off. "Charley," she said in a hard strained voice, "lemme tellye somethin' . . . I think I'm goin' to have a baby."

"But you're crazy. We haven't ever . . ."

"Maybe it's somebody else . . . Oh, God, I'm going to kill myself."

Charley took her by the arms and made her sit down on the sofa. "Now pull yourself together, and tell me what the trouble is."

"I wish you'd beat me up," Emiscah said, laughing crazily. "Go ahead; hit me with your fist."

Charley went weak all over.

"Tell me what the trouble is," he said. "By Jeez, it couldn't be Ed."

She looked up at him with scared eyes, her face drawn like an old woman's. "No, no . . . Here's how it is. I'm a month past my time, see, and I don't know enough about things like that, so I asks Anna about it and she says I'm goin' to have a baby sure and that we've got to get married right away and

388

she told dad, the dirty little sneak, and I couldn't tell 'em it wasn't you . . . They think it's you, see, and dad says it's all right, young folks bein' like that nowadays an' everythin' an' says we'll have to get married and I thought I wouldn't let on an' you'd never know, but, kid, I had to tell you."

"Oh, Jeez," said Charley. He looked at the flowered pink shade with a fringe over the lamp on the table beside him and the tablecover with a fringe and at his shoes and the roses on the carpet. "Who was it?"

"It was when you were in the hospital, Charley. We had a lot of beer to drink an' he took me to a hotel. I guess I'm just bad, that's all. He was throwin' money around an' we went in a taxicab and I guess I was crazy. No, I'm a bad woman through and through, Charley. I went out with him every night when you were in the hospital."

"By God, it was Ed."

She nodded and then hid her face and started to cry again.

"The lousy little bastard," Charley kept saying. She crumpled up on the sofa with her face in her hands.

"He's gone to Chicago . . . He's a bad egg allright," said Charley.

He felt he had to get out in the air. He picked up his coat and hat and started to put them on. Then she got to her feet and threw herself against him. She held him close and her arms were tight round his neck. "Honestly, Charley, I loved you all the time . . . I pretended to myself it was you." She kissed him on the mouth. He pushed her away, but he felt weak and tired and thought of the icy streets walking home and his cold hallbedroom and thought, what the hell did it matter anyway? and took off his hat and coat again. She kissed him and loved him up and locked the parlor door and they loved each other on the sofa and she let him do everything he wanted. Then after a while she turned on the light and straightened her clothes and went over to the mirror to fix her hair and he tied his necktie again and she smoothed down his hair as best she could with her fingers and they unlocked the parlor door very carefully and she went out in the hall to call dad. Her face was flushed and she looked very pretty again. Mr. Svenson and Anna and all the girls were out in the kitchen and Emiscah said, "Dad, Charley and I are going to get married next month," and everybody said, "Congratulations," and all the girls kissed Charley and Mr. Svenson broke out a bottle of whiskey and they had a drink all around and Charley went home feeling like a whipped dog.

There was a fellow named Hendriks at the shop seemed a pretty wise guy; Charley asked him next noon whether he didn't know of anything a girl could take and he said he had a prescription for some pills and next day he brought it and told Charley not to tell the druggist what he wanted them for. It was payday and Hendriks came round to Charley's room after he'd gotten cleaned up that night and asked him if he'd gotten the pills all right. Charley had the package right in his pocket and was going to cut nightschool that night and take it to Emiscah. First he and Hendriks went to have a drink at the corner. He didn't like whiskey straight and Hendriks said to take it with gingerale. It tasted great and Charley felt sore and miserable inside and didn't want to see Emiscah anyway. They had some more drinks and then went and bowled for a while. Charley beat him four out of five and Hendriks said the party was on him from now on.

Hendriks was a squarechested redheaded guy with a freckled face and a twisted nose and he began telling stories about funny things that had happened with the ribs and how that was his long suit anyway. He'd been all over and had had high yallers and sealskin browns down New Orleans and Chink girls in Seattle, Washington, and a fullblooded Indian squaw in Butte, Montana, and French girls and German Jewish girls in Colon and a Caribee woman more than ninety years old in Port of Spain. He said that the Twin Cities was the bunk and what a guy ought to do was to go down an' get a job in the oilfields at Tampico or in Oklahoma where you could make decent money and live like a white man. Charley said he'd pull out of St. Paul in a minute if it wasn't that he wanted to finish his course in nightschool, and Hendriks told him he was a damn fool, that booklearnin' never got nobody nowhere and what he wanted was to have a good time when he had his strength and after that to hell wid 'em. Charley said he felt like saying to hell wid 'em anyway.

They went to several bars, and Charley who wasn't used to drinking anything much except beer began to reel a little, but it was swell barging round with Hendriks from bar to bar. Hendriks sang *My Mother Was a Lady* in one place and *The Bastard King of England* in another where an old redfaced guy with a cigar set them up to some drinks. Then they tried to get into a dancehall, but the guy at the door said they were too drunk and threw them out on their ear and that seemed funny as hell and they went to a back room of a place Hendriks knew and there were two girls there Hendriks knew and Hendriks fixed it up for ten dollars each for all night, then they had one more drink before going to the girls' place and Hendriks sang:

> *Two drummers sat at dinner in a grand hotel one day*
> *While dining they were chatting in a jolly sort of way*
> *And when a pretty waitress brought them a tray of food*
> *They spoke to her familiarly in a manner rather rude*

"He's a hot sketch," said one of the girls to the other. But the other was a little soused and began to get a crying jag

when Hendriks and Charley put their heads together and sang:

> My mother was a lady like yours you will allow
> And you may have a sister who needs protection now
> I've come to this great city to find a brother dear
> And you wouldn't dare insult me, sir, if Jack were only here.

They cried and the other one kept shoving her and saying, "Dry your eyes deary you're maudlin," and it was funny as hell.

The next few weeks Charley was uneasy and miserable. The pills made Emiscah feel awful sick, but they finally brought her around. Charley didn't go there much, though they still talked about "When we're married," and the Svensons treated Charley as a soninlaw. Emiscah nagged a little about Charley's drinking and running round with this fellow Hendriks. Charley had dropped out of nightschool and was looking for a chance to get a job that would take him away somewhere, he didn't much care where. Then one day he busted a lathe and the foreman fired him. When he told Emiscah about it she got sore and said she thought it was about time he gave up boozing and running round and he paid little attention to her and he said it was about time for him to butt out, and picked up his hat and coat and left. Afterwards when he was walking down the street he wished he'd remembered to ask her to give him back his seal ring, but he didn't go back to ask for it.

That Sunday he went to eat at old man Vogel's, but he didn't tell them he'd lost his job. It was a sudden hot spring day. He'd been walking round all morning, with a headache from getting tanked up with Hendriks the night before, looking at the crocuses and hyacinths in the parks and the swelling buds in the dooryards. He didn't know what to do with himself. He was a week overdue on his rent and he wasn't getting any schooling and he hadn't any girl and he felt like saying to hell with everything and joining up in the militia to go down to the Mexican border. His head ached and he was tired of dragging his feet over the pavements in the early heat. Welldressed men and women went by in limousines and sedans. A boy flashed by on a red motorbike. He wished he had the jack to buy a motorbike himself and go on a trip somewhere. Last night he'd tried to argue Hendriks into going South with him, but Hendriks said he'd picked up with a skirt that was a warm baby and he was getting his nookie every night and going to stay right with it. To hell with that, thought Charley; I want to see some country.

He looked so down in the mouth that Jim said, "What's the trouble, Charley?" when he walked into the garage. "Aw, nothing," said Charley, and started to help clean the parts of the carburetor of a Mack truck Jim was tinkering with. The truckdriver was a young feller with closecropped black hair and a tanned face. Charley liked his looks. He said he was going to take a load of storefittings down to Milwaukee next day and was looking for a guy to go with him.

"Would you take me?" said Charley. The truckdriver looked puzzled.

"He's my kid brother, Fred; he'll be all right . . . But what about your job?"

Charley colored up. "Aw, I resigned."

"Well, come round with me to see the boss," said the truckdriver. "And if it's all right by him it's all right by me."

They left next morning before day. Charley felt bad about sneaking out on his landlady, but he left a note on the table saying he'd send her what he owed her as soon as he got a job. It was fine leaving the city and the mills and grainelevators behind in the gray chilly early morning light. The road followed the river and the bluffs and the truck roared along sloshing through puddles and muddy ruts. It was chilly, although the sun was warm when it wasn't behind the clouds. He and Fred had to yell at each other to make their voices heard, but they told stories and chewed the fat about one thing and another. They spent the night in LaCrosse.

They just got into the hashjoint in time to order hamburger steaks before it closed, and Charley felt he was making a hit with the waitress who was from Omaha and whose name was Helen. She was about thirty and had a tired look under the eyes that made him think maybe she was kind of easy. He hung round until she closed up and took her out walking and they walked along the river and the wind was warm and smelt winey of sawmills and there was a little moon behind fleecy clouds and they sat down in the new grass where it was dark behind stacks of freshcut lumber laid out to season. She let her head drop on his shoulder and called him "baby boy."

Fred was asleep in the truck rolled up in a blanket on top of the sacking when he got back. Charley curled up in his overcoat on the other side of the truck. It was cold and the packingcases were uncomfortable to lie on, but he was tired and his face felt windburned, and he soon fell asleep.

They were off before day.

The first thing Fred said was, "Well, did you make her, kid?" Charley laughed and nodded. He felt good and thought

to himself he was damn lucky to get away from the Twin Cities and Emiscah and that sonofabitchin' foreman. The whole world was laid out in front of him like a map, and the Mack truck roaring down the middle of it and towns were waiting for him everywhere where he could pick up jobs and make good money and find goodlooking girls waiting to call him their baby boy.

He didn't stay long in Milwaukee. They didn't need any help in any of the garages, so he got a job pearldiving in a lunchroom. It was a miserable greasy job with long hours. To save money he didn't get a room, but flopped in a truck in a garage where a friend of Jim's was working. He was planning to go over on the boat as soon as he got his first week's pay. One of the stiffs working in the lunchroom was a wobbly named Monte Davis. He got everybody to walk out on account of a freespeech fight the wobblies were running in town, so Charley worked a whole week and had not a cent to show for it and hadn't eaten for a day and a half when Fred came back with another load on his Mack truck and set him up to a feed. They drank some beer afterwards and had a big argument about strikes. Fred said all this wobbly agitation was damn foolishness and he thought the cops would be doing right if they jailed every last one of them. Charley said that working stiffs ought to stick together for decent living conditions and the time was coming when there'd be a big revolution like the American Revolution only bigger, and after that there wouldn't be any bosses and the workers would run industry. Fred said he talked like a damn foreigner and ought to be ashamed of himself and that a white man ought to believe in individual liberty and if he got a raw deal on one job he was goddam well able to find another. They parted sore, but Fred was a goodhearted guy and lent Charley five bucks to go over to Chi with.

Next day he went over on the boat. There were still some yellowish floes of rotting ice on the lake that was a very pale cold blue with a few whitecaps on it. Charley had never been out on a big body of water before and felt a little sick, but it was fine to see the chimneys and great blocks of buildings, pearly where the sun hit them, growing up out of the blur of factory smoke, and the breakwaters and the big oreboats plowing through the blue seas, and to walk down the wharf with everything new to him and to plunge into the crowd and the stream of automobiles and green and yellow buses

blocked up by the drawbridge on Michigan Avenue, and to walk along in the driving wind looking at the shiny storewindows and goodlooking girls and windblown dresses.

Jim had told him to go to see a friend of his who worked

in a Ford servicestation on Blue Island Avenue, but it was so far that by the time he got there the guy had gone. The boss was there, though, and he told Charley that if he came round next morning he'd have a job for him. As he didn't have anywhere to go and didn't like to tell the boss he was flat, he left his suitcase in the garage and walked around all night. Occasionally he got a few winks of sleep on a park bench, but he'd wake up stiff and chilled to the bone and would have to run around to warm up. The night seemed never to end and he didn't have a red to get a cup of coffee with in the morning, and he was there walking up and down outside an hour before anybody came to open up the servicestation in the morning.

He worked at the Ford servicestation several weeks until one Sunday he met Monte Davis on North Clark Street and went to a wobbly meeting with him in front of the Newberry Library. The cops broke up the meeting and Charley didn't walk away fast enough and before he knew what happened to him he'd been halfstunned by a riotstick and shoved into the policewagon. He spent the night in a cell with two bearded men who were blind drunk and didn't seem to be able to talk English anyway. Next day he was questioned by a police magistrate and when he said he was a garage mechanic a dick called up the servicestation to check up on him; the magistrate discharged him, but when he got to the garage the boss said he'd have no goddam I Won't Works in this outfit and paid him his wages and discharged him too.

He hocked his suitcase and his good suit and made a little bundle of some socks and a couple of shirts and went round to see Monte Davis to tell him he was going to hitchhike to St. Louis. Monte said there was a free-speech fight in Evansville and he guessed he'd come along to see what was doing. They went out on the train to Joliet. When they walked past the prison, Monte said the sight of a prison always made him feel sick and gave him a kind of a foreboding. He got pretty blue and said he guessed the bosses'd get him soon, but that there'd be others. Monte Davis was a sallow thinfaced youth from Muscatine, Iowa. He had a long crooked nose and stuttered and didn't remember a time when he hadn't sold papers or worked in a buttonfactory. He thought of nothing but the I.W.W. and the revolution. He bawled Charley out for a scissorbill because he laughed about how fast the wobblies ran when the cops broke up the meeting, and told him he ought to be classconscious and take things serious.

At the citylimits of Joliet they hopped a truck that carried them to Peoria, where they separated because Charley found a truckdriver he'd known in Chicago who offered him a lift all the way to St. Louis. In St. Louis things didn't seem to be so good, and he got into a row with a hooker he picked up on Market Street who tried to roll him, so as a guy told him there were plenty jobs to be had in Louisville he began to beat his way East. By the time he got to New Albany it was hot as the hinges of hell; he'd had poor luck on hitches and his feet were swollen and blistered. He stood a long time on the bridge looking down into the swift brown current of the Ohio, too tired to go any further. He hated the idea of tramping round looking for a job. The river was the color of gingerbread; he started to think about the smell of ginger-cookies Lizzie Green used to make in his mother's kitchen and he thought he was a damn fool to be bumming round like this. He'd go home and plant himself among the weeds, that's what he'd do.

Just then a brokendown Ford truck came by running on a flat tire. "Hey, you've got a flat," yelled Charley.

The driver put on the brakes with a bang. He was a big bulletheaded man in a red sweater. "What the hell is it to you?"

"Jeez, I just thought you might not a noticed."

"Ah notice everythin', boy. . . ain't had nutten but trouble all day. Wanta lift?"

"Sure," said Charley.

"Now, Ah can't park on de bridge nohow . . . Been same goddam thing all day. Here Ah gits up early in de mornin' b'fo' day and goes out to haul foa hawgsheads a tobacca and de goddam nigger done lost de warehouse key. Ah swear if Ah'd had a gun Ah'd shot de sonofabitch dead."

At the end of the bridge he stopped and Charley helped him change the tire. "Where you from, boy?" he said as he straightened up and brushed the dust off his pants.

"I'm from up in the Northwest," said Charley.

"Ah reckon you're a Swede, ain't yez?"

Charley laughed. "No; I'm a garage mechanic and lookin' for a job."

"Pahl in, boy; we'll go an' see ole man Wiggins—he's ma boss—an' see what we can do."

Charley stayed all summer in Louisville working at the Wiggins Repair Shops. He roomed with an Italian named Grassi who'd come over to escape military service. Grassi read the papers every day and was very much afraid the U.S. would go into the war. Then he said he'd have to hop across the border to Mexico. He was an anarchist and a quiet sort of guy who spent the evenings singing low to himself and playing the accordion on the lodginghouse steps. He told Charley about the big Fiat factories at Torino where he'd worked, and taught him to eat spaghetti and drink red wine and to play *Funiculi funicula* on the accordion. His big ambition was to be an airplane pilot. Charley picked up with a Jewish girl who worked as a sorter in a tobacco warehouse. Her name was Sarah Cohen, but she made him call her Belle. He liked her well enough, but he was careful to make her understand that he wasn't the marrying kind. She said she was a radical and believed in free love, but that didn't suit him much either. He took her to shows and took her out walking in Cherokee Park and bought her an amethyst brooch when she said amethyst was her birthstone.

When he thought about himself he felt pretty worried. Here he was doing the same work day after day, with no chance of making better money or getting any schooling or seeing the country. When winter came on he got restless. He'd rescued an old Ford roadster that they were going to tow out to the junkheap and had patched it up with discarded spare parts.

He talked Grassi into going down to New Orleans with him. They had a little money saved up and they'd run down there and get a job and be there for the Mardi Gras. The first day that he'd felt very good since he left St. Paul was the sleety January day they pulled out of Louisville with the engine hitting on all four cylinders and a pile of thirdhand spare tires in the back headed south.

They got down through Nashville and Birmingham and Mobile, but the roads were terrible, and they had to remake the car as they went along and they almost froze to death in a blizzard near Guntersville and had to lay over for a couple of days, so that by the time they'd gotten down to Bay St. Louis and were bowling along the shore road under a blue sky and feeling the warm sun and seeing palms and banana-trees and Grassi was telling about Vesuvio and Bella Napoli and his girl in Torino that he'd never see again on account of the bastardly capitalista war, their money had run out. They got into New Orleans with a dollar five between them and not more than a teacupful of gasoline in the tank, but by a lucky break Charley managed to sell the car as it stood for twenty-five dollars to a colored undertaker.

They got a room in a house near the levee for three dollars a week. The landlady was a yellowfaced woman from Panama and there was a parrot on the balcony outside their room and the sun was warm on their shoulders walking along the street. Grassi was very happy. "This is lika the Italia," he kept saying. They walked around and tried to find out about jobs, but they couldn't seem to find out about anything except that Mardi Gras was next week. They walked along Canal

Street that was crowded with colored people, Chinamen, pretty girls in brightcolored dresses, racetrack hangerson, tall elderly men in palmbeach suits. They stopped to have a beer in a bar open to the street with tables along the outside where all kinds of men sat smoking cigars and drinking. When they came out Grassi bought an afternoon paper. He turned pale and showed the headline, WAR WITH GERMANY IMMINENT. "If America go to war with Germany cops will arrest all Italian man to send back to Italy for fight, see? My friend tell who work in consule's office; tell me, see? I will not go fight in capitalista war." Charley tried to kid him along, but a worried set look came over Grassi's face and as soon as it was dark he left Charley saying he was going back to the flop and going to bed.

Charley walked round the streets alone. There was a warm molasses smell from the sugar refineries, whiffs of gardens and garlic and pepper and oil cookery. There seemed to be women everywhere, in bars, standing round streetcorners, looking out invitingly behind shutters ajar in all the doors and windows; but he had twenty dollars on him and he was afraid one of them might lift it off him, so he just walked around until he was tired and then went back to the room,

where he found Grassi already asleep with the covers over his head.

It was late when he woke up. The parrot was squawking on the gallery outside the window, hot sunlight filled the room. Grassi was not there.

Charley had dressed and was combing his hair when Grassi came in looking very much excited. He had taken a berth as donkey-engineman on a freighter bound for South America. "When I get Buenos Aires goodbye and no more war," he said. "If Argentina go to war, goodbye again." He kissed Charley on the mouth, and insisted on giving him his accordion and there were tears in his eyes when he went off to join the boat that was leaving at noon.

Charley walked all over town inquiring at garages and machineshops if there was any chance of a job. The streets were broad and dusty, bordered by low shuttered frame houses, and distances were huge. He got tired and dusty and sweaty. People he talked to were darned agreeable, but nobody seemed to know where he could get a job. He decided he ought to stay through the Mardi Gras anyway and then he

would go up North again. Men he talked to told him to go to Florida or Birmingham, Alabama, or up to Memphis or Little Rock, but everybody agreed that unless he wanted to ship as a seaman there wasn't a job to be had in the city. The days dragged along warm and slow and sunny and smelling of molasses from the refineries. He spent a great deal of time reading in the public library or sprawled on the levee watching the niggers unload the ships. He had too much time to think and he worried about what he was going to do with himself. Nights he couldn't sleep well because he hadn't done anything all day to tire him.

One night he heard guitar music coming out of a joint called "The Original Tripoli," on Chartres Street. He went in and sat down at a table and ordered drinks. The waiter was a Chink. Couples were dancing in a kind of wrestling hug in the dark end of the room. Charley decided that if he could get a girl for less than five seeds he'd take one on.

Before long he found himself setting up a girl who said her name was Liz to drinks and a feed. She said she hadn't had anything to eat all day. He asked her about Mardi Gras and she said it was a bum time because the cops closed everything up tight. "They rounded up all the waterfront hustlers last night, sent every last one of them up the river."

"What they do with 'em?"

"Take 'em up to Memphis and turn 'em loose . . . ain't a jail in the state would hold all the floosies in this town." They laughed and had another drink and then they danced. Charley held her tight. She was a skinny girl with little pointed breasts and big hips.

"Jeez, baby, you've got some action," he said after they'd been dancing a little while.

"Ain't it ma business to give the boys a good time?"

He liked the way she looked at him. "Say, baby, how much do you get?"

"Five bucks."

"Jeez, I ain't no millionaire . . . and didn't I set you up to some eats?"

"Awright, sugarpopper; make it three."

They had another drink. Charley noticed that she took some kind of lemonade each time. "Don't you ever drink anything, Liz?"

"You can't drink in this game, dearie; first thing you know I'd be givin' it away."

There was a big drunken guy in a dirty undershirt looked like a ship's stoker reeling round the room. He got hold of Liz's hand and made her dance with him. His big arms tattooed blue and red folded right round her. Charley could see

he was mauling and pulling at her dress as he danced with her. "Quit that, you sonofabitch," she was yelling. That made Charley sore and he went up and pulled the big guy away from her. The big guy turned and swung on him. Charley ducked and hopped into the center of the floor with his dukes up. The big guy was blind drunk, as he let fly another haymaker Charley put his foot out and the big guy tripped and fell on his face upsetting a table and a little dark man with a black mustache with it. In a second the dark man was on his feet and had whipped out a machete. The Chinks ran round mewing like a lot of damn gulls. The proprietor, a fat Spaniard in an apron, had come out from behind the bar and was yellin', "Git out, every last one of you." The man with the machete made a run at Charley. Liz gave him a yank one side and before Charley knew what had happened she was pulling him through the stinking latrines into a passage that led to a back door out into the street. "Don't you know no better'n to get in a fight over a goddam whore?" she was saying in his ear.

Once out in the street Charley wanted to go back to get his hat and coat. Liz wouldn't let him. "I'll get it for you in the mornin'," she said.

They walked along the street together. "You're a damn good girl; I like you," said Charley.

"Can't you raise ten dollars and make it all night?"

"Jeez, kid, I'm broke."

"Well, I'll have to throw you out and do some more hustlin', I guess . . . There's only one feller in this world gets it for nothin' and you ain't him."

They had a good time together. They sat on the edge of the bed talking. She looked flushed and pretty in a fragile sort of way in her pink shimmy shirt. She showed him a snapshot of her steady who was second engineer on a tanker. "Ain't he handsome? I don't hustle when he's in town. He's that strong . . . He can crack a pecan with his biceps." She showed him the place on his arm where her steady could crack a pecan.

"Where you from?" asked Charley.

"What's that to you?"

"You're from up North; I can tell by the way you talk."

"Sure. I'm from Iowa, but I'll never go back there no more . . . It's a hell of a life, bo, and don't you forget . . . 'Women of pleasure' my foot. I used to think I was a classy dame up home and then I woke up one morning and found I was nothing but a goddam whore."

"Ever been to New York?"

She shook her head. "It ain't such a bad life if you keep away from drink and the pimps," she said thoughtfully.

"I guess I'll shove off for New York right after Mardi Gras. I can't seem to find me a master in this man's town."

"Mardi Gras ain't so much if you're broke."

"Well, I came down here to see it and I guess I'd better see it."

It was dawn when he left her. She came downstairs with him. He kissed her and told her he'd give her the ten bucks if she got his hat and coat back for him and she said to come around to her place that evening about six, but not to go back to the "Tripoli" because that greaser was a bad egg and would be laying for him.

The streets of old stucco houses inset with lacy iron balconies were brimful of blue mist. A few mulatto women in bandanas were moving around in the courtyards. In the market old colored men were laying out fruit and green vegetables. When he got back to his flop the Panama woman was out on the gallery outside his room holding out a banana and calling "Ven, Polly . . . Ven, Polly," in a little squeaky voice. The parrot sat on the edge of the tiled roof cocking a glassy eye at her and chuckling softly. "Me here all right," said the Panama woman with a tearful smile. "Polly no quiere come." Charley climbed up the shutter and tried to grab the parrot, but the parrot hitched away sideways up to the ridge of the roof and all Charley did was bring a tile down on his head. "No quiere come," said the Panama woman sadly. Charley grinned at her and went into his room, where he dropped on the bed and fell asleep.

During Mardi Gras Charley walked round town till his feet were sore. There were crowds everywhere and lights and floats and parades and bands and girls running round in fancy dress. He picked up plenty of girls, but as soon as they found he was flat they dropped him. He was spending his money as slowly as he could. When he got hungry he'd drop into a bar and drink a glass of beer and eat as much free lunch as he dared.

The day after Mardi Gras the crowds began to thin out, and Charley didn't have any money for beer. He walked round feeling hungry and miserable; the smell of molasses and the absinthe smell from bars in the French Quarter in the heavy damp air made him feel sick. He didn't know what to do with himself. He didn't have the gumption to start off walking or hitchhiking again. He went to the Western Union and tried to wire Jim collect, but the guy said they wouldn't take a wire asking for money collect.

The Panama woman threw him out when he couldn't pay for another week in advance and there he was walking down Esplanade Avenue with Grassi's accordion on one arm and his little newspaper bundle of clothes under the other. He walked down the levee and sat down in a grassy place in the sun and thought for a long time. It was either throwing himself in the river or enlisting in the army. Then he suddenly thought of the accordion. An accordion was worth a lot of money. He left his bundle of clothes under some planks and walked around to all the hockshops he could find with the accordion, but they wouldn't give him more than fifteen bucks for it anywhere. By the time he'd been round to all the hockshops and music stores, it was dark and everything had closed. He stumbled along the pavement feeling sick and dopy from hunger. At the corner of Canal and Rampart he stopped. Singing was coming out of a saloon. He got the hunch to go in and play *Funiculi funicula* on the accordion. He might get some free lunch and a glass of beer out of it.

He'd hardly started playing and the bouncer had just vaulted across the bar to give him the bum's rush, when a tall man sprawled at a table beckoned to him.

"Brother, you come right here an' set down." It was a big man with a long broken nose and high cheekbones.

"Brother, you set down." The bouncer went back behind the bar. "Brother, you can't play that there accordeen no mor'n a rabbit. Ah'm nutten but a lowdown cracker from Okachobe City but if Ah couldn't play no better'n that . . ."

Charley laughed. "I know I can't play it. That's all right."

The Florida guy pulled out a big wad of bills. "Brother, do you know what you're going to do? You're going to sell me the goddam thing. . . . Ah'm nothin' but a lowdown cracker, but, by Jesus Christ . . ."

"Hey, Doc, be yourself . . . You don't want the damn thing." His friends tried to make him put his money back.

Doc swept his arm round with a gesture that shot three glasses onto the floor with a crash. "You turkey-buzzards talk in your turn . . . Brother, how much do you want for the accordeen?" The bouncer had come back and was standing threateningly over the table. "All right, Ben," said Doc. "It's all on your Uncle Henry . . . and let's have another round a that good rye whiskey. Brother, how much do you want for it?"

"Fifty bucks," said Charley, thinking fast.

Doc handed him out five tens. Charley swallowed a drink, put the accordion on the table and went off in a hurry. He was afraid if he hung round the cracker 'ud sober up and try to get the money back, and besides he wanted to eat.

Next day he got a steerage passage on the steamer *Momus* bound for New York. The river was higher than the city. It was funny standing on the stern of the steamboat and looking down on the roofs and streets and trolleycars of New Orleans. When the steamer pulled out from the wharf Charley began to feel good. He found the colored steward and got him to give him a berth in the deckhouse. When he put his newspaper package under the pillow he glanced down into the berth below. There lay Doc, fast asleep, all dressed up in a light gray suit and a straw hat with a burntout cigar sticking out of the corner of his mouth and the accordion beside him.

They were passing between the Eads Jetties and feeling the seawind in their faces and the first uneasy swell of the Gulf under their feet when Doc came lurching on deck. He recognized Charley and went up to him with a big hand held out. "Well, I'll be a sonofabitch if there ain't the musicmaker . . . That's a good accordeen, boy. Ah thought you'd imposed on me bein' only a poa country lad an' all that, but I'll be a sonofabitch if it ain't worth the money. Have a snifter on me?"

They went and sat on Doc's bunk and Doc broke out a bottle of Bacardi and they had some drinks and Charley told about how he'd been flat broke; if it wasn't for that fifty bucks he'd still be sitting on the levee and Doc said that if it wasn't for that fifty bucks he'd be riding firstclass.

Doc said he was going up to New York to sail for France in a volunteer ambulance corps; wasn't ever' day you got a chance to see a big war like that and he wanted to get in on it before the whole thing went bellyup; still he didn't like the idea of shooting a lot of whitemen he didn't have no quarrel with and reckoned this was the best way; if the Huns was niggers he'd feel different about it.

Charley said he was going to New York because he thought there were good chances of schooling in a big city like that and how he was an automobile mechanic and wanted to get to be a C.E. or something like that because there was no future for a working stiff without schooling.

Doc said that was all mahoula and what a boy like him ought to do was go and sign up as a mechanic in this here ambulance and they'd pay fifty dollars a month an' maybe more and that was a lot of seeds on the other side and he'd ought to see the goddam war before the whole thing went bellyup.

Doc's name was William H. Rogers and he'd come from Michigan originally and his old man had been a grapefruit grower down at Frostproof and Doc had cashed in on a couple of good crops of vegetables off the Everglades muck and was going over to see the mademosels before the whole thing went bellyup.

They were pretty drunk by the time night fell and were sitting in the stern with a seedylooking man in a derby hat who said he was an Est from the Baltic. The Est and Doc and Charley got up on the little bridge above the afterhouse after supper; the wind had gone down and it was a starlight night with a slight roll and Doc said, "By God, there's somethin' funny about this here boat . . . Befoa we went down to supper the Big Dipper was in the north, and now it's gone right around to the southwest."

"It is vat you vould expect of a kapitalistichesky society," said the Est. When he found that Charley had a red card and that Doc didn't believe in shooting anything but niggers he made a big speech about how revolution had broken out in Russia and the Czar was being forced to abdicate and that was the beginning of the regeneration of mankind from the East. He said the Ests would get their independence and that soon all Europe would be the free sozialistitchesky United States of Europe under the Red flag and Doc said, "What did I tell yez, Charley? The friggin' business'll go bellyup soon . . . What you want to do is come with me an' see the war while it lasts." And Charley said Doc was right and Doc said, "I'll take you round with me, boy, an' all you need do's show your driver's license an' tell 'em you're a college student."

The Est got sore at that and said that it was the duty of every classconscious worker to refuse to fight in this war and Doc said, "We ain't goin' to fight, Esty, old man. What we'll do is carry the boys out before they count out on 'em, see? I'd be a disappointed sonofabitch if the whole business had gone bellyup befoa we git there, wouldn't you, Charley?"

Then they argued some more about where the Dipper was and Doc kept saying it had moved to the south and when they'd finished the second quart, Doc was saying he didn't believe in white men shootin' each other up, only niggers, and started going round the boat lookin' for that damn shine steward to kill him just to prove it and the Est was singing *The Marseillaise* and Charley was telling everybody that what he wanted to do was to get in on the big war before it went bellyup. The Est and Charley had a hard time holding Doc down in his bunk when they put him to bed. He kept jumping out shouting he wanted to kill a couple of niggers.

They got into New York in a snowstorm. Doc said the Statue of Liberty looked like she had a white nightgown on. The Est looked around and hummed *The Marseillaise* and said American cities were not artistical because they did not have gables on the houses like in Baltic Europe.

When they got ashore Charley and Doc went to the Broadway Central Hotel together. Charley had never been in a big hotel like that and wanted to find a cheaper flop, but Doc insisted that he come along with him and said he had plenty of jack for both of them and that it was no use saving money because things would go bellyup soon. New York was full of grinding gears and clanging cars and the roar of the "L" and

408

newsboys crying extras. Doc lent Charley a good suit and took him down to the enlistment office of the ambulance corps that was in an important lawyer's office in a big shiny officebuilding down in the financial district. The gentleman who signed the boys up was a New York lawyer and he talked about their being gentleman volunteers and behaving like gentlemen and being a credit to the cause of the Allies and the American flag and civilization that the brave French soldiers had been fighting for so many years in the trenches. When he found out Charley was a mechanic, he signed him up without waiting to write to the principal of the highschool and the pastor of the Lutheran church home in Fargo whose names he had given as references. He told them about getting antityphoid injections and a physical examination and said to call the next day to find out the sailing date. When they came out of the elevator there was a group of men in the shinymarble lobby with their heads bent over a newspaper; the U.S. was at war with Germany. That night Charley wrote his mother that he was going to the war and please to send him fifty dollars. Then he and Doc went out to look at the town.

There were flags on every building. They walked past business block after business block looking for Times Square. Everywhere people were reading newspapers. At Fourteenth they heard a drumbeat and a band and waited at the corner to see what regiment it would be, but it was only the Salvation Army. By the time they got to Madison Square it was the dinner hour and the streets were deserted. It began to drizzle a little and the flags up Broadway and Fifth Avenue hung limp from their poles.

They went into the Hofbrau to eat. Charley thought it looked too expensive, but Doc said it was his party. A man was on a stepladder over the door screwing the bulbs into an electric sign of an American flag. The restaurant was draped with American flags inside and the band played *The Star-Spangled Banner* every other number, so that they kept having to get to their feet. "What do they think this is, settin'up exercises?" grumbled Doc.

There was one group at a round table in the corner that didn't get up when the band played *The Star-Spangled Banner,* but sat there quietly talking and eating as if nothing had happened. People round the restaurant began to stare at them and pass comments. "I bet they're . . . Huns . . . German spies . . . Pacifists." There was an army officer at a table with a girl who got red in the face whenever he looked at them. Finally a waiter, an elderly German, went up to them and whispered something.

"I'll be damned if I will," came the voice from the table in the corner. Then the army officer went over to them and said

409

something about courtesy to our national anthem. He came away redder in the face than ever. He was a little man with bowlegs squeezed into brightly polished puttees. "Dastardly pro-Germans," he sputtered as he sat down. Immediately he had to get up because the band played *The Star-Spangled Banner*. "Why don't you call the police, Cyril?" the girl who was with him said. By this time people from all over the restaurant were advancing on the round table.

Doc pulled Charley's chair around. "Watch this; it's going to be good."

A big man with a Texas drawl yanked one of the men out of his chair. "You git up or git out."

"You people have no right to interfere with us," began one of the men at the round table. "You express your approval of the war getting up, we express our disapproval by . . ."

There was a big woman with a red hat with a plume on it at the table who kept saying, "Shut up; don't talk to 'em." By this time the band had stopped. Everybody clapped as hard as he could and yelled, "Play it again; that's right." The waiters were running round nervously and the proprietor was in the center of the floor mopping his bald head.

The army officer went over to the orchestra leader and said, "Please play our national anthem again." At the first bar he came stiffly to attention. The other men rushed the round table. Doc and the man with the English accent were jostling each other. Doc squared off to hit him.

"Come outside if you want to fight," the man with the English accent was saying.

"Leave 'em be, boys," Doc was shouting. "I'll take 'em on outside, two at a time."

The table was upset and the party began backing off towards the door. The woman with the red hat picked up a bowl of lobster mayonnaise and was holding back the crowd by chucking handfuls of it in their faces. At that moment three cops appeared and arrested the damn pacifists. Everybody stood around wiping mayonnaise off his clothes. The band played *The Star-Spangled Banner* again and everybody tried to sing but it didn't make much of an effect because nobody knew the words.

After that Doc and Charley went to a bar to have a whiskey sour. Doc wanted to go to see a legshow and asked the barkeep. A little fat man with an American flag in the lapel of his coat overheard him and said the best legshow in New York was Minsky's on East Houston Street. He set them up to some drinks when Doc said they were going to see this here war, and said he'd take them down to Minsky's himself. His name was Segal and he said he'd been a Socialist up to the sinking of the *Lusitania*, but now he thought they ought to lick the Germans and destroy Berlin. He was in the cloak and suit business and was happy because he'd as good as landed a contract for army uniforms. "Ve need the var to make men of us," he'd say and strike himself on the chest. They went downtown in a taxi, but when they got to the burlesque show it was so full they couldn't get a seat.

"Standin' room, hell . . . Ah want women," Doc was saying. Mr. Segal thought a little while with his head cocked to one side. "Ve will go to 'Little Hungary,'" he said.

Charley felt let down. He'd expected to have a good time in New York. He wished he was in bed. At "Little Hungary" there were many German and Jewish and Russian girls. The wine came in funnylooking bottles upside down in a stand in the middle of each table. Mr. Segal said it was his party from now on. The orchestra played foreign music. Doc was getting pretty drunk. They sat at a table crowded in among other tables. Charley roamed round and asked a girl to dance with him, but she wouldn't for some reason.

He got to talking to a young narrowfaced fellow at the bar who had just been to a peace meeting at Madison Square Garden. Charley pricked his ears up when the fellow said there'd be a revolution in New York if they tried to force conscription on the country. His name was Benny Compton and he'd been studying law at New York University. Charley went and sat with him at a table with another fellow who was from Minnesota and who was a reporter on *The Call*. Charley asked them about the chances of working his way through the engineering school. He'd about decided to back out of this ambulance proposition. But they didn't seem to think there was much chance if you hadn't any money saved up to start on. The Minnesota man said New York was no place for a poor man.

"Aw, hell; I guess I'll go to the war," said Charley.

"It's the duty of every radical to go to jail first," said Benny Compton. "Anyway, there'll be a revolution. The workingclass won't stand for this much longer."

"If you want to make some jack the thing to do is to go over to Bayonne and get a job in a munitions factory," said the man from Minnesota in a tired voice.

"A man who does that is a traitor to his class," said Benny Compton.

"A working stiff's in a hell of a situation," said Charley. "Damn it, I don't want to spend all my life patchin' up tin lizzies at seventyfive a month."

"Didn't Eugene V. Debs say, 'I want to rise with the ranks, not from them'?"

"After all, Benny, ain't you studyin' night an' day to get to be a lawyer an' get out of the workin'class?" said the man from Minnesota.

"That is so I can be of some use in the struggle . . . I want to be a wellsharpened instrument. We must fight capitalists with their own weapons."

"I wonder what I'll do when they suppress *The Call.*"

"They won't dare suppress it."

"Sure, they will. We're in this war to defend the Morgan loans . . . They'll use it to clear up opposition at home, sure as my name's Johnson."

"Talking of that, I got some dope. My sister, see, she's a stenographer . . . She works for J. Ward Moorhouse, the public relations counsel, you know . . . he does propaganda for the Morgans and the Rockefellers. Well, she said that all this year he's been working with a French secret mission. The big interests are scared to death of a revolution in France. They paid him ten thousand dollars for his services. He runs pro-war stuff through a feature syndicate. And they call this a free country."

"I wouldn't be surprised at anything," said the man from Minnesota, pouring himself out the last of the bottle of wine. "Why, any one of us may be a government agent or a spy right at this minute." The three of them sat there looking at each other. It gave Charley chills down his spine.

"That's what I'm tryin' to tell ye . . . My sister, she knows all about it, see, on account of workin' in this guy's office . . . It's a plot of the big interests, Morgan an' them, to defeat the workers by sendin' 'em off to the war. Once they get you in the army you can't howl about civic liberty or the Bill of Rights . . . They can shoot you without trial, see?"

"It's an outrage . . . The people of the Northwest won't stand for it," said the man from Minnesota. "Look here, you've been out there more recently than I have. La Follette expresses the opinion of people out there, don't he?"

"Sure," said Charley.

"Well, what the hell?"

"It's too deep for me," said Charley, and started working his way among the closepacked tables to find Doc. Doc was pretty drunk, and Charley was afraid the evening would start running into money, so they said goodbye to Mr. Segal who said please to kill a lot of Germans just for him, and they went out and started walking west along Houston Street. There were pushcarts all along the curb with flares that made the packed faces along the sidewalk glow red in the rainy darkness.

They came out at the end of a wide avenue crowded with people pouring out from a theater. In front of the Cosmopolitan Café a man was speaking on a soapbox. As the people came out of the theater they surged around him. Doc and Charley edged their way through to see what the trouble was. They could only catch scraps of what the man was shouting in a hoarse barking voice:

"A few days ago I was sittin' in the Cooper Institute listenin' to Eugene Victor Debs, and what was he sayin'? . . . 'What is this civilization, this democracy that the bosses are asking you workers to give your lives to save, what does it mean to you except wageslavery, what is . . .?' "

"Hey, shut up, youse . . . If you don't like it go back where you came from," came voices from the crowd.

"Freedom to work so that the bosses can get rich . . . Opportunity to starve to death if you get fired from your job."

Doc and Charley were shoved from behind. The man toppled off his box and disappeared. The whole end of the avenue filled with a milling crowd. Doc was sparring with a big man in overalls. A cop came between them hitting right and left with his billy. Doc hauled off to slam the cop, but Charley caught his arm and pulled him out of the scrimmage.

"Hey, for crissake, Doc, this ain't the war yet," said Charley.

Doc was red in the face. "Ah didn't like that guy's looks," he said.

Behind the cops two policedepartment cars with big searchlights were charging the crowd. Arms, heads, hats, jostling shoulders, riotsticks rising and falling stood out black against the tremendous white of the searchlights. Charley pulled Doc against the plateglass window of the café.

"Say, Doc, we don't want to get in the can and lose the boat," Charley whispered in his ear.

"What's the use?" said Doc. "It'll all go bellyup before we get there."

"Today the voikers run before the cops, but soon it will be the cops run before the voikers," someone yelled. Someone else started singing *The Marseillaise*. Voices joined. Doc and Charley were jammed with their shoulders against the plateglass. Behind them the café was full of faces swimming in blue crinkly tobaccosmoke like fish in an aquarium. The plateglass suddenly smashed. People in the café were hopping to their feet. "Look out for the Cossacks," a voice yelled.

A cordon of cops was working down the avenue. The empty pavement behind them widened. The other way mounted police were coming out of Houston Street. In the open space a patrolwagon parked. Cops were shoving men and women into it.

Doc and Charley ducked past a mounted policeman who was trotting his horse with a great clatter down the inside of

413

the sidewalk, and shot round the corner. The Bowery was empty and dark. They walked west towards the hotel.

"My God," said Charley, "you almost got us locked up that time . . . I'm all set to go to France now, and I wanter go."

A week later they were on the *Chicago* of the French Line steaming out through the Narrows. They had hangovers from their farewell party and felt a little sick from the smell of the boat and still had the music of the jazzband on the wharf ringing through their heads. The day was overcast, with a low lid of leaden clouds, looked like it was going to snow. The sailors were French and the stewards were French. They had wine with their first meal. There was a whole tableful of other guys going over in the ambulance service.

After dinner Doc went down to the cabin to go to sleep. Charley roamed around the ship with his hands in his pockets without knowing what to do with himself. In the stern they were taking the canvas cover off the seventyfive gun. He walked round the lowerdeck full of barrels and packingcases and stumbled across coils of big fuzzy cable to the bow. In the bow there was a little pinkfaced French sailor with a red tassel on his cap stationed as a lookout.

The sea was glassy, with dirty undulating patches of weed and garbage. There were gulls sitting on the water or perched on bits of floating wood. Now and then a gull stretched its wings lazily and flew off crying.

The boat's bluff bow cut two even waves through dense glassgreen water. Charley tried to talk to the lookout. He pointed ahead. "East," he said, "France."

The lookout paid no attention. Charley pointed back towards the smoky west. "West," he said and tapped himself on the chest. "My home Fargo, North Dakota." But the lookout just shook his head and put his finger to his lips.

"France very far east . . . submarines . . . war," said Charley. The lookout put his hand over his mouth. At last he made Charley understand that he wasn't supposed to talk to him.

SELECTED BIBLIOGRAPHY

Works by John Dos Passos

One Man's Initiation—1917. London: George Allen and Unwin Ltd., 1920

Three Soldiers. New York: George H. Doran Co., 1921

Streets of Night. New York: George H. Doran Co., 1923

Manhattan Transfer. Boston: Houghton Mifflin Co., 1925

The 42nd Parallel. New York: Harper and Brothers, 1930 (Signet Classic CE1344)

1919. New York: Harcourt, Brace and Co., 1932 (Signet Classic CE1508)

The Big Money. New York: Harcourt, Brace and Co., 1936 (Signet Classic CE1353)

The Grand Design. Boston: Houghton Mifflin Co., 1949

Midcentury. Boston: Houghton Mifflin Co., 1961

Occasions and Protests. Chicago: Henry Regnery Co., 1964

The Best Times. New York: New American Library, Inc., 1967

The Fourteenth Chronicle: Letters and Diaries of John Dos Passos, ed. Townsend Ludington, Boston: Gambit Incorporated, 1973.

SELECTED BIOGRAPHY AND CRITICISM

Belkind, Allen, ed. *Dos Passos, the Critics, and the Writer's Intention*. Pref. Harry T. Moore. Introd. Allen Belkind. Carbondale and Edwardsville: Southern Illinois Univ. Press, 1971.

Cowley, Malcolm. "Dos Passos: The Learned Poggius." *The Southern Review*, 9, No. 1 (1973), pp. 3-17. In *A Second Flowering: Works and Days of the Lost Generation*. New York: Viking Press, 1973, pp. 74-89.

———. "John Dos Passos: Poet Against the World." In *After the Genteel Tradition*. New York: W. W. Norton and Co., Inc., 1937, p. 134-46.

Diggins, John P. "Visions of Chaos and Visions of Order: Dos Passos as Historian." *American Literature*, 46 (1974), pp. 329-46.

Geismar, Maxwell. *Writers in Crisis*. Boston: Houghton Mifflin Co., 1942.

Gurko, Leo. "John Dos Passos' 'U.S.A.': A 1930's Spectacular." In *Proletarian Writers of the Thirties*. Ed. David Madden. Carbondale and Edwardsville: Southern Illinois Univ. Press, 1968, pp. 46-63.

Hoffman, Frederick. *The Twenties*. New York: The Free Press, 1965.

Hook, Andrew, ed. *Dos Passos: A Collection of Critical Essays*. Englewood Cliffs, N.J.: Prentice-Hall, Inc., 1974.

Kazin, Alfred. *On Native Grounds*. New York: Harcourt, Brace and World, Inc., 1942.

Leavis, F. R. "A Serious Artist." *Scrutiny*, 1 (1932), pp. 173-79. Rpt. in *Dos Passos: A Collection of Critical Essays*, pp. 70-75.

McLuhan, Herbert Marshall. "John Dos Passos: Technique Vs. Sensibility." In *Fifty Years of the American Novel: A Christian Appraisal*. Ed. Harold Charles Gardiner. New York: Charles Scribner's Sons, 1951, pp. 151-64. Rpt. in *Dos Passos, the Critics, and the Writer's Intention*, pp. 227-241.

Millgate, Michael. "John Dos Passos." In *American Social Fiction: James to Cozzens*. New York: Barnes and Noble, 1964, pp. 128-41.

Morse, Jonathan. "Dos Passos' *U.S.A.* and the Illusion of Memory." *Modern Fiction Studies*, 23 (1977-78), pp. 543-55.

Sanders, David. "John Dos Passos: An Interview." In *Writers at Work: The Paris Review Interviews: Fourth Series*. Ed. George Plimpton. Introd. Wilfrid Sheed. New York: Viking Press, 1976, pp. 67-89.

Sartre, Jean-Paul. "John Dos Passos and *1919*." In *Literary and Philosophical Essays*. Trans. Annette Michelson. New York: Philosophical Library, 1957, pp. 86-96. Rpt. in *Dos Passos, the Critics, and the Writer's Intention*, pp. 70-80.

Trilling, Lionel. "The America of John Dos Passos." *Partisan Review*, 4 (1938), pp. 26-32. Rpt. in *Dos Passos, the Critics, and the Writer's Intention*, pp. 35-43.

Walcutt, C. C. *The Divided Stream*. Minneapolis: Univ. of Minnesota Press, 1956.

Whipple, T. K. *Study Out the Land*. Berkeley: Univ. of California Press, 1943.